RHIANNON'S CIRCLE

THE BOHANNON WITCHES DUOLOGY
BOOK ONE

EMILY BEX

FOUNDATIONS BOOK PUBLISHING

Foundations Book Publishing
4209 Lakeland Drive, #398, Flowood, MS 39232
www.FoundationsBooks.net

Rhiannon's Circle
Book 1: The Bohannon Witches Duology

ISBN: 978-1-64583-102-0

Copyright © 2023 by Emily Bex
Cover by Dawné Dominique Copyright 2023
Book Formatting by Bella Roccaforte

Published in the United States of America
Worldwide Electronic & Digital Rights
Worldwide English Language Print Rights

All rights reserved. No part of this book may be reproduced, scanned or distributed in any form, including digital and electronic or mechanical, including photocopying, recording, or by any information storage and retrieval system, without the prior written consent of the Publisher, except for brief quotes for use in reviews.

This is a work of fiction. Names, characters, businesses, places, events, and incidents are either the products of the author's imagination or in the case of actual locations and historical figures, used in a fictitious manner. Otherwise, any resemblance to actual persons, living or dead, or actual events is purely coincidental

ACKNOWLEDGMENTS

To my friend, Johanna Morrisette, who spent long hours on the phone with pen and paper in hand as I thought out loud to push through writer's block. Unfortunately for her, I need to talk it through when I'm unsure where to take the story. I talk, and she writes down what I'm saying, frequently shouting, "Hold on, hold on! You're talking too fast!" Or worse, scratching out ideas when I would change direction. "So, keep this part, or not?" Trust me when I say no one was happier than Johanna when we finally reached the end.

To my faithful beta readers who gave me feedback on the story before it went to the publisher; Brittany Catlett, Michelle Simpson, Laura Donaldson, Amanda Allen, Jennifer Soppe, Kerri Stanke, Heather Clonch, and Claire Cross. They helped catch the stupid mistakes.

To my readers, who are true Wiccans, who generously shared information on their rituals. I used pieces of their actual practices as jumping-off points for pure fantasy.

To my amazing personal assistant, Debbie Victorino, who helps me spread the word on all my social media accounts and manages TikTok, creating those fabulous videos.

And finally, to all the loyal fans of The Medici Warrior Series, who kept me motivated to sit for hours in front of the computer screen again.

Wiccan Sabbats (Holidays) Calendar

YULE: Celebration of the winter solstice and a time of rebirth and new beginnings.
IMBOLC: Marks the halfway point of the winter season. Time to clear your heart and mind.
OSTARA: First day of Spring, or Spring Equinox. The balance between light and dark.
BELTANE: May Day, the midpoint between spring and summer. Celebrates passion, love, and sexuality.
LITHA: Midsummer or summer solstice. The longest day marks life at its fullest.
LUGHNASADH: (Pronounced Lunasa) Midpoint between summer and autumn. Marks the first harvest.
MABON: Autumn Equinox and the balance between light and dark again. Celebrates abundance.

SAMHAIN: (Pronounced Sahwin) Halloween. The veil that separates the two worlds is at its thinnest, allowing loved ones to pass through to this world.

CHAKRAS

Chakras are 7 energy centers in our body that correspond to the nerves and major organs at that point.
When our chakras are open, energy can run through them freely, and harmony exists between the physical body, mind, and spirit.

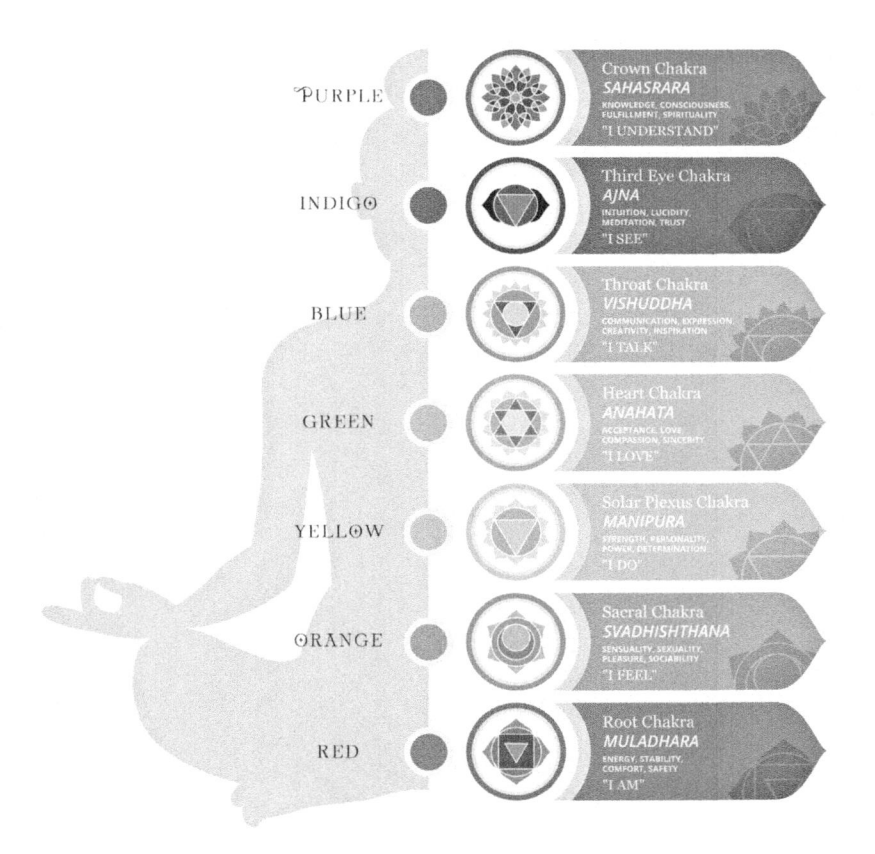

Color	Chakra	Sanskrit	Qualities	Affirmation
PURPLE	Crown Chakra	SAHASRARA	Knowledge, Consciousness, Fulfillment, Spirituality	"I UNDERSTAND"
INDIGO	Third Eye Chakra	AJNA	Intuition, Lucidity, Meditation, Trust	"I SEE"
BLUE	Throat Chakra	VISHUDDHA	Communication, Expression, Creativity, Inspiration	"I TALK"
GREEN	Heart Chakra	ANAHATA	Acceptance, Love, Compassion, Sincerity	"I LOVE"
YELLOW	Solar Plexus Chakra	MANIPURA	Strength, Personality, Power, Determination	"I DO"
ORANGE	Sacral Chakra	SVADHISHTHANA	Sensuality, Sexuality, Pleasure, Sociability	"I FEEL"
RED	Root Chakra	MULADHARA	Energy, Stability, Comfort, Safety	"I AM"

BOHANNON

1

Eilish sat on the porch steps of the expansive wrap-around porch of their home on the Battery in Charleston. She loved watching the sunset, but the oppressive heat and humidity were almost too much to bear. It might be late spring for the rest of the world, but the hot sultry days began early in Charleston. Even in her skimpy sundress and bare feet, she could feel the beads of sweat run down her back. She set her glass of ice tea, filled with lemon wedges and loaded with sugar, down on the steps and raised her hands to lift her long snow-white hair from her neck. She bent her head slightly forward, hoping to feel a breeze on her back, but the air was still and thick. She could hear the faint sounds of Otis Redding playing from inside the house, and she smiled to herself. It could only be her middle sister, Anya. Dropping her hair, it tumbled down her back as she looked up with steel gray eyes to see a tourist taking photos of their house... and her.

She picked up her glass and stood quickly, her hair fanning out as she turned to go back inside. The man taking the photo waved and smiled at her. "I hope I didn't run you off."

Eilish didn't answer but looked back over her shoulder, giving a hard stare, sending out an invisible wave of energy, and watched as the cell phone slipped from his hands, crashing to the sidewalk and heard him curse as he saw the crack on the screen.

Her family had owned this house since it was built in the 1800s, passing it down through the generations, and she couldn't imagine ever leaving it, but the tourists had become an unwanted annoyance in their lives. She knew it wasn't a good idea to use her powers for such frivolous stuff, but it was hot, and she was annoyed with the constant interruptions from the tourists. Some would be emboldened enough to open the gate and come into the yard to get a better picture of the house.

She stepped inside the house and felt the blast of cold air against her bare skin, causing goosebumps on her arms and creating the odd sensation of being too hot and too cold at the same time. Her oldest sister, Seraphina, insisted on keeping the air conditioner working at full speed. They could never agree on where the thermostat should be set between the three of them, but Seraphina pulled rank as the oldest and usually won the battle.

Eilish lifted the glass to her lips and tipped it up, draining the contents as she walked to the kitchen and placed the empty glass in the sink. She heard Seraphina shouting up the stairs to Anya, "Turn that music down!" Eilish rolled her eyes as she heard a door slam shut, and the music was lowered a few decibels. Seraphina stomped into the kitchen, her long black hair twisted in a loosely constructed bun on the top of her head, and Eilish turned to see her disapproving stare.

Seraphina snapped at her. "Put your dirty dishes in the dishwasher. I'm not your maid."

Eilish sighed. "It's one glass, Fina."

Seraphina gave her a cold stare with her oddly colored amber eyes, and Eilish relinquished, putting the glass in the dishwasher.

Seraphina straightened the items on the already immaculately organized kitchen counter. "We need to go into the shop tonight."

Eilish threw up both hands. The sisters ran a new-age shop on Tradd Street called Rhiannon's Circle. Like the house, the shop had been passed down from previous generations. Eilish chuckled to herself at the description of "new age." There was nothing new age about witchcraft. It had been around since the dawn of time. "The shop's closed today. Why do we have to go in? I was planning on going out later."

Seraphina slowly crossed her arms before extending her index finger with her long, painted fingernail, tapping out a message on the countertop to emphasize her words. "It's not for you to argue with me, Eilish. We have a shipment of new items to be stocked on the shelves. You *will* go and help. Go upstairs and tell Anya. I'll be ready to leave soon. I don't intend to spend half the evening waiting for either of you to be ready."

Eilish grunted her discontent and brushed past her sister, who was partially blocking the door. Seraphina never missed an opportunity to remind them that she was the oldest and most experienced witch and would remain in charge. Eilish started up the stairs and could hear the musical refrains from The Platters, a doo-wop group from the 50s, coming from Anya's room. She tapped lightly on the closed door. "Anya?" She heard her sister respond, "Come in."

Eilish opened the door and flopped down across her sister's bed. Anya was dressed in oversized jeans, an old white tank top, and a faded plaid shirt that had seen better days. Her feet were clad in the heavy Doc Martens she wore with everything. "Don't you get hot in all that?"

Anya shook her head, her tangled honey-blonde hair falling across her green eyes when she casually tossed her hair over her shoulder. "Nah. I'm used to it. Besides, Fina keeps this place colder than the morgue." Both sisters giggled before Eilish remembered why she was there.

"Fina says we have to go into the shop tonight."

Anya sighed. "I heard."

Eilish rolled over on her back, looking at the ceiling with the water stain shaped like a butterfly. "Fina doesn't like it when you use your powers to eavesdrop."

Anya scoffed as she lifted the arm from the turntable on her record player, bringing a sudden end to the music. She preferred old record players and vinyl to the new technology. "Well, Fina can kiss my ass."

"Really?" They both looked up to see Seraphina standing in the doorway.

Seraphina stared deep and hard into Anya's eyes. Her head tilted back slowly as her chin jutted out. "And if I didn't keep Rhiannon's stocked over the summer tourists' season, exactly how would either of you survive?" She turned to glare at Eilish, the youngest and still learning her place in the coven, but Seraphina had no doubt she'd discover her full power with time. As siblings do, both her sisters would test her, but they'd never win; she was the eldest and intended to remain in control. "Where do you think you'd find money to buy the clothes and makeup you adore?" Her head snapped quickly to Anya, almost surreal in its quickness. "And you, that vinyl you play constantly costs money." Her smile crept slowly across her face. "As for kissing your ass, who could find it in that outfit? When will either of you learn? The sooner this is done, the sooner we get back to the house and can enjoy the night."

Seraphina spun on her heels and stomped down the stairs, and the sisters heard the massive front door slam behind her as she left the house. Eilish looked at Anya. "We better go. She's in a mood. I don't want to listen to her bitch all night."

Anya grabbed her backpack and slid it over one shoulder. "Come on, then."

Eilish smiled. Anya never went anywhere without that beat-up backpack. As they exited the bedroom door, the music of The Platters started to play again, and Anya looked over her shoulder at the pale apparition standing over the record player. "Oh, hi, Emric. Don't scratch the vinyl."

He nodded and answered. "I'll be most careful, Miss Anya. But it does get lonely when you take leave."

Eilish smiled at him. "We won't be long." The apparition

retreated to a chair in the corner and settled in, looking out the window. "The soldiers will be here soon."

Anya spoke lovingly to him. "There are no more soldiers, Emric. The war is over. The war ended in 1783." Emric nodded but continued to stare out the window, wearing the tattered brown coat of his regiment, the deep, open gash on his head that had taken his life still apparent. Anya reassured him. "We'll be back soon." She waited for a second to see if he'd respond, but the young soldier was lost in his world of battles fought long ago and stepping over the dead and dying. Emric had haunted this house for as long as she could remember but had always been a benign source of energy among them. "Good night then."

The sisters turned and walked down the wide staircase with the elaborately carved banisters of the Victorian-style house and into the front foyer. Eilish stopped to find her sandals and slipped them on before they headed out the door. Summer hadn't even arrived yet, and they were hit by the oppressive heat of the Deep South as they made their way down the broad steps of the front porch and across the cracked sidewalk onto East Bay and walked the few blocks to their shop located in the heart of the tourists' district.

The two girls walked together, a common sight in the neighborhood as the Bohannon sisters were always a source of gossip among the locals. Most suspected they were witches, and the Bohannon House was even on the Charleston Ghost Tours. They never tried to deny the presence of Emric. He'd haunted this house long before they were born, and everyone in the city knew the local legends of haunted houses in Charleston. They ignored the gossip about their witchcraft and laughed it off whenever a local was bold enough to ask outright. Of course, the rumors weren't helped by the fact they ran a shop that sold books on witchcraft, tarot cards, crystals, candles, runes, herbs, and items for casting or breaking spells. As they reached Rhiannon's Circle, they opened the unlocked door and heard the small bell chime to announce their entry. Seraphina looked up from the stack of boxes she'd carried from the back room where they stocked inventory. "It's about time you got here."

Pushing two boxes forward, she directed Anya. "Put these on the shelves in the herbal section. The black bookcase on the bottom, and don't just shove them in there. Arrange them neatly. Pay attention to what you're doing, Anya. I don't want to have to rearrange the chaos you call stocking the shelves when we open tomorrow."

Seraphina opened another box as she heard the loud purring from the floor and felt the cat's soft fur rubbing against her ankles. "Luna, my pet, you'll get your attention when we get home." She picked up the green-eyed black cat and slid her cheek against her silken fur. Setting the cat on the counter, she watched as she made a curious leap over the boxes and found a nesting place inside an empty one. She returned her attention to the work at hand.

"Eilish, this sage needs to be put into the baskets; don't just stand there. It's not as if you've never done this before!" Her sigh was audible and filled with frustration. "Must I always do everything? We'd have nothing if it weren't for my direction and wits." She stopped and fanned herself. "It's much too hot in here!" She walked back to the storeroom in the rear of the shop and found the thermostat had been tampered with again and knew it was Eilish. Adjusting the AC to kick up some much-needed cool air, she heard the soft tinkling of the chimes. "Just what I need, another tourist who can't read the 'closed' sign on the door." Heading full steam for the front of the store, she stopped when she recognized the tall, handsome man standing in the middle of the shop. She almost purred louder than Luna when she saw Warrick. She admired his handsome face and black hair, hanging straight and long, almost to his waist. His mustache and goatee were trimmed to perfection. She absorbed his energy as it flowed around all of them. He exuded power and stature.

"Good evening, Bohannon sisters." Although he addressed all of the sisters, he only had eyes for Seraphina.

Seraphina glided across the old wooden floor as if she were

walking on air. "Warrick, what a pleasant and much-needed surprise."

He chuckled softly as he embraced her for a hug. "It's good to see you intend to make the most of the summer tourist money. I rather like that about you, Fina."

She smiled, and her posture softened. "Well, for my sake, I hope that's not all you like about me. It's a gift, of course, taking their money, and most of them have no idea what they're buying, but what do I care." She noticed his gaze wandering to petite Eilish as she delicately arranged bundles of white sage in the basket. Seraphina wouldn't share his attention and lightly placed a hand on his arm. "To what do we owe this visit, Warrick? Tell me you have something wicked on your mind. Did you miss me?"

Warrick wandered around the familiar shop, picking up items and returning them to their rightful place. Rhiannon's Circle was where every witch in Charleston came for supplies to practice their craft. "I was taking a stroll, saw the light on, and thought perhaps I'd come in and visit my favorite sisters."

Eilish cast a sideways glance at Anya, who acknowledged her with a wink. They both knew who Warrick was here to visit, and it wasn't either of them. He and Seraphina had been hand-fasted for years but had an unconventional marriage. Warrick had insisted they live apart. It was always a source of speculation among the coven members, but it seemed to work for them as a couple. Eilish giggled and answered, "You mean sister... singular, right Warrick?" Luna wove her way around the carefully arranged basket of sage as Eilish brushed her away. "Shoo! I have some catnip for you later."

"Now, Eilish, you know I love all of you, but yes, Fina will always hold my heart. Don't you have someone who draws your attention?"

Eilish looked up at him from where she knelt on the floor. From this vantage point, he looked ten feet tall. "Not me. I'm a free agent, and I plan to remain that way, despite your constant efforts at match-making."

Anya spoke up, "Hello? I'm single and ready to mingle. Why don't you focus some of that match-making attention on me?"

Warrick turned his focus towards Anya and gave her a quick once over in her shabby attire. "You know, Anya, that grunge look went out in the '90s. Perhaps if you dressed more... feminine."

Anya smirked and flashed him her middle finger. "Fuck you, Warrick."

Warrick raised one eyebrow and shook his head. "And maybe clean up your language to something more befitting a young lady of your standing."

Anya returned to her task of arranging the books on the shelves. "I'll find my match, and don't try casting any spells. I'll know if you do."

Seraphina was appalled at how flippant her sisters could sometimes be with Warrick, but she knew he could readily handle them. "Warrick has a point on both accounts. You both need to find suitable mates. You aren't getting any younger."

Warrick chuckled as he turned to Seraphina. "It looks as though the Charleston heat has generated a few prickly attitudes. Let them finish up, and I'll walk you back to the house. I have something to discuss with you about the upcoming full moon. The coven will want to gather to honor the Goddess of the Ostara." He wrapped his arm around Seraphina's waist and guided her to the door as Luna leaped from out of nowhere to rush out the door in front of them.

Seraphina issued her final instructions as she left. "Finish up, and don't leave the packaging strewn everywhere. Warrick and I have some things to take care of." Kissing him quickly, she was more than eager to have his full attention for the rest of the evening, no matter the subject.

Anya and Eilish watched as the two left the shop together, arm in arm. Anya smirked. "How does Fina manage to drag us down here to do all the work and then leave without doing a damn thing?"

Eilish laughed. "Because she's Fina... and we are mere underlings."

BOHANNON

Warrick and Seraphina casually strolled the several blocks back to the house. It was dark now, but the street lights cast a soft glow, lighting their path. The Spanish moss hanging from the enormous live oak trees looked eerie in the artificial light. Luna walked far ahead of them, her tail swishing back and forth like a clock pendulum, counting off the seconds. There was no conversation as they walked hand in hand, lost in their own thoughts. Once inside the house, Warrick spun her quickly in his arms and kissed her softly. Seraphina sighed, with a delicious lick of her lips, as Warrick broke the kiss. Fina inquired. "So, what is it you wished to discuss? Is it Eilish?"

Warrick chuckled low in his throat. "Business later, my goddess. We come first." He led her up the ancient staircase, the stairs creaking under his weight. He was quite familiar with the path to her bedroom. He opened the door slowly for her and led her inside. Closing the door, he absentmindedly waved his hand as the air shimmered slightly, placing a boundary spell around the door. The younger sisters knew better than to interrupt, but Warrick liked the invisible barrier that protected it from entry, granting them privacy.

There was no pretense between them, they'd been lovers for a long time, but it was always something special for them. He loved her, but he loved the power he gained *through* her even more. Warrick went to her, his eyes sweeping from head to toe. She was his goddess; he adored her and loved the power she held. In witchcraft, the women had more power than the men, and Warrick drew power and status in the coven from his relationship with Seraphina. She held the position of High Priestess, as she was seen as the most powerful witch in Charleston, and his bond to her made him the High Priest. Still, Warrick had kept an eye on Eilish; he and Fina knew she had yet to discover her real potential. He was certain Eilish wasn't aware of the degree of her budding power, and they'd like to keep it that way. He and Seraphina had worked hard to maintain their positions in the coven. They shared secrets best left undiscovered.

He strolled around Seraphina, keeping one hand on her waist. Reaching up, he pulled the single stick pin holding the knotted mass of black hair atop her head and watched as her hair tumbled over his hand and to her waist. Pushing it aside, he left butterfly kisses at the base of her neck. "You should never knot your hair in such a mass. You enchant me much more with it down."

Seraphina smiled at him, her amber eyes sparkling as the candles flared to life within the room. She knew what he liked and always gave him his due. She walked to the bed, slipped the spaghetti straps of her black dress over her shoulders, and let the dress drop to the floor. Crawling up on the bed on all fours, she growled like a hungry lioness as he watched. His eyes followed her every movement and finally locked with hers. He stripped quickly and walked toward her. She lay back on the vast antique four-poster bed as her dark hair fanned out around her face.

He crawled between her legs and knelt on his knees as if in prayer. He held out his left hand, letting it hover over her. Seraphina slowly lifted her right hand and held it beneath his, close but not touching, and watched as the thin blue streaks of electricity appeared and crackled softly between their hands. Seraphina closed her eyes and arched her back as she felt the pleasurable energy engulf her body. She could hear the low, deep-throated moan coming from Warrick. And so it began, his powerful strokes brought her body to life, and with each one, the intensity grew. The candles flickered as if a wind had washed through the room as they came together. Warrick kissed her violently when he came, then planted soft kisses on her shoulder and took the ancient pentagram she always wore around her neck between his teeth. It had been handed down from her ancestors, and she never took it off. He caressed the pentagram with his tongue before letting it drop softly between her breasts. He looked into her eyes. "My sweet goddess, you're always here for me to love."

Seraphina tugged his hair to pull him closer to her lips. "And I always will be." The sound of the front door slamming shut brought a moan from her lips. "How subtle."

Warrick winked at her. "I knew they wouldn't be long coming home; they both had that look of waiting to escape when they were at Rhiannon's. Besides that, I have some business to attend to tonight." He stood and began to dress as Seraphina sat straight up in the bed.

"But I thought you wanted to discuss the Ostara ceremony?"

Warrick nodded at her. "I did, but this was much more important." He leaned down and kissed her softly. "There's time, and it does involve Eilish, but I prefer to be alone when we talk. I must go, my goddess."

Reaching out, she touched his arm and pleaded with her eyes. "Must you rush off? What's so important?"

"Nothing that concerns you. You have enough on your mind already." He walked to the door, removed the spell, and closed the door behind him. Seraphina stared silently at the door. She loved Warrick, and they'd been bonded through a hand-fasting ceremony years ago, but he'd refused to take up residence with her. He said he needed his space, and she'd given him that, although it wasn't her preference. She bit back her anger. She was the one who led the coven, not Warrick, and she always resented when he presented himself as being the one in charge. She'd spent their years together weaving a story that made it appear that living apart was her choice because she refused to give up her independence to a warlock. She knew Warrick's position within the coven was elevated to High Priest through his relationship with her, and together, they did make for a powerful team. Still, she wished he'd at least acknowledge that she was the source of his power.

◦⟨≫⟩◦

Eilish and Anya were still standing in the foyer. Eilish kicked off her sandals when they heard the door close upstairs and looked up to see Warrick, still tucking in his shirt as he descended the stairs. Anya smirked as she called out to him. "So, you work out all the details for Ostara?" Eilish bit her lip to stifle her laughter and nudged her middle sister.

Warrick scolded. "I think both of you would be much more considerate if you had males in your life. You both understand your obligations to the coven. Stop acting like spoiled children. Seraphina is much too easy on you both." He made his way to the door and turned to look at Eilish and the devilish grin on her face. "Zavian is ready for you, Eilish. Show him some attention. He'd be putty in your hands if you made half an effort."

Eilish felt her cheeks turn red, and Anya took a step back, knowing this was a sore subject with her sister. "I'm well aware of Zavian's interest. We've been good friends, we grew up together, and I'm afraid his affections are misplaced. I never want to offend him, Warrick, but there will never be a hand-fasting between Zavian and me."

Warrick confronted her, and his voice rolled out in a menacing low tone, squinting his eyes just a hint as he towered over Eilish. "The de Burke family are highly regarded and powerful members of this coven; how dare you act as if you're so far above us. I give you fair warning, Eilish Bohannon, don't force my hand in this matter."

He spun on his heels and stomped out the door, slamming it behind him.

Seraphina had felt the turmoil brewing and stopped halfway down the stairs as Warrick came at Eilish. She had to agree with Warrick. It was time that Eilish settled down. Her powers were coming to the fore much quicker than Anya's, and bonding with Zavian would make her easier to control. As Warrick slammed out the door, she walked down the remaining stairs. "Warrick gives few warnings, Eilish. It's time you heed them and begin to return Zavian's attention. He's quite handsome, so I don't understand your hesitation. I want a match between our families." Holding up her hand, she shook her head. "Don't think you'll change my mind on this. Warrick and I both agree."

Eilish tossed her handbag on the floor and angrily confronted her older sister. "You and Warrick agree? Well, how convenient. I won't be used as some bargaining chip for this coven. I like Zavian. I've always liked him. But I feel no attraction to him, and you know this! I'll bond when I decide... not you, not Warrick, not the coven. Me!" Eilish pushed past her sister and stormed up the stairs to her room, slamming the door behind her.

Anya looked with annoyance at Seraphina. "Why can't you leave her alone? You know she doesn't love Zavian. She'll find her path, Fina."

"Leave her alone? If I left her alone, she'd end up with some warlock beneath her status. It's time for both of you. And if you think Warrick or I will leave this alone, you're wasting your breath. Leave my sight!" Seraphina pushed past Anya, almost knocking her over, grumbling as she went. "Oh, you will see, little sister. You won't defy the powers of Warrick and me together."

As Seraphina walked away, still shouting, Anya mimicked her sister behind her back, silently mouthing the words she'd heard a million times. Anya picked up Eilish's handbag and started up the stairs, muttering under her breath. "We might surprise you, Fina."

Anya knew Eilish had powers she hadn't begun to tap into; the whole coven knew, which was why they were so concerned about her bonding. A strong bond with any of the Bohannon's would increase the coven's power as a whole, just as Fina's bonding with a powerful warlock such as Warrick had increased her powers. The power of the High Priestess was indicative of the coven's strength and longevity, and it was why the High Priestess' choice with whom she chose to bond with was crucial. Anya had her own power, but she wasn't equal to her sisters. Fina flaunted her power, and Eilish tried to ignore hers, not wanting to stand out. Anya had always been ambivalent about being a witch. She used her power when it suited her but had largely ignored the rituals, participating only when Fina made a fuss over it. She reached her sister's door and tapped on it before opening it. "Eilish? You okay?"

Eilish was pacing back and forth, and Emric hovered in the corner, upset by the negative energy the young witch was generating. Anya chuckled. "You're scaring Emric. Calm down. You know Fina. She always has to be the one in control."

Eilish flopped down on her bed and sighed loudly. "But that's the thing! Most of the time, I don't care. Fina wants to run things, and I could care less. But I'm not some, some... prize to be awarded to Zavian. She talks like I have no say in this, and I can tell you now, I won't bond to Zavian!"

Anya sat beside her on the bed and brushed a strand of snow-white hair from her sister's face. "Hey, at least you have someone interested in bonding. I don't exactly have them lining up over here."

Eilish shook her head and smiled sheepishly at her sister. "Then count your lucky stars. I don't think you're missing much." Both girls laughed as Emric quietly left the room, and Luna entered, jumping up on their bed.

"Find your own path, Eilish. Once you bond, they'll settle down."

Eilish lay back on the bed. "You make it sound easy."

Anya leaned back on her elbows and turned her head to her sister. "They can't force a hand-fasting. It screws up the energy. You know that. If you don't bond to Zavian of your own choosing, then none of their plans for strengthening the coven means anything. Take your time. You'll find the right one."

Eilish reached up and twirled a tangled tendril of Anya's honey-blonde hair around her finger. "And you, Anya? What about you?"

Anya shrugged. "Whatever. My power's not as great as yours. The coven isn't as focused on me. The pickings are slim here anyway, let's face it. I mean, Zavian is cute, but he's not my type. When it happens, it happens." They heard a door slam downstairs and Seraphina's voice shouting to them from the foot of the stairs. "Get down here. We have an Ostara ritual to plan!"

BOHANNON

Eilish had pulled on a maxi skirt with a dark blue and white tie-dyed print and an ivory lace-edged tank top. She layered on the long necklaces that included a pentagram and several crystals and amulets. She stacked silver bangles along both of her slender arms. She liked the soft sound of the metal bangles as they clinked together as she moved, like soft bells. Slipping on her sandals, she brushed out her long, white hair, then looked in the mirror. Her large gray eyes peered back at her. She rarely wore makeup, except for special occasions and some of their Wiccan ceremonies. She put on a clear lip balm to protect her lips from the sun and then dropped the lip balm into her hobo bag of a purse. Turning on her heels, she made her way to Anya's room. The mournful sounds of Sam Cooke singing "A Change is Gonna Come" drifted from behind Anya's door. EILISH tapped on her sister's door before opening it. "You ready? We need to open the shop by ten. Fina had some errands to run, so we have to open today."

Anya was wearing a pair of cut-off jeans, frayed at the hem, and had another of her endless supply of plaid shirts tied at the waist. Her jeans sat low on her hips, exposing a small strip of bare skin at her waist. She wore two small pentagrams in her pierced ears. She was seated in a chair, lacing up the heavy Doc Martens. She answered without looking up. "Almost."

She stood upright, shaking out her hair that looked like it hadn't seen a brush in days, reaching for the record player when Emric spoke. "Don't. Let it play." Anya shrugged. "Okay, just turn it off when you're ready." The apparition stood at the window, looking out, lost in his world. Eilish called out to him, "Bye, Emric," but he didn't respond.

The two girls headed down the stairs and out the front door of their house. Luna slipped out with them as they stepped outside, and they were hit with the oppressive wall of heat and humidity.

Anya squinted at the bright sun, pulled a pair of sunglasses out of her backpack, and slipped them on her face. "Wow. It's stifling already. Don't even tell me what the temperature's going up to today."

Eilish answered anyway. "Ninety-eight, and a hundred percent humidity with a late afternoon thunderstorm."

Anya laughed. "I asked you not to tell me."

They walked side by side, talking non-stop as they made their way the few blocks to Tradd Street. The tourists were already out, taking pictures of the houses, the trees filled with Spanish moss, the old churches, and the unique storefronts. They approached Rhiannon's Circle, where a few curious tourists had their faces pressed against the window, trying to peer inside as Anya pulled the keys from her jeans pocket. Eilish looked at the humans and smiled. "You can come in if you want."

A heavy-set woman in a sundress two sizes too small looked up at her. "What's in here? Witch stuff?" Eilish continued to smile, hiding the fact that she'd like to cast a spell or two. "Books on new age philosophy, crystals, incense, sage, that kind of thing. We have some nice wind chimes and some water fountains."

The woman scrunched up her nose and moved on, but not before looking over both girls and giving a look of disapproval. "No thanks."

Anya pushed open the door, and Luna dashed past their feet and into the store, landing squarely on the counter next to the cash register. Anya laughed at the exchange between Eilish and the tourist. "I don't think we impressed her." They both set about readying the store for the morning traffic and handling a few customers before Fina arrived.

As Seraphina approached the shop, she was relieved to see that her sisters had been on time and the shop was open. She'd been on a few errands for Warrick, checking in with a few of the witches in their coven to ensure their preparations for the upcoming ceremony. She always took care of the details. She was, after all, the High Priestess. She walked into the cool air-conditioned shop, carrying her large tote, and heard her sisters' rather noisy chatting. "At least you both got here on time to open, but if you have nothing better to do than gossip, pick up a duster and clean. We'll start to get extremely busy, and Warrick likes things clean and in their proper place."

Luna jumped to a display counter and then into Seraphina's arms. "Ahh, my lovely pet, keeping these two in line, I hope?" As the black cat purred, she returned her attention to her sisters. "Any sales yet this morning?"

Anya shook her head as she picked up a feather duster and started dusting the immaculate displays. "So, this is Warrick's shop then? And all this time, I thought it was ours?"

Setting Luna on the counter, Seraphina turned to Anya. "Stop being a smartass. Warrick is only looking out for our interests. You tend to sell more if you have top-quality goods in an excellent environment. I have some things to work on in the back room, and I'll turn down the air conditioning."

Eilish looked up as the door chimes jingled, and a few tourists wandered in as Seraphina disappeared to the back room. Eilish smiled as they entered, the people enjoying the cool air inside the shop, if nothing else. "Welcome. Look around and let me know if I can help you with anything."

The three humans fanned out, exploring the unusual objects in the shop. One of them asked, "Do you have any salt lamp things?"

Eilish approached and led her to the Himalayan salt rock lamps. "You mean the salt rock? The salt is mined from the left slope of the Himalayan Mountains. When you plug in the lamps, it emits a soft orange-pinkish glow. Kind of like a sunset. It generates negative ions which increase oxygen flow to the brain."

The woman squinted as she looked at the box. "Negative ions? That doesn't sound good."

Eilish shook her head. "No, it's good. Like the air after it rains or how the air feels when you stand near a waterfall. It makes you more alert and increases your mental energy. They also protect against contaminants in the air, things that make you feel stuffy, or make you sneeze or cough."

The woman held the box in her hand, looking back at the lamp on display. "Does it work?"

Eilish nodded. "Our customers love it. People prone to allergies, or who get frequent colds swear by them." The woman tipped the box over and read the price, then shrugged. It was only about twenty bucks, so she decided to take a chance. "Okay then, I'll try it." She returned her purchase to the counter, where Anya rang up the sale.

Zavian strolled from Queen Street to Tradd Street and still couldn't believe the heat still got to him after all the years he'd lived in Charleston. Growing up in Boston, he didn't have this problem. He pushed back the dark blonde hair that hung across his shoulders and past the collar of his t-shirt. He didn't complain because he'd take every opportunity to see Eilish. And today, his Uncle Warrick, the High Priest of the Coven, was too busy to go to Rhiannon's, so he sent him instead. He'd been living with his uncle for many years in South Carolina as an apprentice warlock learning his powers and the customs of the local coven. As he approached the shop, his heart leaped in his chest. Eilish... she was the most gorgeous witch he'd ever laid eyes on. She liked him well enough, but Zavian wanted more, and he was patient. His Uncle had practically promised him that Eilish was the witch he would be hand-fasted to just as Warrick had bonded with Seraphina. Eilish had powers equal to, if not greater than, those of her oldest sister, although she rarely displayed them. Together, he and Eilish would make a powerful couple and be in a position to lead this coven someday. He was looking forward to the ceremony celebrating Ostara. He knew he'd see her there, and the coven would draw on their combined power. He hoped this ceremony would bring them closer, making her see how powerful they were together and their hand-fasting was destined to be. Entering the shop, the chimes rang softly, and a few customers with their packages almost ran into him. Holding the door open for the customers to exit, he could sense Eilish close by. Closing the door behind him, he looked straight into her eyes. "Well, it looks as if business is good today. How are you, Eilish? I like the skirt. Is it new?"

Eilish looked up from straightening the boxes of salt lamps. "Oh, hey! I didn't know you were dropping in today. This skirt? Nah... it's been in the closet for years."

She returned to her tasks, putting the boxes in a pleasant display as Anya looked up from behind the counter. "Hi, Zavian." She unconsciously dragged her fingers through her hair, trying to straighten her tangled locks. She knew Zavian was attracted to her sister, but Anya had had her eye on him for years, not that he ever seemed to notice. Her eyes raked over him. Zavian was tall and lanky. His hair was almost the same honey-blonde color as hers but fell smooth and silky around his face, not the unruly mess she'd been born with. His face was chiseled and angular, with well-defined cheekbones and full lips. His light blue eyes had a sleepy quality about them. She'd always found him sexy. He was in a cotton t-shirt and a pair of loose cargo pants. No human would ever look at him and suspect he was a warlock and the heir apparent to Warrick's title of High Priest. Zavian looked toward Anya and nodded. "Hey. I didn't see you there."

Anya smiled at him but thought to herself, *"no, you never notice me anywhere."*

Zavian started helping Eilish rearrange the salt lamp boxes so he could be close to her. "I thought perhaps you'd like to join me tonight, like, for a movie? Anything you want, someplace we can be together, out of the heat?" He ran his fingers over the bracelets that encircled her small wrist, listening to the musical jingle. "Just something fun together, alone and away from our elders."

Eilish looked straight ahead at the boxes before her, avoiding eye contact. She liked Zavian and didn't want to hurt his feelings, but she didn't want to encourage his affection. "That's very sweet of you to ask. But we have Ostara coming up. I know Fina will keep us busy preparing for that. But I'll see you there, right?" She glanced up at him quickly, seeing the disappointment on his face.

Anya spoke up. "I'll go. I mean, if there's a movie you want to see and want some company."

Zavian tried not to let the disappointment show on his face. He didn't look in Anya's direction but continued to look at Eilish. "I'm sure that if Eilish is busy with Ostara, then you will be as well, Anya." Taking Eilish's hand, he smiled down into her eyes. "Maybe if I ask Seraphina, I'm sure she'd let you off from your duties for just one night."

Eilish bit at her lip. She knew she had no real excuse, and if Fina got involved, she'd only encourage her to go. "I... yeah, okay, I'll ask Fina if I can go." Eilish was aware of just how ridiculous she sounded. She was twenty-five! She didn't need permission to go out with anyone.

Seraphina stepped into the shop from the back room. "Did I hear my name?"

Eilish turned toward her sister. "Uh, Zavian was asking me to go to the movies."

Seraphina had over-heard most of their exchange and knew Eilish would try to wiggle out of going out with him. She approached Zavian and kissed him lightly on the cheek, running her finger along his beautiful jawline. "You get more handsome every time I see you. So, you have asked Eilish out to the movies?"

"I did, but she politely refused. Everyone seems so busy with Ostara that they have no time for anything else. My uncle asked me to deliver this to you, a list of things he wants readily available for the witches to purchase for the upcoming ceremony." He handed her the envelope, which she tucked in her waistband.

Seraphina looked at her youngest sister. "Eilish, I think we could spare your company for one night. Go have fun." She stared at Eilish, daring her to refuse.

Eilish closed her eyes and sighed, resigning herself to an evening with Zavian. She enjoyed his company as long as he stayed in the 'friend-zone,' but she knew he wanted more. "Well, I guess it's settled then. A movie it is. Just let me know what time you're coming by. I'll be ready."

A smile spread across his face. "Pick you up at eight." He kissed Seraphina on the cheek and whispered, 'thank you.' "I need to get going; I have more errands for Warrick. See you later, Eilish." He smiled at her, and his heart was flying. He waved goodbye to Anya and walked out.

Seraphina crossed her arms across her chest. "About time you got smart and started listening. Please do us a favor, put on some makeup, dress up, and show Zavian a good evening. Come along, Luna; we have more work to do. It looks as if the day is getting better by the minute."

Eilish muttered under her breath, "Better for who?"

Anya glanced at her younger sister as Fina disappeared again into the back of the shop, "Come on, Eilish. There are certainly worse things than spending an evening with Zavian. I'd go out with him, but he hardly knows I'm in the room."

Eilish wasn't unaware of her sister's fascination with Zavian. "Then why don't you flirt with him then? Let him know you like him?"

Anya shook her head. "You know he's not interested in me. I

mean, he's a nice guy, and we always get along, but you're the one he has his eye on."

Eilish nodded. She knew it was true. "But I'm not interested in him." She tugged at a strand of her snow-white hair. "Warrick and Fina keep pushing me, and I don't want to hurt Zavian's feelings, but this will never happen."

Anya shrugged. "Maybe it will blow over."

Eilish scoffed. "When did Fina ever let anything blow over?"

BOHANNON

Zavian parked as close to the house as possible, right on time, at eight sharp. He'd driven his classic red Jaguar XKE convertible. He'd spent many an hour restoring it to its former glory. It was his baby. He'd tied his hair back in a loose ponytail since he had the top down, so he checked his hair in the mirror and decided he looked rather handsome this evening. He picked up the small violet bouquet he'd bought for her and hoped she'd appreciate the gesture. He hoped to make this a fun evening for them both. He walked through the wrought iron gate and up the steps of the old Victorian home and let his eyes take in the span of the large wraparound porch. The house was a rare architectural beauty, but it could use some work. Taking a deep breath, he rang the doorbell and hoped Eilish would be ready. He didn't want to waste one moment of their time together.

Seraphina heard the doorbell and came rushing from the kitchen, Luna on her heels as she called out. "Eilish! Zavian is here!" She swung open the front door, which was framed by transom windows on both sides, and welcomed the young man into their foyer. "Welcome! Come in. We've been expecting you. Please, take a seat in the parlor. I'm sure Eilish will be down in a moment."

She led Zavian into the overly feminine parlor filled with elaborately scrolled Victorian-era furniture and heavy drapes that puddled in a soft pile of fabric on the floor. Zavian took a seat in a side chair that didn't accommodate his lanky frame. His uncle's place had nice leather furniture, big, modern, and over-stuffed, that allowed a man to sit comfortably. The cushions on this furniture were stiff and rigid, filled with old cotton batting and horsehair.

Seraphina asked sweetly, "May I get you something to drink? Iced tea, perhaps?"

Luna curled herself around Zavian's legs, purring loudly. Shifting his frame slightly in the chair, the last thing Zavian wanted was something to keep him here one minute longer. "No, thank you, Fina. I'm hoping Eilish won't be too long. We don't want to miss the beginning of the movie." He twirled the delicate bouquet of violets in his hand.

Seraphina looked at the flowers. "Violets, how appropriate. Violets signify faithfulness, love, happiness, and virtue."

Zavian smiled as he gave Seraphina a sideways glance. "You forgot loving watchfulness."

Seraphina threw her head back and laughed. "You are quite the gentleman when you want to be. Warrick has taught you well."

Zavian stood up, unable to sit one moment longer in the chair built by the devil himself. "Don't worry; I promise to have Eilish back at a respectable hour and will be every bit the gentleman."

Seraphina laid her hand on his arm. "I hope not too much a gentleman, but please, Eilish has no curfew. She's a grown woman. Stay out as long as you like."

Eilish heard her sister call to her and sighed heavily. She'd changed into a long, loose-fitting maxi dress in a soft pink that allowed the air to circulate freely beneath her skirt. She picked up a bottle of perfume but decided against it and returned it to the dresser. Zavian didn't need any encouragement, and she didn't need to send any false signals. While brushing out her hair one last time, she stepped into her sandals and headed down the stairs. She heard their voices in the parlor and made her way to the large room with high ceilings. "Hi. Hope I didn't keep you waiting."

Zavian went to her quickly. "Eilish, you look beautiful, but then you always do. I haven't been waiting long, and your sister has kept me company." Realizing he was still holding the violets, he gave them to her. "These are for you. Should we go? I don't want to be late for the movie."

Eilish accepted his flowers and nodded that she was ready to go. He said a quick goodbye to Seraphina as he escorted Eilish out the door. He walked to the Jaguar and opened the car door for her, taking her hand and helping her slide into her seat. "I hope our escape wasn't too obvious, but I thought the sooner we left, the sooner we could be alone and away from the ever-watchful eyes of your sister."

Eilish laughed. "Fina doesn't miss much, that's for sure." She folded the long hem of her skirt around her legs as he closed the door and settled herself in the car. Holding the bouquet of violets to her nose, she inhaled their delicate scent. She understood the meaning of every flower and the message he was trying to convey in this simple gesture. "Thank you for the flowers. They're lovely. You've always been a good friend, always there when I needed someone."

He smiled as he made his way into the traffic. "I could give you so much more, Eilish. The violets remind me of you, delicate, with a quiet beauty." He saw her blush and changed the subject, squirming in his seat. "Besides, I was in a hurry to get out of that parlor. I don't know how anyone can sit on those chairs."

Eilish smiled despite herself. She'd always liked Zavian. She wished his feelings for her weren't so deep, complicating their relationship. "Fina loves that old furniture. Personally, I'd toss it out and completely renovate the interior. She refuses. Says it would destroy the very heart of the house."

Eilish clasped her hair at the base of her neck to keep it from blowing too much in the wind. She should have brought a scarf. She knew Zavian liked to drive with the top down. She looked over at him as he drove. He had classic good looks with his defined profile.

She wished she felt more for him, but it wasn't there. "So, what are we going to see?"

Glancing over at her, he loved how her hair blew about in the night air. "*The Avengers*, of course!" He could hear her laugh as he pulled into an empty parking space and shut off the car.

"Of course. I should have known." After getting out of the car, he walked around and opened the door for her, and watched as she tucked the small bouquet out of sight beneath the seat. He took her hand and helped her out, not letting go of her hand. They walked together to the theater. "So, what's your poison, popcorn or candy?"

"Oh, just a soda, please. I already ate."

He led her to the ticket window, where he paid for their tickets, then led her inside the over-air-conditioned theater. That's the thing with the South. If the temperature hits 60° in the winter, everyone is in a panic and pulls out their winter coats, but 60° seems the preferred temperature setting for everyone's air conditioner in the summer. Eilish rubbed her bare arms, wishing she'd brought a sweater.

Zavian noticed her response to the temperature inside the theater. "A bit chilly in here. Let me warm you." He stood behind her and ran his hands gently up and down her arms, then over her shoulders. "I should have reminded you to bring a shawl." He bought the two drinks and walked with her to the theater, taking her to two seats three-quarters of the way back on the aisle. He snuggled beside her and draped his arm around her, pulling her close. "I'll keep you warm. Just snuggle into me, and you'll soon forget how cold it is."

Eilish set her drink in the cup holder and leaned against him in her seat as his arm slipped around her shoulder. This wasn't how she'd planned for the evening to go, but she had to admit, his body heat did help keep her warm. The movie was all action and special effects, the surround sound vibrating through their seats. Zavian seemed absorbed in the film, and for that, she was grateful. As the movie ended and the lights came up, they made their way through the throng of humans. She looked about and didn't recognize any witches in the crowd tonight.

"Well, that got the blood running. It's still early; let's take a ride or get a drink or something. Which do you prefer?" He noticed her looking around as if she was looking for someone. "Eilish, what do you prefer?" She turned to him as if she hadn't even heard him. He asked again, "Is there someone you're looking for? You seem a bit distracted."

"What? No, just seeing if there was anyone from the coven here tonight. I don't see anyone. Why don't we get a coffee? That would warm me up."

"I'd enjoy that; let's walk. There's a coffee shop several blocks from here." He took her hand, and they walked through the night, his thumb running along the back of her hand as he held it. When they reached the coffee shop, he got them both a coffee and found a small corner table alone where they could talk.

She settled into their seat at the table and looked up to see Wynter and Rain. They were sisters from their coven. The two women looked up, noticed Eilish with Zavian, and waved in acknowledgment. Eilish smiled back at them. "Oh, hey!"

Wynter winked at her. "You make a cute couple."

Eilish was about to explain that they weren't a couple when Zavian said, "We do, don't we?"

Zavian had a huge smile when he answered and took Eilish's hand. "Nice evening; we thought we'd catch a movie and have a coffee. You ladies have a great night." He waited for the two sisters to leave before he started talking. He didn't know if they had the gift to eavesdrop on any conversation, and he preferred to keep this private. As the two left the shop, Zavian turned to her and chuckled. "Well, now everyone in the coven will know we went out tonight."

Eilish smiled, hiding her slight annoyance that the two sisters would certainly gossip, and the entire coven would know before daybreak. "No doubt. I wouldn't be surprised if they've spread the word already."

Zavian turned serious as he held her hand across the table. "There are things I want to talk about, though. About us. I wonder about you and me, well, mostly you. You're always nice to me, but something holds you back." Letting go of her hand, he took a sip of his coffee and proceeded as she looked at him from across the small table. "Is there someone else in the coven you like more than me? I live with my uncle, but I can provide for us. We can live right here in Charleston and be close to your family. Tell me what you want, Eilish. I'll do whatever it takes to make you happy. Please tell me you know that."

Eilish scraped her nail across the wax-coated paper coffee cup, listening to him talk. He asked about their relationship, and she knew this conversation would come sooner or later. She listened carefully to his words as he explained the logistics of how they could be together. Not once did he mention the word love. She knew Zavian was fond of her, but she wondered how much of his assumptions about their future together were just part of his upbringing. After all, she'd been coached to bond with Zavian for years, and she was sure he'd been getting the same instruction. "Zavian, you know I care about you, and I have no doubt you'd take care of me. You've always been a good friend, someone I could count on to be there for me. I hope you know I value that. And to answer your question, there's no one else in the coven that's caught my eye. Maybe I'm just not ready. I mean, I feel close to you, and I, you know... I love you like a friend. But I don't feel romantic love for you. I can't promise that will change. If you want to see someone else, I think you should. You deserve someone who will love you in that way."

Reaching out, he stroked her cheek and looked into her eyes. "I love you, Eilish, but far beyond a friend. No one else remotely captures my heart as you do. Give me a chance to show you romantic love, please. You need to give us a chance." He was frustrated with her response. Why couldn't she see how much he cared for her? "I'll soon be done with my apprenticeship. My powers are as great as

Warrick's. You're destined to be my High Priestess. This is what Warrick and Seraphina have arranged."

She looked up at him. "Who are you concerned with here, Zavian? Me, or Warrick and my sister? I know I've been prepped for you for as long as I can remember, and I'm sure you have been as well. Are you sure what you feel for me is love and not obligation? Do you come to me of your own free will or because Warrick thinks it's what you should do? If I weren't here, if I weren't part of the equation, who would you be seeking out?"

Zavian shook his head in frustration and stared at her. "That's your response? I tell you I love you, have always loved you, and you think I do this out of obligation? I don't know who I'd seek out. I've never loved anyone but you. I fell in love with you long ago, but obviously, that wasn't reciprocated." He stood and paced, shaking off his agitation. "Don't blow this off before giving us a chance. Besides, Warrick has promised you to me."

Eilish frowned. "What does *that* mean? There are only two of us in this relationship. Don't you think I have a say? And for the record, I'm not Warrick's to promise, or Fina's either. I'll make my own choices when the time comes. Stop being a jerk. Sit down. I'm not rejecting you. I'm saying I'm not ready to bond with you. I may never be ready to bond with you. I want you in my life, Zavian. Don't make this so difficult."

Sitting down, he sighed. "I'm trying to understand, Eilish. I know we can both be happy. I'm trying to understand your reluctance. You're your own person, as am I, but we have restrictions and rules. There are things the coven will expect from both of us." He chuckled. "That damn Bohannon stubborn streak is very powerful in you."

Eilish relaxed as he calmed down and returned to his chair at their table. "I don't know how this all plays out, Zavian. I don't have the gift of foresight. But I won't be anyone's puppet. I've been groomed to assume Fina's role as High Priestess someday, just as you are being groomed to fill Warrick's shoes. I know what my sister wanted. I understand that our hand-fasting would have made us both more powerful for the coven, but I'm not going to live my life for the coven. I have a responsibility, and I'll honor it, stepping into Fina's shoes when the time comes. My powers are greater than Anya's. It would have been much easier on me if she'd been born the more powerful of the Bohannon sisters. I wish she had, but it is what it is."

She took a sip of her coffee and looked out the window into the night as a few people were passing by on the other side of the glass. Eilish blinked her eyes a few times and was caught by the irony. She always said watching humans was like watching fish in a fishbowl, just moving about their lives, completely unaware of what was on the other side of the glass. If they only knew how thin the veil was that separated them. "I need time to process all this. And I can't promise anything. Maybe my feelings will change, and maybe they won't. I know it's not the answer you're looking for, but it's the only answer I've got. You know Zavian, Anya is quite fond of you. Have you ever thought about... you know, maybe asking her out?"

Zavian sat back in his chair and knew nothing would change her mind tonight, but he had no intentions of giving up. Was she serious? Anya? He knew Anya had something of a crush on him, but Anya didn't fit into his view of his future. "There's only one person who has the power to become my High Priestess, and that's you." He snickered and shook his head. "And you can't be serious. Anya? Can you actually see us together? Because there's no way."

Eilish listened to him as he settled back in his chair. "I can see you together. I mean, Anya is quite pretty. She dresses like that on purpose to put people off. You know that, don't you? And she's mastered the art of the sarcastic comeback. It's her weapon for keeping people at arm's length. When has Anya, or any of us, not been there for you when you needed us? Our families seem destined to be intertwined in some way. We'll always support the de Burkes."

Reaching out, he stroked her hand. "I meant no disrespect. I'm sorry. Anya is sweet, and she's always been a good friend. I want you, and I'm willing to wait. Perhaps with time, as you say, things will change. I don't want to ruin our friendship with this between us." He let go of her hand, knowing he didn't want to push any buttons tonight. "You know we could end up like Uncle Warrick and Seraphina, they bonded, but they maintained separate households. Warrick said that if they lived together, they'd kill each other. But they clearly love each other and share a passion for each other. How ironic. The High Priest and Priestess are instructing us, and they're not exactly setting a great example."

Eilish gave him a reluctant smile. "You know Fina; she sets her own rules. She understands the combined power of the High Priest and Priestess to protect the coven, but she's not about to give up her independence. She loves Warrick, but she'll never relinquish control. I guess I inherited more of that stubbornness than I realized." She paused a moment and finished off her coffee. Living like Seraphina and Warrick wasn't what she wanted for herself. She wanted real love. She wanted someone who'd be excited to see her at the end of the day, someone eager to share her life. She dismissed the thoughts from her head. She changed the subject. "So, are you ready for Ostara? Has Warrick started instructing you on how to lead yet? Fina is already frazzled getting prepared. She loves these ceremonies and doesn't like giving up the power."

"Uncle Warrick also likes his power. I'll be assisting as well. He's running my ass ragged, though, on running errands and checking on things. Don't you look forward to the day when neither can control us, and we are finally in our power?"

Eilish shrugged. "Not really. I mean, I was born into this family, so my fate as a witch was sealed. It's all I know. Fina says I should be honing my powers more, learning to control them, but I've never had much interest. Don't you wonder what's out there?" She waved her hand in a broad sweep across the shop window. "Wouldn't you like to travel and explore and not worry about the coven's needs?" She slumped down in her chair, knowing she'd never be free of what she was and the responsibility that would be laid on her shoulders.

It broke his heart to see her disillusioned. "Eilish, come on, don't feel so down. I enjoy serving the needs of the coven. It's who and what I am. It's an honor to serve. I've accepted that. And once you do, you'll see things differently." Standing up, he took her hand. "Come on, let's get out of here. It looks like they're trying to close up."

Eilish allowed him to take her hand and lead her from the shop as they returned to his car. She tilted her head back and looked up at the moon. It was almost full. They'd celebrate Ostara soon.

Zavian stopped and looked at her as the moon shone down; her hair looked silver in the moonlight. His heart raced because there was nothing more beautiful to him than Eilish. He could see the moon reflected in her eyes, absorbing the energy, and he knew she felt her power. "You look beautiful under the moon, Eilish; you're going to make a stunning High Priestess."

They finally reached the car and headed back to the house. Walking her to the door, he fidgeted slightly and smiled. "Thank you. I had a wonderful night. I hope we can do this again soon." He kissed her softly before she realized what he was doing.

Eilish leaned into his kiss. She felt his hands slowly caress her back and the heat from his mouth as his full lips covered hers. She returned his kiss and waited for the spark, but she felt nothing. As Zavian stepped back and turned and walked away, she looked after him and sighed. She opened the door to the foyer and stepped inside the house, closing the door behind her. She leaned with her back against the door as she heard the engine of the Jaguar roar to life outside. She wished for the hundredth time that she felt something... anything, for Zavian. She felt more than saw her sister's presence at the top of the stairs and looked up to see Anya.

Anya asked, "Did you have a good time?"

Eilish stared back at her, her face blank. "It was okay. Like always." The two locked eyes, caught in the dilemma of a man who fell in love with the wrong sister. Eilish finally broke the silence. "You know we could cast a spell..."

"No!" Anya interrupted her sister. "I don't want him out of your pity." Anya turned on her heels and walked back to her room, slamming the door.

Eilish started up the stairs. "Anya, no . . . I didn't mean it like that!"

Seraphina entered from the kitchen, wiping her hands on an apron. "I thought I heard voices. I was making the ritual cakes for Ostara. They're baking now. How was your date?"

Eilish looked over the banister at her sister. "My date? My date was the same as every date, Fina."

Seraphina's smile disappeared. "Get over yourself, missy. Who do you think you will bond with? Warrick brought his nephew here from Boston just for you. The other warlocks in the coven are twice your age. Beggars can't be choosers. You do what you need to do."

Eilish headed up the stairs. "Maybe I'll just run away."

Seraphina followed up the stairs behind her, raising her voice. "And do what? How long would a witch survive among humans without her coven? You'd be an outcast."

Eilish continued up the stairs. "I'm already an outcast." She saw Emric as he dashed back and forth in a panic at the top of the stairs. He always got upset when the sisters argued. She walked past him to her room and closed the door behind her. She repeated under her breath, "I'm already an outcast."

⁂

Warrick paced as he kept his eye on the clock. He heard the sound of Zavian's car as he pulled into the driveway and listened as the mechanical sound of the convertible roof rose into place. Zavian had hardly stepped inside the house before Warrick was asking questions. "So? How did it go?"

Zavian shrugged. "It was okay. We had a nice time."

Warrick got in his face, backing him against the door. "A nice time? That's the best you can do? Have you even bedded her yet?" Warrick poked his finger hard into Zavian's chest. "I didn't bring you here from Boston just to give Eilish Bohannon someone to take her to an occasional movie. You have a job to do, now do it!"

Zavian frowned. He didn't want to start a fight with his uncle; he always ended up on the losing end of any argument with Warrick. "My job? Eilish isn't a job. Jeez, no wonder she feels pressured."

Warrick glared back at him. "You know what I mean. If you're not up for the challenge of seducing her, then let's get that on the table right now. All I see is you following behind her like some stray pup. Do you need a spell?"

Zavian pushed past his uncle on his way to his bedroom. "I'm not going to win Eilish's heart by casting a spell. I'm not going to trick her into bonding with me. Believe it or not, I care about her!"

Warrick heard him slam his bedroom door as he shouted after him. "The clock is ticking, Zavian. Fina and I won't wait forever!"

BOHANNON

It was late evening on the night of the full moon, and the sisters scrambled to get everything together for Ostara. Warrick and Zavian had arrived in Warrick's van. Warrick kept the small table used for an altar in the back of the van. The legs of the table had been cut in half, so it sat low to the ground.

Each sister had her list of items needed for tonight's ritual. Eilish gathered the elemental representations of the universe that would be placed on the altar: salt to represent the earth, incense to represent air, a red candle to represent fire, and water. In addition, she added a stack of small, shallow bowls to the basket.

Seraphina had packed up the small ritual cakes she'd baked, enough for everyone in the coven. The cakes were small and plain. She'd loaded up a case of wine that Zavian quickly lifted to his shoulders and carried out to the van. She carefully counted out the small glasses, ensuring she had enough as she placed them in boxes. After quickly counting one last time, she added a few extras, then had Warrick carry the two boxes containing the glasses to the van.

Anya gathered one gold and one silver candle to represent the god and goddess and the quarter candles for the four Watchtowers; black for North/Earth, yellow for East/Air, red for South/Fire, and blue for West/Water. She dug through the kitchen drawer, found a pack of matches, and tossed it in the basket, although Eilish and Seraphina could usually light the candles without matches. She carefully laid the three wands in the basket, as each sister had her own, making sure the wands didn't touch. The wands were as unique in their magic as the witch who owned them. She removed the jewel-embellished gold chalice from the china cabinet, carefully wrapping it in a dish towel before placing it in the basket. She grabbed the broom reserved for ceremonies from the kitchen pantry and some fresh sage sprigs. She put the sage in the basket and leaned the broom against the wall next to her basket. Checking her list, she noticed an item she had missed. "Oh, the feather!" Returning to the pantry, she retrieved the eagle's feather from the top shelf and laid it with her other supplies.

She checked her list to ensure she had everything when Seraphina spoke up. "White candles. Nine of them. We're casting a fertility spell tonight for Beckett and Esca."

Anya nodded. "Right, I almost forgot." She returned to the pantry and retrieved the box of candles, sorting through it to collect nine white ones, then wrapped them in a towel and laid them in the basket. She gathered the velvet pouch containing a single pearl and the abalone shell. The men had returned from loading the van, and the three sisters stood in the kitchen as Seraphina called out all the items they should have gathered, and each sister nodded. Seraphina looked about, slipping the basket of cakes on her arm. "Okay then, I think we're ready." Eilish and Anya each picked up their baskets, and Zavian grabbed the broom as Warrick led them to the van.

The items were stored in the back of the van, and the five of them climbed inside. Warrick drove as Seraphina sat next to him in the passenger seat. Zavian was wedged between the two sisters on the bench seat in the back. He reached to take Eilish's hand just as she lifted it to brush back her hair. He wasn't sure if it was a coincidence or a conscious move on her part, but he didn't make another effort. Warrick made his way through historic Charleston and across the Cooper River Bridge on their way to John's Island and the massive live oak tree called Angel's Oak. It was the spot where they always held their ceremonies for the moon.

They were silent as they drove, each in a form of meditation as they readied themselves for the ceremony. Warrick drove down the narrow gravel road on the island and pulled the van off to the side of the road as they approached the massive four-hundred-year-old tree, its lower branches bowed down with their weight, level with the ground in some places. He noted that a few cars were parked off the road, their lights off. Inside the van, Warrick and Zavian pulled black hooded robes over their clothes while the three sisters discreetly removed their summer garb and pulled the sheer white gossamer gowns over their heads. Once their gowns were on, they removed their underwear, nude beneath the gowns. The women wore their hair down tonight, another symbol of their feminine energy. Each carefully placed the flower halo crown of fresh sage and primrose atop their heads. Even the male warlocks understood that the power of the sacred feminine was far superior to any force they could conjure. Warrick averted his eyes as Seraphina changed, even though he'd slept in her bed for years. The ceremony was sacred, and he gave her privacy in her preparation. Zavian kept his head down with his eyes closed as the two sisters changed their clothes on either side of him, resisting the temptation to watch Eilish undress.

As the High Priest and Priestess exited the van, followed by Zavian and the other two sisters, they heard the collective sounds in the dark of other car doors opening. The witches and warlocks from their coven were exiting their cars, following them barefoot across the grass. The warlocks, all dressed in the same black hooded robes, formed a wide circle around the tree, while the witches, all dressed in the same ghostly gossamer, their heads bare and hair down, gathered in an inner circle.

Anya approached the center of the circle, holding the broom, and walked clockwise, sweeping from the center outward to cleanse the space of negative energy. "Sweep out evil, sweep out ill, where I do the lady's will. Besom, besom, lady's broom, sweep out darkness, sweep out doom. Witch's broom, swift in flight, cast out darkness, bring in light. Earth be hallow, air be pure, fire burn bright, as water cures. A sacred bridge this site shall be, as I will, so mote it be."

As she chanted, a low, soft drone could be heard from the circle of warlocks. As Eilish entered with her wand, Anya held the broom skyward and slowly backed from the cleansed space. Standing in the center of the circle, her nude silhouette visible through her thin gown, she lifted her wand above her head, drew a pentagram in the air, and watched as the symbol she created glowed slightly in the dark sky before fading to nothing. She lowered her wand and etched the pentagram into the soil at the base of the tree. "Blessed be, instruments of light, tools of magic with power and might." The drone of the male warlocks deepened as they began drawing more energy from the young, white-haired witch.

Zavian carried the small table to the center of the circle, near the base of the tree, and placed it on the ground. He removed the items from Eilish's basket, placed a shallow bowl on the altar, and filled it with salt. He poured a second bowl full of water next to it. He set a red candle upright on the altar and laid the incense stick next to it before slowly backing out of the circle's center.

Eilish knelt before the altar and held her hand over the water and salt, slowly passing her hand over the shallow bowls three times before holding her hands still to bless the elements. She concentrated her energy, and a sparkling light appeared to glow from the water as she recited, "Elements of earth and water, I consecrate thee. In the name of the lord and the lady, I bring their blessings upon us now. So mote it be."

She poured the consecrated salt into the blessed water and turned her attention to the red candle. Feeling her power, she ignored the book of matches on the altar, pointed her forefinger at the tip of the red candle, and watched in silence as the flame flickered to life. "Element of fire, cleanse this space and those who gather here. In the name of the lord and the lady, I now bring their blessings upon us. So mote it be."

She picked up the stick of incense and held it to the flame, watching as the tip caught fire, and the fragrant smoke rose in the air. Holding the incense stick in both hands, she lifted it skyward as the smoke trailed off in the night air. "Element of air, cleanse this space and those who gather here. In the name of the lord and the lady, I now bring their blessing upon us. So mote it be." The drone of the warlocks, repeating their chant, picked up volume and energy.

Eilish placed the incense upright in a holder and then picked up the bowl of water, salt, and a sprig of fresh sage. She walked clockwise around the circle as the males moved inward, widening the circle's circumference as they joined hands with the females. She dipped the sage into the consecrated water and sprinkled the coven as she passed. "Powers of water and earth, purify, cleanse and bless those who gather here." She returned the bowl to the altar and picked up the incense, walking clockwise around the circle again, using the large eagle feather, a sign of her authority, fanning it in an outward motion to disperse the smoke from the incense over the coven. "Powers of fire and air, this circle grace. Purify, cleanse, and bless those that gather here." The low, droning sound from the warlocks continued as Eilish walked back to the altar, laying down the incense and the feather.

She held her wand out at waist level, facing East, then walked clockwise three times around the circle. As she walked, the coven could see the small beam of white light that glowed from the tip of her wand, burning brighter with each rotation she made. It was just another indication to them of the young witch's power. "Maiden, cast your circle white. Weave a web of healing light. Round and round the circle's cast, joining present, future, past. Mother, cast your circle red. Weave the strands of family threads. This sacred space shall now be bound as I cast this circle round. Old crone, cast your circle black. Weave the wisdom that we lack. Thrice is the circle cast this night and now begins my magic rite."

Eilish moved to the center of the circle as the males stopped the low drone, and all was silent. She stood with her wand pointed skyward and called out, "As above." The coven answered, "As above." She lowered her wand so it was pointing to the ground. "So below." The coven responded, "So below."

Zavian had watched her through this portion of the ceremony. He was struck by her beauty as the outline of her slender body was visible through the sheer white gown. Her face was softly lit by the glow from the candle and the moon's soft light. As always at night, her snow-white hair looked almost silver. She took his breath away. He watched from beneath his black hood as she rejoined the circle created by the coven and took his hand. He gave her hand a soft squeeze she didn't return.

Seraphina stepped forward into the circle and gathered the elemental candles. Walking clockwise around the coven's inner circle, she moved to the North and planted the black candle into the ground, stepping back and quickly lighting it with her finger, calling on the Guardians of the Watchtowers. She then walked East and planted the yellow candle as she started marking the four quarters. She spoke boldly, "Hail mighty ones of the Eastern Tower. Guard this circle with your power. Powers of air weave the ground. Between the worlds, the power bound. Till I send it at the last, Guardian, keep it strong and fast." She repeated the ritual, placing the red candle in the South, and the blue candle in the West, calling on the Guardians of water and fire.

She returned to the altar and picked up the gold god candle, her power strong now, as the candle ignited with a mere nod of her head. Standing strong in the circle's center, she lifted the gold candle to the sky. "I call to the god. Spark of the spirit eternal. Lord of the wild hunt. Judge of gods and men. Shining god of the sun's rays, who walks with me through all my days. Into my circle, I invoke thee to bless and guide all I do. Hail and welcome." The coven chanted, "Hail and welcome."

Seraphina placed the gold candle on the altar and picked up the silver goddess candle as it ignited with her touch, her power growing. The coven stood in awe of their High Priestess, and Warrick watched her, knowing no witch here came close to the Bohannon's power. He had made sure to secure his position in the coven years ago by bonding with Seraphina and doing whatever was necessary for the two of them to reign. He heard Seraphina begin the following chant. "I call to the goddess, beauty of the green earth. White moon among the stars, mysteries of the water. Shimmering goddess of the moon's light, who guides me through the dark of night. Into my circle, I invoke thee to bless and guide all I do. Hail and welcome." The coven repeated, "Hail and welcome."

Seraphina placed the silver candle next to the gold one, then poured some wine into two shallow bowls before filling the jewel-encrusted goblet. She lifted the golden goblet above her head. "I drink to the god and goddess." She took a sip from the goblet and said, "Blessed be." The coven echoed her, "Blessed be."

Returning the goblet to the altar, Seraphina turned and held her arms out to her side. "We will use our collective powers to invoke a fertility spell for Beckett and Esca. Come forward, please."

The couple stepped forward, holding hands. Beckett and Esca had been hand-fasted two years ago and had yet to produce a child. They had approached Seraphina after the last Ostara about the need for a fertility spell, and she had granted their request. Ostara was the time for fertility, birth, and renewal and the most conducive time for casting a spell for fertility. Anya and Eilish broke from the circle and approached the altar. Eilish picked up five white candles, and Anya grabbed the remaining four, plus the matches. The two witches created a smaller circle within their sacred space as they placed the white candles in the ground. Eilish lit each candle with a touch from the tip of her finger while Anya struck a match to light hers. Once the circle of white candles was completed, the two young witches returned to their place in the larger circle formed by the coven. Seraphina nodded as she placed the abalone shell on the altar, and gently laid the single pearl inside, as the coven members turned in unison, their backs to the young couple and rejoining hands. Beckett and Esca stepped inside the circle of white candles and disrobed, standing nude before Seraphina. Seraphina stood in front of Beckett, placing her left hand over each chakra, the seven centers of spiritual power located in the body, starting at the top of his head and moving down his torso, drawing on her energy as she saw each chakra glow. She repeated the ritual with Esca, focusing on the sacral chakra, the center for sexual energy, to remove any negativity. She stepped forward so the couple was behind her as they both lay down on the ground and began to make love. Seraphina dropped her robe to the ground as it puddled at her feet. She lifted her hands above her head and tilted her head back, looking at the moon. "With one mind, we call to thee. With one heart, we long for thee. Child of earth, air, fire, and sea, into our lives, we welcome thee."

The women in the coven repeated the chant in unison, their voices sweet and melodic, as they let go of the warlock's hands and danced freely and sensuously. The warlocks stood still and returned to creating the low, constant hum that sent out a powerful vibration. The chanting and the continuous drone became louder as the couple in the center of the circle reached their climax, crying out with the ecstasy of their union. The coven stood still and silent as Seraphina and Esca slipped back into their gossamer gowns, and Beckett donned his black robe. Seraphina placed her hands on their heads and closed her eyes. She could feel the power of the united egg and sperm within Esca's womb and opened her eyes to smile at them. She could see the joy in both their faces as they silently returned to the circle, and the coven turned back to face center, welcoming them back into the fold. Seraphina extinguished the white candles with a glance, the smoke curling upward, mingling with the Spanish moss in the ancient tree.

Anya and Eilish stepped forward again and worked quickly with Seraphina in a routine they had repeated many times, distributing the ritual cakes and wine. Once all had been served, Seraphina held her ritual cake for all to see and then spoke, "May I never hunger." She took a bite, as all in the coven did the same. She held up her glass of wine and said, "May I never thirst." She tipped the glass to her lips to drink, and all in the coven drank from their glasses. As the cake and wine were consumed, Seraphina said, "Blessed be." The coven repeated her refrain.

Warrick stepped forward to close the ceremony and release the Guardians of the four quarters. Starting in the North, he walked counter-clockwise in a circle as he extinguished each candle with his finger, tapping the flame down. His voice was deep and loud. "To all those of the Northern sphere, I release you now; may you depart from here." The chant was repeated as he walked to each quarter, and the colored candles burned no more. He stood in the center next to Seraphina and took her hand. "I give thanks to all of thee, god and goddess, and guardians of the North, South, East, and West. Depart in peace, and blessed be." The coven called out, "Blessed be!"

Warrick and Seraphina approached the altar, where Warrick continued in his booming voice. "I give thanks to the gods for guarding our circle and joining our rite. Hail and farewell." He extinguished the gold candle with a tap of his finger. Seraphina said, "I thank the goddesses for guarding our circle and joining our rite. Hail and farewell." She extinguished the silver candle.

Lifting her wand, Seraphina walked counterclockwise and drew the energy of the ceremony back into her own body. "Circle round, now be unbound as I make my way around. I now dissolve this sacred space and send all powers back to place. Circle round, now be unbound as I make my way around. Stay if you can. Go if you must, with perfect love and perfect trust. My work is finished for the night, and now I end my magic rite."

Warrick stepped forward, marking an end to the ritual. "The circle is closed but not unbroken."

He watched as the members of their coven slowly broke away from the circle, returning their empty glasses to the altar, and chatting quietly among themselves, as they slowly returned to their cars.

Ian sat on a high branch in a live oak tree located a discreet distance from the witches and watched the ceremony. He'd only been in Charleston a short time before the white-haired witch had caught his eye. There was just one problem, vampires and witches never mingled. Cavorting with a mortal was bad enough, but a witch caused all kinds of problems. He'd been watching her for a while now, and despite all the alarm bells going off in his head, he knew he was smitten. He'd seen her with the blonde warlock but could tell from her body language that the relationship wasn't physical, at least not yet, and not ever if Ian had anything to do with it. He'd watched her slender nude form, silhouetted against the candles and the moonlight throughout the ceremony, then watched as all the witches packed up and left. He lay back, cradled in the branches of a tree that was possibly older than he was, and lit up a cigarette as he spoke aloud to himself. "Ian, what the fuck are you doing?"

BOHANNON

As the van rolled to a stop in front of the sisters' home, Seraphina immediately started issuing orders. She directed Warrick and Zavian to unload all the boxes and bring them inside. Strolling ahead, she opened the scrolled wrought-iron gate, leaving it open for the others, and walked briskly to the front porch, unlocking the door. Luna slipped outside and explored the wrap-around porch, chasing after the lightning bugs that flittered about. Anya grabbed her backpack, and Eilish picked up her large tote containing their ritual gowns, jumped down from the van, and headed inside.

Seraphina called to them from the porch. "Hurry up, you two; we need to get this done; tomorrow, we'll have to wake early to clean up and still get the store opened on time." Seraphina heard their mutterings as they walked past her into the house. She ignored them. It wasn't the first time she'd heard it.

Zavian carried several boxes to the porch and piled them up close to the door, his eyes constantly on Eilish as he imagined how beautiful she looked tonight in that sheer gown, standing in the moonlight. She looked like the goddess she was born to be. Eilish returned to make another trip to the van, and Zavian quickly caught up to walk beside her. "You were magnificent tonight, Eilish. You captivated everyone in the coven."

Eilish remained focused on removing things from the van as she answered him. "Oh, thanks. I love the Ostara ritual. It's one of my favorites. Seraphina said the fertility spell worked. So that will be wonderful for Beckett and Esca." She took one last look into the back of the van. "Looks like we got everything." She turned and started walking back to the house with Zavian on her heels.

"I had no doubts! You could feel that Seraphina was in her full power. That will be you, someday." When they reached the porch, Warrick lifted the boxes and carried them inside to the kitchen as Seraphina orchestrated the events, issuing orders.

Warrick cast a sideways glance at Fina, knowing she still felt her power. "My goddess, there's no need to instruct us as if we were moving the planets back in alignment. I know where these things go." He kissed her quickly as he passed her and turned to stare at Zavian and Eilish. He was pleased with how they'd struck up such an easy conversation between them, and Zavian's attention to her had been laser-focused. Warrick directed his attention to the two younger sisters. "I was quite pleased with both of you tonight. You're learning well to master your powers. I thought this was a particularly powerful Ostara. And thanks to Seraphina, we'll have another member in our coven soon." Turning to Seraphina, he suggested they all have a drink before they parted ways for the night.

Seraphina removed some clean glasses from the cabinet, working around the boxes stacked on the countertops. Anya retrieved a bottle of white wine from the fridge and popped the cork, handing it to her sister to pour. As Seraphina filled the glasses, she instructed everyone. "Take a seat in the parlor. We'll chat a bit before everyone leaves. Here Anya, help me carry the wine glasses." Warrick grabbed his glass as Seraphina and Anya carried the extra glasses back to the parlor. Zavian and Eilish followed them. They each found a seat, leaving the sofa free, so Eilish was forced to sit next to Zavian. Eilish wasn't unaware of their ambush tactics.

Zavian turned to Eilish, tipping his glass to hers. "To the future High Priest and Priestess." Eilish was shocked by his proclamation and remained silent, deciding not to make a big deal of it.

Warrick raised an eyebrow. "Is there something you wish to tell us, Zavian? Perhaps some long overdue news we've been waiting to hear?"

Zavian took a long sip of the wine and smiled at Eilish. "No news, Uncle, just that I think Eilish will make an excellent High Priestess and that she'll bond with me in time. You and Fina can conduct our hand-fasting ritual."

Warrick sat watchfully and saw the glow in Zavian's eyes. Eilish had cast her own spell on him tonight. He had to admit she was a stunning creature in her gossamer gown and white hair. She looked like some forest nymph dancing in the moonlight. And like Seraphina, she was channeling her full power. "I agree, she'll make an excellent High Priestess, but what exactly does 'in time' mean? Time is running out with each second our two families wait. Neither of you is getting any younger, and my patience is running thin." He took Seraphina's hand and looked at Eilish. "I thought this would have been worked out by this time. Tell me, Eilish, what exactly are you waiting for?"

Eilish took a sip of the wine, feeling her anger rise to the surface. She hated being confronted and pinned down. Seraphina was pushy, but Warrick took everything to the next level. She lowered the glass and stared back at Warrick with her steel-gray eyes. She wanted to tell him she was waiting for hell to freeze over, but she knew that would start an argument. "I'll wait until the time is right for me, and not a second sooner, Warrick. And if that answer doesn't suit you, then perhaps you should find a different witch."

Zavian quickly jumped to her defense when his Uncle's face began to turn red, his anger about to pour forth on all of them. "Please, Uncle Warrick, let's not argue. It's been such an enjoyable evening. Eilish and I have talked at length, she's not ready, and I agreed to wait. What's a few months' time? We care for each other very much, and both of us agree that this constant pressure only makes us more hesitant. We're all tired, and everyone has worked so hard to prepare for Ostara."

He placed his arm around Eilish's shoulders and kissed her softly. "Come on. I'll walk you up to your room. Where's your bag? I'll carry it up for you. You've had a long night, and you look tired; you need some rest." He stood up to take her hand and looked at his Uncle. "Not tonight, please, Uncle; we're just asking for some time. Things are well between us."

Warrick waved his hand as if brushing it all aside. "I'll think on this tomorrow, but I expect a definitive answer before the next Ostara."

Eilish downed the remaining wine in the glass and stood up quickly. She should have known this gathering couldn't pass without some pressure being applied as to what her intentions were regarding Zavian. She headed for the stairs as Luna ran ahead of her, and Zavian carried her tote bag, rushing behind her to keep up. Eilish was glad to escape Warrick's cross-examination but not so eager to have Zavian on her heels. She entered her bedroom and sighed as Zavian came in behind her and placed her things on her bed. Eilish apologized. "I'm sorry I lost my temper, but I'm tired of feeling pressured."

They both saw Emric exit the room as he felt the mounting tension. Zavian spoke softly to the apparition. "Sorry, Emric. It's okay..." but Emric had brushed past him in a rush to exit. Zavian apologized to her. "I didn't mean to upset him."

Eilish raised her hand as if to brush away some invisible force. "Don't worry. He'll be fine. Emric doesn't like conflict, and between Seraphina, Anya, and me, we keep him in constant turmoil. I don't know why he stays." She laughed softly as she sat down on her vanity table stool, eliminating any possibility of Zavian sitting next to her. "Thanks for standing up for me. I get so tired of everyone pushing me. I'll make my own decisions in my own time. Jeez... I can see why he and Seraphina don't live together. They would constantly be butting heads, and neither knows the meaning of the word compromise."

Zavian saw the angst this had caused her, but he wouldn't give up easily. He'd continue to strive to win her heart. Laying his hand on her shoulder, he kissed her cheek and whispered softly. "I can only defy him for so long, Eilish. He's set on this."

He exited and sighed heavily. He'd have her no matter how long it took. But make no mistake; he was, above all, her defender and protector. Heading down the stairs, he passed Anya on her way up. "Good night, Anya." Walking into the parlor, he found his Uncle and Seraphina clutching each other's hands in a solemn conversation. "No need to wait on me, Uncle. I'll walk home. I need some air. Good night to you both." Walking out on the porch, he took a deep breath of the humid night air and vowed to the moon that someday, Eilish would be his forever, his High Priestess.

BOHANNON

The construction crew worked in the sweltering heat of the Charleston summer. Ian had seen the witch with white hair around town for some time and noted she and her sister walked daily past this old house under reconstruction. It wasn't difficult to get hired onto the construction crew. He stood atop the roof of the house at the intersection of Tradd and Meeting Street and pulled his thick, dark brown hair back into a bun to keep it off his neck. He could immediately feel the cooler air against the sweat on his neck. The contractor he worked for was no stranger to the antebellum and even the few pre-Revolutionary war homes that populated the historic district of old Charleston. The houses were all uniquely beautiful but constantly needed upkeep and repair. For Ian, it gave him the means to blend in with the mortals and a way to cross paths with the witch.

It was only 9:30, and he was already removing his t-shirt and tossing it aside. The sun had baked his skin to a caramel brown. He kept an eye on his watch. He knew to expect the two girls who walked past the house every day about this time. He'd befriended Carter, a mortal, who walked gingerly across the roof as sure-footed as a cat and started ribbing him good-naturedly. "Better pay attention to what you're doing and stop looking for those girls. Besides, I told you, everyone around here knows they're witches."

Ian shook his head and chuckled. He played along, but if Carter only knew the truth of it. "You saw them fly on a broomstick with your own eyes? Cause, otherwise, I don't believe in that witch stuff."

Carter punched his arm lightly. "Not that kind of witch. Hey, I'm just telling you what people say."

Ian knelt in his torn jeans and work boots and removed the roof tiles. "Since when did you start listening to what people say, Carter?"

Carter laughed and tipped the water bottle to his lips, taking a long drink before pouring some of the water over his head to cool down. "Suit yourself, Romeo. Just don't say I didn't warn you."

Carter knelt beside him as they used small crowbars to pry loose the shingles and toss them into a large metal collection bin on the ground. Within minutes, the men could hear the soft chatter of the two sisters who routinely walked past the house every day before ten. Ian looked down as the young women passed and heard the cat calls from the other workers on the ground floor. Ian laughed as the blonde one with round sunglasses flashed them the finger, and the one with the snow-white hair only turned her head slightly, barely acknowledging the men's presence. Ian asked the question, thinking out loud, "Where do they go, you reckon?"

Carter looked up and used a bandana to wipe the sweat from his eyes. "They have a shop. Some witchy store a few blocks up on Tradd. They live back on East Bay near the Battery. Even if they're not witches, they're too rich for our blood, bro. Which one you got your eye on?"

Ian nodded his head in Eilish's direction. "The one with the white hair."

Carter chuckled. "Good. Cause I prefer that snarky one. She don't take shit from nobody."

Ian laughed and followed her with his eyes as she walked away, her white hair caught in a light breeze, and he watched as she tilted her head back to enjoy the momentary relief from the heat. "You can make enough money running a shop down here to buy one of these houses?"

Carter shrugged. "Old money, I think, inherited. Not sure. There are three of them, though. Three sisters. Last name is Bohannon. The way the locals tell it, the family came over from Ireland, and they were among the original settlers of Charleston."

Ian watched the girls until they were no longer visible through the branches of the trees and returned his focus to removing shingles. He knew there were three sisters. He'd seen them at the ceremony on John's Island but didn't mention that to Carter. "You think their ancestors came here during that potato famine? Those people were poor."

Carter shook his head. "Well, that depends on which story you want to believe. The folks 'round here say they were driven out because they were witches. They were being hanged or drowned, or whatever the fuck it was they did to witches. So they got on a ship and sailed to America. Landed here in the port city of Charleston and been here ever since."

Ian tossed more shingles over the side and heard them hit with a thud in the metal dumpster. "Bohannon. You know their first names?"

Carter laughed. "Dude, what do I look like, fucking Wikipedia? You want to know, go find out for yourself. But let me know if you need a wingman. I'd be up for a go at the snarky one."

Ian chuckled, wondering how long he could maintain his cover. "You don't seriously believe that witch stuff, do you? I mean, look at them."

Carter looked up, gazing down the sidewalk where the two girls had passed, and shrugged. "Don't know. They don't mingle with the locals much; I know that."

Ian smiled. "Maybe I like a challenge."

Carter laughed at him again. "Shit, brother, it's going to be an entertaining summer; I'll give you that much." He emptied the remaining water from his water bottle over Ian's head, and Ian laughed.

At noon, Ian grabbed his t-shirt and climbed down from the roof. He got to his truck, where he kept a cooler filled with ice and water. The other workers wandered off around the grounds, most eating a lunch they'd packed for themselves, seeking relief from the heat under a tree. Ian used a bandana to dip into the cold water and wipe off his face and neck. He usually pretended to take a short nap in the truck to avoid questions about lunch, but he wondered if he could find the witch store Carter had been talking about. He looked down at his holey jeans and the dirty t-shirt and thought this was probably not how he wanted to look the first time he met her. He realized that somewhere between 10:00 a.m. and noon, a decision had been made. He was definitely going to find that girl with snow-white hair.

BOHANNON

The morning dawned thick and muggy, and the early dew had converted to steam and could be seen rising in a mist from the street. It was a typical Charleston summer and would be another day of oppressive heat. The construction crew was on the job at sun-up, trying to get work done before the temperature rose. Ian had volunteered to clean up some of the nails and roofing materials that had missed the dumpster as they had been haphazardly tossed down the previous day. He didn't mind; it seemed a bit cooler on the ground, and working there gave him the occasional opportunity to stand in the shade. Still, he'd already pulled off his t-shirt and tossed it under the base of the tree. He checked his watch, and it was close to ten. He kept glancing in the direction of the sidewalk, looking down toward East Bay. He could see the sisters approaching.

"Hey Ian, you missed some," Carter yelled down at him, laughing as he saw the girls now closing the gap between themselves and Ian.

The sisters were laughing over an incident this morning when Luna had gotten under Seraphina's feet while she was rushing about in the kitchen, and she almost went down. Fina was cussing, and Luna took off for the stairs, and the younger sisters' laughter only darkened Fina's mood. It didn't help that the incident occurred at the end of another one of Fina's lectures about when Eilish would get serious about Zavian.

As their laughter faded, Eilish said, "I hope she gets over it before she comes in today. She said she had a bunch of errands to run, and she might not see us until this afternoon."

Anya nodded, brushing her hair from her face. "What are you going to do, though? She and Warrick are really pushing this whole thing with Zavian."

Eilish turned solemn. Since Ostara, she hadn't heard a sentence from Fina's mouth that didn't contain the name Zavian. She sighed heavily. "I don't know. I told her to back off, but you know Fina. I might as well be talking to a brick wall. She and Warrick are both relentless." She cast a sideways glance at her sister. "I'm sorry, Anya. I know you care for him. I don't know what to do."

Eilish heard a man's voice calling out from the rooftop. She looked up to see a man standing dangerously close to the roof's edge, silhouetted against the bright sun. She cupped her hand over her eyes to block the glare, squinting into the sunlight when she bumped into someone on the street. He bent over, picked up scrap material from the construction site, and stood up abruptly, apologizing profusely. Eilish immediately recognized him as a vampire but tried to hide her shock. It had been a while since she'd seen any vampires in Charleston, and she hoped this didn't mean trouble for the coven. "Oh! No... it was me. I'm sorry. I wasn't watching where I was going."

Eilish took in the vampire. He was tall and bare-chested, skin bronzed by the sun, a day-walker, unaffected by the killing rays of the sun and free to roam night or day. His dark brown hair was long, thick, and wavy. It had a just tumbled-out-of-bed look. The muscles in his chest and arms were well-defined, and sweat glistened off his tanned skin. He wore jeans that hung low on his slender hips and a pair of work boots laced over his ankles. His eyes were as dark as his hair. She locked eyes with him as he apologized and felt like someone had cast a spell on *her* for a change.

Ian reached out to steady her when they collided, ensuring she didn't fall. "Hey, are you all right? I didn't mean to startle you, but..."

His eyes met hers, and he knew she saw him, knew what he was, but he was stricken. She looked straight through him with those soft gray eyes. He felt like he'd been hit by a bulldozer. This wasn't how he envisioned their first meeting, and he apologized again. "I was just trying to clean up here, so no one got hurt." He was hypnotized by her and couldn't take his eyes off her. A few seconds felt like hours.

Anya saw the vampire a second too late to prevent Eilish from bumping into him. She felt the instant chemistry between them and muttered under her breath, "Oh, brother."

Eilish was saying she was fine, no harm done, and realized she'd reached out and placed her hand on his upper arm to steady herself when she bumped into him. He felt like steel. She quickly withdrew her hand as if she'd been burned on a hot stove, and come to think of it, the sensation felt similar. "It was totally my fault. Forgive me."

Anya slid her arm through her sister's. "Come on; we need to get to work." She looked at the vampire and said, "See ya," as she dragged Eilish off down the street, leaving Ian looking after them. Anya waited until they were about half a block away and out of range before speaking. "He's a fucking vampire! What were you thinking?"

Eilish shook her head, her arm still locked with Anya's. "I don't know. Did you see him? Anya... he's gorgeous."

"And a vampire. Don't forget that part. We don't mingle with vampires, remember?"

Eilish nodded, and despite her best instincts, she turned her head and looked over her shoulder. He was still standing there, legs slightly spread, arms held slightly away from his body, and staring back at her. She thought to herself; he *felt what I felt*. She turned her head back around and continued walking with her sister. "Vampire. Right."

Ian watched them walk away. He felt immobilized, as if he were standing in hardening cement. He was aware he was breathing heavier, and his heart was pumping hard inside his muscled chest. He fought the desire to follow after her, and then she looked over her shoulder, her eyes the color of softest gray, and he could swear the sun sparkled through them.

Carter shouted at him. "You gonna stand around down there all day? I told you, you better get that piece out of your head."

Carter's voice broke through his trance, and he shook his head to clear it. He looked up to see the mortal standing on the roof with his hands on his hips. "Yeah, I'm coming."

He headed up the ladder but was already thinking about how and when he could see her again.

Anya pulled the store keys from her pocket and opened the shop, hearing the familiar jangle from the old-fashioned bell that hung above the door. The sisters entered and got the store ready to open. Anya unlocked the cash register, although it held almost no cash. Most of the transactions were digital. Eilish had gone straight to the back of the shop and returned with a box of new books they'd ordered. She slid the heavy box onto the counter, and the two sisters started removing the books about the healing powers of crystals and placing them on the shelf.

Anya became aware of her sister's silence and looked over to see a tear on her cheek. She dropped the book and focused all of her attention on her sister. "Eilish! What's wrong? Are you okay?"

Eilish quickly brushed away the tear and answered almost angrily. "I don't want Zavian. I'm not going to be forced into this bonding, Anya; I'm not! I'll run away first! I'm so tired of making excuses."

Anya hugged her sister. "Then stop making excuses. Just tell her outright."

Eilish shook her head. "I *have* told her."

Anya said, "No. You dance around it. As you said, you make excuses. You say things like, when I'm ready. You're so busy trying not to hurt Zavian's feelings that you don't say what you mean. You need to have this out with Fina once and for all. It won't be easy. Fina will fight you tooth and nail, so stand your ground."

Eilish sat down on the floor in front of the bookcase, feeling dejected as she placed the books on the shelf. "I've tried. She even told me I could bond with Zavian and continue to live at home like she does with Warrick. That's not what I want."

Anya looked down at her sister. "This doesn't have anything to do with the vampire, does it?"

Eilish shook her head. "No. He reminds me of the possibilities in life. That there are others out there that I could feel something for."

Anya stood with her hands on her hips. "Don't get too tied up in the fairy-tale, sister. All unions have their problems; you know that."

Eilish nodded. "I know. I don't need a knight in shining armor. I don't want the troll under the bridge either."

Anya threw her head back and laughed. "I can't believe you compared Zavian to a troll. Your judgment has been seriously impaired."

Eilish smiled. "He's not a troll. You know what I mean. He's not the one for me." She cast a wicked glance up at her sister. "I could cast a spell for you. You know I can."

Anya pointed her finger at her. "Don't you dare! I've told you before I don't want your leftover pity fuck."

Eilish laughed. "Well, technically, he's not a leftover since we've never had sex."

Anya glared at her. "I'm not kidding, Eilish!"

Eilish stood up from the floor, brushing off her long skirt. "I'd never do that without your permission. You know that. Besides, you'll find someone."

Anya rolled her eyes. "In a book, maybe." The door jangled as the first customers of the day started to come in, and the sisters got to work.

BOHANNON

Carter had teased Ian about his "witchy little piece" for the rest of the day. Ian needed no help keeping her in his mind. She was inside his head every minute. He'd thought about her all night, trying to talk himself out of this insane obsession, but to no avail. He was a mercenary warrior and belonged to no coven, so he had more freedom than most. But he didn't kid himself. Hooking up with a witch would bring all nature of shit down on his head. He took the ribbing from Carter like a champ, but it only reminded him of his intense desire to have another encounter with her. He had watched her walk by again that morning, and when noon struck, he walked in the direction of his truck, and Carter followed him. "Let's grab our coolers and sit under the tree. Damn heat is hell on the roof today." When Ian didn't answer, Carter stopped walking. "What the hell has you all riled up? Did she cast a spell on you? Told you to watch out for those sisters."

He nudged Ian in the ribs, which was Ian's tipping point. "Yeah, you know this shit is getting old. Lay off the witch and spell shit. She looks different from other girls; it doesn't make her a witch."

He turned and walked to the truck, and his mind was made up. Looking back at Carter, "I'm going to get something to eat. Not in the mood for what I brought today."

Carter laughed and threw his hand up. "Have fun on your little adventure. You ain't foolin' me!"

Ian climbed into the cab of his truck and peeled off the tee that was soaked through and stuck to his muscled frame, and threw it in the passenger seat. He took his bandana from his back jeans pocket and grabbed a bottle of water, held it out the window, and drenched the bandana. Cleaning off his face and neck of the dirt and sweat, he felt half decent. In this heat, he always kept clean tee shirts in the truck. He grabbed a black one and pulled it over his head. His jeans and boots were dusty, but nothing to be done about that. He checked the mirror and decided to take the elastic band from his hair, shaking out his dark brown wavy curls. He climbed out of the truck and started walking up Tradd, trying to figure out which one of these places looked most like the store Carter had described. Hell, he had no damned idea what he was doing, and only one thing on his mind... her.

He strolled down Tradd as if he knew where he was going. He felt the heat from the sidewalk penetrating through his booted feet on the pavement. He'd only walked a few blocks and hadn't seen anything that looked like what he was looking for. He passed a book shop, an antique shop, and a little jewelry store that looked like they displayed local artists' work. Nothing called to him. He crossed the street and decided to walk on the opposite side and see what he could find. He kept stopping to look at the window displays but saw nothing that looked like items a witch would buy. He shook his head at the bizarreness of his thoughts. He'd almost decided he'd lost his mind when he looked up and saw a very Celtic-looking hand-carved wooden sign that read Rhiannon's Circle. Two women walked out, and he heard the soft tingling of a bell over the door. They were smiling and laughing, carrying bags containing their purchases. He remembered the conversation with Carter and the sisters' Irish heritage and knew deep in his gut that this was the place. He straightened his broad shoulders and walked inside the little shop, the frigid air immediately hitting him like a soothing balm. He closed the door behind him, and when he looked up, he saw her seated on a stool behind the counter.

He was lost for words. What the hell? He hadn't thought this damn thing through. He quickly looked away and began to look at the stuff inside the shop under the pretense of shopping. There were colored rocks, books, dried herbs tied in bundles, and candles. He heard several water fountains set up for display and small wind chimes that sang with the slight breeze created by the air conditioner.

Eilish did a double-take when she saw the vampire from the construction site walk into the shop, make quick eye contact with her, and then start browsing through the display of crystals. Anya entered from the rear of the store when she heard the bell and stopped in her tracks. She turned to look at her sister and raised her eyebrows.

Eilish shrugged and whispered softly, "Just a coincidence."

Anya answered softly, "Doubt it."

Eilish approached the vampire, standing with his back to her, and she couldn't help but notice how he filled out the t-shirt and jeans. He didn't follow the youth trend of wearing baggy jeans but instead was wearing jeans that accentuated his physique. He was everything Zavian was not, and she couldn't deny her attraction to him. "Can I help you with something?"

He turned and looked straight at her. He held out his hand, which contained a polished black stone. "Oh, hi. I was, umm, just looking at these." He held up the rock between his fingers and smiled. *Christ, Ian, you need to come up with a better pick-up line than this.* "You work here? Do you remember me? I'm sorry about the other day. I should have been paying more attention."

Eilish smiled at him. "Oh, I remember you." In her head, she was thinking, how could I forget? Not every day do you encounter a vampire. "If you'd been paying attention, we might not have met."

She took the piece of hematite from his fingers and felt the spark when her fingers touched his and knew he felt it too. She noticed how strong and tan his hands looked. "This is hematite... a stone for self-control and decision-making." She looked up at him coquettishly, unable to remember the last time she flirted. "Do you need self-control?"

Ian hardly heard her words because all he could do was look at her lips when she smiled. *Is she flirting with me? Oh, yes, she is!* Grinning back at her, he tilted his head as his hair fell forward. "Depends; sometimes I have total control of the situation, and other times..." He shrugged as he laughed. "Other times, it's more fun to let others have the control." Reaching into the basket, he withdrew another greenish-brown stone with bright red rust colors running through it. "And this one?"

She smiled. "Ah, you found a special one. That's dragon's blood jasper. Pretty, isn't it? It's only found in Australia. The legend says these stones are the remnants of ancient dragons, the green being the dragon's skin and the red representing his blood. These are healing stones but are also thought to promote courage and strength. Especially good if you are going into battle, I think. Are you planning a battle...I'm sorry, I didn't get your name?"

He couldn't take his eyes off her; everything about her hammered into him like hot lava, her voice, her eyes, the way her hair moved when she spoke. "My name is Ian. Ian Cross. No battles on my calendar right now. Is this your place? I see you walk by our construction site every day with your friend. I always wondered where you were going." Rolling the stone around in his hand, he felt its polished hard surface and thought he'd slay a damn dragon barehanded to spend one night with her.

"Well, Ian Cross, my name is Eilish, and that is my sister Anya."

Anya waved. "Don't mind me. By all means, carry on."

Ian tore his eyes away from Eilish long enough to glance in Anya's direction. He could read her thoughts and heard the hesitation behind her casual response. She wasn't quite as eager to have a vampire in the shop as her sister was.

Eilish laughed. "We have another sister, Seraphina, and the three of us own this place."

"It's nice to officially meet you, Eilish. That's a unique name. Gaelic, right? All of your names sound Gaelic." He smiled softly at her and felt the sparks from her fingertips as she removed the jasper from his hand. He'd never felt anything like this before. He'd felt attracted to many women, mortal and immortal, but never a witch.

Eilish nodded when he said their names sounded Gaelic, and she placed the stone back in the basket. She started talking about the various stones and crystals to fill the awkward pause. "Every stone has its own physical properties and carries specific power or energies. Was there something you were looking for?"

"Uh, you know. I was just curious when I saw the shop. I really didn't know what was here." He reached into a different basket and pulled out a pink crystal marbled with white throughout. He placed it in her delicate hand and felt the heat from her soft skin. She wore many bangles that jingle jangled softly when she moved her arms and hands. His hand lingered, his fingertips touching her palm, and she felt the sharp snap of electricity as he made contact with her skin. He stared into her gray eyes. "And this one?"

She smiled and took his hand, placing the polished quartz in his palm and closing his fingers around the stone, clasping his one hand with both of hers. He felt her energy flow through his entire arm.

She leaned into him. "Do you feel it?"

Oh, he felt it, and he was pretty damn sure it had nothing to do with the stone. It felt like he'd grabbed the loose end of an electrical cord. He wondered if she was doing it on purpose, but her face remained neutral.

Eilish continued to speak to him. "It returns your own body heat. This is rose quartz, and it's the stone for the hopeless romantic. Actually, it's about love in its many different forms. Love that's transcendental, self-love, love for the family," she paused briefly, "passionate love. What's on the menu, Ian Cross?"

She felt entranced by this man and knew she was treading into dangerous territory. She heard Anya from behind the counter issue another soft, "Oh, brother...." Eilish was having too much fun flirting with this man and ignored her sister's comment.

Ian felt his heart explode. This couldn't be happening. He felt like they were the only two people in the world right now, encased in a bubble. He just knew it felt real and incredible, and he didn't want it to end. Her hands were so soft, holding his rough hands. He placed his free hand over hers, the quartz enclosed in their grasp. "This is the one. I want this one."

She stared back at him, and before he could lose his nerve, he asked her out. "Eilish, would you like to go for a drink with me later, after work?"

Eilish's smile disappeared. There was no way she could go out with a vampire, but she desperately wanted to spend more time with this man. And Seraphina? How would she keep this from her? "I, uh, I can't tonight. Perhaps another time?"

Ian watched as her expression changed, and the energy flow she'd been sending through his arms dropped dramatically. His heart fell. Of course, she wouldn't go out with a vampire, and he was aware of the warlock who already had designs on her. He let go of her hand as he held on to the crystal. "Yeah, sure. Another time." He fumbled in his back pocket, thinking he should just get the hell out of there. "So, do you take credit cards? I want to buy this quartz."

She looked at him, aware he'd come to the shop to seek her out. She could read his disappointment but knew she shouldn't encourage him. This situation had disaster written all over it.

Anya answered, "We take all forms of currency; checks, cash, credit, or debit."

Eilish glanced at her sister before she spoke again. "This is complicated. We both know this is...." She left her words hanging.

Ian finished her sentence, both of them acknowledging the unspoken. "Complicated. Yeah, that would be an understatement."

Still reluctant to let him leave, she heard herself suggest that he could give her his number.

He smiled at her as he walked to the counter and placed the rose quartz crystal on the counter. As Anya rang up his purchase, he grabbed a piece of scrap paper from the counter and quickly wrote out his address and phone number.

Anya took the crystal and placed it and the receipt in a bag. She looked at Eilish and raised one eyebrow before addressing Ian. "So, do you want this symbol of your undying love gift-wrapped?" Eilish glared at her as Anya laid the bag featuring Rhiannon's Circle logo, address, and phone number on the counter. Anya tapped the bag with her finger, drawing his attention to the logo. "So you both have no excuses now."

Eilish rolled her eyes as her cheeks turned pink. Anya seemed intent on making both of them as uncomfortable as possible.

Ian almost burst out laughing at Anya. Carter was right about this one, and snarky didn't begin to cover it. He turned to Eilish and placed the piece of paper in her hand. "We both know there are a thousand reasons why you shouldn't, but call me anyway."

Looking back at Anya, he nodded. "Thanks for all of your help."

He walked to the door with more swagger than when he walked in. He turned as he exited the store and flashed her one last smile. Walking out, he strutted down the street carrying the bag and knew she'd call him.

Eilish followed him with her eyes, and Anya spoke up as the door closed behind him. "This is all very nice, Eilish, but you seem to have conveniently forgotten Fina. I know I encouraged you to be frank with her about Zavian, but a vampire?"

Eilish dropped her head, folding the paper and slipping it into her skirt pocket. "I didn't forget." She turned to Anya. "I'm going to see him. I don't know when, but I'll figure it out, and you'll cover for me."

Anya shook her head in disbelief. "He's a fucking vampire! Fina won't stand for it."

Eilish answered with exasperation. "I know that! That's why you're going to cover for me."

Anya was muttering under her breath when Seraphina came through the door, hearing the tail end of the conversation. "What's this? What are you two plotting that Anya needs to cover for you?"

Eilish looked up in surprise. "Nothing... I was thinking of buying this really cool skirt in that boutique down on King. It's a tourist trap, and it costs a small fortune. I was just saying how much I wanted it, but it's so over-priced in the height of tourist season."

Seraphina gave her a questioning glance, not buying a single word. Eilish was a powerful witch, one that wasn't even aware of just how much power she held yet, but she was a terrible liar. "Hmmph. You'll have to do better than that, Eilish. Now bring me a cold drink from the back, and turn that air conditioning down!"

BOHANNON

After a long day at work, the sisters had wrapped up their dinner together and cleaned the kitchen, after which the two younger ones had retreated to their rooms. Seraphina needed to talk with them but was unsure how the conversation would go. She stepped out onto the screened porch on the back of the house, surrounded by the enclosed courtyard, the ceiling fan creating a cooling breeze. Setting down the tray which held the pitcher of sweet tea and ice, she poured tea into the three tall glasses. Grabbing a slice of lemon from the small bowl, she carelessly dropped it into her glass and walked back inside the old Victorian house. While standing at the bottom of the stairs, her voice boomed as if she were using a megaphone. "Eilish, Anya. Come down now! Stop whatever foolish nonsense you're doing. Meet me on the back porch." As Luna purred, Fina looked down to find the cat sitting on her haunches and staring at her. "Come along, pet. I don't have a treat for you now; we have a plan afoot."

Eilish had pulled the precious piece of paper from the pocket of her maxi skirt and was gently smoothing it out to reveal Ian's cell number, written boldly in black ink. She picked up her phone and programmed his number into her contacts. She carefully folded the paper and placed it in the drawer of her nightstand. She might have a use for it someday. Some spells could be cast with an item a person had held in their hand. She heard Seraphina calling from the bottom of the stairs. "Okay, coming!"

Eilish started down the hallway and stopped at her sister's closed door. Tapping before she entered, she found Anya stretched out on her bed, her legs crossed at the knee, headphones on, and silently mouthing the words to a song only she could hear. Eilish waved her arms above her head and spoke loudly. "Hey! Anya!"

Anya looked her way, pulling the headphones off as the sound of the Chi-Lites could be heard singing, "Have You Seen Her?" Eilish spoke through her laughter, "You're on another planet when you put those headphones on. Come downstairs. Fina is calling us."

Anya slid off her bed barefoot, wearing her trademark cut-off jeans with frayed edges and a tank top with a faded imprint of The Clash that boldly stated 'London Calling.' Together the two sisters headed down the stairs and out to the back veranda. The courtyard behind their house was lush with plants and trees, creating an oasis of shade during the day. The brick wall that enclosed the courtyard was covered in ivy and protected it from outside visitors. There was a lion's head fountain mounted on the far wall, where water poured forth from the lion's mouth in a constant stream year-round, splashing into a shallow pond below where several Koi fish swam languidly in the cool water.

The two girls joined Seraphina on the screened-in porch, which protected them from the South Carolina mosquitoes that were large enough to carry them away. Anya grabbed a glass of sweet tea and handed another to Eilish as the two girls settled into the wicker chairs, filled with mixed-matched cushions of varying patterns and colors. The wind chimes in the trees caught the slight breeze, their bell tones sending out their soothing vibrations. Anya sat with one leg draped over the arm of the chair, and Seraphina gave her a disapproving look which Anya ignored. Eilish sipped the cold, sweet liquid that was the staple of the South before looking up at her oldest sister. "What's up?"

Seraphina leaned back in her chair, the old wicker creaking in protest. "I received a call from Warrick last night. He needs Anya."

Seraphina turned to look at the middle sister. "Are you even paying attention?" As Anya nodded, her shaggy mane tumbled into her face, and Seraphina continued, speaking directly to her. "It seems Asher's youngest child is sickly again. Apparently, Lizbet is at her wit's end to take care of Molly and maintain some degree of sanity in the house with the older two boys. You know how out of control her boys are." She took a sip of her ice-cold tea. "Personally, I think she needs to take them all in hand and give them a sleeping potion. The few times I visited, they seemed to run like wild beasts, disarranging things and making a horrible mess." Sighing, she continued. "Nevertheless, Warrick wishes for you to use your skills as a healer, then stay with Asher and Lizbet for a week or so to give them a break. You need to help Lizbet with the kids; she's overwhelmed. As for the little one, I know there's an immunity problem; the child seems to catch everything, but this episode appears to be more serious if they asked Warrick for help."

Anya moved her leg from the arm of the chair and dropped both feet to the floor while leaning forward. "Of course, I'll help her! Molly has always been a sickly child. Do you know what's wrong, Fina? I can take my herbs, brew her a tea." Eilish listened and nodded. Anya's powers to heal were the strongest of the three of them. It was her gift.

Seraphina shook her head. "No, but I'm sure you'll figure it out once you're there. You're a gifted healer, Anya. More than likely, one of those sniveling boys got sick and passed it around. Males are just so disgusting when they're young... mud, frogs, and this unexplained fascination with boogers. Molly has never been able to fight off anything. She's a weakling. I doubt she'll ever become much more than a burden to Lizbet. But do your best, Anya. Warrick is relying on you."

Picking up the tall glass of tea, now sweating with cool drips of water, she held it to her forehead and sighed with relief. She turned her attention to Eilish. "I complained to Warrick that I cannot run the shop in the busiest season of the year without Anya. So he's generously volunteered for Zavian to assist during Anya's absence. Wasn't that just the sweetest gesture?"

Eilish looked momentarily stunned. But of course, they'd need help. They were heading into summer, their busiest season. They counted on the influx of tourist dollars to even out the slower months, but the idea of having to work day after day in close quarters with Zavian wasn't appealing. She immediately felt guilty, understanding it would be selfish of her to complain. Lizbet needed Anya's help, and Fina needed help with the shop. Who else would be available other than Zavian? She responded with reluctance. "That was very thoughtful. The coven always pulls together, as it should."

Anya tipped her glass up, the ice sliding forward and tapping against her nose as she emptied the last of the sweet tea. "So when do they expect me? I'll probably need to stop in the shop and pick up fresh herbs before I go."

Seraphina nodded, glad for once they hadn't argued. "As soon as we can arrange it. Warrick and Zavian should be here shortly, and Warrick will drive you and me over to Asher's. I think perhaps you should go into the garden. Pick some fresh lavender, chamomile flowers, and perhaps some comfrey leaf. If Molly is suffering from the heat, you can make a soothing bath for her. It will relieve her anxiety and help her to sleep. Look in the wicker hamper in the pantry; I put fresh herbs in there today. Collect whatever you need, and pack a small bag; you'll be there for a week or so. Go."

As she watched Anya leap into action, she turned her attention back to Eilish. "Make the most of your time with Zavian. I won't be in the shop tomorrow as I have some duties for the coven. I appreciate that I received no temper tantrums from you. It's quite a nice change for once."

"Fina, you know I want to help. And I certainly don't begrudge Anya for leaving to help Lizbet. I appreciate that Zavian has volunteered his time, or perhaps Warrick volunteered it for him. Either way, I know we need help in the shop. Just don't expect sparks to fly, okay? I know you and Warrick want things to move along between us, but I'm not making you any promises. We'll be fine... Zavian and me. We'll work together. He knows where I am in this relationship and has respected my need for space."

As soon as the words left Eilish's lips, Warrick and Zavian walked around the side of the house and opened the gate into the courtyard. Seraphina waved at them. "There you are. I was wondering what took so long."

Warrick climbed the stairs, opened the screen door as it creaked on its hinges, then leaned over to kiss her and smiled. "My goddess, you are almost glowing. You light up the night sky. And how was our rescue mission to Molly accepted?"

Seraphina nearly purred. She planned to have him spend the night with her, and the most devious sexual thoughts went through her head. "Anya will be gathering some healing plants from the garden, and she should be ready soon. She's upstairs packing now." She turned to Zavian, "Thank you for volunteering to help with the shop, it's so busy this time of year, and Eilish is overjoyed for your company."

Zavian smiled. "I'm more than willing to help out." He stood beside Eilish's chair. "So, overjoyed, is it?"

Eilish gave him a doubtful glance. "You heard my sister, I'm positively overjoyed." She chuckled, "No, really, thank you for helping. I do appreciate it."

Anya returned from inside the house and started picking fresh herbs from their courtyard garden. Eilish had a fleeting thought that this would put a damper on her plans to sneak away to see Ian. She needed to get word to him somehow. Remembering her manners, she focused her attention on Zavian. "Would you like some tea, Zavian?"

He smiled broadly at her, sitting down in the chair vacated by Anya. "Of course." He'd accept her invitation to drink most anything as long as he could be in her company.

BOHANNON

Anya had packed her things and left the house to help Asher and Lizbet with Molly. The rest of them had stayed late, sitting on the porch, talking, and listening to the sounds of the tree frogs and the cicada filling the night air. Eilish yawned and said she needed to get to bed if she was ever going to make it to work tomorrow, and Zavian reluctantly said his goodbyes to her. He tried to kiss her, but she turned her face slightly at the last moment so his lips graced her cheek.

Warrick waited until the young couple was out of sight when he whispered to Fina. "Why don't you tell Eilish to let Zavian stay the night? You need to put more pressure on her." Fina shook her head. "I push her enough. Eilish may appear docile to you, but I assure you she can be stubborn. It's a balancing act. Let me manage her. You worry about Zavian."

He lifted Seraphina's hand to his lips and kissed the palm of her hand. "And what are *your* plans for the night, my goddess?"

Seraphina smiled wickedly at him, pulling him in close to kiss him. It was clear Warrick would be spending the night. Eilish walked Zavian to the front door as Luna followed, weaving in and out between her legs. "I'll see you at the shop tomorrow. I'll try to get there a little before ten, so I can open and get things ready."

He nodded. "I'll be there."

She watched him as he turned and walked away, wishing she could feel something for this man. Sighing, she closed the door and almost mindlessly cast a boundary spell preventing anyone from entering. She made her way up the stairs and could hear the sounds emanating from Fina's bedroom. "Well, that didn't take long." She entered the bedroom and closed the door to block the sounds of sexual pleasure and wished she had Anya's headphones.

Emric was squatting in the corner, his arms wrapped around his knees, rocking back and forth, looking anxious. "It's okay, Emric. It may sound like a battle, but it's just Warrick and Fina."

The pale apparition bowed his head down on his knees. The sisters had tried many times to free Emric, to let him pass through to the light, but he remained bound here, trapped in fear. Eilish felt sorry for him. She undressed, tossed her clothes aside, and climbed nude between the sheets. Her last thought as she drifted into darkness was that she needed to talk to Ian.

<hr />

As the sun shined brightly through the bedroom window, Eilish woke to the alarm and got up to hurriedly get ready for work. She could already smell coffee brewing downstairs. Warrick was an early riser, and Fina would have gotten up with him and fixed breakfast. She showered and dressed quickly, grabbing her handbag and slipping it over her shoulder. She rarely bothered with makeup as her delicate features didn't need any enhancement. She made her way down the stairs and into the kitchen, where Fina and Warrick sat making goo-goo eyes at each other over their empty breakfast plates. Eilish grabbed a slice of buttered toast from the plate and said, "I'm out. Will you be coming in at all today, Fina?"

Eilish looked at her sister's disheveled look and knew there hadn't been much sleeping going on last night. Fina's powers would be at a peak now if anyone needed anything. Seraphina looked at her with sleepy eyes. "Maybe; I'll see how the day goes. If I finish up with the coven early, I'll drop in."

Eilish nodded and turned on her heels, leaving the house. She walked alone down East Bay and made a left on Tradd. It felt odd to be alone. It was rare for her not to be in the company of at least one of her sisters.

Ian knelt on the roof, his tee shirt clinging to the sweat on his back. His hair was in a messy bun to keep it off his neck, and a few wavy curls hung loose, dripping with sweat. He was working the roof's edge near the road, and Carter was working the other side. He was grateful for the quiet. His head was filled with thoughts of her today. She hadn't called him. She'd said it was complicated, but he was sure she'd call. At least she hadn't eliminated the possibility completely. He'd hardly slept, waiting for the phone to ring. He looked up and saw her walking towards him alone. This was an excellent opportunity. He quickly climbed down the ladder and approached her. "Hey, you going to work?"

Eilish had been lost in thought and looked up suddenly at the sound of his voice, surprised to see him standing on the sidewalk in front of her. "Ian! Yes, I'm headed to the shop now."

He loved the smile and enthusiasm in her voice when she greeted him. It gave him some hope. "Where's Anya? Is everything okay?"

"We have some friends... a couple whose youngest child is ill. Anya went to help them out for a while. I was going to call you, but it was really late when things settled down at the house last night." Eilish looked around. The coven in Charleston wasn't large, but for her to be seen chatting casually with a vampire wouldn't go unnoticed. "This could make things challenging. Anya was my wingman." She laughed softly. "My older sister, Seraphina, is pretty guarded about... uh, well, most everything. She'd never approve of me seeing you. Anya was going to make excuses for me. I wanted you to know that, so you wouldn't think I was ignoring you." She looked at her watch. She was running late and pretty sure Zavian was already waiting for her to open the store.

Ian didn't miss how she seemed to stumble over her words or looked around to make sure no one saw them together. "I see. Well, I hope the child will be okay." He looked down and kicked at a crack in the sidewalk. "Look, Eilish, if this is too complicated, don't worry about it. You don't need to make excuses for me." Looking up at her, his smile was gone. "Sorry if I misread you, but I thought we had a connection."

Eilish was taken aback by his response. "No! Ian, I... You didn't misread the situation. I think we have a connection, too. But I told you, it's complicated." She looked down at the sidewalk. She'd never mingled with vampires before. She'd only had occasion to cross paths with a few. Both species had strict "no trespassing" rules. Looking back up, she locked eyes with him. His eyes were the darkest brown she'd ever seen. "I have no right to ask this of you, but I'm asking. Be patient with me, please."

He saw the pleading in her eyes and heard the sincerity in her voice. He reached out and took her hand, holding it, feeling the immediate jolt of her energy. "You have every right, and I can be patient. You're worth the wait. And next time you're thinking of calling, no matter what time it is, call. I'll always answer." He leaned in and gave her a small kiss, immediately regretting the decision. His mouth watered, and his gums ached as he fought the need for his fangs to punch through. He'd never been this close to a witch, and he didn't expect her scent to trigger such a strong need to feed. "I better get back to work, and you need to open the shop." Letting go of her hand, he looked into her eyes and smiled.

Eilish smiled back at him and watched him as he walked back to the house. He had a swagger in his walk she'd often seen with human males, leading with their broad shoulders as if they could barrel through anything in their way. She spoke out loud to herself. "You better keep that swagger, Ian Cross. You're going to need it."

She turned and picked up her pace, despite the heat, trying to get to the shop on time.

As she approached Rhiannon's Circle, she saw Zavian waiting patiently, his back leaning against the shop's outer wall, his hands in the pockets of his cargo shorts, and his feet crossed at the ankles. His head was tilted down, and his blonde hair fell forward, obscuring his face. Eilish took a second to assess him and his lanky frame. He seemed to be all arms and legs, attached to a thin torso. She had a flash of Zavian's walk in her head, a long, lanky stride. No swagger. She cleared her head of thoughts of Ian as she called out, "Hey! Sorry, I'm late." She dug inside her handbag and withdrew the keys, unlocking the door. "Come in where it's cool. I'll give you a quick orientation to the cash register. You won't have any problems with the customers. You'll be able to answer any of the questions from the humans... just, you know, keep it light."

BOHANNON

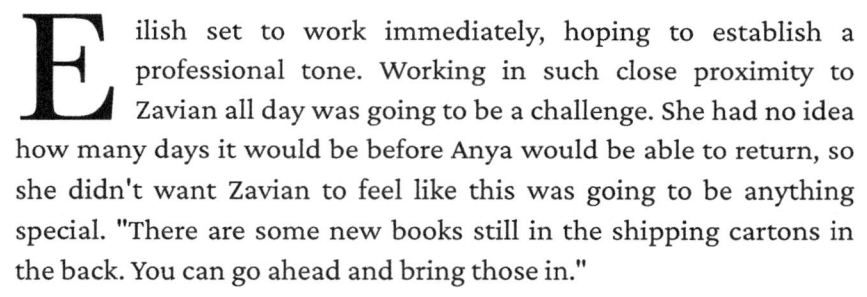

Eilish set to work immediately, hoping to establish a professional tone. Working in such close proximity to Zavian all day was going to be a challenge. She had no idea how many days it would be before Anya would be able to return, so she didn't want Zavian to feel like this was going to be anything special. "There are some new books still in the shipping cartons in the back. You can go ahead and bring those in."

She directed her attention to the cash register and started balancing the previous day's receipts against the transactions. Most of their sales were credit or debit, so they rarely kept much cash. She opened a small safe to add money to the register. Zavian kept trying to start a conversation, but Eilish would shake her head, a slight frown on her face like she was concentrating, making the task appear more complicated than it was. "I can't talk and do this at the same time."

Zavian busied himself with placing the new books on the shelves but kept glancing at her. When she finished, she batched all the credit and debit card slips and put the prior day's cash into a bank deposit bag. She'd make a bank run later. Fina would do the rest of the shop's accounting this evening.

Zavian felt like it was safe to talk now. "Are you mad at me?"

"What? No, I just needed to pay attention to what I was doing. We run a business here, Zavian. We didn't come to play." She wasn't mad, but she was starting to feel annoyed at the idea of having to keep him at bay and was already wondering if there was something she could do to help Anya get back sooner. Eilish hadn't explored her skills with healing, but she was feeling motivated to try.

Zavian stood up with the empty boxes. "Okay, well, the books are in place. You need these boxes?"

She shook her head. "Just break them down and stack them in the storeroom. They'll get recycled."

The bell over the door jingled, and Eilish looked up with a bright smile, glad to see a customer who could act as a buffer between her and Zavian. Her smile quickly vanished when the customer was Warrick. "Oh, hi, Warrick. Did you need something?"

"Nope. Just checking on my two favorite love birds. How are things going?"

Zavian returned from the store room in the back, a broad grin on his face. "It's going great! I mean, I don't know what I'm doing, but Eilish will teach me the ropes." He stepped next to Eilish and placed one arm around her shoulder, giving her a squeeze.

Eilish wiggled free of his grip. Directing her comment to Warrick, she said, "Okay, first of all, we're not love birds." Turning to Zavian, she said, "And this is a place of business. You need to conduct yourself in a professional manner."

Zavian laughed. "There's no one here!"

"It doesn't matter. You get comfortable with your behavior, and you forget. When I'm here with Anya or Fina, it's business. Understand? We leave all the sister drama at home. The customer doesn't need to see that."

Warrick looked down his nose at her. "Well, aren't we feeling a little high and mighty today? I'm sure Fina wouldn't object to a little professional fraternization if it advances the cause."

Eilish snapped back at him. "I object, Warrick! And there is no 'cause,' as you put it!" The wind chimes started to swing, and the items on the display shelves began to vibrate in response to her anger. Eilish took a deep breath and closed her eyes. She could feel her energy building and didn't want things to get out of control. She calmed herself before speaking again. "I'm sorry. I didn't mean to get so angry, but we've had this conversation. I appreciate Zavian being here and his willingness to help, but don't turn this into something it isn't."

Both Zavian and Warrick had been startled by the energy force field that had flowed through the room like a giant ripple in a pond. Eilish didn't have her wand and hadn't even lifted a finger. Her mood alone had created the energy field, and she was only mildly annoyed. Zavian thought he never wanted to see her get really mad, and Warrick was thinking the opposite and wondered just how much power she could harness.

Warrick spoke calmly. He'd appease her for now, but he'd make sure Fina heard about this. If she thought for one minute that her fate wasn't tied to Zavian; she had another thought coming. "Looks like someone had too much caffeine in her coffee this morning. You know I mean no harm." He browsed through the herb baskets until he found fresh chamomile and valerian root. He handed the sprig of chamomile and the roots to Zavian. "Brew our sweet Eilish some tea. She's missing her sister, I'm sure, and it's left her at odds."

Zavian was eager to help and took the chamomile and valerian to the store room to brew the tea.

Eilish took a seat on the stool behind the counter and rubbed the bridge of her nose as she felt the beginnings of a headache. She'd suppressed the release of energy when she was angry, and now she'd pay for that. The truth was, the tea would help.

Warrick placed his elbows on the counter and leaned across from her. "You don't have to make this so hard, you know. Zavian adores you, and really, what are your options? Adriel? Lowan? Most of the males are already bonded. Unless you leave our coven for another warlock, you know those unions never work. It always creates conflict, and we can't have you in conflict with your sisters, now can we? Stop fighting the inevitable, Eilish. You're smart. Smart enough to see the handwriting on the wall. If you need some time... well... take some time. Just don't take too long."

Before she could respond, Zavian returned with the tea and placed it on the counter in front of her. "Be careful. It's really hot."

The door jingled again as a real customer came in, fanning themselves from the oppressive heat. Warrick said, "Well, let me get out of your way. You have work to do", as he turned to leave the store.

Zavian responded to the customer, coming from behind the counter to assist them as Eilish blew on the tea before taking a sip. She wanted to cry because, deep down, she knew Warrick was right. Her options were limited.

BOHANNON

Eilish and Zavian had been working together in the shop for three days now. They'd established a routine, but Zavian was like a puppy under her feet. He hadn't been inappropriate, but his desire to please her, to help her at every turn, as if she couldn't lift a book from a shelf, was extremely annoying. She was exhausted at the end of each day with how much she had to hold back her temper. It made her feel guilty because he'd done nothing wrong. She was gritting her teeth by the end of each workday, eager to close shop and get home and away from him. She felt like she couldn't breathe. She was watching the clock, waiting for their 8:00 p.m. closing time. They stayed open later in the summer to accommodate the tourists. While she felt relief when the clock struck eight, she could tell Zavian felt deflated. She closed up and locked the cash register as he did some last-minute straightening of merchandise, then they left together as she flipped the "closed" sign over and locked the door.

"You don't need to walk me home, Zavian. I'm sure you have things you need to do since you've been tied up in the shop this week. I can walk alone. I'm fine."

"Eilish, do you really think I'd ever let you walk alone at this time of night? Besides, Warrick would never let me hear the end of it." He took her hand and began to stroll with her toward the sisters' home. "Any plans for the weekend?"

She slipped her hand out of his under the pretext of looking for something in her handbag. She pulled out some lip balm and applied it as they walked, then used both hands to grab onto the straps of the hobo bag. "This time of night? It's still daylight outside! Besides, you know I'm perfectly safe on my own. I never intentionally use my witchcraft in public, but I wouldn't hesitate to defend myself. But I have no doubt you'd never hear the end of it from Warrick, regardless of the time of day." She cast her eyes at the old house where Ian had been working. The construction crew was long gone. She'd seen Ian a few mornings on her way to work, but with Zavian on her heels, he'd kept his distance, and for that, she'd been grateful. "No plans for the weekend. At least not yet. I need to talk with Anya. See how things are going and when she'll be back home."

Zavian sighed; he knew she was frazzled with having him in the shop so much, but he wasn't about to give up. "First, I don't feel like I've been tied up in the shop. I like helping. You have to admit; it's been busy." He strolled beside her and knew she was walking faster than usual. "Eilish, why don't we go out for the weekend? Anything you like. We could leave town if you want." Before she could answer, he grabbed her elbow and stopped her, turning her toward him. "Anya will be gone, Fina will undoubtedly be with Uncle, and you'll be bored." Looking into her eyes, he smiled. "We have to try to make an effort, remember. Trust me when I tell you, it will keep Uncle off your back, and besides, I'm not that bad to hang out with, am I?"

Eilish felt suffocated by him. Zavian had been a big help in the shop, and she couldn't have managed the tourists' trade without him. But the last thing she wanted was to spend more time with him. "Well, I don't know for sure that Anya will be gone. As I said, I need to talk to her tonight. She could be coming home, and you won't have to work the shop anymore."

Zavian knew she was looking for an excuse. He let go of her elbow, and they began the short distance to the house. "Talk to Anya tonight. Let me know. I'll come in and help you out as long as she's gone." As they approached the house, he saw the lights on inside. "Looks like Fina is home. I should pop in and say hello." He'd do anything to stay in her company as long as possible.

She couldn't think of any reason not to invite him in. "Yeah, sure. Fina will be glad to see you." She opened the wrought iron gate to the sidewalk that led to the expansive front porch, climbing up the few stairs. Zavian remained at her side every step, and Eilish felt like she could scream. This was what being hand-fasted to him would feel like, having him present every minute of her life. She opened the front door and felt the blast of sub-freezing air hit her in the face. God forbid they ever had a power failure, and Fina lost her precious air-conditioning. "Fina! We have company!" Luna came running to greet her, winding her way between her legs before sniffing at Zavian's sneakers.

Seraphina heard the loud call from her youngest sister and smiled. She strolled down the staircase as if she was entering the finest ballroom. "Well, isn't this the most wonderful sight, seeing the two of you return together from a hard day's work. I hope business has been booming."

Zavian quickly rushed to her and took her hand to help her down the last step. "Very busy, and I'm enjoying myself!"

Fina smiled at Zavian with a devious twinkle in her eye. "I'm glad to hear it because Eilish will need more help. Warrick and I are going off for the weekend. I was just packing a few essentials." She turned and grinned wickedly at Eilish. "You shall have the entire house to yourself, dear sister. Isn't that wonderful?"

Eilish felt her heart sink. Usually, a Fina-free weekend would be a joyous occasion for her and Anya. But this time, it had probably removed any excuse for not seeing Zavian. "But Anya? She might be coming home. I'm sure she's exhausted with Lizbet's kids."

"Well, she may be exhausted. Have you seen those children? Like a pack of wild beasts! That house is a total disaster. But she won't be home this weekend. I spoke with Anya, the baby is fine now, but Lizbet is worn to a frazzle. I promised her Anya would help out." Seraphina stretched out on the settee and patted the seat beside her. "Come, Luna." She didn't miss the grin on Zavian's face or her sister's look of grim resignation. "Eilish, don't look so ridiculously heartbroken; it will give you and Zavian a lovely weekend together."

Zavian took Eilish's hand and grinned. "Fina insists; you know what that means; we can plan anything you wish."

Eilish smiled back at him with a smile that didn't reach her eyes. "Yeah, sure. We can go out for dinner on Saturday. You better make reservations, though, since it's tourist season. Maybe the Morgan Creek Grill on the inter-coastal waterway. They have great food." If she was going to be stuck with Zavian, she might as well get a good meal out of it.

Zavian kissed her on the cheek. "Perfect, I love that place. Get some rest. I'll make reservations and let you know tomorrow." Walking to Fina, he didn't miss the wicked smile on her face. "I'm out of here. Eilish must be tired of me by now." Seraphina laughed, "Never, my dear Zavian, never."

As he kissed her softly and walked out the door, Seraphina stood and stared at Eilish. "Warrick gave you time, but time is quickly running out. Get with the program. Zavian is more than willing. Make him happy, and stop looking like you lost your best friend. Warrick isn't going to wait forever, and neither am I."

Eilish didn't bother to answer. It would only lead to an argument. She started up the stairs and went into her bedroom. Emric was kneeling in the corner, rocking back and forth, his arms wrapped across his chest in a self-hug as he consoled himself. He was listening to one of Anya's records, "Tears on My Pillow" by Little Anthony. Eilish sighed as she tossed her handbag on her bed before collapsing in a heap on the bed herself, wrapping her arms around her pillow and listening to the sad lyrics of the song. "You don't hold the exclusive rights to sorrow and sadness, Emric."

He stopped in his rocking motion and looked up at her. "What, Miss Eilish? Did I do something wrong?" Eilish looked back at him and wondered what it must feel like to be trapped for eternity in misery. She felt like she might soon find out. "You're fine, Emric." He went back to his rocking, hugging himself tighter. "Yes, Miss Eilish."

BOHANNON

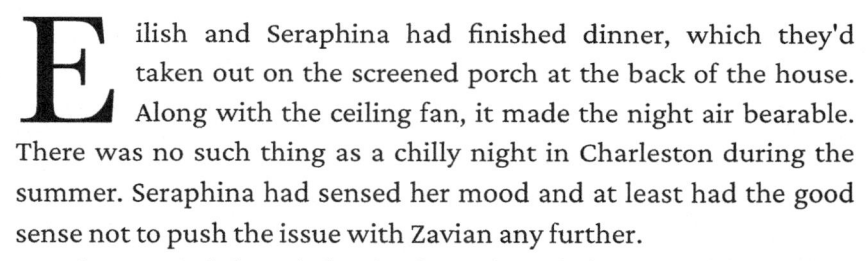

Eilish and Seraphina had finished dinner, which they'd taken out on the screened porch at the back of the house. Along with the ceiling fan, it made the night air bearable. There was no such thing as a chilly night in Charleston during the summer. Seraphina had sensed her mood and at least had the good sense not to push the issue with Zavian any further.

They carried their dishes back inside and cleaned up the kitchen in silence when Eilish said, "If you don't need me for anything else, I'm going to go call Anya. See how she's doing."

"She'll be doing fine, although I wonder how her patience is holding out. I need to finish packing. Warrick and I will be leaving early in the morning." As Seraphina made her way to the stairs, Eilish wasn't far behind her as Seraphina looked back at her over her shoulder. "Piece of advice, Eilish, take this opportunity and make the most of your time with Zavian. At some point, you need to realize that you seem to be the only one who can't see your destiny." She headed into her bedroom before issuing one final comment and closing her door. "We won't be returning until late Sunday evening. I expect a much different response from you when I return, especially toward Zavian."

Eilish ignored Fina's comments. There wasn't any response that would satisfy her anyway. She went to her room, closing the door behind her. Emric wasn't around, but she knew he wasn't far. He never left the house and rarely went downstairs. She fished her cell phone out of her handbag and hit dial for Anya. The call was about to roll over to voicemail when a frazzled Anya answered. Eilish could hear what sounded like about a hundred kids in the background, although she knew Asher and Lizbet only had three kids. "You all right, sis? It sounds like you're out-numbered over there."

Anya was about to scream when she finally got to her phone. "Eilish! Hold on. It's like Ringling Brothers over here!" Anya turned her head to the side and yelled, "Lizbet, can you keep them quiet? Sister is on the phone!" Anya closed the door of the small bedroom she'd been given. She'd seen closets bigger than this, but at least she could escape the chaos. "Can you give me a spell to remove voice boxes?"

Eilish laughed. "Actually, I can give you a spell that will silence them all. It wears off in about an hour, though. What time do they go to bed?"

Anya paced the room as she talked. "Like, never. I have no idea what in hell they needed me for. Curing Molly was easy, but I didn't know I was signing up for 'Maids R Us.' Asher and Lizbet act like this is their second honeymoon, and I'm supposed to babysit!" Anya flopped on the bed and sighed. "What's up with you?"

"Nothing much. I'm on Zavian overload. He's in the shop all day, walks me home at night, and now I have to go out with him this weekend. Please tell me you're coming home soon. What was wrong with Molly anyway?"

"Sucks to be you. I'd love to have someone falling over their feet to be with me. Sorry, well, not really." Anya sighed, "Molly had some respiratory thing. Remember, she was premature, so she's never been that strong. If you could see the condition of this place, the complete disorganized chaos, and the fact that it's never quiet, you'd understand. She's okay for now. It's me you should worry about.

Lizbet said Warrick promised her a week. I won't be back for a few, sis."

Eilish felt so deflated she could cry, but she didn't want to add to Anya's burden. "Oh... I'd hoped, you know, you'd be home soon. I miss you, and Emric's beside himself. He's found every sad song in your record library. He may fade away if he doesn't hear some decent doo-wop music soon. So, the end of the week then?"

Anya could hear the defeat in Eilish's voice. She knew she was counting on her to get back as soon as possible. "Afraid so. In the meantime, I'm trying to teach Lizbet some basic herbal teas for Molly to build her immunity, but these rug rats are like nasty little trolls. Hang in there."

Anya heard something hit the door and whipped it open to find two filthy boys fighting over a jumping frog and, in the process, knocking over a vase filled with dead flowers. "Get to the bathroom. It's time for your baths. Right now, before I turn you into tadpoles and throw your wee butts into the pond!" Watching as they took off screaming for their father, Anya growled into the phone. "I could strangle them! I have to go. Have fun on your date with Zavian. Do me a favor, and remind me never to get knocked up!" She hit the end call icon and headed for the stairs thinking that she couldn't get someone to look at her, let alone get preggo.

Eilish heard the call end and dropped the phone on the bed. She sat up and noticed Emric had returned and was standing at the window, staring out into the night, while holding his musket over his shoulder. Eilish stood beside him, watching the cars drive slowly up and down East Bay Street. Emric spoke, mostly to himself, "The soldiers are coming." Eilish sighed and laid her forehead against the glass. "I hope so. Maybe they can rescue both of us."

BOHANNON

Ian's mind wouldn't rest; no matter what he did, Eilish occupied every thought. He'd worked his ass off all week in that damn construction job to get a glimpse of her. He couldn't ignore how the gangly blonde warlock had been by her side all week, hanging on her every word as they walked past and watching as the warlock damn near slammed his skinny ass into a street lamp, looking at her while she spoke. He needed to leave this situation alone, just let it go... but he wanted her. Hell, he couldn't even get her alone. He knew where she lived, and what she did, and yet still, this was a really bad fucking idea trying to hook up with her. A witch, of all things! "Way to go, Ian. Rile up every damn witch and vamp in the damn state, why don't you." He needed to talk to Ryker. He'd known the vampire for a long time. They weren't exactly the greatest of friends, but hell, they were both mercenaries and had worked a few assignments together. Ryker was older and had lived all over the place, but he seemed to like Charleston and ended up hanging out here for years. If not for this hellish heat, this place would be a great hunting ground for any vampire. Deciding to check out Ryker's usual hangout, he showered and threw on some jeans and an aged-to-perfection rock tee shirt.

Driving down King Street, he found a parking spot and locked up the truck. The joint was packed as usual, but he knew Ryker would be scoping out his prey at the Burns Alley Tavern. After entering, he elbowed his way to a spot, checked out the crowd, and saw Ryker doing his usual "Lonely Romeo" routine, just waiting for the goods to get drunk and stupid. Ian grabbed a Midnight, the salvation of the vampire, concocted by the master who ruled the Medici coven. It was a great blend of blood and wine. It took the edge off until a vampire could feed. He slid onto the stool at the small table. "Ryker, I figured I'd find you here. How are the pickings tonight?"

Ryker had his eye on this one girl standing at the bar with a group of her friends. She was the curvy type, and he admired how she filled out her jeans when Ian slid into the seat across from him. "Don't screw up my mojo, brother. I was just waiting to get that brunette at the bar isolated from her friends. What the hell are you doing here?"

Ian eyed the girls at the bar. "Brunette's now, is it? Just hanging out, hoping to find you here, scoping out the ass." Ian took a drink of his Midnight and began to wonder if this was such a good idea. He would have to be careful about who knew he had a raging cock for a witch.

Ryker took his eyes off the girl long enough to look at Ian. It had been a while since they'd run into each other, and he had a feeling that tonight's encounter was no coincidence. He swallowed down some Midnight and reached for his cigarettes when he remembered the No Smoking policy and cursed under his breath. "So... heard you were working construction. What the hell is that about? You down on your luck or something?"

Ian leaned his elbows on the table, wondering what the hell he was about to let loose. "It's about a girl. Look, bro, you've been around here a long time. It's always the same bullshit night after night. Don't you ever come across someone that's just different? You have to have her, and nothing is going to stop you? I don't know; maybe I'm fucking going insane in this damn heat."

Ryker ran his hand over his face, then shook his head. "Fuck, brother, please don't tell me this is some damn love connection. Look around. It's a fucking buffet in here. A lot of tourists, women looking for a good time to let their hair down. You make a quick hit. It's one and done. If you found something that's caught your eye, then just take it; what's the problem?"

Ian shifted his weight on the stool, not sure Ryker would understand. How in the hell did you tell a brother that you wanted more than a quick hit, and he was already past the one and done; he wanted all of her. "More than caught my eye, brother. She's different, something special. Her long white hair and gray eyes rattle the beast inside me. You ever heard of the Bohannon sisters?" Grabbing the Midnight, he downed it in one gulp.

Ryker shook his head. "Nah. Are you into sisters? That's cool. How many? I managed a three-way last weekend. It took me until Wednesday to recover." He threw his head back, laughing loudly.

Ian shook his head; nothing that came out of Ryker's mouth surprised him. "I'm not into all the sisters, just one. But there's a snag. She's a witch, and a powerful one at that. Every time I touch her, it lights my whole fucking body up. I know it's a bad idea, but damn, she rocks everything inside me. There's a fucking neon sign in my head, flashing on and off, telling me to run like hell and never look back. Just not that easy, I want her, but there's some fucking warlock on top of her day and night."

Ryker dropped his head forward, beat it hard three times against the table, then looked up slowly at Ian. "I know I've had a lot to drink, but I didn't just hear you say, 'witch'. Tell me you didn't say witch. Come on, Ian, you lost your fucking mind? Did she cast a spell or something? We've got no defense against witches other than brute strength and speed, and they can even shoot that down if they see it coming. And it's almost impossible to erase their memories." He pushed the bottle of Midnight back in Ian's direction. "Take another drink, brother. Your brain is muddled."

Ian grabbed the bottle and took a swig, and passed it back. "If I can get her alone, I can handle this. She likes me. I know that. This warlock likes her too, but she hasn't been with him yet. I think she's keeping him in the friend zone. I can win her over; I worry about what might come down on all of us when I do. And stop looking at me like that."

Ryker slid down in his chair, staring back at Ian. "You're serious about this. Man, I thought you were kidding, but you're serious. Holy fuck, Ian." He was quickly losing his buzz from the Midnight. Despite the No Smoking policy, Ryker lit a cigarette and took a deep drag, dropping his head back to exhale the smoke and ignoring the stares of the annoyed patrons. "Ian... it's not just her. I mean, there's the whole fucking coven. You'd have more than one pissed-off warlock on your hands. You could start a species war. Man, I don't even know what to say other than this is the worst fucking idea of the century."

Ian stared at Ryker hard. "She's worth it. Maybe it's about time I make sure she knows that. And let some fucking warlock know I'm not scared of his shit." Ian looked at the bar and the girls, giggling and drinking themselves into oblivion. He knew he'd never have found Eilish in a bar. It wasn't her scene. She knew who she was, and that gnawing beast inside him reassured him that once he won her over, she'd fight to keep him, and vice versa. "I'm heading out, bro. It looks like your brunette is ripe for the picking. Not much fun in such easy prey. I need more challenge, and I think I found my woman for that."

Ryker reached out and grabbed his arm, pulling him back into the chair. "Hang on, rawhide. You better think this through before you go rogue. I got your back, brother, but I can't fight off a coven, and neither can you. You're thinking with your dick now. If you're intent on destruction, then you at least need a plan."

Ian knew he was right; he needed a plan and a damn good one. Grabbing the bottle, he took another long swallow of Midnight. His body was aching. He needed to get his shit together and feed soon. But the ache for Eilish was even worse than his ache to feed. "I've got some inroads, but I'm not that far with her yet. This is going to take patience. Do you have any brilliant ideas?"

Ryker laughed. "Oh yeah, my first brilliant idea is for you to get the fuck out of town, but I don't think you'd listen. Before you go off half-cocked, I'd say go slow. Real slow. You don't even know this witch's intentions. How much is she into you? What's she willing to risk, if anything? She has as much on the line as you, brother. As soon as her coven gets wind of you, they will surround her, try to isolate her." Ryker shook his head. "And this warlock. You got no idea what their relationship is. Just because you don't think they've been together could mean nothing. She's expected to bond. Different from us. Can you feed from her? Fuck, I don't even know. All we got now are questions with no answers. Slow your roll, brother. There's stuff you need to figure out before you dive in."

Ian just looked down at the floor. Ryker was correct; there was much more to this than he'd thought. He looked up at Ryker and spoke with a determination he didn't feel. "I don't know what happens, except this is dangerous for both of us. But if I don't try, it will drive me mad; I know that for sure. I've got some thinking to do. Thanks, bro." As he stood up to leave, he knew one thing, he was walking into a minefield of unknowns.

BOHANNON

16

Eilish had been counting down the hours. She'd gone out with Zavian over the weekend, and now it was going on seven days of having him in the shop. Today was Zavian's last day! Anya would finally be coming home later tonight. He'd been helpful, more than helpful, but he'd become comfortable with having her close at hand day after day. They'd had a casual dinner after work a couple of evenings at Fina's insistence. She said after everything Zavian had done to help them out, it would be rude of her to turn down an invitation, not to mention she had no good excuse for not going.

As they both worked to close up the shop for the night, he eagerly asked her out again. "I can't tonight. We sold through so many herbs this week; we're going to run out before our next shipment comes in. Fina told me to go see Cressa. She's expecting me. She has an herb garden, and I can pick some fresh herbs to get us through until our order arrives. Besides, Anya's coming home too. I haven't seen her in over a week. Thanks, though, for the invitation and all the help this week. I couldn't have managed without you."

Zavian didn't like her response to his date request, but he knew she was anxious to see Anya. They were inseparable most of the time. He'd enjoyed the week alone with Eilish without Anya and her snide comments. "Are you sure? I could help you with the herbs and walk you to Cressa's. I don't mind. I like walking with you. It has been a wonderful week being together."

Eilish felt suffocated by him. "Well, Cressa was hoping for some girl talk... you know, just the two of us. But thank you. I'll be sure to tell Fina how much help you've been." She flipped the closed sign over and locked the door. She stood a moment with her handbag on her shoulder. "Okay...so, see you around."

Ian had seen her every damn day with the warlock going into the shop. He hoped this wasn't permanent because neither of her other sisters had been with her all week. He didn't dare call out to her when she passed the construction site every day. He didn't even raise his hand to acknowledge her. But he knew she was aware of him.

He shadowed himself, making himself invisible to humans and witches alike, blending like camouflage into his surroundings, and waited across the street from their shop. He'd been doing this all week after work, hoping, for once, the warlock would take a damn hike. As the lights went out, he saw them both emerge together, and as luck would have it, Eilish went in the opposite direction of her home *and* the warlock. "About fucking time!"

He began to follow her but kept himself shadowed so no one could see him. Where the hell was she going? He saw her enter a private residence and sighed. "It's going to be a long night; settle in. You've finally got your shot, don't get stupid now." He took a position a few houses back where he could watch and wait for her to leave.

Eilish knocked on Cressa's door before opening it and calling out, "Hey, it's me!"

Cressa came out of the kitchen to greet her. "I've been waiting for you. Fina said you'd be by after the shop closed. Come on outside. The herb garden has done really well this year. Pick as much as you want." Cressa grabbed a few mesh bags as the two women exited the screen door onto the back porch.

Eilish admired her garden. "Wow, Fina said you'd expanded your garden this year. This looks amazing." She walked into the garden with Cressa on her heels. Eilish picked through the herbs, selecting nettle, sorrel, clary sage, lemongrass, and comfrey, placing the fresh clippings into the mesh bags. "This is great, Cressa. We can't thank you enough. We've been swamped in the shop this week."

Cressa looked about her garden, pleased with the results of her labor. "Plenty here. Come any time. Would you like to stay for tea? I can offer iced tea or hot tea, you choose."

"No thanks, Anya's coming home tonight. I haven't seen her in over a week." Cressa gave her a quick hug. "Well, tell her hi for me, and both of you come for a visit soon." Eilish assured her they would and took her leave. Cressa's house was close to Waterfront Park, where the Cooper River joined the Charleston Harbor. The humidity had dropped, and the evening air didn't feel so oppressive. She decided to walk down to the park and enjoy the breeze that usually came off the water. She tucked the herbs into her handbag and headed toward the river.

Ian saw her when she left and overheard their parting conversation. Apparently, Anya had been away, which was why the warlock had been helping in the shop. He watched her walk toward the Cooper River and followed her. Once he was close to the park, Ian quickly moved to get ahead of her and grabbed an empty park bench, ideally situated, to see her coming at him. He threw his arm casually over the back of the bench, one leg crossed over the opposite knee, and hoped he looked relaxed and could pull off the façade of a coincidental meeting.

Eilish entered the park and noticed the crowds of tourists had mostly cleared out. It was prime dinner time for the restaurants, so there was only a smattering of people in the park. She walked out to the edge and leaned over the rail, inhaling the salt air and enjoying how the breeze lifted her hair. There was a sailboat on the river, moving with the current into the harbor. She turned to make her way back to East Bay when she saw Ian sitting on a park bench, staring out at the river. Had he seen her? She'd noticed he'd intentionally avoided drawing attention to himself when she walked to the shop with Zavian every morning, and she'd been grateful for that. She took a few steps in his direction, "Hey."

Ian looked up and saw her, pretending to be surprised, as his heart skipped a beat. It seemed like years since he'd been this close to her. "Eilish, hey, it's good to see you. What are you doing down here?" He felt his heart slamming in his chest. She was beautiful, her silky white hair blowing softly in the slight breeze coming off the water. She looked like a woodland nymph who could only come out to roam under a full moon, delicate and fragile, but he knew better.

Eilish stood still, deciding whether to sit next to him or offer an excuse and head back home. "I was running errands and decided to stop in the park on the way home." She saw him pat the empty space next to him on the park bench, giving an invitation to join him. She could think of a million reasons why she shouldn't, but she found herself walking in his direction. She sat near the outer edge of the bench, as far from him as the bench allowed. He was relaxed, his arm stretched across the back of the bench, while she sat tensely on the edge of her seat. She looked him over, still in jeans and his work boots, his chest stretching his t-shirt, the muscles in his tanned arms prominent. "How about you? Are you waiting for someone?"

Ian smiled over at her, looking directly into her eyes. "No, just hoping some beautiful woman would come along and want some company, and here you are." Chuckling, "Actually just came down hoping to catch a cooling breeze." He could feel her tension, and her body language indicated she wasn't relaxed. That was obvious in how she was curled up as far from him as possible. "Look, Eilish, I'm just going to be honest here. I know you're not comfortable sitting here talking to me. We can always walk; the park isn't crowded. Or maybe..." He moved his arm from behind her. "You're waiting on someone?"

She shook her head. "No. No one." She looked about, comforted that a few people were seated on other benches and an occasional couple would walk by. She thought it best to stay where they could both be seen. "This is good. Here is good. I, uh...I appreciate that you didn't try to speak to me this past week, you know, with Zavian there. Zavian's in my coven. He was helping out in the shop while Anya was helping another coven family." She shifted back on the seat slightly and placed her handbag on the ground. "We can't be seen together, Ian. My sister knows you're a vampire, and she's cool, but the coven, and my older sister, Fina." She shook her head. "This is dangerous for both of us, I think."

"So Zavian is the one walking you to work every day. But let's not kid ourselves; you and I know he is more than helping out. He wants you." Rubbing the palms of his hands on his jeans, he looked back at her, those gray eyes absorbing him. "It is dangerous, deadly dangerous for both of us. But I feel this connection; I can't deny it. I want to see you, and we can go slow. But if that's not what you want, I'll respect that. I won't like it, but I'll respect it. We both know that witches and vampires don't make a happy cocktail, and both factions will call it an all-out war. But I belong to no coven. I'm a mercenary. I have no idea what I'm getting myself into, but I'll take the risk...for you." Reaching up, he slid his hand softly against her cheek.

He was right, she did feel a connection, but she hadn't seriously considered acting on it. Still, she tensed up slightly when he brushed his hand across her cheek. "Go slow?" She stared back at his dark brown eyes. "I feel the connection, but what are you suggesting? That we could be...a couple?" She bit at her bottom lip. "How? How could we ever hide that?"

Ian couldn't miss the way she tensed up at his touch. He stood up and walked around the bench. "I don't know the answers, Eilish, but I know that I want to be with you, get to know you, no matter what that takes. I've been around a long time, long enough to have encountered numerous witches. Vamps and witches, we've learned to keep our distance, respect each other's territory and give a wide berth. But you're different, something special. I can feel it. What is it you want from your time here on this earth?" He sat back down and gazed at her. "Tell me, where do you see your life going? Working in that shop? Bonded to a warlock? I want to know all about you, what you dream about, what you need to feel whole, to make your life happy and worthwhile. The same questions I ask myself."

Eilish stared back at him. He was asking questions that haunted her. What *did* she want? Not Zavian, and not a relationship like Fina's and Warrick's. But Ian was a vampire. Could she even have a life with a vampire? "I don't know where I see my life going. I only know where I don't want to go. I feel like my whole life is already mapped out for me though, by the coven, by my older sister. Like the choices have been made, none of them by me." She looked down at her hands. "I'll rule this coven someday. It's my birthright, whether I want it or not. My sister Seraphina is High Priestess of our coven, and I'll be expected to follow."

"Impressive to rule a coven if that's what you really want. But who rules by your side? That should be your decision." Standing up, Ian decided he should let her be. It needed to be her choice. He never wanted to pressure her. She was getting enough pressure from the coven already. "Look, I'm sure you probably need to get home before questions are asked and before anyone might see us out here. You have my number. It's your call." He wanted to kiss her so badly that his bones hurt. He didn't want to walk away from her, but they both needed to think about what they were doing. "Good night, Eilish. I enjoyed this little time we had alone together."

She was startled when he stood up. She didn't want him to leave. She wanted to sit here, hold his hand, lean her head on his shoulder and not worry about whether they were seen. She looked at him standing before her as the sun went down, casting a golden glow on everything. He looked like no one she'd ever seen. She reached out and took his hand, holding it gently, delaying his departure. "This is so complicated. I need some time."

His whole body felt alive with a rippling current running through his veins. She was powerful, and he wasn't sure she knew what she did to him, but it felt amazing, and he wanted more of this. Pulling her up to face him, he squeezed her hand. "I've got all of eternity." He leaned in and kissed her on the lips, and he felt like he wanted to teleport her far away and never bring her back. He felt her return the kiss, lean into him, and he felt the surge of energy rolling off of her. She made it hard to breathe. Breaking the kiss, he said softly, "Tell Anya my work buddy, Carter, will be damn glad she's back. He has his eye on her." Smiling, he turned and walked away, the taste of her still on his lips.

Eilish staggered slightly when he let go of her, then stood dumbfounded as she watched him walk away. She'd felt that kiss through every cell in her body. She touched her fingertips to her lips. They still tingled. She'd never felt that with Zavian, or any other man for that matter. She watched him until he disappeared in the dark, then she picked up her handbag and started walking home. She kept looking over her shoulder, thinking maybe he'd change his mind and chase after her, but he wasn't there. He'd said the ball was in her court. The next move was hers, and she had no idea what she should do. "Anya. I need to talk to Anya."

BOHANNON

Eilish walked faster the closer she got to her home, keeping her fingers crossed that Anya would be there already. She ran up the porch steps and swung open the front door, feeling the usual blast of arctic air. She shouted out, "Anya?" Luna appeared and rubbed against her legs as Eilish carried her handbag into the kitchen and placed the mesh bags containing the herbs on the kitchen counter. Seraphina was washing some vegetables in the sink. "Fina, do you want the herbs dried or fresh?"

Fina stopped and looked up. "Fresh, I think. Leave them on the counter, and I'll wash them before putting them in the fridge. I'll take them into the shop tomorrow." Eilish moved the mesh bags over closer to the sink. "Is Anya home?" Seraphina nodded, "She's upstairs, unpacking. She said she would take a shower to remove all the peanut butter and jelly." Eilish turned to leave the kitchen. "Okay, I'm going upstairs then. Don't bother fixing me anything for dinner. I'll fix a sandwich or something later."

Eilish rushed up the stairs as Luna chased behind her like they were playing a game. She could hear the rhythmic Jamaican beat of "Jump in the Line" by Harry Bellefonte long before she got to Anya's door. Eilish tapped on the door and didn't get an answer, so she opened the door slowly to find her sister wrapped in a towel, her hair still wet, as she danced a wild calypso around her room. Eilish laughed as she leaped, landing in the middle of Anya's bed, followed by Luna, who was in the mood to play. Anya was lost in the sounds of the music, dancing with her eyes closed. Eilish had to shout to be heard. "Welcome home, sis!"

Anya's eyes opened wide, and she made a dive for the bed. Luna took a flying leap to escape to the floor, and they laughed. "You have *no* idea how happy I am to be home. Sleeping in my own bed, and Fina is the only one yelling and screaming!" Rolling over on her stomach, she looked at her sister and grinned. "So, uh, want to tell me all about the wild escapades you had with Zavian?" Jumping up from the bed, she laughed and grabbed her robe, throwing it on. The ratty old chenille robe was the worse for wear, but she loved it.

Eilish dropped back on the mass of pillows Anya had stacked at the head of her bed. "Oh god, Anya. That was the longest week of my life. Zavian was a big help, but he was always on my heels. I mean, literally on my heels. If I turned around in the shop, I'd bump into him. He came by every morning to walk with me to work, stayed in the shop with me all day, and walked me home most nights. Fina insisted I go out to dinner with him when he asked. I feel so guilty. He's a nice guy; he's just not *my* guy. But I've had enough of Zavian. Tell me about you. How was your week?"

Anya shook her head. "Oh no, no way are you going to ask me how my week was. It was a lot worse than yours. Try dealing with two dirty trolls and a clingy toddler. I love Asher and Lizbet, but they need birth control. I was thinking of you, though. I missed you so much. I don't think I laughed once or listened to any music. I had no time to myself. It was boring and tiresome." She ran her hands through her damp hair and looked at her sister. "I know he isn't your guy, but just once, I wish some guy would look at me like Zavian looks at you." She saw Eilish about to answer, and she held up her hand. "I know, I know. He does seem to fall over himself when he's around you. And I do feel sorry for you, but Eilish, there really isn't much out there to choose from unless you go to another coven. I'm on your side; you know that."

Eilish felt deflated. "So what are you saying? Do you think I should bond myself to someone I don't love because the pickings are slim? I'd end up living like Fina and Warrick. What's the point of that? I'd rather be alone."

Anya regretted her words and sat on the bed beside Eilish. "I'm not saying that at all. And living like Fina and Warrick isn't living at all. I don't know what that is, but it isn't what I want either. I wish I were as strong as you. And besides, I'm sure you wouldn't have wanted to trade places with me this week!" She poked her sister softly on the arm and laughed. "Fina said you visited Cressa after closing the shop. You two must have had a good talk. You were late coming home."

Eilish gave her a sideways glance before holding up her hand and extending her little finger. "Pinkie swear?"

Anya knew what that meant. Pinkie swears were their private secrets and never shared. Extending her pinkie, she linked it with Eilish's. "Pinkie swear. Give it up!"

"I did see Cressa, but I didn't stay. I cut the herbs we needed, then left. I walked to Waterfront Park to clear my head and ran into Ian." She waited, hesitant to add more until she saw Anya's reaction.

Anya's eyes widened in disbelief when she heard her sister mention Ian. She then closed them into slits as she stared at her sister. "The vampire? Eilish, you didn't go near him, did you?" Anya shook her head, her heart racing. This wasn't like Eilish at all. She knew Ian had come into the shop, and Eilish had flirted with him, but being alone with him was dangerous.

Eilish looked out the window as she spoke, so she wouldn't have to make eye contact with her sister. "He was sitting on a park bench, and I sat next to him and talked." She paused a minute before continuing. "He understands me, Anya. I think he feels as lost in his world as I feel in mine. He kissed me when he got up to leave... a real kiss. He said the ball was in my court, and I don't know what to do."

Anya felt her heart ache for her. She'd always be supportive, but this was a very dangerous situation she was walking into. Anya laid her hand on her back. "Vampires have the potential to kill us, Eilish, we can put spells on them, but I understand your attraction to him. He's different, and he's hot. But this is dangerous beyond belief. If anyone, I mean anyone, finds out about him, Fina and Warrick will flip out; they'll draw the coven in and protect you to where you're never alone. It's possible they could even drive him out or start a war between the covens. Does he belong to a coven?"

Eilish shook her head. "No, he's a mercenary. He's a warrior, but he doesn't belong to any coven. I understand the dangers; at least, I understand everything I've been taught about vampires. But I don't feel in danger when I'm around him, and you know I would. He's different, and I'm not just saying that because I'm attracted to him. I feel safe with him. Whatever this is, whatever's happening between us, I think it's real."

Anya stood up and paced. "So, you're serious about him then?" She didn't know exactly what to say; she'd never seen Eilish take an interest in a guy like this. And she could tell by the tone in her voice that she was thinking about it. "I want you to be happy, but you have to think about this seriously, the danger you put all of us in. Can you even see yourself with a bloodsucker, even if he's built like a tree you can't wait to climb? Are you absolutely sure he isn't tricking you?"

Eilish pulled her knees to her chest and tucked her head down. "I'm not sure of anything, except I don't want a life with Zavian." She looked up, "Would he have to feed from me? I know he has to feed. I know their desire to feed is tied to their desire for sex. We know they feed from humans all the time, and they don't kill humans. They're able to erase the humans' memory of the encounter. But they're so taboo in our culture, seen as not pure because we draw our power from the earth and the celestial bodies, and they draw their power from blood. He's not evil, Anya. I can feel evil."

"Well, there are a lot of "thinks" in all of this, and we aren't sure of the answers. I don't know if he can feed from you or what that might cause to happen. If you have sex with him, he's going to want to take your blood, that much we know for sure. I mean, can they abstain from that?" Anya began to pace, her mind racing with the questions in her head and the dangers her sister seemed to be actually considering. Suddenly she stopped pacing and quickly went to the bed and sat opposite Eilish. "Do you remember when we went with Fina, and she went to this old crone...what was her name? It was a long time ago..." She grabbed Eilish, "It was Henwen! Do you remember where it was? She's old and wise; she'd know about the vampires, or at least the consequences. I mean, hell, she's old enough to have known a few vampires, don't you think?"

Eilish nodded. "Henwen, yes, I remember. We were really little then. Fina went to her for some advice right after our parents were killed, and she took over the coven. We were in a shack in a swamp somewhere. I asked Fina about her once, and she said I'd know when I needed to know. I can't remember where it was. I'll have to find her, but you're right; Henwen would know everything." Eilish twisted a strand of her hair around her finger as she pondered the idea of trying to find Henwen. "Would you go with me?"

"Well, I'm not letting you go alone. This will take both of us if you're serious about Ian. I want you to be happy with the man you choose. I'll stand by you, but this must be taken in small steps. Without stirring up any suspicions, I'll see if I can find out where Henwen is." Anya took a deep breath, hoping that once Eilish learned what she needed to know from Henwen, it would convince her this was the worst idea possible.

Eilish could see the doubt in her sister's face, and even she had to admit this was a bad idea. "You know Anya, that guy at the construction site that always cat-calls you, and you flash him the finger? He really likes you. Ian said to tell you Carter has missed you. That's his name...Carter. I know he's human, but he is cute."

Anya sat straight up and couldn't hide the slight grin. "I think one of us trying to hook up outside the coven is enough for now, don't you? He's such a typical male moron, not interested!" Despite her words, Anya was bursting inside; she liked the looks of the sexy blonde guy that was constantly tormenting her. She actually wanted the attention. "And don't worry, he'll continue to get the finger; it's my best weapon!"

Eilish laughed. "Well, not your best weapon." She nudged her sister, still laughing. "Can you imagine Fina, though? Me with a vampire, and you with a human? She'd self-combust." Both girls collapsed in a fit of giggles on the bed.

BOHANNON

Anya had thought about Eilish and the crone after their conversation earlier that evening. Her top priority would be to get the location of Henwen's place. She knew if she was smart about it, she could pull it off, and the perfect person to give her information and never remember or think another thing about it would be Lizbet. She looked at the clock and knew that Lizbet would still be up. Dialing her number, she hoped the holy terrors hadn't tied her to a chair!

Lizbet had the baby Molly on her hip while one of the boys hung on her leg. Asher was sitting two feet away from the ringing cellphone, his head in a book and oblivious to the world. "Asher! Get the phone!" When he failed to look up, she tossed the dish towel on the counter and dragged her leg behind her as her son clung to her as she made her way to the cellphone. Frazzled, she answered the phone just as she heard a crash from the other room. She replied, "Hang on." She turned again to Asher and yelled, "Asher! Will you see what your other son has destroyed in the living room?" Asher looked up and blinked his eyes a few times as he returned to the reality of the chaos around him. "Yeah, sure." Lizbet returned her attention to the ill-timed call, but there was no good time for a call in this house. "Hello?"

Anya could hear the chaos in the background, grateful she was home. "Hey Lizbet, it's Anya. I thought I'd call and check on Molly. Is she doing okay tonight?"

Lizbet looked at the toddler, who had grape jelly all over her face and needed a bath. "She seems fine. Her appetite is back, and I haven't heard her wheezing." The boy clinging to her leg was whining about not being able to find his pet lizard. "Uh, is there something you need, Anya? Things are a little out of control here."

Anya grinned; perfect timing! "Well, actually, yes, I need some special herbs, and I know the crone Henwen will probably have what I'm looking for, but I can't remember where she lives. Do you know by any chance?"

"Henwen? Gosh... I haven't seen Henwen in years. She never leaves her house." Her middle son was still clinging to her leg, asking about his lizard, when she snapped, "Go look for the lizard! I have no idea where he is!" She sighed loudly, getting back to Anya. "Sorry about that... Henwen lives out in Stumphole Swamp, over in Elloree. She has an old shack back there someplace, but you'd never find it unless you know the way. She never comes to the coven rituals anymore. I haven't seen her in years. They have some swamp guides...human, though, so be careful. You could probably hire a swamp guide to take you out there."

Anya sighed. Nothing about this situation was going to be easy, but she was going to do whatever she could to help Eilish. "Thanks, Lizbet, you sound a bit busy; hug Molly for me. I'll talk to you soon." She heard Lizbet yelling as she hung up and laughed out loud. "Your vacation is officially over, Lizbet!" She went to Eilish's room and tapped on the door. "Eilish, are you asleep yet?"

Eilish was changing into her pj's when she heard her sister. "Come on in. But be warned, Emric's in one of his moods."

Anya entered and saw Emric rocking in his usual spot. She quickly closed the door, not wanting Fina to hear them. "Emric, everything's fine. Go to my room. You can listen to some music. Don't scratch the record and keep it turned down low; we don't want

Fina yelling at us." She watched as he walked out through the closed door. "Was he really bad while I was gone?"

Eilish folded back the bedspread and then slipped beneath the blankets. She needed blankets in the middle of summer to counteract Fina's air conditioning. "He found every sad song on every album you own. He's looking for the soldiers again."

Anya shook her head. "Poor Emric, but I have some good news. I called Lizbet to find out if she knew where Henwen lived. Don't look surprised; she won't even remember by morning that I called her. It sounded like the normal chaos over there. Henwen lives in Elloree, in the Stumphole Swamp. But don't get too excited. We need to find a swamp guide to boat us over there."

Eilish plumped up her pillow. "That's good, actually. It's far enough away that we won't have to worry about being seen. I never hear anyone speak of Henwen much these days. We should be pretty safe. We'll have to come up with an excuse to take the car out. Fina rarely takes it out of the garage. Other than that, we shouldn't have a problem."

Anya sighed. "I'm glad you think that will be easy. Fina will ask a million questions, so we better come up with a plan. We'll be gone awhile. Hopefully, the swamp guides will know where Henwen's shack is."

"The swamp guides know every inch of the swamp and the people who live there. They'll know. Maybe we just tell Fina we're taking a day off. You need a break from Lizbet's kids, and I need a break from working all week with Zavian. She owes us one. She and Warrick can run the store for a change."

"Good idea; she won't argue about having Warrick around her all day. Personally, he would drive me to the nut house, but hey, we're talking about Fina here. I'll see if I can convince her to let us have the car." She said her good nights and headed back to her room, wondering how she'd gotten into this mess, but she wanted Eilish to know what she was facing before jumping into the frying pan with the bloodsucker.

BOHANNON

Anya decided she'd ask Fina for the day off and access to the car. She could hear Fina humming to herself in the kitchen, and that had to be a good sign, right? Strolling into the kitchen, her Doc Martens treading lightly, she saw Fina making sweet tea. As much as she drank, you'd think the 'sweet' would have gotten into her veins at some point. Anya slumped her shoulders, dragging her feet and walking like she was the living dead. "I need a day off. And I swear Eilish is worse than me. Please don't yell at me for sleeping in late; we could both use a day to get out of this town and relax."

Fina stopped stirring the tea in the large clear glass pitcher and added some freshly cut lemon wedges. She looked at Anya in her cut-off dungarees with a well-worn t-shirt underneath and shook her head. "Well, you sure look like you need a day off." She glanced at the clock, which read 9 a.m., while filling a glass with ice cubes and pouring the impossibly sweet concoction into her glass. "Could have let me know sooner. Now I'll have to scramble, but I talked to Lizbet earlier this week, and I know those kids ran you ragged. Go ahead. I'll call Warrick. He won't like it, but he'll help me in the shop today."

Anya tried to hide her shock. This had been much easier than she'd thought. Now there was just one more hurdle. "Well, we sure as heck aren't walking. Can we have the car, Fina? Like, we seriously need to just bust outta here. Do you even know where the keys are to the jalopy?"

Fina took a big gulp of the tea and wiped her forehead with her apron, although how she could be hot in this meat locker she called a house was beyond reason. She set down her glass, lifted the lid to the canister of fresh flour, and stuck her hand deep into the white powder, fishing around until she retrieved the keys. She held the flour-coated keys over the sink and blew hard, creating a cloud of white powder. She wiped off the remaining powder on her apron before handing the keys to Anya. Anya stared back at her with a frown. "You hide the keys in the flour?" Fina shrugged. "Who would think to look there?" Anya shook her head, glad to have the keys to the old Cadillac De Ville, "Oh, I don't know, the Pillsbury Doughboy?" Fina smirked. "Don't be a smart-ass."

Anya grabbed the keys and resisted the urge to run like a bullet from the kitchen. She poured herself a sweet tea and headed back up the stairs with Luna chasing her like it was the damn Indianapolis Speedway. "One of these days, Luna, you will get tangled up in someone's feet and end up rolling down the stairs." She made her way to Eilish's room and knocked but didn't wait for an answer. She found Eilish sitting on her bed, sliding on some sandals. Dangling the keys in front of her, she giggled. "Lookie, the keys to the black bullet! Fina said she'd get Warrick to help, so get your booty ready. As soon as she leaves for the shop, we are out...of...here!"

Eilish looked up, surprised. "Wow, I didn't even hear any yelling." She grabbed one of her trademark long maxi skirts and a tank top before layering on her bangles. She heard the music of Aretha Franklin singing "Ain't No Way" coming from Anya's bedroom and knew Emric was feeling calmer since Anya had come home. Emric didn't adjust well to any changes in the household. They both waited until they heard Fina leave the house before going downstairs and out the backdoor to the old carriage house used as a detached garage. They swung open the old doors as they creaked on their hinges, revealing the shiny black 1959 Coupe de Ville. Zavian had ensured the car stayed in tip-top working order through the years. The sisters rarely needed the car, as they walked everywhere around town or rode with Warrick or Zavian. Anya held up the keys. "I'm driving!" Eilish laughed and climbed into the passenger seat, waiting for Anya to start the engine so she could turn on the air conditioning. The initial blast of hot air from the vents felt like a hundred degrees. They lowered the windows until the air conditioning started to cool the car. Eilish tucked her handbag on the floor by her feet as she looked over at Anya, backing the car out of the garage and onto East Bay, "You know the way to Elloree?"

Anya was happy she got to drive what she lovingly called the "hearse" that neither of them ever got to drive much. It was always the males toting them around, it seemed. "I think so. It's off Interstate 26 West. Look, are you sure about this? We can always just go to Edisto beach or something instead." She finally got the old black bullet out of the drive and onto the road.

"No. I want to go. 'In for a penny, in for a pound,' as Mom used to say. Or at least what Fina says Mom used to say. I don't have many memories of them. I wish I did. Besides, it's an adventure. We never do anything."

"Oh, it's an adventure, all right." Anya pulled up to a traffic light, getting ready to turn on the interstate, when a group of young guys started blowing their horn. "What do these jackasses want?" They were motioning her to roll down the window. Anya decided why not? Adventure, right? Rolling down the window, she stared at them. The dude in the passenger seat was hanging out of the window and yelled, "Nice fins, baby!" Anya quickly looked up at the traffic signal, and made it change to green, then flipped them the bird and hit the accelerator. "What a bunch of dicks! And people wonder why I'm not hooked up with anyone...if this is what the pickings are like, I'll die an old crone!"

Eilish laughed as the cars in the intersection were thrown off by the sudden light change, and the guys could still be heard calling after them. "They're not all bad, you know. That guy, Carter? He's hot, and don't tell me you haven't noticed. I know he's human, but what the heck, you don't need a commitment or anything."

As Anya got onto the interstate, she kept the pedal to the metal. She wanted to see the state troopers try to catch this old hearse with her behind the wheel. "Yeah, well, he's cute, but let's face it, your bloodsucker probably just said that as another way into your circle. Human males lack intelligence if you ask me, think with their cocks, and have no balls." Anya threw back her head and laughed. "And besides, I have yet to find one who knows who Chuck Berry is. Speaking of which, we got a long ride. Can you put some music on? Just use my iPhone." Before she knew it, Anya was dancing in her seat as she drove, singing "Old Time Rock n' Roll" with Eilish at the top of their voices.

BOHANNON

20

They'd finally made it to Elloree and Anya had slowed down to navigate the entrance and find where the swamp guides were supposed to be. "Ahh, there it is!" An old wooden shack sat alone amongst a few parking spaces. The words "Swamp Tours" was hand-painted in red on the side of the shack, fading to an almost unreadable script. "This looks like a real classy joint, Eilish. I mean five-star accommodations right here." The parking spots were small, and there were few of them. Anya shook her head. "Well, I hope they aren't overbooked today 'cause the hearse will take up at least two parking spots." Shutting off the engine, Anya looked at Eilish. "Last chance to bail, sis."

Eilish looked out the car window at the shack and wondered what was holding it upright. It looked abandoned. She wondered if they'd made this drive for nothing when the door to the shack opened, and a grizzled old man exited the door. His skin was brown from the sun, and his teeth yellowed from chewing tobacco. She watched him spit on the ground as he stood staring at them. He shouted at them. "Well, y'all want a tour or not?"

Anya and Eilish started to giggle, and Eilish slapped her sister's arm. "Shh, he might hear us. Come on." The girls opened the doors of the black Caddy and walked in his direction. Eilish asked softly, "Are you the tour guide?" He spit again and nodded. "Y'all spray fer skeeters?" The sisters looked at each other before Eilish looked back at him. "What?" The old man shook his head. "Skeeters, girl. Y'all cain't go out in no swamp unless ya sprayed up fer skeeters. Skeeters big as a crow out dare. Suck ya dry."

Eilish shook her head. "Uh, no. We didn't think about that. We can drive back to a store and get a can of mosquito spray." An old hound dog wandered out of the shack just as the man spit again, barely missing the old dog. "No matter. I gots some here. Charge five bucks ta spray y'all down... each." Eilish nodded, reaching in her handbag. He watched her carefully. "I only takes cash. Don't gib me no bad checks and none of dem credit cards." She nodded as she pulled a ten-dollar bill from her wallet, and the man disappeared inside to get the spray.

Anya stood with disbelief and concern about going anywhere with this dude. She leaned in close to Eilish and whispered, "I feel like I'm playing a major role in a B movie called, *Curse of the Swamp Creature.*"

Eilish giggled and quickly tried to wipe the smile from her face when the man returned with an industrial-sized tank of chemicals with a hose and spray nozzle. "Close yer eyes and hold yer breath." They barely had time to comply before he started spraying them down, the chemical smell stinging their nose. Anya was coughing, and Eilish was blinking her eyes, feeling a bit of a sting. Clearing her throat of the thick film of chemical spray, Eilish asked the tour guide, "So, how long is the tour?"

The man set the tank down. "Well now, dat depends, don't it? Whar y'all wantin' ta go?" Eilish reached in her handbag for a tissue, wiped some of the spray from around her eyes, and handed a clean tissue to Anya. "Do you know where Henwen lives?"

The man put his hands on his hips. "Henwen, is it? Y'all know Henwen? She expectin' yee? Henwen don't take kindly ta strangers."

Eilish was having some second thoughts about their plans to visit Henwen. "We do know her, but she's not expecting us." The old man nodded, "Humph. Well den, I be charging y'all fifty dollars." Eilish responded without thinking, "Fifty!"

He shrugged. "Y'all wants ta go, or not?" She counted out the money and handed it to him, as he shoved it into the pocket of his dungarees as she answered, "We want to go." He looked down at the dog and said, "You going or stayin'?" The old dog returned to the shed, and the man closed the door. "Name's Cyrus, by the way. Come on down here to my boat. Y'all ever been in a swamp?" Both girls shook their heads. "Well den, keep y'alls hands and feet in da boat. Snakes. Gaters."

He led them to a flat bottom boat that looked like it could sink any minute, and they both carefully climbed in and sat close together on the wooden bench seat. Cyrus stepped in, picked up a large pole, and used it to push the boat away from the dock and out into the marshy water.

Anya looked over the edge of the so-called boat and couldn't see a damn thing in the murky marsh as she addressed Cyrus. "I'm Anya; she's Eilish." Anya looked at her sister and rolled her eyes. "So how far is it to Henwen's?"

The man reached into his back pocket and took out a tin of snuff, scooping up another finger-full and sticking it in his mouth. "Yep, Bohannon's. I knows who ya are. Henwen lives back aways. She don't like people comin' aroun'. Don't y'all two be tryin' nothin' either. I gots my own ways about me."

Anya bit her lip, trying not to laugh, but she was a bit spooked that he knew about them. "Roger that!"

Cyrus maneuvered the boat deeper into the swamp. As the marsh grass got thicker, they entered a dense forest of bald Cypress trees covered in Spanish moss. The only noise was the sound of the pole being used to propel them through the swamp and the occasional flutter of wings as a startled bird took flight. Cyrus nodded his head to the right, "Copperhead. Poisonous." He steered the boat forward as the two sisters watched the snake slither through the water and away from the boat.

They had been in the swamp for over an hour, and Eilish was holding tight to Anya's hand, wondering if they'd ever see dry land again. Despite whatever chemical he had doused them with, both girls slapped at the mosquitoes that were drawn to them like bees to honey. They noticed the mosquitoes never landed on Cyrus. Eilish was about to ask how much further when Cyrus finally spoke up. "Up ahead. Dats Henwen's shack".

The girls turned their heads to look in the direction he indicated to see a shack on stilts that sat about a foot above the water and had a small front porch. It was raw wood, and if it had ever been painted, there wasn't a speck of paint left now. The roof was made of tin and was completely rusted. Eilish looked back at Cyrus. "Can we call you when we're ready to return?"

Cyrus laughed. "Girl, ain't no fancy phone service out here. Besides, y'all didn't mention no return." Eilish stared dumbfounded. "How do we get back?" Cyrus spit over the side of the boat. "Well, now's a fine time ta be havin' dat thought, now ain't it. Y'all want me ta wait, take y'all back. Dat'll be a hundred bucks." Eilish knew she was being swindled and didn't have more than thirty left in her wallet. She turned to Anya. "Do you have another seventy?"

Anya could not believe this place, nor this Cyrus. She zipped open her fanny pack in between swatting at the mosquitos and other flying swamp bugs. "I got this one, sis." Anya pulled out five twenty-dollar bills and waved them at Cyrus, just far enough that he couldn't reach. "Just to be clear, when we come out of that shack, we will see you here waiting, am I right? Because I'm not sure how long this might take. It would be a pity to spend the rest of your life as a boring toad in the swamp."

Cyrus laughed as he took the money and shoved it in his pocket. "I be here, or I won't. Tryin' to figure if y'all two city slickers was smart enough ta tell someone where y'all was going or not." He saw the look of surprise on their faces and realized what he suspected was true. They'd come alone, and no one knew they were here. He could just go on back to his shack, but Henwen had her ways too. It was best not to get in a tangle with the witches. Others had tried and failed, and he didn't figure his luck would be any better, even if these two were a bit green. "Go on, git. Cain't wait to see how delighted Henwen will be to see ya."

As they exited the boat, Anya wasn't sure that any of this was such a great idea. "I've got to tell you, sis, none of this sounds too good. I hope that damn vamp is worth all this mess, and another thing, if you two ever hook up, he owes me a hundred bucks." As they walked toward the shack, Anya grabbed Eilish's arm. "Wait, what are you going to say to her? She's no ordinary, run-of-the-mill witch. Tell me you have a plan."

Eilish was staring at a dead cypress tree that had been turned into a totem of animal skulls; there were pentagrams made of sticks hanging from the branches and a wind-chime of long bones hanging from the porch. She'd only met Henwen when she was maybe three, and Anya was five. Seraphina had come to see her after their parents had been killed, and Fina was about twenty at the time. Fina not only had to assume control of the coven as the new High Priestess, but she was also burdened with raising her two young sisters. Everything Eilish had ever learned about Henwen had come from word of mouth from others in the coven. She wasn't prepared for what she was walking into. All the witches she knew lived in the city among humans and rarely did anything to draw attention to themselves. "Uh, well, my plan was just to talk to her." She grabbed Anya's hand as they walked across the creaking dock that swayed under their weight.

Anya suddenly felt like this was a bad idea, but she was curious about the crone and what she'd tell them if they ever got in the door. "Well, let's go talk because I seriously don't want to be here after dark, at least not with Cyrus." She squeezed Eilish's hand.

Eilish knew better than to enter another witch's circle without an invitation. They never had to think about that at home. Everyone in the coven knew each other and visited frequently. She stood still and searched her mind for the incantation, pretty sure Henwen was already aware of their presence. Eilish called out loudly to the witch inside the shack. "Blessed be thy feet, that have brought thee in these ways. Blessed be thy knees, that shall kneel at the sacred altar. Blessed be thy womb, without which we would not be. Blessed be thy lips, that shall utter the Sacred Names. Blessed be thy third eye, that sees all. To our Blessed Crone Henwen, allow these humble witches into your circle."

The two sisters stood side by side, waiting, as they heard the boards creak from inside the shack and the loud caw of a crow. The old woman appeared in the doorway; her hair white and wiry, what little of it could be seen under the black scarf draped around her head. She was hunched over, barely five feet tall, but neither sister would ever mistake her diminutive size for lack of power. She used an old knurled tree branch as a walking stick, worn smooth through the years. She stared at the two girls through narrow slits, her face so wrinkled it was impossible to imagine what she may once have looked like when she was young.

Henwen sighed loud enough for them to hear. "Knew y'all'd come bringin' ya problems. The Bohannon's, y'all be the death of me yet."

Anya watched the crone, felt a shiver run through her, and gave her sister a sideways glance. Eilish knew Henwen was about to reveal to them a lot of things they'd never heard before.

BOHANNON

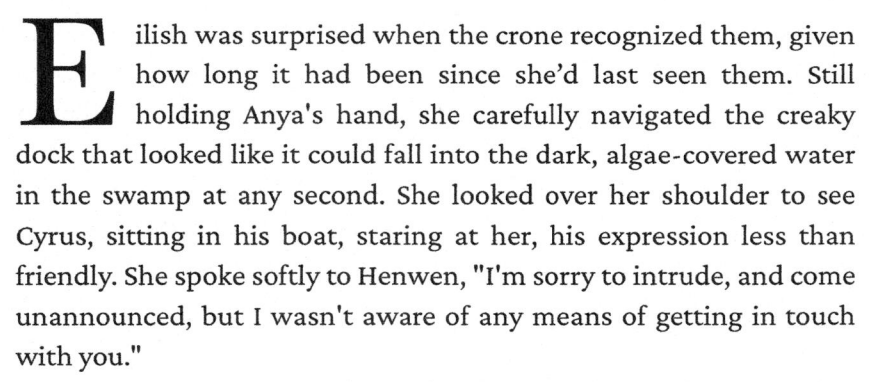

Eilish was surprised when the crone recognized them, given how long it had been since she'd last seen them. Still holding Anya's hand, she carefully navigated the creaky dock that looked like it could fall into the dark, algae-covered water in the swamp at any second. She looked over her shoulder to see Cyrus, sitting in his boat, staring at her, his expression less than friendly. She spoke softly to Henwen, "I'm sorry to intrude, and come unannounced, but I wasn't aware of any means of getting in touch with you."

Henwen held a piece of sassafras between her teeth, gnawing at it as she answered, "Been waitin' fer ya." She turned and entered the shack without further comment. Eilish's hand was damp, and she wasn't sure who was more nervous, her or Anya.

Anya stared at the crone; her crooked body fit the crooked stick she walked with. Her mere appearance was enough to make anyone else dive for the swamp. She looked at Eilish and mouthed, "Waiting on us?" She followed her sister into the shack.

The girls had to stand a second to let their eyes adjust to the darkness. The shack had two windows that allowed for cross-ventilation, but on a day like today, there was no air moving in the swamp. There was no electricity out here, at least not to this shack.

The furniture consisted of an old table with a ladder-back wooden chair, a sofa that looked like something that had been abandoned beside the highway, and a pallet of old blankets and pillows in a corner. A makeshift wooden countertop held an old bucket, an oil lamp, and a few cheap pots and pans. There were a few pegs on the wall where Henwen had hung a few other garments and old towels. Each wall had been whitewashed with a pentagram. Henwen slowly made her way to the one chair when she told the girls to have a seat. Eilish looked questionably at the old sofa. It sagged in the middle, and she could smell the mildew. Not wishing to be impolite, she moved towards the sofa, clinging tight to Anya. The two sisters sat down, sitting close to each other, looking back at Henwen.

Eilish tried to make conversation. "I'm surprised you recognized us. We were so little the last time you saw us." Henwen chewed the sassafras stick. "Didn't recognize yer faces, recognized yer energy. Y'all witches today, livin' among da humans, y'all fergit more dan ya know. Tryin' so hard ta blend in, don't even know da half of y'alls powers, let alone how ta use 'em. Figured y'all'd come sooner or later wiff yer questions 'bout yer parents and Seraphina." The crone watched their expressions and realized the visit had nothing to do with either of those things.

Eilish stumbled over her words. "Questions about our parents? They were killed in a coven war. Did you know them?"

Henwen nodded once. "Course I knowed 'em. Know all y'all and yer secrets."

Anya sat on the couch and cringed, this was *worse* than a B movie, but she tried to settle her trepidation. "Secrets? What secrets?"

Henwen laughed. "Dey's always secrets, girly. Y'all come here ta tell me 'bout some school girl crush ya gots on a vampire like y'all think ya da first? Vampires seduce. Dat how dey hunt dey prey. Ain't ya learned nuthin'?" Anya stared back with her mouth open, for once at a loss for a sarcastic come-back. She pointed at her sister. "Uh, she's the one with the vampire crush. I'm just her wingman."

Henwen shook her head. "So, spit it out, den. What y'all come all da way out here ta know? Cuz I sure hope ya ain't waistin' my time ta find out if ya kin fuck a vampire. Vampires an' witches. Forbidden fruit. Always wantin' whatcha cain't have."

Eilish looked back at her, stunned for words. It wasn't exactly the question she had, but close. "Uh, well, sort of. Has a vampire and a witch ever, you know, bonded? What if he doesn't see her as prey? Can he feed from her?"

Henwen stared out the door, silent for so long Eilish was beginning to wonder if she'd even heard her question when Henwen looked over at her. "True love is it, girly?" Henwen shook her head. "Well, I guess dat will turn Seraphina's hair gray. I kin see she has leff some gapin' holes in yer education. Dare ain't nothin' ta keep ya from da vampires if dat's what ya want. Over da years, we foun' it best not ta congregate. We had some battles over territory, but dat's 'bout it. Hard 'nough tryin' ta blend in wiffout a fuckin' vampire on yer arm. Ya won't be da first, or da last, ta explore what's better leff alone. But he cain't hurt ya. Yo magic be stronger dan his physical strength and any giffs he holds. He could drain ya, but only if ya dumb enough to lay dare. Dat answer yer question?"

Eilish nodded. "I think so. Maybe. Mostly? Do vampires know our magic is more powerful than their physical strength?"

Henwen laughed, her cackle carrying through the silent swamp. "Well, unless ya foun' yerself a really dumb one. He cain't hurt ya unless dat his intention, an' I sure hope yer instincts be strong enuff ta recognize another's intent, regardless of dey species. Same fer you. Bondin', matin', whatever da fuck ya wanna call it, ya cain't hurt him unless ya call on yer power ta do so. Just remember dat. Ain't no spell he immune to. Ya hold all da power."

Eilish nodded. She did know that vampires held no immunity from their spells. "But what if we... bonded, and we had a child? Would he be vampire or witch?"

Henwen rubbed her forehead. "Y'all goin' down a treacherous path, girly. Ya bring a vampire into yer coven, whatcha think is gonna happen? Ever'body welcome him wiff open arms? Da coven will gather ta bless da newborn cuz ya be da High Priestess. Da baby be a witch, wiff da physical strength of da vampire. Prolly teleport. Always a day-walker. But don't expect da coven ta celebrate yo handfast ta no vampire. Most times, a witch be exiled from da coven fer such. But y'all Bohannon. Changes everythin'."

Anya had relaxed a little and was hanging intently on Henwen's every word. "Well, I'd hook up with him just to yank Fina's chain if it was me."

Henwen turned her attention to the other sister. "Sounds ta me like Seraphina is da one yanking yer chain, girly." Henwen looked back at Eilish with her pale complexion and her pale gray eyes. "I knowed y'alls mama. I remember when ya was born. She say she knowed when ya was in da womb ya had mo powers dan her, and yo mama was one of da most powerful witches ta come from da Bohannon's, and dats sayin' a lot. So, I'm wonderin'... how come Seraphina is High Priestess?"

Anya was caught off-guard. "Wait, are you saying what I think you're saying? Momma knew that sis was more powerful, and so does Fina?" She turned to face Eilish on the couch. "That would explain the push with Zavian, and don't even think that Warrick is a dumbass either. He's part of this. His power is weak, and that would make you easier to control."

Eilish looked confused. "But Fina is High Priestess because she's the oldest."

She heard Henwen's cackle. "Is dat what she tole ya? Hellfire, girly; if it was based on age, I'd be da fuckin' Queen of Sheeba by now!" Henwen threw back her head and laughed. "So I was right. She never tole ya 'bout Rhiannon's Circle."

The two sisters looked at each other, more confused than ever. Eilish looked back at her. "That's our shop. Of course, we know about it. We work there almost every day."

Henwen leaned back in her chair, a knowing smile on her face. "Well, I has to gib da Bohannon's credit. Dey be smart ones, fer sure.

Dey put it right out dare...like dey be daring da world ta figure it out." She looked at the confused stare of the two sisters. "She ain't tole y'all nuthin', has she? Clever, how da Bohannon's name da store after da one thing dey gots to hide. Rhiannon's Circle ain't 'bout no shop, it's a grimoire, a book, passed down from one generation of Bohannon's ta another. It's what y'alls parent's died protectin', and it sounds like Seraphina has it now."

Anya was on the edge of her seat and was hit with the most incredible feeling of betrayal. She stood up quickly and paced around the small shack. "She has this book and *never* told us? She's protecting it? From who, us?" She stopped pacing and stared at the crone. "So, does this book hold power or something?"

Eilish shook her head. She'd never heard anything about a book. She looked back at Henwen. "What's so special about this grimoire?"

The crone knew she was opening a can of worms, but the truth would come out sooner or later anyway. "Dat book holds spells an' incantations long lost to da witch community, an' only recorded in dat fuckin' book. Dat what makes da Bohannon's so powerful. Dat what got dem driven out of Ireland. Yer great-great gran'parents came here, settled in Charleston, played it low key fer a while. But ya cain't suppress da power of da grimoire. Weren't long befo yer gran'ma, den yer mama, now Seraphina, was High Priestess. Da Bohannon's have tried ta remain under da radar. Kept dey power local when dey coulda knocked out ever' coven in da country. Least now ya know why all da witches kiss yer ass. Only thing now is, whatcha gonna do 'bout it?"

Eilish was overwhelmed with the information. "Do I need to do anything? I mean, Fina says I'll be the next High Priestess. Maybe she's just waiting to tell me about the book then."

Henwen smiled. "Guess dat's up to you, den. Now git on outta here. Tole ya all I know. Y'alls problem now. Git on befo Cyrus gits tired of waitin'. I don't plan on havin' any overnight guests, an' I ain't sharin' da last of my possum meat wiff ya, either."

"Come on, Eilish, let's go." The sisters stood up to leave, but

Eilish knew better than to leave another witch who had bestowed knowledge without leaving a token. She reached deep inside her handbag and retrieved a raw stone of turquoise, a stone that granted power, luck, and protection, and placed it in Henwen's hand. "Thank you."

The crone nodded but offered no more words. The girls walked outside, both of them in a state of disbelief. Anya quickly looked and saw that Cyrus was still there. "Come on, before Cyrus decides he's had enough, it's getting dark out, and the last thing I want to do is be stuck in this swamp. I know you're a bit shaken. Hold my hand; we have to get back in that rickety surfboard he calls a boat."

Eilish felt numb. She'd come here to find out what could go wrong if she decided to pursue a relationship with Ian and got a lot more than she'd bargained for. Cyrus held out his hand as each sister had to grab onto him to steady themselves as they stepped back into the flat bottom boat.

Cyrus had heard most of what was said inside the shack. Witches. Vampires. He'd seen it all living out here on the swamp and steered clear of their troubles. He didn't want to draw the anger of either species. Mostly, they let him be as he'd provided a service. He grabbed his pole and started pushing the boat back through the murky waters. The two sisters sat silently as they returned.

BOHANNON

The girls made it back safely to Cyrus's shack, the air still and heavy. It was dark as they made their way to the black bullet. Neither had uttered a word since getting inside the boat and returning. They were lost in their thoughts of the revelations Henwen had revealed to them. But Anya was stunned to realize all the questions she now had and was dying to confront Fina. As she began the drive back to Charleston, she flipped the AC on high and frequently looked over at Eilish. She could imagine what was going through her sister's head if she was this stunned. Her sister stared straight ahead, looking through the windshield, and she had to pull her out of this. "I know you've got some answers on your vampire, but I imagine he's the least of your worries right now. What are you going to do, Eilish? About Fina and this book? By rights, the position of High Priestess is yours. She's robbing you of that position." She glanced again at her sister, finding her expression the same, as though she hadn't even heard her. "Eilish, did you hear me?"

Eilish nodded, then wiped away a tear. "Yeah, I heard you. I feel kind of torn, you know? I'm shocked by the revelation of this book, and it's something our parents died protecting. So clearly, its value is beyond measure. But I'm more shocked... no, that's not the word; I'm hurt. I feel betrayed by Fina. Not about the High Priestess thing, you know I never really cared about that, and I still don't. But she lied to us, withholding information about our parents, the book, and our lineage in ruling the coven. I mean, I was only three when our parents died. I couldn't have ruled the coven anyway. Fina would have had to take it on, wouldn't she? Could a child rule a coven?" Eilish shook her head. "We can't let Fina know what we learned, at least not now. There's more to this; we can't show our hand yet. We don't know where the book is. We don't know what Warrick's involvement is. We don't know if the rest of the coven knows. And right now, we don't even know if Fina is our enemy or our beloved sister." Eilish laid her head back against the headrest and closed her eyes, glad her sister had the wheel.

The air in the car was suddenly laden with sadness and betrayal. Anya had to abide by Eilish's request not to confront Fina, but that wouldn't be an easy task. "I'm worried about you, Eilish. This makes your problems with Ian seem like nothing. I personally want to confront Fina right now with everything we know. I won't because first, we need to know where the book is; that will be the key to confronting her and the lies. Maybe she had a good reason, but at this point, I can't imagine what." Reaching over, she softly squeezed Eilish's hand while steering the caddy with the other. "Two things bother me, and one is why? Maybe we were too young at the time, but then she *never* told us, and she never groomed you for this in any way. She *knew* you had this power. Selfish is what it is." She sighed heavily, trying to keep her temper under control. "And I have no doubt Warrick knows it all as well. He has always ridden on Fina's coattails. And when you do take over, he needs you bonded to Zavian. Zavian's powers are weak, and Warrick has always run his life. Keeping you tied to Zavian gives Warrick a way to hang on to power in this coven. He thinks he can control you through Zavian, or at least maintain power through association."

Eilish looked over at her sister. "Do you think Zavian knows?" Anya shook her head. "Nah. Zavian is pretty guileless. I think his interest in you is sincere, but let's face it. Without his association with the Bohannon's, his standing in the coven would be pretty low. He's shown almost no real potential as a warlock. His power would come through you."

Eilish felt like someone had shoved a stake through her heart. Could Fina really be using her in such a way? Manipulating her hand-fasting because it helped secure Fina's future, not hers? Fina had raised them both, ensured the family had a secure income, kept a roof over their heads, and food on the table. She'd had to assume the role of mother to her two younger sisters, albeit not always the most loving, but she'd always seen to their education, safety, and well-being. Aside from the loss of her parents, Eilish remembered their childhood as happy. Was Fina that devious? Or was she just so confident her secret would never be discovered? Would there ever have come a day when she would have relinquished her power and shared the secret of the book?

Eilish had more questions swirling in her brain, and they were questions she didn't want to deal with. "Warrick knows about the book. He has to know. It's why he clings on. Bonded to her, but not because he loves her, because of the power she brings. That's why he doesn't live with her. And Fina pretends it's her idea because it's embarrassing to her that Warrick chooses to live apart. And you're right; it's Warrick as much as Fina pushing this match with Zavian. Warrick may not know where the book is. If Fina is that devious, she'd never tell anyone, including Warrick."

The more they talked, the more Anya became aware of how long this had gone on and how much Fina had hidden from them their entire lives. "I feel sad for Momma and Daddy. Possessing that book was the reason they lost their lives, and she lied about all of it, Eilish. She may have lied to keep us safe, and we were too young to understand, but still, look at us now. You're a threat to her, sister dear, a very big one, and one we have to figure out with a sure-fire plan. I know you don't want to be High Priestess, but it's your destiny, now more than ever." She looked at the headlights coming at her and shook her head. "How is it possible that no one in our coven ever said anything? Are they that afraid of us or Fina?"

Eilish stared at the lines painted on the highway as the car sped past them, making it look like it was the lines that were moving past them, and the car was stationary, the world spinning beneath them. It was hypnotizing, and she would have preferred just to zone out, stare at the lines and let her mind go blank. But Anya's question penetrated her thoughts. With a sudden clarity of thought, Eilish spoke what she knew had to be true. "Henwen said the Bohannon's were driven from Ireland over that book. No witch could stand against the powers held inside that book, regardless of how powerful. No one would ever dare confront Fina. Every coven has a High Priestess, and we've met a few, but no coven kowtows to their priestess as our coven does to Fina. The coven must be aware of the book or at least have heard enough rumors to suspect it's true. I've never seen another witch even dare to question Fina in all my years, and that's just how Fina likes it. They may think we know, but it wouldn't matter. They can't risk getting on Fina's bad side. Whatever we do, we won't get help from the coven."

Anya drove, mulling over the points Eilish had made. It all began to make sense. Their entire life was a mystery of unanswered questions, and the only one who knew the answers was Seraphina. "We have to find that book, somehow. I don't know how yet, but wherever it is, you have the power, sister. Henwen was right. You have the power."

Eilish opened the car window and felt the wind blow against her face, lifting her hair in a white halo around her head. "That's the problem, sis. I don't want the power."

BOHANNON

Ian stood upright on the roof, stretching his back and looking back the length of the sidewalk for the tenth time to see if she was coming. She'd told him when he'd seen her in the park that her older sister was coming home. He assumed everything would return to their normal routine, and he'd see the two of them walking to work together, but no one yet. He'd left the ball in her court and was wondering now if he'd made a huge mistake pretending to accidentally meet her there. Maybe he'd moved too fast for her, and she was avoiding him and had taken another route. He shouted at Carter over his shoulder. "I'm going down for a cold drink."

Carter had been watching him looking for the girls all morning. It was a few minutes past 10, and the girls were never late. He knew the one with white hair had been with the tall skinny dude all last week, and the blonde one with the smart mouth was gone. He'd missed seeing her as well, and they both had wondered where she was. Strange how you could get wrapped up in someone else's drama when you only saw them for a few seconds every day, but the girls walking by had become something they both looked forward to. Carter shouted back to him, "Yeah brother, I'm sure it's a cold drink you're after." He laughed as Ian climbed down the ladder.

Ian sat on the tailgate of the truck, pulling off his sweat-soaked t-shirt and grabbing some water, pouring some of it over his head. He was facing the direction of what should have been Eilish and her sisters' route towards them. Carter was right behind him, grabbing bottled water from the cooler. Ian spoke. "That didn't take long." He looked at his watch and knew it was well past their regular time. He never took his eyes off the sidewalk. They should have been here by now. "The long-haired skinny-ass dude was a friend of the family. He won't be back this week. And the one you like is called Anya. She was visiting elsewhere, but she's back now. And don't tell me you weren't watching for them as well, damn it."

Carter grabbed a bottled water from Ian's cooler and emptied the bottle in about four swallows before wiping his mouth on the shoulder of his shirt. "Anya. How'd you find that out?" He tucked that name away in his brain, glad to have it.

Ian shrugged. "Went down to Waterfront Park after work; she just happened to be there strolling around alone." Ian let his mind wander to those moments with her, right next to him, and that kiss. He wanted a whole lot more of those. "She sat with me, and we talked. Fuck Carter; she's hot. She likes me; I like her. Where in the hell are they?"

Carter was surprised to hear Ian had met up with her. He looked down the sidewalk, and there was no activity all the way down to where it intersected with the Battery. "Well, if they're coming, they're really late, and they're never late. Maybe it's some kind of witch holiday, and they have the day off. Ever think of that?" Carter chuckled as he tossed the empty water bottle into the back of the truck. "Or maybe she's not as enamored with you as you think, and they took an alternative route. Damn, now you're even spoiling *my* game."

Ian picked up his shirt and threw it at Carter with a laugh he didn't feel. "You might be whistling a different tune once I convince her to go out with me." Ian watched as Carter shook his head and headed back to the roof. The rest of the day moved slowly, and Ian's mood never improved. She had to know he waited for her to walk by every day. If she wasn't going to be working today, wouldn't she have told him that last night? He knew this was a bad idea. Trying to connect with her was dangerous. It was insane, but the feelings he got from her wouldn't leave him alone. As the work day ended, he said goodbye to Carter and headed home. After taking a shower, he made his way to Rhiannon's Circle. He knew the shop closed around 8 p.m., so he hung out across the street and waited for them to close. He wasn't going to give up easily. He saw the door open and out walked what must be the older sister and another older dude. They locked up and got into a nearby vehicle. Eilish hadn't come to work at all, which only made him feel worse. He wanted her, and he'd do whatever was necessary to make it work.

BOHANNON

As they arrived back home, both of them seemed to be lost in their thoughts. After three tries, Anya finally got the jalopy backed into the garage. "Sometimes this thing is like parking a tank." She shut off the engine and sat looking at Eilish. "So, what's the plan? Because you know Fina will ask us a million questions about what we did today, especially coming back after dark."

Eilish almost wished they hadn't gone to see Henwen. She wished she could erase from her mind the information they'd learned about Rhiannon's Circle. "We can't let her know we saw Henwen, not ever. Promise me, Anya. I wish I didn't even know about this book. Maybe Fina has a good reason for keeping it from us. I don't want to think she's betrayed us all these years. That breaks my heart. I mean, it's always been the three of us against the world. That's what she used to say. Besides, I never cared about the High Priestess thing anyway. It's important to Fina, and she can keep it as far as I'm concerned. You said something about Edisto Beach when we started out this morning, so let's just say we went there...rented a beach umbrella, sat on the beach, read, went for lunch, and took a nap in the afternoon listening to the waves. That's low-key. We don't need anyone to collaborate on our story. It was just the two of us. Okay?"

Anya stared at her for a moment. "Sure, it's for the best we never speak of any of this. I know you don't want to be a High Priestess, but I wish you'd think differently about it. This is for the good of our coven, our future. Someday you'll want children, don't you ever think about it? Having a home with someone you love and having babies, let's face it, we aren't getting any younger." Shrugging her shoulders, she looked straight ahead. "Just sayin', you know?" Deep inside, Anya dreamed of someone to love her as much as she could love them.

Eilish ran her finger along the car window. "I think about it sometimes. Fina never had kids and never asked for a fertility spell, so it must have been her choice. Or maybe it was Warrick's." She shook her head. "Honestly, I tried not to think too far ahead. I didn't like imagining a future with Zavian, and there wasn't anyone else. Now there's Ian, but despite what Henwen said, we both know that's a really bad idea."

"Does that mean you've made a decision? You're not going to see him?"

Eilish sighed. "I haven't made a decision. But you know he has no idea what he's getting into. Fina will try to destroy him, and so will Warrick. He's not immune from their spells. I know he's strong, but they can really hurt him. I'm not sure it's even fair to drag him into this. I can only protect him from so much."

Anya turned to look at her sister and could feel her sadness. "Okay, well, enough of this. Edisto beach it is; come on, let's get inside; I don't know about you, but I need a shower!"

Eilish grabbed her handbag from the floor. "Oh crap! I forgot we probably smell like that chemical Cyrus sprayed on us. We'll need to get upstairs quickly. If she asks, just say we bought some bug spray at the beach because the midges were so bad." The two girls climbed out of the car and closed the doors to the garage. The doors were never locked, and Eilish replaced the boundary spell on the garage.

They climbed the steps to the screen porch on the back of the house and could smell that Fina had been cooking. Eilish looked at her sister. "We'll have to make a beeline for the stairs, don't stop; just say we have to wash off the sand and bug spray."

Warrick had come with Fina after working with her in the shop all day, and she kissed him goodbye as the girls walked in the back door. "Well, haven't we been gone a long time? And just where did...what's that smell? It smells like you fell into a swamp!"

Warrick looked at the girls and smirked. "How nice, the scent of bug spray and two sweaty, bedraggled sisters. I certainly hope your day off was a pleasant one and you feel better. Although I enjoyed my day with Fina, and the store was bustling, don't count on me being a regular. I have things to do, so don't expect another vacation day soon. Tourists are overloading the city." Kissing Fina one last time, he wrinkled his nose at the girls as he brushed past them on his way to the front door.

Anya rolled her eyes at Warrick, glad that he was leaving. "We were at the beach, Edisto, to be specific. And the bugs were terrible, so we just got some spray...you know, the perfume of Charleston."

"Well, you both need to clean up before this house smells like bug spray. I cooked dinner. Warrick and I already ate. I left yours in the fridge. I never liked the beach, myself. Sand and bug spray, I don't see what you see in it." Shaking her head, she left the kitchen and headed upstairs. "Eat something, then get some sleep. I want that shop opened on time in the morning!"

Both girls decided on a quick shower before eating the dinner Fina had prepared. After coming back down in their robes, Anya removed the plates from the fridge and popped them into the microwave. Even though Fina had retreated to her bedroom, the girls knew better than to speak of their adventure within possible earshot of Fina in case she eavesdropped. Anya placed the hot plates on the table, and it was clear Fina had stopped at the Farmer's Market. There was fresh squash, Vidalia onions, and a mix of steamed broccoli and cauliflower. They heard Fina call down to them when she heard the microwave beep. "There are fresh tomatoes on the windowsill!"

The two girls made eye contact. Fina was tuned into them. Eilish poured two glasses of sweet tea as Anya sliced the tomato before they both sat down to eat and made small talk about their "day at the beach" for Fina's benefit. Luna wrapped herself around the chair leg, purring loudly, but quickly left when she discovered there was no chicken or fish to be shared. After the meal, they rinsed their plates and returned to their rooms. Tomorrow they'd resume their routine of walking to Rhiannon's Circle to open the shop and have more privacy to talk.

BOHANNON

Both Eilish and Anya woke in the morning, anxious to get out of the house and away from Fina. Anya knew that neither of them had slept well. As they left the house, Fina shouted for them to get moving; she'd be along shortly. As they walked together, Anya found Eilish walking faster as they approached the house where her vampire was working. "Eilish, I know Fina said to get a move on, but I don't feel like jogging to work! Are we bypassing the vamp, or do you have a plan?"

"I'm not ready for this, Anya. My brain is scrambled right now. The last thing I need is more complications. The best thing for me to do is just walk past that house as quickly as I can and ignore him. It's unfair to pull him into this drama until we both know what's going on with Fina."

Eilish glanced ahead at the house. She was staring into the sun, but she could tell the silhouette on the roof was Carter, not Ian. She crossed her fingers, hoping maybe Ian was working on a completely different section of the house today, and they wouldn't even see him. She didn't want to hurt his feelings, but ignoring him was the best thing for both of them. She felt Anya catch up to her as the two of them walked side by side. Just as they passed the house, she saw Carter stand upright and lift his shirt to wipe the sweat from his eyes. In a micro-second, she saw him as he took one step back, and his foot started slipping over the roof's edge. The sisters' gasped as they watched him struggle for his balance. Eilish saw Ian appear from nowhere and knew he'd moved faster than their eyes could detect to try to grab Carter, but he was too late. As Ian was reaching out to grab him, Carter slipped off the side of the roof and was in a three-story free-fall to the ground. Eilish screamed out, "No!"

Carter had been keeping watch for the girls. He thought he'd seen motion out of the corner of his eyes and was wiping his brow to remove the sweat. The sun was blinding him, and he wasn't aware of how close he was to the edge when he stepped back and felt himself falling. It happened so fast that he hardly had time to think, but he knew he was in for a hard fall with a lot of pain and broken bones.

Anya saw him start to fall, and her heart raced. She threw a spell with the flash of her hand and a wave of energy flowed out from her extended fingertips, like a ring of concentric circles when a stone is thrown into a pond. She held her breath as she watched his rapid fall come to a halt, inches above the ground, then gently laid him down. It had happened so quickly that her response was reflexive, and she didn't have time to think about what she'd done. Both sisters ran to his aide, but there was a brief moment when Anya made eye contact with Carter as he lay on his back, looking back at her with a combination of awe and confusion. Their eyes met, and it made Anya's heart leap, even though she'd broken a rule never to use magic around humans.

Carter had prepared for the pain of impact when it felt like someone had hit the brakes, and he landed like a feather. He saw the two sisters rushing in his direction and locked eyes with Anya. He knew she'd stopped his fall. He was already fighting the adrenaline rush of falling when he realized all those rumors he'd only halfway believed about the Bohannon's were true. He didn't know how, but Anya had probably saved his life or, at the very least, kept him from breaking his back. He sat up slowly, checking for injuries. He jumped to his feet as Ian rushed toward him. "You okay? I couldn't get to you in time."

Carter nodded, not taking his eyes off Anya. His face reflected his confusion, "Yeah, I'm good."

Ian knew one of the sisters had intervened and quickly figured out from the eye contact that it was Anya. As Anya reached out and touched Carter's arm, inquiring if he was okay, he felt a jolt of energy pass through her fingers, and he pulled his arm away in reflex, immediately regretting the move. "I'm good. Thanks to you."

Anya felt her heart fall when Carter jerked his arm away. She knew he was confused and decided it was best to leave it that way. Her heart was still racing from the worry she felt when she saw him fall. "Well, I've heard of trying to get a lady's attention, but don't you think that was a little much?" She gave him a smirk but was glad he was fine.

Carter was at a loss for words, trying to sort out what had just happened, but glad she didn't seem to notice he'd pulled away. He was shocked by the sensation of her touch but now intrigued even more than before.

Ian stood beside Eilish and reached out to take her hand, but she gently slipped her hand from his. It wasn't the response he was looking for. "By the way, this is Eilish." Pointing to Anya, he smiled at her, "And this is Anya. Meet Carter, the flying carpenter." Ian tried not to show his disappointment at Eilish's rebuff, but he felt like someone had just ripped his heart out. "Lucky you two were walking by." He nudged Eilish. "I guess you're going to work?"

"Yeah, just opening the shop. So, you're okay, Carter?" As he nodded, Eilish quickly scanned up and down the sidewalk. They never used their magic in public and now risked being exposed. They were aware of the rumors, but talk was one thing, and the proof was another. Right now, the Bohannon's were just another curiosity like the city ghost tours. No one really took it seriously. Usually, they wouldn't have interfered in the problems of humans, but she knew Anya had a crush on Carter, although getting her to admit it would be like pulling teeth. Eilish felt uncomfortable that Ian even referred to their magic, although she was pretty sure Carter had figured it out on his own by now. She grabbed her sister's hand. "We should be going. We'll be late."

As they walked away, Carter yelled, "Wait." Both girls turned their heads, but he could see the white-haired one tugging at Anya's arm. "You want to go for pizza later? I mean, maybe all four of us?"

Anya gave him a look as if she had time for such nonsense. "Well, I think you might want to practice your flying skills; flapping your arms helps." She turned away, and the two sisters were on their way as both guys stood staring at them with confused faces.

Carter turned to Ian as the girls walked away. "Dude, they really are witches," Ian responded with no emotion. "I know." Carter persisted, slugging Ian in his solid biceps. "No, I mean for real. Did you see what happened? I barely touched the ground! How'd she do that?"

Ian shrugged, watching Eilish's hair blowing softly in the wind as she walked away. Carter persisted. "Don't you care?" Ian sighed, "I care. I care a lot. Just not sure it's reciprocated." He looked over at Carter. "You have an in now, though. That witch just saved your ass, in broad daylight, where anyone could have witnessed it. Witches don't involve themselves in the problems of humans, risking exposure." Carter looked at him as Ian climbed back up the ladder to the roof. "How do you know so much about witches?" Ian looked down at him, wondering how long it would take before Carter realized he was a vampire.

BOHANNON

Eilish felt rattled after the incident with Carter as she almost dropped the key opening the shop door. As the girls got inside, she flipped the store sign to 'open' and then turned to her sister. "What were you thinking? You completely stopped his fall in plain sight! What if someone had seen us? There were cars driving by, Anya."

Eilish tossed her handbag on the counter and brushed her hair back from her face. She was already feeling conflicted about Ian trying to take her hand in public. The incident had happened close to the shop, where every witch in Charleston visited at some point. They could have seen them, and while a human wouldn't recognize a vampire on sight, a witch would. She paced the floor, feeling like things were unraveling.

Anya stared at her sister. "I don't know; it all happened so fast, and I didn't even think about it." Anya walked to the back and brought out a box of items that needed to be put on the shelves. "All of this is your fault. You had to go and get hooked up with some bloodsucker. I'm sorry you're upset. I wasn't thinking. Carter could have gotten seriously hurt." Anya began to put the crystals in their proper place, arranging them in their baskets. "Why does this bother you so much?"

Anya had her back to her as she answered, keeping herself busy with the crystals. Eilish watched her sister's fingers spark as she touched each crystal, still carrying the residual energy of stopping Carter's fall. "Fina doesn't even let us use our magic to get a dish from a top shelf inside the house! She did that to make sure we didn't use magic out of habit. You could have slowed his fall, maybe, but he was totally suspended above the ground for a few seconds. You did it without thinking." A light bulb went off for Eilish. "Wait. You like this guy, don't you? You *did* do it without thinking because you really like him. You can flash him the finger all you want, but you're attracted to this guy. That's it, isn't it?"

Anya hung her head and stood there, her back to her sister. Eilish was right. She did like Carter. Her voice was soft, almost a whisper. "So what if I do? Nothing will come of it. Even if I tried, there's no chance it would ever work. But I'm tired of only going out with people from our coven, people who've known us our whole lives. Even if I was interested in someone from our coven, it's always the same. I don't regret this life, Eilish. I just wish I didn't feel so alone sometimes. Let's face it, if I'm honest, if I'm being myself..." She shrugged, "Guys don't seem to be attracted to me. It's just who I am." She turned to face her sister, "I'm sorry. I wasn't thinking. I know that put us in a bad position."

Eilish immediately regretted using a sharp tone with her sister and went to her, embracing her in a hug. "No, I'm sorry. I didn't mean to snap at you. I just got scared. Ian had tried to hold my hand, and you used your magic in public. I panicked because I felt like a thousand eyes were on us. It's not your fault." She let go of her sister and locked eyes with her. "But we've got a real problem here, sis. I don't know what I'm going to do about Ian, and now you're attracted to a human. We could get them both killed. Ian at least has a fighting chance, but Carter? That would be like throwing raw meat to the wolves."

Anya shook her head, "Don't worry; he probably won't even speak to me after today. But I think you have a real chance with Ian, the way he looks at you, he's more than interested, if you ask me. There's a connection between you. I feel it. But that makes it more dangerous because if I can feel it, so can any other witch around you." She smiled to ease the tension and worry on her sister's face. "Besides, I don't think Carter would fancy going out with me if he knew he was risking his life!" She laughed, hoping it would lighten the mood. "But it was sweet of him to ask us out for pizza. I wish we could say yes."

Eilish shook her head. "You know we can't be seen in public with humans. Encounters with humans have to be transactional, such as store clerks, or waiters. Even then, we have to be careful not to be too friendly. And it doesn't matter how I feel about Ian. It doesn't change things."

Eilish walked behind the counter and sat on the stool. She placed her elbows on the counter and covered her face with her hands. "I don't know what to do. No... that's not true. I *do* know what to do. I need to tell him to leave me alone, but my heart is torn. I need to send him on his way, make it clear there's nothing here for him, but the truth is, I really like him. There's no path for us that doesn't spell disaster. And no path for you and Carter either. The witches would be threatened by Ian, and Carter would just be seen as so beneath you. They would begrudgingly accept Carter into the coven if you hand-fasted with him, but they'd never accept Ian. Even Rhiannon's Circle couldn't change that. It wouldn't matter how much power I had. No coven is going to follow a witch bound to a vampire."

Anya cocked her head to the side. "Rhiannon's Circle, if you have the book, you have the power. Henwen said you have more power than Fina. I know you don't want to be the Priestess but think about all the things we could have. No one would come against you with that kind of power; look at Fina now. They fear her or what she could do because we are the Bohannon's. Don't look at it as a curse, but maybe a way around all this."

Eilish looked up at her sister. "There's just one problem. We have no idea where that book is, and I'm pretty sure Fina didn't just tuck it next to the cookbooks in the kitchen."

Anya grabbed her hands and shook them. "Then we need to find it! We can do it. You know we can! Of course, she hid it, but let's face it, we could find it together. We have to do it discreetly. I'm game if you are!"

Eilish pulled her hands away. "Anya! This is no game! I couldn't predict her response if Fina discovered what we were doing. Or Warrick's. Cripes, even Zavian would run and tattle. I could understand why Fina didn't tell us things as children, but to keep it hidden now means she never meant for us to discover it. Fina loves being High Priestess. And Warrick loves his power even more. Neither of them is going to roll over on this. If we go after that book, we must be prepared to either be destroyed by Fina or lose her. It's not out of the realm of possibility, you know. Bronwyn told me once years ago that Fina killed the High Priestess of the Adelgrief coven in Beaufort. When I asked her why, she just shook her head, said never mind, she shouldn't have mentioned it. I've tried to get her to talk about it, but she says nothing. She told me to forget I ever heard it. How come no one talks about that? Are you ready for whatever horrors Fina could rain down on us?"

Anya realized very quickly that Eilish might never consider finding the book. "Here's what I know, sister; I've got nothing to lose. I'm 27 years old, and you aren't far behind me. So all I have to look forward to is being a crone living in the swamp with Cyrus as my chauffeur." She looked her sister straight in the eyes. "Are you willing to fight for Ian, live the life you want, or be forced to live with Zavian forever? Think hard about that." As she turned to go back into the stock room, she yelled over her shoulder. "And you need to start thinking like Fina. She hides the jalopy keys in the flour canister."

Eilish followed her sister into the stock room. "Are you serious? Anya, look at me. Do you understand what you're saying? If we do this, and I do mean *we*, because there's no way I'm tackling this alone, we could permanently divide our family. There's no coming back from this. If we go after that book, there's no guarantee we can even find it, but if we do, Fina will not shrug it off and let things return to normal. It's the end of us...the three of us. And as much as Fina can be a pain in the ass, she's still my sister, and I love her."

Anya stood her ground. She didn't want Eilish to give this up. "I love her too, but if she hid this book all these years just to stay in power, I'm not sure that love is reciprocated quite the same. And if you think for one minute I'm going to miss this adventure, think again. It's time we got on with our lives, sister. I want something different in my life, something beyond this shop and living under Fina and Warrick's shadow. I'd like to make my own decisions, and I know you feel the same. We're not betraying her. She's the one who betrayed us our entire lives if what Henwen says is true." She hugged her sister as she heard the bell jingle over the door. "And another day in the life of the Bohannon sisters begins. Is this what you want 20 years from now?" She walked out of the stock room to help the day's first customers and hoped that Eilish would find the courage to become the witch she was destined to be.

BOHANNON

As the workday came to a close, the girls had been busy all day with a steady stream of customers. There hadn't been a chance to have any further conversation, but Eilish was thinking hard about what Anya had said. It wasn't easy to accept that Fina had betrayed them. She felt there had to be a sound reason for Fina's action, even if Eilish disagreed with it. Maybe she just needed to be clear and let Fina know how she felt about Zavian. As the girls locked up the shop and headed home, Eilish addressed her sister. "I've been thinking about what you said this morning. I don't think Fina's decisions were designed to hold us back intentionally. I think she's doing what she thinks is best, even if she's wrong. I just need to speak out. I've let her run things...we both have...and she's gotten used to everything going her way. If I explain how I feel about Zavian, I mean, a real heart-to-heart talk with her, that could change things. Don't you think?"

Anya stopped in her tracks. "You are actually going to confront her and disobey her persistent orders of hooking up with Zavian. Well, good for you!" Anya couldn't help but be proud of Eilish. It was a step in the right direction and one that was long overdue. "I believe she needs to understand we're no longer teenagers, and we have minds of our own. It won't solve all your problems, but it's a start.

Maybe we both need to cut the proverbial apron strings. We've both allowed her to make decisions on our behalf. It was fine when we were young, but she got used to it; hell, we all got used to it. I'm behind you, whatever you decide. Do you want me to join you or disappear for the evening?"

"I don't think you should be in the same room. Fina feels like we're ganging up on her when we do that. But I would appreciate it if you could stick around. I may need moral support. Telling Fina no isn't easy."

Anya agreed. "That sounds like a plan. I can hang out on the front veranda or at the top of the stairs. I can be there in a flash if you need me. But stick to your guns. She isn't going to take this lying down, and neither will Warrick." As they approached the house, they entered from the front door. Anya whispered, "Good luck, you can do it."

Eilish stood dumbfounded. She'd thought she could ease into this. She could hear Fina in the kitchen. She laid her handbag on the bottom step and headed into the kitchen. "So, you didn't come to the shop today. Anya and I thought you were coming in. It was hectic. We've sold through some inventory. You're going to need to place some orders."

"Where's your sister? Dinner is ready. I spent the day with Warrick, if you must know. Coven affairs, nothing you need to concern yourself with. I'll look into the inventory tomorrow. I'm glad to see business is picking up more." She stepped outside into the hallway and yelled for Anya to come to eat. As they began their meal together, Fina noticed the two girls seemed quieter than usual, but she paid no mind. The shop kept them busy and out of her hair.

Anya finished eating quickly, then begged off and went to her room. Seraphina turned to Eilish. "Help me with the cleanup. It won't take long with the two of us."

"Sure. Thanks for cooking. You're a good cook, Fina." Eilish scraped the plates and handed them to Fina to rinse. "Um, could we talk about something? I mean, can you listen to me for a while and just hear me out? Don't comment until I say what I need to say?"

Immediately Fina had her suspicions about this conversation. "What's this about? Of course, I'll listen." Fina continued to rinse and noticed that Eilish's hands were shaking. This couldn't be good.

Eilish wasn't sure where to begin. "Okay, well, it's about Zavian. I really need you to hear me, Fina. I care about Zavian like he's my brother. He's been nothing but kind to me, but I'm just not attracted to him. I've gone along with this charade just to keep the peace because I know you and Warrick both expect a hand-fasting. Even Zavian expects it. But I can't. I can't imagine my whole life tied to Zavian. I really need you to accept this. I don't know who I'll bond with, but you need to let go and let me find my own way. There's someone out there for me. You just need to let me find them on my own."

Fina stopped what she was doing, setting the dish aside. "Are you finished? Because I have a few things to say. How *dare* you even consider saying such a thing? Warrick and I have done nothing but consider your future and personal circumstances to make you the best possible match." Fina grabbed the plate from Eilish's hands and shook the plate in her face. "Let go? I'll never let go of you, little sister, your place in this coven is vital, and your bonding is for the benefit of this coven *and* the Bohannon family."

Fina's voice rose in pitch, and her eyes were slits in her face. "Playing a charade, Eilish?" She threw the plate across the room as it shattered into pieces. She heard Anya's footsteps bounding down the stairs as she flew into the room. Seraphina turned on Anya. "You have nothing to do with this, Anya. Get out now!" She pointed to the entrance of the kitchen. "Move!" Anya stepped back into the doorway but didn't leave.

Seraphina spun around and got an inch from Eilish's face. "So, what's his name? Tell me! I demand you tell me what you've been up to. I bet you two never went to Edisto Beach; you were out meeting someone else! Don't think you can outsmart me, little sister; my wrath will drive you to the ground!"

Eilish was caught off-guard by Fina's anger. She'd seen her fly off the handle with others, but she'd never been the focus of her sister's anger before. "What? We didn't meet anyone at the beach. We never meet anyone, anywhere! That's the whole point, Fina! You've controlled our whole lives, and we've let you, but we're not kids anymore. But you better hear this; if you hear nothing else, I won't be bonded to Zavian. I don't know who's in my future, but I *do* know who isn't, and there's nothing you, or Warrick, can do to change that!"

Seraphina's face was red with anger. "You *will not* dictate to me. I'm Priestess of this coven, and you *will* follow my lead. I don't understand you, Eilish. After everything that I've done for you, raising you on my own, shaping your future and that of our coven. Do you think this was easy, a walk in the park? Yes, you are both well past the age of bonding, but I have protected you, taught you, and guided you for a higher purpose. And what do I get for giving up my own life for you? A slap in the face."

She walked around the room in a stride only a queen could pull off. "You'll never find another like Zavian. You can lead him on a leash. He'll bend to your every will. You'll be powerful and stand beside me. He adores you, and you decide this isn't good enough? You'll regret this for the rest of your days, Eilish. Warrick will hear about this, and believe me, if you think either of us will take this lying down, you can think again. You *will* bond with Zavian. Enough of this chatter, you need a tincture and some sleep, and this will all be forgiven in the morning."

Eilish was livid and screamed at her sister. "Forgiven! *I'll* be forgiven? For what? Having an independent thought? For thinking I had some say over my own life?" The dishes in the cabinet started to rattle, and the teapot on the stove began to whistle as the water came to a boil. Luna exited the room like her tail was on fire, and even Anya stood in the doorway with her mouth open. She knew her sister needed to rein in her anger before she brought the whole house down on their heads. The pans on the stove flew across the room at warp speed, leaving large dents in the walls, yet Eilish seemed oblivious to the chaos she was unwittingly creating. Anya spoke softly, not wishing to draw that negative energy in her direction. "Eilish. Stop. That's enough, now."

Fina was stunned at her power, realizing how little energy it was taking for Eilish to create this chaos. Eilish took a deep breath while closing her eyes and trying to calm down. The teapot whistle dwindled slowly, and Eilish opened her eyes. "This isn't over, Fina. Don't think I'm changing my mind." She turned on her heels and walked out of the kitchen with Anya right behind her.

Fina was stunned by her sister's display of power and realized just how much greater it was than her own. Eilish was beginning to come into her own, and steps would need to be taken. Fina needed to see Warrick, and Zavian would have to push harder and be more present in her life. Warrick would have to convince Zavian to move faster. He needed to stop being so low-key with Eilish and step up his pursuit. Eilish was right; this was far from over, and it would take Fina and Warrick together to get this nonsense of not bonding with Zavian out of her head.

BOHANNON

Eilish ran to her room, grabbed her handbag from the bottom step on the way up, and then slammed the door behind her. Emric was stunned to see her so angry. He'd felt the tremors of her anger all the way upstairs. He quickly left her room and headed for Anya's space. Eilish collapsed on her bed in tears. How could Fina even think she could dictate who she'd be bonded to? With time and her unwillingness to commit, she'd thought the subject would blow over, or Zavian would get tired of chasing after her and find someone else. Anya tapped on her door as she opened it. "You want to talk?" Eilish sat up on the bed and turned on the lamp on the nightstand, shaking her head no. "Not right now. I just need some space."

Anya paused as she saw how broken Eilish looked. "Okay then, but you know where you can find me." Eilish nodded as Anya quietly closed the door. She wiped at her tears as she dug in her handbag and pulled out her phone, scrolling through the contacts. Except for some service repair companies they routinely used, all her contacts were other witches and warlocks from the coven...except one. It only drove home the point of how isolated her world was. She stared at Ian's name on her phone. She'd been attracted to him since the first time she'd seen him, and she knew the feeling was mutual. It was more than physical; there was a connection whenever they locked eyes, which drew her to him. She thought she could love him if given a chance, but was she willing to destroy everything to find out? Before she could talk herself out of it, she hit dial and waited to see if he would answer.

Ian's day had been long, hard, and hot. Carter falling and the quick retreat of the two sisters had left him feeling more confused as each hour passed. He knew this relationship with Eilish would never be easy, but there were more issues than he'd ever imagined. When Eilish pulled her hand away, it was a stab in his heart to realize that they couldn't show the slightest affection for each other in public. As he kept running the day's events over in his mind, his hope of ever being with her dwindled. He'd told her it was her decision to make, and her actions towards him that morning could mean she was bowing out. He got up from the couch, paced the room, and ended up on the front porch. The night air was slightly cooler but not by much when his cell phone rang. He looked at the number and didn't recognize it. He contemplated a few seconds if he should let it go to voice mail but decided to answer. "Hello."

"Hey, you got a minute?"

Ian heard her voice, and his emotions were mixed; there was hope and also dread. "Sure, my evening is free."

"I need to talk...face to face. Could you meet me? Like, now?"

Ian's only thought was to move slowly and carefully. He could tell from her voice that something was wrong. Was she in danger, trouble? "Yes, I'll meet you wherever you feel safe."

"Thank you. Meet me in St. Michael's graveyard, the big church on the corner of Meeting and Broad. It will be quiet there, and it's late; we shouldn't run into anyone. Just give me about 15 minutes to get there. Okay?"

Ian nodded. "I know where it is. I'll be there." He hung up and took a deep breath. It was time for him to find out if he would be given a chance to be with her or if he'd have to let this go. He locked the door and used his skill to teleport inside the graveyard, scoping out anything on his way. Teleporting was a means for him to travel faster than the human eye could see and would give him time to surveil the graveyard before she arrived. The place was deserted, just as he'd hoped. He stayed shadowed inside the entrance, remaining invisible to both mortals and witches until she arrived.

Eilish tossed her bag over her shoulder and tip-toed down the stairs, stepping around the creaky steps. It was a skill she and Anya had practiced when they were teenagers and wanted to sneak out. She could hear Fina was still in the kitchen as she slipped into the foyer and slowly opened the door onto the front porch, stepping outside. She hurried down the front porch steps and onto East Bay, making her way to St. Michael's church. As she approached the graveyard, she glanced around before opening the elaborate wrought iron gate and stepping inside the old cemetery. Ian was waiting for her, leaning against an old tree. Eilish looked over her shoulder to ensure she hadn't been followed and reached out her hand to him. "Let's move towards the back, where we won't be seen."

Taking her hand, he began walking among the long dead who were buried here and the crumbling tombstones, leading her to the far back of the graveyard. No one could see them in the rear. It was surrounded by an old wrought iron fence and tall trees that were hundreds of years old. "No one's inside the graveyard. I checked it out before you got here."

Eilish sat down on the grass under the tree and laid her handbag to the side, and Ian joined her, sitting close but not crowding her. She appreciated that he was letting her lead. There were already enough people in her life trying to dictate her next move. "Thank you for coming. It's been a rough day, but Ian, we really need to talk."

Ian looked at her as he sat beside her, and she let go of his hand. "I'm here. Talk to me. I'm happy you asked to see me, good or bad. I appreciate it. I know that we need to talk, Eilish. So just say what you want to say. I'll listen and try to answer anything you have to ask. Like I said, I'll respect your wishes."

Eilish leaned back against the tree, closing her eyes and gathering her thoughts. Now that she was here, she wasn't sure where to begin. "Well, let's just start with the obvious. I'm attracted to you, but you know that, and I can feel your attraction to me. My heart tells me this could go somewhere, but my brain tells me this has disaster written all over it. Before I destroy other relationships in my life, I need to know what this is. You've got an eternity. Whatever happens between us, you can move on as if nothing happened. But the stakes are much higher for me. This can't be a game, Ian. If you want a fling, then say so. I need to know if this is just curiosity over what you think it might be like to make it with a witch or a passing attraction you'll move on from. I can handle that if that's all it is. You're not the first...well, you're the first vampire, but you're not the first fling. Just tell me, where do you see this going, and please, don't string me along."

Ian sat watching her as she spoke. He didn't look at her with a yearning but with caring and understanding. He could tell decisions had to be made, and he'd be truthful with her, whatever they were. "I feel more than an attraction to you, and my heart tells me the same. My brain is trying to be cautious and knows this is life-threatening for us both. My heart tells me it can be done if we both want it." Ian pulled up his knees and rested his elbows on them. "I can live an eternity, but I can also be killed. And, if we were to decide to be together, I'd take that risk." He sighed heavily and looked up at the shining moon. "But Eilish, you won't live for eternity. I can turn a mortal, but I can't turn a witch. At some point, I'll lose you. I'd have to live with that knowledge our whole lives together. I can't change what I am. The stakes are very high for you; believe me, I understand that. I suspect there are many things I don't even know. I'm no expert on witches, but I know you have great power and could also harm me if you chose to. This isn't a game for me or some curiosity. I could seek that out at any time. There's something much deeper that's calling out to me." He stood and turned to look at her, then crouched in front of her, softly taking her hand in his. "Where we go from here is up to you, and I'll do everything I can to make it work if you want us together, and if not, believe me, it will be a loss I'll feel for a long time to come."

She squeezed his hands, hanging on to him like a lifeline. "That's all I needed to hear. But you do need to understand that the coven will reject you...us. They may come after us. And I think there are things you need to know before you commit to anything. Do you know who I am? I mean, not my name, but do you understand who the Bohannons are?"

Something inside him exploded like a burst of fireworks, and he couldn't control the slight smile that crept across his lips. She was going to say yes. This would be a long road; he had to go slow with her and whatever else came with managing their relationship. "I know enough to understand they'll come after us. I have skills, and I know some of them will be useless against witches. I know you're Eilish Bohannon; you have two older sisters." Shaking his head. "But I'll be honest with you. I have no idea who the Bohannons are. Tell me about these Bohannon sisters. Tell me what I'm up against."

Eilish sighed, more from relief that he hadn't run away already. "Better sit down. It's a long story." Ian settled in next to her, still holding her hand. "The Bohannons are from Ireland originally. Witches, like vampires, are born. Many humans practice our arts, follow Wiccan traditions, and some get quite good at it...drawing on the power of nature. But their access to the source of power is limited. The Bohannons go back many generations. A lot of families die off or bond with humans, so their offspring have less power, but the Bohannons stayed strong and only bonded from within their coven. They reached such a pinnacle of power in Ireland that the other covens turned against them and drove them out. My family and our coven have been here since the 1700's, and settled here in Charleston. Nothing has changed from the old ways, and our power has continued to grow. Like vampires, covens can be allies or rivals, so my sisters and I have tried to keep things quiet and not rock the boat. Just live and let live, you know? My parents were killed when I was really young over a power struggle. Anya and I were too young to remember the coven war, but Fina has made sure we understood the details. Ever since then, my sisters and I have tried just to keep the peace. Everyone knows who we are; we don't need a big display to show the other covens what we're capable of. But there's just one thing..."

Ian knew whatever was coming wouldn't be good, but he wanted to keep her talking. He wanted her to tell him everything. They both needed to go into this with open eyes and no secrets. "Your cultural structure sounds a lot like vampires, in a way." He squeezed her hand softly. "But there's always 'one thing,' so tell me, all of it. We can't have secrets from each other. It could be life-threatening for us both if we do."

Eilish nodded. "Witches aren't born with equal power. The females are always stronger than the males, and the female with the strongest power in the coven is designated as High Priestess. She commands the coven. A Bohannon has always been the High Priestess since as far back as recorded history. The male she bonds with assumes power through her and becomes the High Priest. Right now, my sister Fina is the High Priestess of our coven. She assumed that role in her twenties because my parents were killed. Anya and I were only toddlers then. But I'm the sister that was born with the most power. I'm the legitimate heir to the coven. Honestly, I don't care about it, or at least, I didn't. But now my sister is trying to force my hand, force a bonding with Zavian. Zavian is weak. Not as a person, I don't mean to speak ill of him, but his powers as a warlock are weak. My sister is bonded to Warrick, and Zavian is his nephew. They want our bonding as it will raise Zavian's status and weaken mine. Fina and Warrick think they can control us then and keep their place in the coven." She looked over at him, waiting to see his reaction. "Too much drama, I know."

He laughed. "Doesn't every family, vampire, witch, or human

have family drama?" He stood up and pulled her up with him. "Come on, let's walk; the damn ground is hard!" He held her hand as they walked. "You know, Eilish, I'm glad you told me this. It helps us both. But if you were trying to scare me off, you failed. I already don't like Zavian; it's nothing personal. But anyone with eyes can see he's not for you. I come from a culture where the males are dominant and typically rule their covens. I'm a mercenary warrior; I travel from coven to coven, helping other masters if they need more warriors for territorial wars. Not much of that is happening around the States right now, though. Fina and this Warrick sound a bit daunting. I can see why you're scared. It's a big battle to fight, but with the combination of us together, will that give us any leverage?

Eilish stopped walking and turned to him. "Maybe. You're not immune to the spells of even the weakest witch. I can protect you from many things, but I can't prevent them. But there is something...it would give us leverage."

"Well, that's something at least. Go on, tell me, I'm curious now."

"My parents died protecting a book. It contained spells long forgotten by most covens and is one of the reasons the Bohannons have remained in power for so long. Whoever has the book has the power to control their coven and all covens. It's both a blessing and a curse. Fina has it now, and it's why she remains the High Priestess, not me. By all rights, she should have handed it over when I came of age, but she's not only keeping it, she's kept it a secret. She doesn't know that Anya and I found out about it. I really didn't care about the book or being High Priestess, but getting that book is the only way to control my destiny."

Ian stopped walking and looked at her. He took her other hand and held both in his. "Are you saying you should be High Priestess, and if you find this book, you can take over the coven? Wow, Eilish, that's a pretty big thing to tackle on your own. I'm not saying you can't handle it, but taking control of your coven from your sister will be a war. I now understand why you wanted to tell me all of this. It hasn't changed my mind, but this will be daunting if you can do it. The question is....do you want me along to help you?"

She stared up at him. "I think the better question is, do *you* want to be along to help? You're right when you say this will be a war...a war between Bohannons. That's never happened before, and it will fracture the coven. Other than Anya, I don't think I'll have many allies. Witches don't turn against the High Priestess; it's too dangerous for them. This won't be quick or easy, and people could die."

Ian could feel the power of energy rising up his arms; her strength and courage made him feel as if, together, they could take on the world. He leaned down and kissed her, soft and slow, not breaking the touch of her lips against his. He placed his hand around her waist and pulled her close. Touching her made his body feel like he was on fire. He knew he had to go slow, but damn, he wanted her to see that he'd be there; no matter what, he'd fight alongside her and help. Breaking the kiss, he whispered, "I'll be there, beside you; I'll fight with you. Say yes, Eilish, say that you want me there with you."

Eilish returned his kiss and wrapped her arms around him. Vampires had an unnatural strength, and she could feel that in him. He felt solid as steel, and it was comforting. Her powers came not from the physical, but from the energy pulled from nature. Maybe together, they could change the course of things. "Yes, my answer is yes. But promise me, you'll be careful. I know you're a warrior, but this won't be like any war you've ever fought before." She looked up at the moon. "It must be close to midnight. We've been talking for a long time. I should get back. Fina probably just went to bed and isn't aware that I'm gone." She led him back to the cemetery gate.

"I'll be here for you, Eilish; I promise that." As they walked towards the gate, he passed a tombstone, old and worn, but his eyes caught the name. "Wait." He tugged at her hand and let go. He crouched down and ran his fingers over the name. Standing up, he sighed. "Good ole Charlie. Charles Rutherford, I knew him when we fought in the Revolutionary war. We both lived through it, but I didn't know he was buried here. Damn, he was a good guy."

Eilish stopped and looked at the headstone, covered in lichen and moss, the name almost worn away by time. The dates under the name were 1742 -1792. "You knew him? He was a friend?"

"Yes, a friend. I was mortal then, not a vampire. I befriended him during the war. We lost touch afterward, each going our separate ways. Now that I think about it, he did tell me he was from Charleston. He must have had family here and returned." Shaking his head, he smiled. "We kept each other going during the war. Had each other's back. This really brings back memories. I haven't thought about him in a very long time."

Eilish looked back at him. "You were mortal?"

Ian nodded. "I was wounded during the war. I was lying on the battlefield in Yorktown, bleeding out. I knew I was dying and thought at least I died fighting. This man, this vampire, just appeared out of nowhere. He bit into my neck, and I could feel my life draining away. I thought I was hallucinating. I lost consciousness, and my body was just piled in a heap with the other dead until we could all be buried. When I came to, I thought I had just survived somehow. I got up from the pile of corpses, and everyone was gone. It was the middle of the night, and I went looking for my regiment, but the battle had ended, and they had moved on. I wasn't even sure how much time had passed. It wasn't long before I discovered I needed to feed. I never returned to my family. I was counted among the dead at Yorktown, so I just left it alone. I had to figure stuff out on my own, but I found a few covens that took me in along the way. In the end, I preferred being on my own, so I never swore allegiance to any one coven."

Eilish squeezed his hand. "That sounds like a lonely life, Ian."

Ian shrugged and chuckled. "Well, it's been interesting."

Eilish held her hand out over the grave and spoke softly. "Oh, you soul of Charles Rutherford, greatly majestic, behold, I have come that

I may see you. I open the Summerland that you may now enter the land of the living."

A pale wisp of white haze appeared to rise from the grave, and gradually take the shape of a man. The man looked confused, not recognizing the young woman standing by his grave. He looked at the man, squinting his eyes as he searched his memory. "Ian?"

Ian had no idea what Eilish was doing, but he watched in amazement as she chanted and jumped back slightly when the ghost of Charlie appeared. Her power was unreal. He knew that conjuring spirits was a rare gift, and only the most powerful witches could master it. Even then, it typically called for the power of the entire coven for the witch to channel a spirit. He stood speechless for a moment, in awe of her power and trying to comprehend that his friend had just risen from his grave. "Yes, Charlie, it's Ian. Don't be afraid. This is Eilish. We don't wish you any harm. I found your grave by accident and remembered our times together in the war. You returned home then?"

Charlie smiled. "I did. I got married. We had kids. The war took its toll, though. Only lived to be 49." Charlie looked around and could see vehicles of some sort moving past the church graveyard, nothing like the horse and buggies of his time. He looked back at Ian and the girl. "A vampire. You're a vampire now. That explains a lot." He looked at Eilish. "And a witch. You conjured me up, I guess." He nodded at Ian. "Different times. Good to see ya, Ian, but be careful. The world is a more dangerous place in many ways, and you're headed down a dangerous path." He turned to Eilish and tipped his head, "No offense, ma'am."

She smiled back at him. "None taken." The apparition faded as the wisp of vapor returned to the ground.

Ian stood silent for a long time, looking at the now empty space that Charlie had once occupied. His mind was trying to wrap around the event that just took place in front of him and the oppressive warning that was given. He turned his head and looked at Eilish. "I didn't know witches could raise the dead."

Eilish shook her head. "Not raise the dead, but raise the spirit. Your friend Charlie is still dead. And very few witches have the power to draw the spirits of the dead. They're drawn to me. Does that freak you out?"

Ian laughed. "I've not lived a very conventional life myself. I've learned not to be surprised by much in the world, but you brought him here for me. Thank you. I suppose his warning is clear. But with that, so is your power and what's to come."

Eilish smiled as she took his hand. "Well, you can't say I didn't warn you, Ian Cross. There's a ghost who has taken up permanent residence in our home... Emric. He was a soldier in the war too. Anya and I have tried to help him get back to the spirit realm, but he won't go. Some unfinished business in this world, I suppose. It's not too late to change your mind."

Ian smiled, "You startled me, but it didn't change my mind. I'm in this for the long haul, right beside you, Eilish Bohannon, ghosts and all." He smiled and kissed her once again as they came to the gate.

She reluctantly let go of his hand as she stepped through the gate and back onto the sidewalk. "The secrecy doesn't change, at least not for now. I can't confront Fina until I know where the book is, and I haven't the slightest idea where she has it hidden. We have to keep the relationship under wraps until I control the book, assuming I can."

"Don't worry; my very survival has been dependent on keeping secrets. I just need to watch out for your older sister and the skinny-ass warlock who follows you around. I would ask to walk you home. I know that's not allowed, but know that I would if I could."

Eilish looked up and down the sidewalk, making sure it was clear of pedestrian traffic, then stood on her tip-toes and kissed Ian softly. She knew he felt the surge of electricity, even with the soft kiss. "I'll be safe, trust me. Don't you give up on me now."

He felt the jolt from the kiss and was beginning to get addicted to that feeling. "Never." He stood a long time after she was gone, staring after her. "Well, Ian, you just dropped yourself into one shitload of a mess, but damn if it doesn't feel fine." He shadowed himself and followed her, making sure she arrived home safely. He'd won her over and would hold to every promise he'd made to her, even if it killed him.

BOHANNON

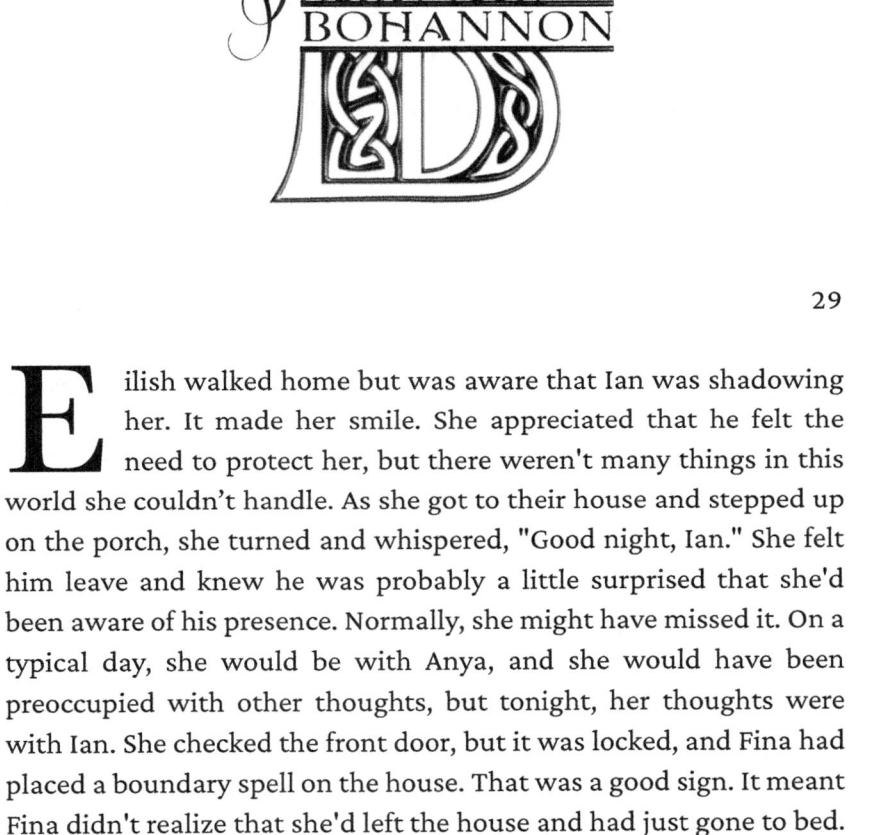

Eilish walked home but was aware that Ian was shadowing her. It made her smile. She appreciated that he felt the need to protect her, but there weren't many things in this world she couldn't handle. As she got to their house and stepped up on the porch, she turned and whispered, "Good night, Ian." She felt him leave and knew he was probably a little surprised that she'd been aware of his presence. Normally, she might have missed it. On a typical day, she would be with Anya, and she would have been preoccupied with other thoughts, but tonight, her thoughts were with Ian. She checked the front door, but it was locked, and Fina had placed a boundary spell on the house. That was a good sign. It meant Fina didn't realize that she'd left the house and had just gone to bed. She dug in her handbag for the house keys and removed the spell with a few words and a flick of her hand. She quietly slipped inside, closing and locking the door and replacing the spell. Luna greeted her with a meow and a loud purr. Eilish scooped her up in her arms and carried her upstairs, setting her gently on her bed. She turned on the lamp by her bed and started to get undressed, pulling a nightgown over her head. As she climbed into bed, Anya stuck her head in the door.

"Hey sis, where have you been? Are you all right?" She stepped inside the door and closed it softly behind her. "Fina just went to bed. She never noticed you were gone. Where did you go?"

Eilish patted the bed, indicating her sister should join her. There had been so many nights when they were young when they'd snuck into each other's rooms to share a bed at night. "She put a boundary spell on the house, so I figured she didn't know I was out. I'm glad you're still awake. I'm sure you heard the whole fight with Fina. She's not giving an inch, so I went to see Ian. He met me in the graveyard at St. Michael's."

Anya's eyes grew wide. "Did I hear you right? My baby sister sneaks out and meets a vamp in the graveyard?" Anya shook her head, "Wow, you're really taking some chances. So, you're serious, then? I knew you were upset with Fina. I don't blame you. I think it's time she understands that Zavian is not your chosen path. So, what happened?"

Eilish sighed. "I told him everything about us and about the book. I figured if we were going to pursue this, he had to know what he was getting himself into. He'll be at risk, and he needs to know that. I'm going to see him. We haven't worked out the details yet, of how and where. Just once, I'm going to do something for myself and not for Fina or the coven."

Anya grabbed her and hugged her tight. "Eilish, I'm so happy for you, even though it's dangerous. But you do know I'm with you, no matter what happens." She pulled away and looked down. "Ian seems like a nice guy. So, did he kiss you?"

Eilish smiled. "He's a good kisser. I'm pretty sure he's had lots of practice." She tugged at her sister's sleeve. "So, what about Carter? You can't hide that you like him. I think if we haven't scared him away, then you should see him."

"Oh, I wish I could, but who knows after the fall. He may think we're both crazy. I do like him. He's hotter than a tin roof on a Charleston summer day!" They both laughed. "Well, it's really late; get some sleep. Maybe we'll see them on our way to work in the morning."

"Good night, sis." Eilish slipped beneath the covers as Anya tiptoed out of her room. Luna curled up on the foot of her bed, purring in contentment. As Eilish reached to turn off the lamp, she saw Emric standing in the corner. "Good night, Emric." He nodded as he stared out the window. "Good night, Miss Eilish. I'll stand guard. I got guard duty." Eilish looked at him for a few minutes. "You know you can pass over any time you want. I can help you." He violently shook his head. "No, ma'am! I got guard duty!" She gave him a sad smile. "Okay then. I'll rest better knowing you have everything under control. See you in the morning." He nodded calmly as she turned off the light. "Yes, ma'am. I never leave my watch."

BOHANNON

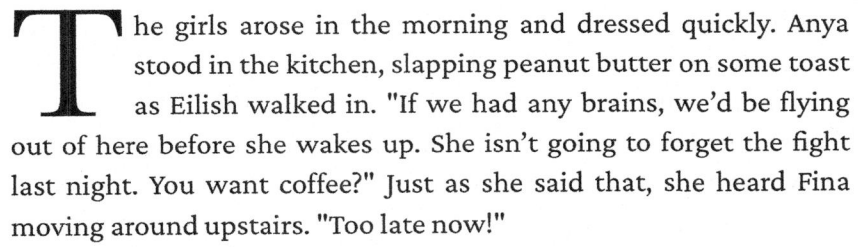

The girls arose in the morning and dressed quickly. Anya stood in the kitchen, slapping peanut butter on some toast as Eilish walked in. "If we had any brains, we'd be flying out of here before she wakes up. She isn't going to forget the fight last night. You want coffee?" Just as she said that, she heard Fina moving around upstairs. "Too late now!"

Eilish had to giggle at her sister's breakfast choice. She'd been eating peanut butter on toast since she was about five. She poured herself a mug of hot coffee as Fina entered, still in her robe. "Pour me a cup while you're at it." Eilish poured the second mug full and added milk and sugar before handing the mug to Fina. She was glad her sister was calm and acted as if last night's fight had never happened. Eilish slipped a pear into her handbag to eat later and sipped at her coffee. "Are you coming in today, Fina?"

"Yes, I'll be in as soon as I eat a decent breakfast." She gave a side glance at Anya. "I want a list of what inventory we need to order. That will be the first priority when I get in, and things will only get busier with the summer months."

Anya decided to keep her smug comments to herself and oblige Fina. "Consider it done. You ready to go, Eilish?"

Eilish emptied the mug with a few big swallows of the coffee, nodding her head as she placed the empty mug in the sink. "Ready." She grabbed her handbag, tossed it over her shoulder, and followed Anya out of the kitchen. The two girls stepped out on the front porch and were hit with the wave of oppressive heat. "It's not even ten yet, and it's already unbearable." They walked side by side up the sidewalk toward their shop. Eilish kept looking at her sister, who had her eyes glued on the house under renovation. "Looking for someone?"

Anya never took her eyes off the house. "To be honest, I'm a bit nervous. I mean, what if he completely ignores me now? That would be my luck. Who can predict humans?" As they came closer, Anya slowed her pace and could see Carter on the roof. Ian was picking up scraps in the yard and throwing them in a huge dumpster. "Well, someone is definitely waiting for you."

Ian stopped what he was doing and turned to watch her approach. He'd already abandoned his t-shirt, and was wearing a pair of old jeans that sat low on his hips, pulled even lower by the hammer he had slung through a belt loop. He was tanned a golden brown, and his skin glistened with sweat. Eilish had never had a tan in her life. She burned in the sun. When she was little, the coven referred to her as their moon child because she was so pale. Her complexion, paired with her white hair and gray eyes, made her striking to look at. She raised her hand and waved at him. He shifted his weight to one hip and placed his hands on his hips, waiting for her to reach the house. Eilish recognized the alpha pose and his ease of movement. She caught some movement in her peripheral vision and noted Carter was coming down the ladder. Eilish nudged her sister. "There you go, sis. Signed, sealed, and delivered."

"Well, at least he's using a ladder this time and not coming down like Batman." Anya smiled as Carter hit the ground and walked toward her with a smile on his face. Maybe this was a good sign.

Ian grinned. "Good morning, Bohannon sisters." He walked toward the two sisters. Carter followed behind him, with his hair in a messy bun and his body rock solid. Anya liked the dirty blonde look of his hair and the sweat glistening off his skin. She could smell his musky male scent as he approached her.

"Hey, Anya. Come over to the truck. I need some water." As he walked to his truck, Anya glanced at her sister and followed him while looking up and down the street to make sure no one was looking. She watched as Carter reached inside the truck and pulled out a water bottle filled with daisies. "These are for you. Thank you for yesterday."

Anya's face lit up, and she almost giggled because the flowers were in a water bottle. She found it endearing. "That wasn't necessary, Carter, but thank you, very sweet."

Carter smiled at her as he kept shifting from one foot to another. "I'd really like to get to know you better. Would you like to get some pizza?"

Anya truly wanted to say yes. "Well, I can't be seen in public with you, Carter. It's dangerous." Eilish and Ian walked up just as she was answering.

Carter could see the disappointment on her face. He glanced at Eilish and Ian. "Well, we can always order in if you want to come over to my place." Anya looked down at the ground and then up and down the street again. She wanted to say yes, but the panic Eilish displayed yesterday when she'd stopped Carter's fall was ringing loudly in her head. Carter decided to throw in something that might help her say yes. "Ian and your sister can come over as well. We can all come to my place and order pizza." Anya looked at Eilish with a pleading look. "Looks like we have a dinner invite. What do you think, sis?"

Eilish glanced at Ian. "I'm game if you are. Are you sure you can wait that late to eat? We'll have to come after dark. Less chance of being seen. No offense, but the coven doesn't respond well to fraternization with humans."

Ian nodded. "I'll be there." He wanted to slip his hand around her waist and pull her close but knew that was off-limits in public.

Anya smiled. "Sounds like pizza night to me." Carter nodded his head while grinning. "How about 9:30. I live over on Legare. I rent out a little apartment in the house. I'll be on the porch waiting for you." Anya smiled as she sniffed the flowers in the water bottle. "See you then. Thanks for the flowers. Eilish, we need to open the shop; Fina will be coming soon."

Eilish smiled at Ian. "See you tonight then." He winked at her, and she felt herself blush. She felt Anya take her hand and tug as they needed to get to the shop before 10. The two girls hurried off, and Eilish looked over her shoulder as both men stood watching them walk away. "I can't believe we just did that!"

Anya giggled. "Me either; this is going to be one for the record books. He gave me flowers in a water bottle. What will I do with them? Fina will question everything."

Watching the girls walk away, Ian looked at Carter. "Flowers in a water bottle. Dude, what in hell were you thinking?"

Carter slapped him on the back. "Hey, got her to say yes, didn't it? And you get bonus time with Eilish, so don't knock it." Ian shook his head. "I hope you know what you're doing, 'cause these are no ordinary women." As Ian went back to work, Carter took to the ladder. "Just how I like 'em, bro."

BOHANNON

Carter took one last look around his sparsely decorated apartment. It was a place to sleep and eat at its best. He'd been cleaning and trying to make it look presentable when Ian and the sisters arrived. Just as he finished, he heard the banging on the door and answered to find Ian standing there with a bottle of wine. "Hey, come on in. You didn't need to bring anything. I got plenty of beer."

Ian shrugged. "Not much for beer. I just brought my own." Carter reached for the bottle, saying, "You want me to put it in the fridge?" Ian pulled away, setting the bottle on the coffee table. "Nah. You don't need to refrigerate it. We, uh, I drink it room temperature."

Carter eyed the bottle that was labeled Midnight, and the wine seemed a much deeper red with less transparency than wines he'd seen, but what did he know? He never cared much for wine. "Yeah, sure. Let's go outside and wait for the girls. They should be arriving any time. It will be easier for them to find us if we're visible."

The sisters walked together through the early dusk of another hot Charleston night. Eilish gave her sister a sideways glance. "Cute dress." Anya fired back, "Don't start!" Eilish laughed, "No, I mean it. It looks nice. I didn't know you had a dress!" Anya ran her hand over the skirt. "I keep it for emergencies, like a funeral or something."

Eilish threw back her head and laughed. "Well, I hope this date is more fun than a funeral." Anya shook her head. "You never know." Eilish reached out and grabbed her hand. "Come on, sis. The guys are waiting." They turned the corner and could see both men sitting on the front porch, deep in conversation. Ian looked up, and Eilish waved. Carter stood up from his chair as the two sisters started up the sidewalk to the house. "Hey. Hope we're not late."

Ian grinned. "Just in time." He walked up to Eilish and led her to the porch. "Any problems with your older sister?"

Eilish shook her head. "No, we just said we were going out for pizza and not to wait up. Technically, that wasn't a lie. Besides, she had plans with Warrick tonight."

Anya stood staring at Carter, who seemed distracted by her dress. She felt nervous and wondered if the dress was too much. "So, are you inviting us in, or are you just going to stare?" Her smile disguised her insecurity.

Carter was caught off guard by her appearance. He'd only seen her in cut-off dungarees and Doc Martens. She'd never made an effort to look remotely feminine, and the cotton sundress she wore showed off her slender figure. "No! Come in! We've been waiting for you." As Anya stepped onto the porch, she placed her hand under his chin, closing his mouth. "Careful, you'll catch flies."

He chuckled at her. "I never saw you in a dress before." Without asking, she opened the screen door and entered his house. "Don't get used to it. Do you have anything to drink?"

Ian chuckled as he led Eilish to the door. "Looks like we're all going inside." He tapped Carter on the shoulder as he went indoors with Eilish. "Come on, bartender. Don't leave them waiting. Bad form." Carter nodded and followed them into the house. "I've got a fridge full of cold beer, some bottled water, maybe some sodas, and Ian brought some wine."

As Anya walked inside, she looked around the meagerly appointed room. His furniture looked like it may have been salvaged from assorted yard sales. She turned to Carter. "I'll have a beer." Eilish piped up, "I'll have bottled water." Both sisters noted the bottle of Midnight on the coffee table and knew it was for Ian alone. Ian said, "Just grab me a glass and a corkscrew."

Anya followed Carter into his tiny kitchen. "I'll help. Just show me where the glasses are." Carter grabbed two beers and a bottle of water. "Right in the cabinet above your head." He watched as Anya pulled out three glasses. "Do you have a corkscrew for the wine?" Carter frowned, trying to remember where he'd last seen it. "I think it's in that drawer next to the sink. I have no idea why I have it, but I remember buying one some time ago." Anya yanked the drawer open and rummaged until she found it. "Ah-ha, found it." They headed back into the living room to see Ian and Eilish sitting side by side on the couch.

Anya handed her sister the bottled water and gave Ian the corkscrew. She plopped into an oversized armchair and reached out for the beer. Carter handed her the glass and sat on the arm of the chair. One sofa and one chair were all he had, and he rarely entertained, so seating had never been a problem. "Normally, I just drink beer from the can, but I'll step up for the occasion. Besides, no dishes to wash." He watched as Ian opened the bottle of wine and poured the liquid into the glass. It looked dark and thick. He spoke up. "Should we order pizza now or wait? Who's hungry?"

Anya didn't hesitate. "Let's order; then we can talk while we wait for the delivery. What's everyone's preference?" Ian shrugged, "No preference, get whatever you like; I fed before I came." Carter laughed. "You fed? Like at the trough? That sounds civilized." Ian rephrased his words. "I mean chowed down when I got off work. I didn't pack much for lunch and couldn't wait." Anya piped in, "Men, always hungry!" She laughed. "I'm a throw everything and anything you have on it."

Eilish piped up, "Except anchovies. No anchovies...or pineapple.

Other than that, you can order anything." Carter nodded, pulling out his cell phone to place the order and looking at Ian. "Really, dude, you don't want pizza? I want to make sure I order enough. You might get hungry later."

Ian grinned. "I might grab a piece later, go ahead and order. You know you want to have plenty of leftovers." Ian took Eilish's hand and kissed her palm, then continued to hold it. "I'm happy you're here; thank you for taking the risk; I know this is dangerous for you both."

Eilish felt his lips against her palm, and a chill ran through her. "Dangerous for you, too. Maybe even more." She realized she'd maybe said too much and looked down at her hand in his, wishing things could be simple.

Carter watched the interaction but finished placing the pizza order on his phone. "Okay, done. Should be here in thirty minutes." He took a drink from his glass, then asked, "So what do you mean by dangerous? Because you're witches? You've been here forever. Everyone in Charleston knows about the Bohannons. What's the big deal?"

Anya looked at Eilish and knew the time would come when he'd start asking questions. "Because witches don't normally hang with humans. It's dangerous because Eilish is sort of promised to another warlock, our friend Zavian. She's well, she's supposed...." Anya left the sentence hanging and looked at Eilish. "I think maybe you should tell Carter. I don't know how much you want to reveal, sis."

Carter looked confused, shifting his gaze from one sister to another. He noticed Ian wasn't fazed and continued to sip slowly from the wine. Eilish answered. "Like Anya said, we live among humans, interact with them, but don't bond. Or mate...uh, date, or marry. We stay within our coven to keep the bloodlines pure. Social interaction is discouraged to avoid developing any emotional attachments. We're aware that rumors circulate when we stay in a community for a long time, and the humans will speculate. A lot of them, like you, think it's just rumors and superstition. We try hard not to display our powers in public like Anya did when she broke your fall. Speculation is one thing, but humans get nervous when they realize we have real power."

Carter drained the contents of his glass. "So, what kind of powers are we talking about here?" Eilish thought before she spoke. Carter had already seen a display of Anya's power, but she had no idea where this relationship between the two of them would go. Best to keep the information to herself. "You know, the usual. We can cast spells on people or even on places."

Carter could sense she wouldn't reveal much more as he stood up, heading for the kitchen. "I'm going to grab another beer." He looked at Anya. "You ready?" She shook her head. "I'm good. I'll get another one when the pizza comes." As he left the room, the two sisters made eye contact. Eilish issued her a warning. "Be careful, sis. The coven won't be kind to him."

Ian sensed the sisters' unease to reveal too much. As Carter returned to the room and got comfortable again, he looked at him. "Carter, listen to me. You need to know a few things. Covens are a strong influence in their society. If they know you're hanging around Anya, the coven will come together, protect her, and try to eliminate you. This is dangerous for them; what Anya did for you was extraordinary, but you need to understand you can't go strolling around Charleston with Anya on your arm. You'll have to meet away from all prying eyes. I only say this because you need to know before you get too serious with her. You put us all at risk, so you must know and follow the rules." He looked at Anya and then Eilish and squeezed her hand tight.

Carter took a drink from his beer. "Yeah, okay. I get it. But what makes you an expert?" Ian stared back at him, wondering how he'd respond to the truth. He slid his glass of Midnight across the coffee table in Carter's direction. "Drink." Carter looked confused. "Nah, man, I told you, I wasn't into wine." Ian responded, "Drink anyway." Carter looked annoyed but picked up the glass and took a sip before quickly spitting it out. "What the hell, dude!" He wiped his hand across his mouth. "That's not wine. Too thick." He searched his memory, recognizing something familiar in the taste. "Gross, it tastes like blood or some shit."

Anya bit her lip and knew Ian was laying the cards on the table. This was going to be an all-reveal shit show. She would either leave here and never see Carter again, or she'd have someone of her own. She laid her hand on his thigh and looked to Eilish, who nodded in agreement that Ian needed to let the proverbial cat out of the bag.

Ian knew the wine tasting would make Carter roll with them or freak his ass out, but they had no time to play games. Ian took a large gulp of the Midnight from his glass, then swirled it in front of him as the thick liquid clung to the sides of the glass. "This is called Midnight, a special blend of two ingredients. It is made by a vampire named Medici." Ian looked at Carter and held him with his eyes. "You heard the rumors about the witches, and you've accepted that they're real. I hope that you also respond to the fact that vampires are real. The wine combines blood and alcohol, specifically made for vampires to ease the hunger until they can feed." Ian released the hold on Carter and waited quietly with the sisters for whatever was going to happen next.

Carter looked from person to person and noted that the sisters hadn't reacted to the news. He looked at Anya. "You knew about this?"

She nodded. "We can recognize witches and vampires on sight. To you, we just look like another human." Carter looked at Eilish. "And you're okay with this?" Eilish gave him a soft smile. "Well, *I'm* okay with it; the coven won't be any more than they'll be okay with you. Ian is no threat to you, Carter. Well, don't piss him off. I'd stay on his good side."

Carter shook his head, trying to absorb this new reality. He stood and paced the floor. He looked at Ian as he sat quietly next to Eilish as if all of this was normal. "Dude, you drink blood? From people?"

"Relax, Carter. I know this is a shock to you, but yes, I feed from humans. I seduce a woman I'm attracted to, make sure I get them someplace unseen. I don't drain them; I don't kill them. I get what I need from them, erase their memory and send them on their way. I don't turn them into vampires. I was once mortal like you, but I was turned. Most vampires are born, but a few of us are turned. We have covens as well."

Carter looked at him with confusion. "Dude, you've worked with me every day for months. What about all that stuff about vampires not being able to be in the sun."

Ian shrugged. "Every vampire is born with a gift. I'm a daywalker, probably because I was mortal. But it gives me the freedom to move about day or night."

Carter emptied his glass and was slightly calmed by the sisters' seemingly unconcerned attitude with this news. "But you said born, most vampires are born... like babies?" Ian chuckled, "Like babies. Most of the crap you know about vampires was created by the vampires to help them hide in plain sight. We made up all the mythology about coffins, crosses, and silver bullets. We're not the walking dead. We live, bleed, and even die eventually, but we can survive hundreds or thousands of years."

Carter stood and paced the floor. "So, how old are you then?"

"Young, by vampire standards. I'm around 250 years old. I was a soldier in the Revolutionary War. I was shot through with a musket ball and was bleeding out on the battlefield. Some vampire drained and turned me in the middle of the night. I thought I was hallucinating. Never saw him before or since. No idea why he singled me out. Woke up the next day in a pile of the war dead. I found a coven that took me in but living in that community didn't fit me, so I struck out on my own. Now I hire out as a mercenary to any coven looking for help during a coven war. Our covens are patriarchal and highly structured, unlike the witch's covens, which are dominated by females. The warlocks draw their power and status within the coven based on the female they bond with. This is real, not a game; we're all at risk here."

Carter sat back down on the arm of the chair and felt Anya's hand on his thigh. He'd heard the rumors about the Bohannons his whole life and didn't place much stock in them. He'd figured it just came from the fact they ran that witchy voodoo shop. He was just getting used to the idea that witchcraft was real when Ian dropped this bomb. He rubbed his hands over his face, wondering what he'd stepped into. He looked at Anya, "So why me?" Anya looked up at him. "You're cute, and you were flirting. Even when I gave you the finger every day, you kept flirting. I liked you. I still like you." He nodded his head and looked at Eilish. "Well, when you two decide to stir up shit, you go big."

Eilish chuckled. "Tell me about it."

BOHANNON

The doorbell rang, and Carter was glad for the interruption. He needed a minute to gather his thoughts. He took the pizza delivery as Anya jumped up and ran to the kitchen, calling out, "I'll get some napkins and a knife." Carter opened the boxes and laid them on the coffee table as Anya returned and handed paper towels to Eilish and Carter. She held up the knife. "You want me to slice?" Carter nodded as he sat back on the arm of the chair. "Yeah, sure."

Anya completed cutting through the sliced pizza, passed one slice to her sister, and then handed one to Carter before she took one for herself. She took a healthy bite and made an "mmmmmm" sound as the spicy, hot pizza touched her tongue. Eilish watched Carter as he ate in silence, not making eye contact. She knew the news about Ian had rattled him a little. "Are you okay, Carter?"

He nodded. "Yeah...I guess. I mean, I didn't see this vampire thing coming." He looked at Ian as he sat quietly, ignoring the pizza and sipping on that crap he called wine. Ian made eye contact with him, sensing his unease. "Go ahead. Ask me whatever you want to ask. I'm no threat to you, brother. You've worked beside me for months now. You know me."

Carter shook his head. "Well, apparently, I didn't know you well enough."

Ian chuckled. "Nothing's changed."

Carter said, "Everything's changed." He took another bite of his pizza as he contemplated a million questions in his head. "Okay, so explain this day-walker thing?"

Ian set his glass on the table. "All vampires have a gift, a special skill. I'm a day-walker. It just means I can be in the sunlight. There are different gifts, like dream-walking or sin-eaters. We can use that gift for evil or good, depending on the situation. We don't get to choose our gift; it comes with the territory. Most vamps are born; only a few of us have been turned."

Carter wasn't feeling particularly relieved by the information. "Okay, well, I don't even want to know what a sin-eater is. I thought you were all like the walking dead and shit."

Ian laughed. "We're not dead; we feel, we bleed, and we have hearts that beat. But you can kill us, and not with garlic or a cross. A bullet can take us out." He glanced at Eilish. "And I'd think even a damn good wicked spell, so I wouldn't piss off either of these two."

Carter chewed on his pizza but barely tasted it. "So, like 250 years. Dude, you're 250 years old. What the fuck?"

Ian poured another glass of the Midnight. He took a long deep swallow. "Yeah, it's not easy, it's lonely, and you're constantly looking over your shoulder, staying out of everyone's way. You don't bring attention to yourself. A master can get really shitty if you come into their territory and start stirring up crap. Since I'm a mercenary, it's like being a nomad; you just keep moving around. There are a lot of things I can do. But we can always save that for another day. I'm no threat to you, but you're at risk. You are the least prepared to protect yourself. Witches and vampires don't associate; we stay the hell out of each other's way. The Bohannon coven is strong, and neither of us will be welcomed."

Carter looked at Anya, who was already on her second slice of pizza. She seemed completely unfazed by this conversation. Carter spoke to her. "You seem okay with this." Anya shrugged. "Because this isn't news. I grew up with this stuff. To us, you're the weird one. In our world, we're all normal, and it's humans we have to be careful of. You're not a very accepting species. You tend to kill off people you don't understand. You know, the witch trials were real, although all the women that were hung weren't even witches. Just the thought of something being off and humans go batshit. We know all the rumors about us, but most people enjoy the rumors. We're a curiosity, something to gossip about. Something they can speculate about. But they don't think it's real, and we try to keep it that way. Same with Ian. Vampires stick to their covens; we stick to ours. We're all safer if we keep it on the down-low. Just how it is."

Carter nodded, laying his unfinished slice of pizza back in the box and getting up to grab another beer. "So how does this work then? You and me?"

Anya looked at his back as he walked away. "This is your choice, now. You know everything, so it's your choice to be with me or not. We can't be normal as a couple if that's what you want to know. We have to be careful." She watched him walk back in and sit back on the arm of the chair.

Ian watched him carefully, judging his reaction. "One other thing you need to understand, women rule the witch covens, but males rule the vampires." He looked at Eilish. "Want to come with me for a while? I think these two need some alone time. They have a lot to discuss and mull over."

Eilish nodded and wiped her lips with the paper towel. "Are you okay with that, Carter? You might feel better if you and Anya had some time alone. She can answer your questions, and you'll have some privacy."

He nodded. It was clear he had some decisions to make. But he was aware that they had let him into their circle. He knew things now that could put them at risk, which made him a threat to them. "Yeah, maybe some alone time would be good."

Eilish stood up, and Ian grabbed her hand. "Okay then, we'll take off. See you at home, sis."

Ian turned to look at Carter. "No harm from any of us, bro. I know your brain is churning. Anya will need to go home alone. You can't drive her or walk with her. She can handle herself. Just do me a favor and don't play with her. Make a decision. Stay or go. I'll see you tomorrow." He walked outside ahead of Eilish. "I'll walk around the side of the house. Follow me once I'm out of sight. I can teleport us. No one will see." He glanced up and down the street. It was empty, but a few houses still had lights on. He was going to be alone with her, and he wasn't wasting one minute of it.

BOHANNON

Ian walked around the side of the house. It was another muggy, humid night. Eilish followed him without hesitation. He wrapped his arms around her waist. "Don't be afraid. I'm going to teleport us to my place. It's a safe place to go where we won't be seen. Hang on tight; this is a quick trip."

As Eilish put her arms around his neck and wrapped her legs around his waist, Ian had to take a deep breath. Holding her this close pulled on him. Her blood smelled like gardenia, bergamot, and a touch of citrus, and he felt the ache in his gums. Good thing he wasn't going far. Taking off, he teleported quickly, faster than a human could tolerate, but this woman in his arms wasn't human. He landed inside his house and set her down gently. Her legs slid from his waist to the floor, but her arms remained around his neck. Her hair was like a beacon in the night. It was soft and long, and his heart felt like it would explode any second. He leaned into her cheek and kissed her softly. "Hope that wasn't too traumatic?" He smiled into her gray eyes and knew he had to go slow, but he was fighting the demands of his nature.

She smiled. "I've never been teleported before. Interesting. And despite all the myths to the contrary, we really can't fly off on a broom. Unfortunately, I'm as earthbound as any human. So, I guess you have an advantage."

Ian chuckled. "Maybe my only advantage." He looked around the room, sweeping his arm out to indicate the space. "Well, this is it, my humble abode. I rent this house. I never stay in any place for long. Come in and get comfy. I know we don't have much time, but any time I have with you is precious to me." He took her hand and led her to the couch. They sat side by side as he threw his arm over the back of the sofa and ran his hand gently through her hair. "I apologize for throwing out my identity at Carter without warning, but I felt he needed to know."

She nodded. "No, I agree. It's a bit of a risk to tell him, but Anya already opened that can of worms when she broke his fall. He has a right to know what he's getting into. I really hope we didn't scare him away. Anya likes to play it off like nothing ever gets to her, but she likes him. She's really pretty, but she goes out of her way to downplay her looks. Self-protection, I think. She builds a wall and doesn't let anyone in, yet she is always hoping someone will try. Maybe it's a middle sister thing; I don't know."

Ian smiled at her. He knew that Anya showed her bravado through smart-ass remarks. Eilish was unlike her sister; she knew her power and hid it well. "I noticed she got dolled up more than usual tonight. I know she likes Carter; he likes her too. I don't know his intentions long-term. He's never talked about it. I only met him on the construction job, so I don't know much about him. He seems cool enough, but I hope he doesn't just toy with her." He took her hand and then looked into her eyes. "I know we're treading into dangerous territory here, and I'll do whatever I can to protect you and your sister." He raised her hand to his lips and kissed it. "I'm in this with you to the end, wherever that leads us. Anya as well."

Eilish leaned her head on his shoulder. "I don't think Carter would hurt her, not intentionally. He doesn't seem the type. We're pretty good at reading humans. Her only danger with Carter is a broken heart if things don't work out between them. He'll either make a choice to follow this path or not. We have to let him make that decision. But you sound all in. I'm not sure you understand the full ramifications either. You know I'm attracted to you, but I hesitated to pull you into this. This isn't going to be easy, Ian. Not even a little. When Fina finds out, she and Warrick will come for us, all of us."

Ian stared at her. She still had doubts about him and if he'd see this through. "Eilish, I'm a vampire. I know what I'm facing. But you need to understand something. I've been around a long time, and I've seen and done things I prefer not to discuss. But I have never in my whole life had a woman make me fall to my knees before. Warriors are discouraged from making emotional attachments, and mercenaries are never in one place for very long. I spent my life avoiding affairs of the heart. I feed and leave. You know the drill. I knew the first time I saw you that this was different. You knew it too. I could see it in your eyes. I knew you were a witch. I've heard your story, but my heart tells me this is where I want to be. This is the path I want to follow. Let them come, Eilish. I have no fear if we're together. You're the one, and I'll fight to my death to be with you. And if I lose this battle, the only thing I'll regret is leaving you behind in this world." Ian leaned in and kissed her, his hand sliding softly up her face as he let his tongue wander across the lips. He saw her close her eyes and felt her hesitate for only a second.

Eilish was caught off guard by the kiss. It wasn't unwanted. She'd thought about kissing him many times. She relaxed as his lips touched hers and felt her energy build like a ball of heat in her chest that spread outward. She slid her hand through his hair and cupped the back of his neck, pulling him close into the kiss. She felt the snap of electricity as their tongues touched and the tingle in her fingertips and knew he'd feel the energy her body gave off.

Ian felt the soft jolt of energy through her fingers, but when she wrapped her tongue around his, it felt like sticking his finger in a wall socket. His head jerked back, but she held him firmly, making the kiss even more intense. What the hell was happening? For a brief moment, he couldn't believe what he was feeling. He was a vampire, and he was used to being the one who manipulated women to his will. But he'd never felt anything like this. He groaned softly and felt her hand drop from the back of his head. He broke the kiss and shook his head slightly. He stared back at her and licked his lips; the tingle was still there. But damn, did it feel amazing. "If that was to scare me, you missed by a million miles. If it was meant to turn me on, you succeeded." This was something Ian had never encountered before, and his heart only beat faster.

She gave him a shy smile. "Oh, my sweet, Ian. That was nothing. I think my power level was at a one. It rises with my emotions." She brushed his hair back from his face. She didn't use her powers often, but she was well aware of what lay beneath the surface. She'd always let Seraphina lead and was happy to do so. But testing Ian's limits for pleasure would be a journey she'd enjoy. "I can bring a whole new meaning to the term turning you on."

BOHANNON

Carter felt more than a little overwhelmed with this new information about Ian. He'd known Ian for a few months and had never seen anything unusual, but the only thing he knew about vampires was what he'd seen in the movies, and Ian had said that was all pretty much bullshit. He was picking up the pizza boxes and his half-eaten pizza and carrying them to the kitchen to toss in the trash. Anya followed behind him with their empty glasses and placed them in the sink. He stood quietly, looking out the kitchen window into a small courtyard. He spoke without looking at her. "So, you guys knew. You knew all along he was a vamp?"

Anya knew that Carter's mind was full....and confused. It was one hell of a lot to get hit with at once. Her heart felt heavy for him. She knew that he was the one in control of this decision. "Yes, we're familiar with vampires, and they with us. We don't hang out together, but we can recognize them on sight, just as they can recognize us." She looked down at the floor and shuffled her feet. "Are you angry about that, Carter?"

Carter shook his head, still staring into the distance as his blond locks tumbled around his face. "No, not angry. Just confused, I think." He leaned against the kitchen counter and looked at her. "I was just getting used to the whole witch thing. I mean, I'd grown up with the rumors about the Bohannons, but they're like the ghost stories in Charleston. You take it with a grain of salt. Like maybe it's true, but probably a lot of exaggeration just to make things interesting for tourists. I mean, I've seen your shop. I know people burn sage to cleanse their houses and stuff like that, but I never really thought about witches having any actual power until you broke my fall. Jeez, Anya, that's some superhero shit. But I thought, okay, I can go on this ride, but tonight, Ian springs this vampire shit. I could tell that you and Eilish were already aware since you didn't even react, so you clearly felt you weren't in danger. I think that's the only thing that kept me from wanting to run out of the house. You weren't afraid of him, but for a moment, I was thinking, is this three against one?" He shook his head again. "It's a lot to take in."

Anya went to him and laid her hand on his arm. "Ian means us no harm; none of us do, Carter. He told you so you'd know before you jumped into all of this. He wanted you to know the truth. And to be honest, you should know, because it's a dangerous step to take, even being seen talking to me. We don't know each other very well, but I do know that when you began to fall, I couldn't stop my powers. I didn't even think about it. I just did it before I even knew what was happening. I didn't want to see you hurt." She ran her hand up and down his arm. His biceps were hard as rocks. "I still don't want to see you get hurt, so please know, if you don't want to see me, I'll understand." She removed her hand and stepped back. She didn't want to influence his decision, but it wasn't easy; she wanted those arms around her.

Carter looked into her green eyes. He'd always been attracted to her rebellious streak. Strangely enough, he didn't feel threatened by either sister, and Ian had never done anything to indicate his intentions were anything he should fear. But didn't Ian say he seduced his prey? He was probably good at manipulating people. "So, you trust Ian? I mean, you said yourself that the witches and the vamps don't mingle. I have to say, I never spent much time thinking about vampires and never thought they were real. I think I was more open to the idea of witches... well, open to the idea in my own way, not stopping people from falling mid-air. But it seemed like more of a possibility. But vampires? You're okay with this?"

Anya smiled. "Yes, I'm okay with it. My sister likes him, and he seems to care about her as well. I'm not afraid of him if that's what you mean. I know that you're friends with Ian. Do you feel as if this revelation will change your relationship with him? " She walked to the fridge and grabbed another beer, and held it up to him. "Want one? You look like you might need another one."

He took the beer and popped the top, taking a long drink. "Thanks." He wiped the back of his hand across his mouth, and Anya couldn't help but notice the fullness of his lips. He had sensual lips.

Carter thought about what she was saying, processing the information before he answered. "I don't know how I feel, to be honest. I feel like I need a re-set button. I mean, he said he feeds from people. Are they hurt? Are they afraid? I know he said he wipes their memory, but what happens to them afterward?"

Anya grabbed a beer for herself, took his hand, and led him into the living room. She flopped on the couch and patted the seat next to her. She turned towards him as he sat next to her and looked into those gorgeous eyes. A few stray tendrils of dirty blonde curls hung over his eye, and she sighed. She wanted to touch him. "When Ian feeds, he stakes out a place, looking for someone he's attracted to, or maybe someone who is easy and open enough to engage in a conversation. Most vampires have a sexual preference. Ian would always choose a woman unless he were in a very precarious situation. His prey isn't hurt. He lures them, flirting, and he can use his eyes to put them in a trance-like state where they aren't able to look away until he releases that stare. When vampires feed, it's a very erotic feeling for both of them, so they usually have sex with their prey. It's always consensual. It's against their code to take someone who rejects them, although I know some rogues that don't play by the rules." Carter looked confused. "Rogues?" Anya shrugged, "Vampires who live outside the dictated structure of their culture, outlaws." Anya watched his face as she explained. She wished Carter had asked Ian these questions. She took a swig of the beer and continued. "Anyway, after the sex, they erase their memory, so they remember very little about the experience. If they see the vampire again, it may trigger a response tied to something pleasurable, but the events won't be clear. It doesn't hurt the humans, or as the vampires call them, the mortals. It's like rewiring the brain's circuitry and helps protect the vampire. It's pure survival."

Carter nodded, listening intently to her explanation. "He left out the sex part." He leaned back on the sofa, trying to mentally calculate how many women Ian had been with. He'd said he was over 200 years old, so Carter guessed the number was pretty high. Ian was a good-looking guy, and Carter didn't think he'd have to work too hard to get women in his bed, even if he wasn't a vampire. "So, Eilish is okay with this? This sex thing?"

Anya looked down at the floor. This was getting intense now. She stood up and walked around the room, her energy rising. "Well, there's a difference between witches and vampires." She took a deep breath. "Carter, this isn't easy to say, but we have more power than the vampire. We are actually dominant when it comes to sex." Anya sat back down. "My sister has a lot of power, a lot more than me. So, I think if they ever get together, let's just say Ian will probably be in for a new experience. But I'm sure he won't be complaining." Anya blushed a bit and took another sip of beer.

Carter gave her a sly smile. "You tryin' to tell me something, darlin'?"

Anya cocked her head to the side and winked at him. "Maybe. The question is, have we run you off permanently, or are you brave enough to tangle with this witch?"

Carter set his beer on the coffee table and turned to face her. "Well, I'm not so sure about Ian yet, but I'm more than ready to see what you have in store for me. Just promise that if I don't live up to your expectations, you won't turn me into a frog or something."

Anya grinned. "Get your damn fairy tales straight, badass; that's 'The Princess and the Frog'." Anya leaned in close, running her tongue across her lips. "But I'll tell you this..." she slid her hand softly along his jaw. "You won't forget it." She kissed him on the lips and felt her energy rise slow and sure and let him feel what was in store.

Carter felt the jolt of energy when their lips touched, and she gently pressed her palm against his chest, pushing him back against the sofa. He felt his skin tingle under the pressure of her hand, and when she inserted her tongue into his mouth, it felt like a small electrical charge. He was immediately hard for her and slid his arm around her waist, pulling her against his chest. He felt like he couldn't breathe and was locked to her like a drowning man hanging on to his only life source. He didn't know what lay in store for him with this girl, but suddenly, life as a frog didn't seem half bad.

BOHANNON

Ian felt the power within Eilish, and he was intrigued by her energy and how it came across to him. The kiss alone felt like a lightning bolt. How in the hell would being inside her feel? He slid his hands under her shirt and slowly kissed down her neck. He was already hard as a rock, and that kiss had enough power to send his predator instincts into overdrive. He lifted her blouse and snuggled between her breasts. They were taut and ready for attention, and he knew she was as well. He lifted her blouse over her head, and she didn't object. He suckled each nipple and felt the energy increase in the room, and he could only imagine how intense this might become. He loved that he could create this reaction in her.

Eilish tried to remain relaxed, knowing her emotions dictated her power. The stronger her emotions, the less control she seemed to have, and she didn't want to scare Ian off. She'd had sex with a few humans before, but they never came back a second time. "Go slow," she whispered. "This will feel different for you."

He gave her a look that said he welcomed different, but she wasn't sure he was ready for her. She ran her hand through his hair and could hear the crackle of static electricity. She took a deep breath, trying to pull back on her power. His mouth working magic on her breasts created a sensation that was hard to ignore. She stopped him long enough to help him remove his shirt. She ran her hand down his rock-hard chest and saw the small arcs of light from her fingertips. She heard him gasp in surprise. "Does it hurt?" He shook his head, and she watched as his eyes turned red. Eilish knew she could trigger his beast, but the beast was no threat to her. His voice was gruff when he answered her, hearing the beast emerge, that part of him that was more vampire than man. "I can only control the beast so much."

"Don't try to control it. I don't want you to control it." He shook his head. "Eilish...you don't understand." Her mouth covered his as she mumbled, "Teach me."

She knew he felt her power when his tongue explored her mouth, but he didn't pull away; he gripped her tighter. She placed her hand at the base of his head and held him tight to her lips as she released the full force of her power. She felt his body jerk, like an electrical current ran through him, as she levitated slightly off the sofa, and in an instant, she flipped him over so he was on his back and straddled him. He had a startled look on his face as she undid his jeans and slid them off his hips, not surprised to discover he didn't wear underwear. She removed the rest of her clothes as he kicked his jeans to the floor. Ian was breathing rapidly, and his fangs had punched through, but she knew he wouldn't feed from her. Not yet. The sex alone would overwhelm him.

"Should I continue?" She asked. He nodded. "Even if it kills me." She laughed. "I'll try my best not to do that. That would be a bad end to a first date." She straddled him again, and Ian realized she was the alpha, and he had mixed feelings about that. He'd always been the predator, the pursuer, the one who took what he wanted. It felt strange to be on the receiving end.

He felt his beast rise to the surface and fought hard to push him down. He wanted out, and Eilish had assured him she could tackle him with ease, but he wanted this experience to be between the two of them. When she climbed on top of him and looked into her eyes, he saw the power she wielded, the sexual desire, and the absolute control she had over him. He now knew how his prey felt, a loss of control, yet a desire to continue. His growl was guttural as he slid his hands over her breasts and then slid slowly inside her. He felt like he was in another realm. The electrical charge raged through his body and ran through his veins. His breath quickly left his body, and his beast disappeared. He was overwhelmed with her energy and sexual desire. He could feel it, traveling along every nerve. His voice was breathy and strangled. "Eilish."

Eilish didn't waste time with foreplay. She knew what she wanted, and she doubted Ian could tolerate much more stimulation as it was. She slid down his body and wrapped her lips around his cock and felt his whole body go rigid as he arched his hips and tilted his head back, his mouth open and his fangs on full display. They presented no threat to her; she had control of him now. She closed her mouth around him, her tongue lapping at him as she sucked gently, then released him before he could come and straddled him again. She braced herself with both hands on his chest as she rode him to orgasm, a bright light of energy projecting out into the room as they came together. She felt his body relax under her as he was still gasping for breath, and the light faded away, leaving them in the dark. She laid her head down on his chest, listening to the hammering of his heart. "Are you okay?"

Ian tried to control his breathing, but everything happened in such a flurry of intensity that he'd tried to let himself go and enjoy the ride. His fangs retracted, and his eyes returned to normal, but his heart was still hammering. This was definitely something he'd never experienced before. "I'm still alive. Thank you for sparing my life." He grinned and kissed the top of her head. "I don't know if you've ever been with another vampire, but you may have killed a few if you were. Are you okay?"

Eilish kissed him. "You're my first vampire, but I went easy on you. We'll have to build up your endurance." She laid her head back on his chest. She loved how firm and solid he felt. Warlocks didn't draw power from their physical strength, so Ian's muscular build was a turn-on. She lay quietly as he regained his composure. "We should probably talk...about us, about Carter. We've created a real prescription for disaster here."

"Funny you should say that. I was wondering about something similar. If your sister is having sex with Carter, it will surely kill him. But knowing Carter, he'll think it's the best way to go out." Ian laughed and pulled her up, so her head lay on his shoulder. He kissed her forehead. Her white hair was like a beacon in the dark room. He let his hand run through it softly. "Us. I like the sound of that. I know what's going to happen, Eilish, or at least an idea. I don't regret it, do you?"

She nestled into his neck. "I don't regret it, but you don't know what's going to happen. If we stay together, we have to keep everything hidden; even with that, it's impossible that we won't be discovered at some point. I'm under pressure to bond with Zavian, and that situation will come to a head soon. If Fina discovers...no, *when* Fina discovers I'm with you, she will come after us. This isn't a game. Your only real power against her is your ability to escape, to teleport away. But you need to understand, if she, or any witch, has something you possess, an article of clothing, a lock of hair, anything...they can cast a spell no matter where you are. You aren't safe, Ian. I can undo a spell, but you will still be bound to it until I can release you from it. I can't ask you to stay. It's too much to ask of anyone, and I'll understand if you decide to leave."

Ian growled. "If I had the power, I'd take out Zavian's ass right now, just being very honest with you. Deep down, I know you will have to play this game with him. But I've seen him with you, he wants you, and no one is pushing him to hook up. He wants you." He sat up, and Eilish moved to sit up with him. Grasping her face softly, he looked into her eyes. "Hear me, Eilish, I can only protect you with what powers I have, but know one thing. I will leave this Earth if it means I have to fight for us, to be with you, stay with you. I'm here. I'm not leaving." He leaned in and kissed her with every bit of energy he could muster. The kiss was possessive and claimed what he wanted. He needed her to understand, he'd found what he'd been looking for, and he'd fight to the death for it.

Eilish succumbed to his kiss and read his thoughts. *Good,* she said to herself, *because you might have to.*

BOHANNON

Anya and Carter said their goodbyes, and it wasn't without its energy and passion. Carter didn't like the idea of her walking home alone, but Anya said she'd text Eilish and find out where she was so they could go home together. Anya looked at her watch and realized it was close to 2 a.m. They'd been out most of the night, and hours had passed since Eilish and Ian had left. She texted her sister and told her she was just leaving Carter's place and where they could meet. She kissed Carter again and finally heard the little beep that a message had been returned from Eilish. She looked at Carter and smiled. "Don't worry; I'm sure Ian will shadow us home undetected. Once we get there, I'll text and let you know I'm okay." Carter walked her to the door and stood on the porch as she walked back the way she'd come, realizing this had been the weirdest and yet the best damn night of his life.

Eilish was in a light sleep with her head on Ian's chest when she heard the slight ping of her phone. She sat up and dug for her phone in her handbag as Ian roused from sleep. "Everything okay, babe?"

Eilish looked at her phone and read the text from Anya. "Yes, it's

Anya. I need to go. We told Fina we were going for pizza. Staying all night would create too many questions." Ian ran his hand slowly up and down her back. Even in the dark room lit only by moonlight, he could see the contrast of his dark tan against her pale skin. He sat up beside her. "I'll go with you."

Eilish stood and started getting dressed, shaking her head. "No, shadow us, maybe. We can't take the chance of being seen with you. It's already going to be hard enough explaining what we were doing until 2 a.m."

Ian pulled on his jeans and was looking about for his shirt. "Yeah, I can do that." Eilish texted her sister to wait at the corner of Legare and Tradd, she and Ian would teleport to her, and they'd walk from there. As Ian was tying his work boots, Eilish wandered into his kitchen and opened the fridge, hoping to find something cold to drink. The fridge was completely empty. "Don't you have anything to drink?" Ian followed her into the room, flipping on the light. "Uh, no. I wasn't expecting company. I got water from the tap or Midnight."

Eilish laughed. "Why do you even have a kitchen?" He shrugged. "It comes with the house." Eilish removed a glass from the cabinet and filled it with tap water. "Ice? Do you have ice?" Ian opened the freezer and saw that he'd never turned the ice maker on. "Sorry, no." He flipped the switch so it would make ice. "Next time."

She leaned against the kitchen counter and sipped at the water, watching him move about the kitchen he was clearly unfamiliar with. "So where are we anyway. I couldn't keep my bearings when you teleported me here." He walked to her, placing one hand on the counter on either side of her, trapping her inside his arms. "Uh, Beaufain Street. I rented this place because it's next to the College of Charleston. I don't have to go far to hunt. Probably not a good idea, but it was easy. I just have to make sure I erase any trace of my encounters, so they don't recognize me on the street someday."

Eilish placed the empty glass in the sink as his answer about where he lived only served to remind her of how he fed and had sex.

She had to remind herself it wasn't personal, but she still felt a tingle of jealousy. "Yeah, that makes sense, I guess."

He saw the mood shift and gave her a soft kiss. "You know it means nothing." Eilish locked eyes with him and felt their connection to each other. "I know...I... I'll adapt."

He brushed his lips across her neck, feeling her pulse accelerate as he did so. He'd never fed from a witch, but if it was anything like the sex, he was all in for the discovery. "Maybe you won't have to." Eilish gently pushed him away. "Discussion for another time. We need to get going." He nodded. "Does that mean there will be another time?" She looked surprised. "Of course. Did you think otherwise?" He gave her a smile that would melt butter. "Just checking. Come on, let's go get your sister." He scooped her up and teleported back to Legare and Tradd where Anya stood under the streetlight.

Anya saw her sister appear with Ian from out of nowhere. "Neat trick. Now disappear, or whatever it is you do." Ian chuckled, "I'll shadow you." Anya grabbed her sister's hand as she answered him. "Whatever."

The sisters started the walk home together as Eilish tugged at her hand. "Come on; we're going to have a lot of explaining to do. Even if Fina is asleep, she'll hear us come in." They walked hand in hand as Ian shadowed them a few steps behind.

As they picked up their pace, Anya giggled. "Well, I don't know about you, but pizza night was a success. Now, all we have to do is get past Fina. And I'm assuming Ian is all in?"

Eilish looked over at her sister in the moonlight. She could see how much Anya cared for Carter already, and clearly, it had been a good night for them. "Ian's in. But right now, I'm worried about Fina. We need a story. There's no pizza place open at this hour of the night. What are we going to say we were doing all this time?"

Anya stopped in the middle of the sidewalk. It was quiet, and a slight breeze was blowing softly. Looking up at the moon, she scrunched up her face. "Well, obviously, we weren't thinking ahead." She could feel Ian close by and knew she should watch her tongue.

Eilish squeezed her hand. "This is serious, Anya! What if Warrick is there? It's too late to say we were with someone from the coven because we don't have time to create an alibi. It will just have to be the two of us. It can't be anything she can check."

Eilish heard Ian's voice as he spoke up. "Just tell her you went to the waterfront. It was a beautiful night, and you went for a walk after the pizza place closed. You just sat and talked and didn't realize how much time had passed." Eilish nodded. "It's our best option, I guess. Can you work with that, Anya?"

Anya nodded. "Yeah, that works. Come on."

They saw lights in various windows throughout the house as they got home. It wasn't unusual for Fina to leave the lights on if she'd gone to bed before they'd returned. Anya heard Ian speak up, saying he'd leave them now, and felt him leave. She turned to Eilish. "Break the protection spell, and let's get this over with."

Eilish stepped up on the porch and removed the protection spell with a flick of her wrist. She turned to Anya and held her finger to her lips. "Shhh." She quietly opened the door and stepped into the foyer, with Anya on her heels. As she closed the door and replaced the spell, they both heard Fina's voice from the top of the stairs. "About time you two got home. Must have been some great pizza."

Fina started down the stairs. It was rare for her sisters to be out so late without the coven. She didn't worry about their safety; they could both take care of themselves, but coming home at such a late hour raised questions. Eilish looked up, "Oh, I hope we didn't wake you. We just lost track of time. We ran into Wynter and Rain at the pizza place and just sat talking until the place closed." Eilish immediately regretted pulling Wynter and Rain into this story. Now she'd need to cover her tracks. "We went to the waterfront when the pizza shop closed and just sat and talked. We totally lost track of time."

Fina looked from one sister to the other, trying to read their faces. If they were lying, they were doing an excellent job of it. "You could have called."

Anya headed for the stairs. "We just lost track of time. I didn't know we had to punch a time clock to come and go from our own home."

Fina stared at her back as she started up the stairs. "It's a cell phone; you could have used it." She turned and looked at Eilish. "And I suppose your cell phone had no signal?"

Eilish shrugged. "We didn't think about it, Fina. Haven't you ever been caught up in a conversation and lost track of time? All we've done all summer is walk from the house to the shop and back again. It was just good to get out. You take off with Warrick all the time. Give us a break." She walked past Fina on the stairs, following Anya as they made their way to their bedrooms.

Fina watched her walk up the stairs. Something had happened, but she couldn't put her finger on it. "What Warrick and I do does not concern either of you unless I feel it's necessary to tell you." She raised her voice so both of them could hear. "And don't think you'll be dragging in the morning; we have a shop to run!"

Eilish and Anya both rolled their eyes and headed for their separate bedrooms. Anya quickly texted Carter and told him she was home safely; all was well, and she'd had a great night. His response was simple and made her smile, *'Just one of many.'* She texted Eilish: *Give Wynter and Rain a heads up about tonight. Don't give Fina any reasons to stop me from seeing Carter again.*

Eilish closed the bedroom door behind her and let out a deep breath. She knew Fina was suspicious but didn't have anything to go on. Emric was at the window, staring out. "A vampire. Did you know there was a vampire out there?"

Eilish shushed him. "Shh! Yes, I know. He's harmless. Don't mention it to Fina, okay?" Emric looked back at her. "It's important, Emric! Keep this to yourself, or I'll force you to pass over." Emric looked back at her with dismay. None of the sisters had ever threatened him before. "Of course, Miss Eilish. I can keep a secret."

Eilish locked eyes with the ghost, making sure he understood the importance of keeping his mouth shut. She went to the window, looked out, and saw Ian standing on the sidewalk in front of their house. She shook her head no, and he faded from view. She heard the soft ping from her cell phone and got Anya's message. She curled up on her bed and immediately sent a text to Wynter and Rain so they'd see it as soon as they woke up. *Hey, if anyone asks, you were with Anya and me at the pizza place last night until it closed. I'll fill you in later.* Eilish leaned back against the headboard and closed her eyes. Nothing about this was going to be easy.

BOHANNON

Fina was in the kitchen drinking coffee. She had made some muffins for breakfast, but there were no signs of the girls. She knew this would happen. She began to bang pots and pans, and even that didn't rouse them. She finally went upstairs with Luna on her heels and began yelling and banging on doors. "Get up. You have a store to run today. And make it fast. I *knew* this would happen, running around all hours of the night!" She heard their moans and grumblings. "You have 10 minutes; Warrick is picking us up and dropping you both off at Rhiannon's; we have errands to run today." As she descended the stairs, she bent to pick up Luna. "Come along, pet; we have finally roused the dead."

Eilish rolled over and covered her head with the pillow. She'd only had about four hours of sleep. She heard one of Anya's Doc Marten's hit the bedroom door with a loud bang as she'd thrown the heavy shoe at the door to protest Fina's screaming. She reluctantly sat up on the bed and rubbed her eyes. They felt glued shut. She dragged herself to the bathroom and jumped in the shower, leaving the water on the cool side. After a quick rinse, she ran a comb through her long hair but didn't bother to blow it dry. She scrubbed her face, brushed her teeth, and then threw on a tank top and a loose-fitting maxi skirt. She was sliding the bangles on her arms when Anya appeared at her door in a tie-dyed t-shirt and a pair of cut-off dungarees, already wearing her sunglasses. Anya deadpanned. "One of these days, I'm going to kill her."

Eilish giggled. "Remind me never to wake you before you've had a full night's sleep." Anya lowered her glasses, peering over them. "And bring coffee." Eilish grabbed her handbag and slung it over her shoulder. "Come on, before she comes back again."

The two girls shuffled down the stairs and into the kitchen, where Warrick was already hovering, and Fina had two mugs of coffee ready for them on the counter. Anya grabbed one immediately, filling it with milk and sugar before taking a big gulp. Eilish sipped hers black. Warrick paced, looking at his watch and annoyed with the delay. "This is no way to run a business. It would help if you were on time. We have errands to run; hurry up, and I'll drop you two off at the shop. You're already late. The shop should have opened ten minutes ago!"

Fina gathered up her things and headed for the door. "Bring your coffee. You can drink it in the van. We don't have time to dawdle!"

Anya rolled her eyes at Eilish, and the two sisters followed them, climbing into the van, which felt like an oven. Warrick slid behind the driver's seat as Fina sat in the passenger seat. He turned the AC on full blast as Fina lowered her window slightly to allow some air inside. The van rumbled to a start as Warrick drove them to the shop. The van passed the old house that was under construction, and the younger sisters looked out the window as they passed. Carter was on the roof and didn't notice them, but Ian was on the ground and looked up, making eye contact with Eilish as they passed. He hoped the girls hadn't gotten in trouble. Warrick pulled up in front of the shop, and the girls climbed out. Fina issued last instructions before the van pulled away, and Eilish removed the protection spell and unlocked the shop door.

They entered the shop and appreciated the blast of cool air. Eilish flipped the sign to 'open', and they dropped their bags behind the counter. Both sisters looked at each other, knowing this ruse couldn't be maintained forever. Eilish checked her phone. "I sent a text to Wynter and Rain last night. They both responded this morning with 'no problem,' but Rain said she wanted to hear the real story. What are we going to do, sis?"

Anya groaned and pulled her sunglasses over her eyes once again. "We're going to make coffee first; I'm dying here." She walked to the back office and set the coffee pot to brewing. She wasn't sure what they were going to do, she'd planned to take it one day at a time, but the first night out and *bam*, almost caught red-handed. She dragged herself back in and flopped on the stool. "I doubt Fina will bring it up again unless we screw up." She laid her head back and closed her eyes as the smell of the hot brewing coffee wafted throughout the shop. "Let's just hope Fina and Warrick are gone *all* day. I will need all day to regroup, but I need coffee, now!" As she slid off the stool and walked back to the store room, she heard the chimes over the door jingle and knew a customer was there already. "Great, can't even get a decent cup of coffee before it begins."

Eilish forced a smile as a few tourists trickled in. "Let me know if I can help you with anything." The customers browsed through the merchandise as Eilish considered their dilemma. There were only so many excuses she and Anya could come up with for leaving at night when all of them had been such homebodies. Seraphina was smart, and it wouldn't take her long to get suspicious, not to mention that Eilish would need to work on spending some time with Zavian. This seemed an impossible mess. She really liked Ian and wanted to see him, and she knew Anya was smitten with Carter, but there was no way they could bring a human, let alone a vampire, into their coven. She was lost in her thoughts when a customer placed a book on the counter and broke her train of thought. "Miss? Could you ring this up?" Eilish was snapped back to reality as she apologized and rang up the purchase just as Anya returned with coffee. Fina would never approve of them drinking coffee in the store front, but then, Fina didn't approve of a lot of things.

Ian recognized the old van as it drove by and the driver and passengers. He'd seen them all at the ceremony when he was following Eilish, long before she knew he existed. As lunchtime came, he told Carter he knew they'd been in the van with their older sister, probably heading to the shop. He told Carter he would go to the shop and check it out, make sure the girls were okay. Carter reluctantly stayed behind, knowing he'd be useless if a problem arose. Ian cleaned up a bit, let his hair down, and decided to walk, even though it felt like hell outside. He slowly opened the door to the shop, and the cold air hit him. He scanned the shop to make sure there weren't other customers. Anya lifted her head when she heard the door chime and saw Ian walking in. "Oh wow, I didn't expect to see you in here." Ian grinned, and his eyes found Eilish as he answered Anya. "Just checking on you both. I got worried when I saw you in the van."

Eilish looked back at him nervously, hoping no one from the coven popped in. This wasn't Ian's first visit, but it was his first visit since they'd been together. "Hey. We're both fine. Fina woke up when we got in. I'm not sure she's completely buying our story, but she didn't suspect we'd been with anyone. Ian, this is going to be a problem. I don't know how to sneak around without raising her suspicions. We have to be careful."

He reached across the counter and took her hand. "I am being careful. But I was also worried. I just needed to know everything is cool with your big sister." He let go of her hand. He could feel her nervous energy. "Would you prefer I not come here?"

Eilish shook her head, filled with mixed feelings. She wanted to see Ian, but having him in the shop was a big risk. She was about to answer him when the small bell over the door jingled and she looked up to see Zavian strolling in. He stopped in his tracks when he saw the vampire. He knew both Anya and Eilish would know he was a vamp, but the guy didn't appear to be making any trouble. He picked up on Eilish's nerves and watched as Anya returned to the back room. Both sisters were behaving oddly. Zavian spoke boldly. "Hey. I know Warrick and Fina are out for the day. Thought I'd stop in and see if you needed any help." He kept his eyes on the vamp, who remained with his back to him. Eilish gave him a forced smile. "We're good. It's been pretty slow so far."

Ian still had his eyes glued on Eilish when he heard the door chime and saw her face. He felt her fear spike, and the forced smile was unmistakable. He heard the male voice and knew it was the warlock, Zavian, and his beast sat up and wanted a piece of him. Ian closed his eyes and tapped down the beast. This wasn't the time. Ian watched as Zavian walked behind the counter and kissed Eilish on the cheek while running his arm around her waist. Ian raised his eyes to Zavian and stared him down. Eilish's anxiety level could have blown the roof off the place, but Ian knew he had to play it cool.

Zavian stared back at the vampire. "Well, this is something you don't see every day, a vamp in a witches' store."

Ian casually crossed his arms over his chest. "Sometimes, we use your items to enhance our power."

Zavian huffed. "Yeah? You think a few crystals and some sage will save you?"

Eilish nudged him. "Stop. He's a customer."

Zavian stared down the vamp, not feeling at all the need to be courteous. "One less customer won't hurt the business. Get what you need and get out."

Ian didn't budge. Who the hell did this fucking skinny-ass, long-haired warlock think he was? Ian chuckled. "And do you own this store? You know, sometimes I've encountered witches who have manners." He raised his hands. "But no problem, I was just asking the beautiful lady if she could accommodate me with something." Ian wanted to jump the counter and rip the bastard's head off, but he knew he couldn't make a move.

Zavian possessively placed his arm around Eilish's waist and gave the vamp a hard stare. "Don't own it yet, but let's just say it will be in the family."

Eilish stood rigid, giving Ian a pleading look not to start anything. "Zavian, please. You don't need to speak to our customers that way." Zavian pulled her closer, feeling her slight resistance. "You're being much too naïve, Eilish. Vamps only mean trouble." Looking back at Ian, he issued an order. "You're bad for business. Better if you just leave."

Ian didn't miss the look on Eilish's face. He'd leave, but only because this would lead to more grief for her if he didn't. But Zavian's time would come, and Ian now had an even bigger reason to see him dead. His eyes slid to the arm around her waist and then back to her eyes. "Thank you for your help; you were very accommodating until he walked in. Have a pleasant day." His eyes slid to Zavian. "You can fuck off." Ian turned his back and walked out the door, slamming it harder than necessary. He walked back to the work site and knew his face was still showing anger when Carter shook his head and said, "Oh shit."

※

Eilish broke free of Zavian's grasp and responded angrily. "That was completely unnecessary! He wasn't causing any problems. We've had vamps in here before. Why do you feel compelled to create conflict when none exists? This isn't your shop, Zavian, and don't act so damn sure it will be 'in the family' as you say."

Zavian was perplexed at her anger. This was odd for Eilish. "Don't act so sure? I'm very sure, and you should be as well, Eilish! What in the hell do you need vamps sniffing around here for? They are trouble, but I shouldn't have to remind you of that." Zavian walked around the store, his frustration nagging him. "And what do you think Uncle Warrick will say when I tell him the crap that when on in here today? I wasn't creating conflict, I asked him to leave nicely, and he resisted, or did you miss that part?"

"Nicely? You call that nicely? You were rude. You don't own the shop, and you don't own me, and I'd appreciate it if you stopped acting as if you did! So, run and tell Uncle Warrick. The last time I checked, the only name on the deed to Rhiannon's was Bohannon... not de Burke!"

The wind chimes rang out as her wave of anger created an energy vortex that shivered across the room, and the candles lit automatically, their flames flickering. Anya re-emerged from the back room and stepped close to her sister, whispering, "Calm down."

Eilish took a deep breath, closing her eyes and trying to settle her anger before it got out of control. "Sorry. I'm sorry. I didn't mean to yell, but you over-stepped."

Zavian felt the room vibrate and knew her anger was rising. He reached out and took Eilish's hand. "I'm sorry. I did overstep, and that was wrong, but I wanted no problem with him. I just wanted to make sure he didn't start anything with either of you. I'd never tell Uncle Warrick, you know that. But seriously, Eilish, when are we going to stop fighting this? I sometimes don't understand you." He let go of her hand and looked at Anya. Anya gave him a look that could fall any witch. "It might be a good idea, Zavian, if you just left. You made your apologies, but right now, Eilish is upset. And I ain't too happy either, but thanks for stopping in."

She moved Eilish away from Zavian and to the back room to give Zavian a further push to go out the door. She heard the chimes jingle and knew he'd left. She hugged her sister. "What in hell have we got ourselves into?"

BOHANNON

Carter had watched Ian take off for the shop and wondered if that was a good idea. He kept an eye on his watch, waiting for him to return. Ian had only been gone about thirty minutes when he saw him walking back towards the construction site, and he could tell from his stride he was angry. "Shit. I hope he didn't fuck this up already!" Carter climbed down the ladder and hit the ground just as Ian entered the yard. "Dude, what happened? Whatever it was, it doesn't look good."

Ian hadn't cooled off walking back to the job site. He was even more pissed off. Arrogant fucking Zavian. He ripped his t-shirt off and flung it at his truck. "What happened was...fuck, I went to the shop just to check on them both. Everything was fine. Then that fucking Zavian came in. You know, the one who thinks he's going to mate with her? He walks in like he owns the damn place and orders me to get the hell out." Ian's blood was boiling; the more he thought about it, the madder he got. "Eilish took him down a notch, but he kept at me. Nothing happened, but Eilish was begging with her eyes for me to leave." Ian kicked the dirt with his boot. "I feel like ripping his head off!"

Carter looked over his shoulder as a few other workers looked up to see what all the commotion was about. "Hey, keep it down. We're supposed to keep this under wraps, and we're not off to a good start." He stepped in closer to lay his hand on Ian's shoulder but saw the soft glow of red in his eyes and stepped back. "Come on, Ian. Get a grip. They said no public contact. We need a plan, brother, and this ain't it. We were only with them one night, and now that Zavian dude is already on alert. Don't fuck this up. I really like Anya."

Carter leaned against the truck and shook his head. "I didn't sleep much after she left. I never had to hide the fact that I was seeing somebody before. I don't know how to sustain this. We can't go out together. How can I spend time with her? I mean, I think she'll get pretty tired of sneaking into my place just to have sex and leaving in the middle of the night. Sounds like their older sister keeps pretty close tabs on them, so that doesn't sound like a sustainable plan anyway." Carter looked down; his feet crossed at the ankles in his heavy work boots, his arm crossed over his chest. "She said this would be dangerous for all of us. The last thing I want to do is put Anya in harm's way." He looked up at Ian. "Tell me you have a plan."

Ian shook his head. "Yeah, I fucked up, I admit it. I think, for one thing, we may not be able to see them together. Causes too much suspicion. I'm going to try to text Eilish tonight; hell, I can't even call her; someone in that house might hear us. I need to convince her that we need a plan, something solid. But I know she has to keep up this facade of seeing Zavian to keep her older sister happy." He started to walk back to the house. "Come on; we better get our asses back to work."

Carter threw up his hands in frustration. "Great. That works for you. Guess I'm on my own here." He watched as Ian walked away and didn't respond. Carter reached into the truck and pulled a water bottle from the cooler, taking a long drink before pouring some of the cold water over his head to cool off. On a whim, he pulled his cell phone from his jeans pocket and sent Anya a text. *You okay?* It only took a few seconds before she responded. *Got a little tense here, but I'm fine. I'll call this evening when I have more time. Love you.* She attached an eggplant emoji, and it made Carter laugh. He shook his head and paused a second before answering. *Love you too.*

He stared at his message, knowing she was reading it. He put the phone back in his pocket and walked back to the ladder. "All the girls in Charleston, and you fall for a witch. Great move, Carter."

BOHANNON

The sisters walked home in the evening light. It had begun to cool down as the night approached, and the sounds of crickets and tree frogs began to sing their night songs. Anya found Eilish to be a bit quiet. She'd been so for most of the day after Ian had left. Zavian had taken his leave soon after, and Eilish had remained remote and lost in her thoughts. "You sure have been quiet. Have you even talked to Ian since this morning? I mean, text him or anything? I'm sure he's cooled off by now." She glanced at Eilish as they walked, but her sister's eyes remained on the sidewalk ahead. "Eilish, did you hear me? Don't be angry with me; I'm on your side, remember."

She shook her head. "No. It got busy, and I didn't want to be interrupted. I need to call him. I'll call him tonight. We can't let this happen again. I know Ian didn't mean to start anything, but he can't come to the shop anymore. Carter either, for that matter. We have to maintain distance. And you know Zavian, he probably complained to Warrick five minutes after he walked out the door. I wouldn't be surprised if Fina knows already. We should be prepared for an ambush, so put on your best innocent face."

Anya agreed by nodding her head. "Well, that's easy to play off. We've had vamps in the store before, I mean, it's not that unusual, and maybe Zavian wouldn't have known that. I do think he was rude as hell, to be honest. But I'll keep my mouth shut about that unless you bring it up. And while we are on the subject, we need to get Wynter and Rain. We need to talk to them about using them as a cover; we don't need them going to Fina or Warrick blabbing about us lying either." As they got closer to home, Anya sighed. "I know you like Ian, and I'm already in this with Carter. I'm staying in because, for once, I have a guy I really like and want to keep as long as he'll stay." Anya just hoped Carter *would* stay throughout the chaos that was coming because it was coming in one form or another.

They rounded the corner onto East Bay and saw Warrick's van. Eilish looked at her sister. "Get ready. It may mean nothing. They were together all day." Eilish opened the gate, and they walked up the sidewalk to the front porch. Eilish could feel there was no boundary spell on the house, so she knew Fina and Warrick hadn't been home long, and they were expecting their arrival. Eilish took a deep breath and opened the door, calling out, "We're home!"

The two sisters followed the sounds of conversation to the kitchen, where Warrick sat at the table, which had been set for four, and Seraphina was getting ready to prepare the plates for dinner. Seraphina looked up at her younger siblings. "Sit down. Dinner's ready, and I don't want to serve this cold. You know I hate re-heating things; it's never the same."

Eilish looked at Anya and responded with a slight shrug. Maybe Zavian had kept his mouth shut for once! The sisters took their place around the table as Seraphina served the vegetarian fare. Fina liked to take advantage of the fresh produce from the farmer's market during the summer. She tried to limit the amount of meat they ate, feeling that eating the meat of some dead animal would interfere with their powers. She'd always frowned on her sisters' love of pizza and its overly processed ingredients. Nature's bounty was the healthiest diet for any witch.

Eilish started eating right away, not believing her good fortune that it was possible Fina hadn't heard about Ian coming into the shop. "This tastes great, Fina."

Fina gave Warrick a quick glance and then responded, "Thank you, I'm glad to see you both home and eating a decent meal tonight." Picking up her glass, she sipped slowly at the iced tea laced with copious amounts of sugar. Her eyes peered over her glass at Anya. "Was the shop busy today?"

Anya looked up and laid her fork down. "Yes, Fina, the shop was busy. You should know that. It's tourist season."

Warrick cleared his throat. "Well, it seems as though you had more than tourists visiting the shop today." He looked at Anya, and she stared back. "If you mean Zavian, yes, he stopped in, but he wasn't there long."

Anya stared down at her plate and began eating more vigorously, hoping they weren't hinting at something, but her gut instinct told her they knew. Warrick turned his gaze to Eilish. "Zavian had quite the tale to tell me once he got home. Anything you wish to add to that, Eilish, like perhaps an unusual encounter?"

Eilish stopped eating and looked up at Warrick, deciding the best defense was a good offense. "As a matter of fact, Warrick, there is something I'd like to add. Perhaps you should spend more time schooling Zavian on his manners. We had a vampire in the shop today. It wasn't the first time, and I'm sure it won't be the last, as Fina can tell you. He was a curious customer, like all the tourists who wander in, and Zavian turned it into an international incident, practically throwing him out of the store. We've never had a problem with the vampires, at least not in all the years I've worked in the shop, and I sincerely hope Zavian's behavior today doesn't change that. He was rude and inconsiderate. The only good thing I can say is there weren't any humans in the store to see his completely uncalled-for behavior."

Warrick sat back in his chair and crossed his arms over his chest. Fina laid her hand on his arm. Warrick gave her a look, and she returned that look with one that communicated, 'Don't open your mouth.' Fina smiled at Eilish. "I know, dear sister, that Warrick will have a word with Zavian about his inappropriate behavior. But I must put in my two cents worth. If you gave Zavian even the least amount of attention, he wouldn't have been in the store, to begin with."

Anya tried not to laugh by biting her lip. "Zavian does tend to get in the way at times. He isn't meant for retail, if you get my drift."

Warrick shrugged off Fina's hand. "I will have a word with him, my goddess. I only wanted to get the girls' opinions on the incident. And let us say this matter is settled, shall we? But, I do agree that Eilish should be showing Zavian more attention. This playing hard to get is quite old, don't you think?"

Eilish sighed. "Who said I was playing?" She shook her head, knowing this would just lead to an argument of a different kind. "Okay, I get it. I'll spend some time with Zavian, but don't expect sparks to fly. I honestly don't see Zavian in my future. But I know what you expect, and I'll see him if it will calm things down. Just don't get your hopes up."

Anya could see that Eilish was trying to get everyone to shut up and move on. Standing, she said, "Well, I'm exhausted; I think I will take a shower and listen to some tunes in my room." As she walked off, Warrick and Fina watched her leave. Fina sighed. "Well, seeing him is better than ignoring him, Eilish. Go on up if you wish. Warrick will help me clean up this evening." Warrick smiled and nodded. "The things I do to please her."

Eilish pushed her plate aside and followed Anya. She could hear Warrick arguing with Fina about letting her off the hook too easily. She knew they'd managed a narrow escape this time. Now she just had to make sure there was no next time. It was time to call Ian.

BOHANNON

Eilish walked past Anya's bedroom and could tell her sister wanted to talk. She held her finger to her lips to indicate silence and mouthed the word, "Later." She could still hear the faint conversation from the kitchen. She looked at her sister and whispered, "Play some music." Anya nodded and pulled out an album from her massive vinyl collection. Eilish stood and watched until she heard The Temptations singing, "Papa Was a Rolling Stone." She gave Anya a thumbs up and went to her room, closing the door. Emric stood sentinel at the window, but Eilish smiled as he started to sing along to the music softly. He'd probably heard that song played a hundred times. She curled up on her bed, pulled her cell phone from her handbag, and hit dial, waiting for Ian to pick up.

Ian sat on the couch, restless and wondering why in hell he'd tempted fate earlier at Rhiannon's. He sipped the Midnight, but it didn't seem to help his mood. He'd pulled out his phone a thousand times today, determined to call her, but he couldn't do it. It was her move, and he sighed as he looked at the time on his phone again. He threw it on the table beside the couch and stood up, pacing, trying to calm himself; when his phone rang, he rushed to pick it up and saw Eilish's number. "Hello, my lovely enchantress, are you still talking to me, or is this the fuck-off call?"

Eilish chuckled, despite the seriousness of the situation. "We're still talking, but Ian... you can't ever do that again! Please, I love seeing you, but coming into the shop was a bad idea. Everyone in our coven pops in there from time to time, and I never know when Fina will show up, not to mention Warrick or Zavian. I was able to talk my way out of this one, but now I have to put in more time with Zavian to calm things down."

Ian sighed with relief that she hadn't gotten in trouble but wasn't happy to discover he'd forced her into more contact with Zavian. He hated that damn warlock. Every time he closed his eyes, he saw how his arm went around Eilish, claiming her. "Eilish, I'm sorry. I don't know what I was thinking. It was the wrong move, and I put you in a really bad situation. I don't like him; I don't like him around you. But I know we have to play this game. Forgive me, please. I overstepped, but damn, he fired me up. He thinks he owns you, and that got to me."

Eilish bit at her lip. She wished she had an easy solution to this problem. "Anya and I are going to talk with Wynter and Rain; they're sisters and members of our coven. We've known them our whole lives and used them as a cover for when we all got together last night. We'll have to tell them something and keep them in the loop so we can continue to use them in the future. We can't tell them the truth; we can't say we're seeing a vampire and a human. Even they wouldn't cover for that. We'll have to tell them we see warlocks from a different coven. They both already know I'm not happy about this situation with Zavian, so that won't be a hard sell. But in the meantime, you and Carter need a lower profile. Or better yet, an invisible profile."

Ian chuckled into the phone. "I'm good at being invisible. Listen, can you trust these sisters to help cover for you? I don't want you getting yourself into more than you can handle. I know you're strong, baby, but seriously, this situation scares me, asking people your older sister controls to lie and cover for you. But we have to be able to see each other somehow. I've been thinking about this. I think it is a good idea if we don't all see each other at the same time. We need to break this down, so there's no suspicion. It may help to have at least one of you at home while the other is out. " He sighed, "I'm not trying to tell you what to do, but I'm trying to find some solutions to see you."

Eilish nodded, even though he couldn't see her silent agreement. "No, I understand. It will need to be a combination. Sometimes just me, and sometimes just Anya, but to be honest, Anya and I do so much together; we must be careful of that too. We don't have to all four be together, but we will need to have nights where both of us leave the house together because that's our routine." Eilish sighed. "We stayed home a lot unless it was coven activity, so even this sudden social activity will draw attention, no matter how we do it."

Ian paced the floor. "Eilish, we can do this. Please don't let my stupid mistake make you think differently. I promise you; I'll be on my best behavior from this point forward." He was silent for a moment when Eilish didn't respond immediately. He took a deep breath and, in a softer tone, voiced the words. "Eilish, I love you."

She was silent on the other end. She wasn't expecting his declaration of love. She realized her feelings for him ran deeper than she'd let herself acknowledge because this all seemed so impossible. The truth was, she didn't want to love him because the barriers to being with him seemed insurmountable. It meant the destruction of everything she'd grown up with. She wiped away a tear on her cheek. "And may the Goddess Rhiannon help me, but I love you, Ian Cross."

BOHANNON

The sisters' grabbed a quick breakfast, only to be told by Fina that she was spending the day with Warrick again. No surprise there. They had come to expect her absence in running the shop. The girls left together, shouting their goodbyes to Fina as they left the house and started walking towards the shop. Eilish linked her arm around her sister's as they walked. "I talked to Ian last night and told him under no circumstances could he ever come in the shop again and to be sure to tell Carter. We dodged a bullet this time. I think we need to call Wynter and Rain and see if they can drop by the shop. I hate lying to them and making them a part of this, but we'll need someone to cover for us from time to time. We're going to have to split up. You see Carter one night when I stay home, and I'll do the same with Ian. But we will have to continue to go together sometimes, too."

Anya chuckled. "A plan, we have a plan? Better late than never; I guess. I like that idea, at least for now. I hope Ian and Carter understand how dangerous all this is, but to be honest, it's exciting!" They continued to walk, and Anya felt lighter on her feet as they got closer to the construction site. "I think Wynter and Rain will be okay with it, don't you? They aren't exactly fond of Fina and Warrick. But you'll have to do some fast-talking; they know you're supposed to be hooking up with Zavian."

Anya felt her heart beat faster as she saw Carter on the roof and Ian close by. Both had their shirts off, but she had major tunnel vision for her blonde bad boy. His skin glistened in the morning sun on his tanned, golden skin. She had it bad, really bad.

Carter looked up and saw them coming, an ear-to-ear grin on his face. Ian saw the grin and looked in the direction he was staring. "Bro, you need to keep that monster in your pants; play it cool. We are supposed to be invisible. So, chill out and let them walk by."

Carter laughed. "Dude, I can't make all this invisible." He made a grand gesture with his arm, sweeping from head to toe. "The ladies love what the ladies love. And don't tell me you don't know what I'm talking about. But I hear you. I can play it cool." He kept an eye on Anya as she approached the house and gave her a wink as they passed. Ian looked down at Eilish, waiting for her to acknowledge him. She turned her head slightly, making eye contact, their eyes communicating the unspoken words.

Anya smiled and kept walking, but she knew at least that Carter had been waiting for her. "This is so damn hard. I want to run up the ladder and kiss him. How is this ever going to work!" She looked over at Eilish. "Doesn't it just kill you to walk past them?"

Eilish nodded. "It does. And it's not going to get any easier." She tugged at Anya. "Come on. He saw you, and that will have to be enough for right now." It took all her willpower not to look back over her shoulder. She could feel Ian's eyes on her as they walked away. The sister's reached the shop and set up for the day. They had some early customers who were trying to get out before the sun got too hot. As soon as they had a lull in the tourist traffic, Eilish slipped her phone out of her handbag and called Wynter. The two sisters lived together and, like she and Anya, spent most of their time together. She asked if they could both pop in the shop sometime today. Wynter indicated that wouldn't be a problem because she wanted more details on what was happening. Eilish ended the call and let

Anya know they'd come by. "We have to tell them we see warlocks from another coven. That's it. No details. Understand?"

Anya stood with her hands on her hips. "Got it, warlocks from another coven. Madly in love with a blonde warlock who looks like some bronze god." She shuffled to the back room, yelling, "This should be interesting, Eilish." As the day progressed, there were spurts of customers, and then there would be a lull. Some came in just to get out of the heat, others were there to purchase, and others just browsed. Finally, the door opened with a jingle, and the two sisters walked in. Anya looked at Eilish and whispered, "This is your ballgame. I'll back you, whatever you say."

Wynter walked into the shop with her sister on her heels. She looked around at the familiar display. "Are you getting ready for Litha? It's almost summer solstice."

Eilish nodded. "Fina is already preparing. It should be a good ceremony." Rain ran her hand through the bins of crystals, creating a display of different colored sparks from her fingertips as each crystal generated different energy. "So, what's going on with you two? Wynter and I have been speculating ever since we got your text."

Eilish looked over at Anya and then dived in. "Okay, well, you know I'm promised to Zavian, right?" The two sisters nodded as Wynter spoke up. "Not a news flash, Eilish. The whole coven knows. What's going on?"

Eilish came from behind the counter. "Well then, it's probably no secret that I'm not crazy about the idea." Wynter shrugged. "There's some gossip. Some think you're just not ready, but you'll eventually bond. Especially the elders. They're counting on it."

Eilish shook her head. "I don't love him, and I don't think I'll ever love him." Rain flipped through some books on herbal healing as she responded, "You wouldn't be the first that had a loveless bonding. Besides..." She looked up from the book, "what are your options? We have more women in the coven than men, and most of the men are older."

Eilish nodded, "I know, and therein lies my problem. I sort of...we both sort of hooked up with a couple of warlocks from another coven. I'm not going to name any names because this will just create a shit storm. But the bottom line is, we're both going to keep seeing them. It may not lead to anything. It could just be an infatuation, but I'm not ready to tie myself to Zavian yet. So, what we need to know is, can we count on you to cover for us from time to time? We'll need to give Fina some believable excuses for why we're going out so much at night, and I want to know if we can count on you."

Rain looked at her sister as they silently communicated with each other, and Wynter nodded. Rain placed the book back on the shelf and turned her full attention to Eilish. "On one condition then." Eilish nodded, "Yeah, sure, just name it." Rain walked up to her and lifted a strand of her snow-white hair, letting it trickle through her fingers. "Since you obviously have no interest in Zavian, surely you won't mind if I move in." Eilish locked eyes with her. "Honestly, anything you can do to distract Zavian from me would be a blessing. Please, use all your witchy wiles to seduce him." Rain smiled. "Then we have a deal. Just make sure we know when we're supposed to be out with you, and we've got your backs."

Anya almost laughed out loud. Rain and Zavian, well, that should be interesting. "Well, that's all settled then." Once the sisters left, Anya looked at Eilish, and they started laughing. "Seriously, Rain likes Zavian. You got so lucky on that one! But at least we can get out more, and I think they'll back us, but I have to be honest here. I'd love to see Rain seduce Zavian!"

Eilish made a face. "Please don't put that image in my head." The bell over the door jingled, and another customer walked in as the two sisters shifted gears and returned to the business of running the shop.

It was almost time to close when the bell jingled over the shop door, and a human woman walked in with a small child, about five. She held the child's hand and looked about the shop nervously. Eilish wondered at first if they had wandered into the wrong store. "Can I help you find something?"

The woman bit her lip and walked to the counter, dragging the child with her. She whispered across the counter, her face twisted in torment. "I heard you were witches. Everyone says so. I heard one of you is a healer."

Eilish cast a glance at Anya. "Uh, no. We sell a lot of things that, uh, well, we believe in the power of certain crystals and herbs, but we're not witches."

The woman shook her head, close to tears. "You don't have to pretend with me. Everyone says you are witches, and my daughter..." She looked at the sickly child beside her. "You have to help me. You have to help her. Please, I'll pay you anything you ask."

Anya peered over the counter at the child, small for her age, her skin pale with dark circles under her eyes. Without touching her, she knew the child had some affliction with her blood. The witches saved their skills for use inside the coven and never exposed themselves by revealing their powers to humans, but the child pulled at her heartstrings.

Anya looked back at Eilish, her eyes reflecting her conflict, and spoke softly. "Maybe once?"

The woman spoke up, "Please... she's..." She looked at the child, grabbed a pen from the counter, and wrote across the back of the paper shopping bag. 'She's dying. Leukemia. The doctors said there was nothing left for them to do.'

Eilish bit at her lip and gripped Anya's hand. She turned to the woman at the counter. "Excuse us a minute." She led Anya to the store room in the back of the shop. "Anya, we can't help her. It's too dangerous! If you heal one human, the next thing you know, we'll have them lined up at the door!" Anya nodded, "I know, sis, but did you see her? I'm pretty sure I can help. I can't just let a child die when I know there's something I can do." Eilish paced back and forth, "Okay, but she has to understand; she can tell no one. Tell her if she reveals that you healed the child, you'll reverse it, and her child will die. If you don't make the consequences for spreading the fact that you're a healer dire, then she'd eventually talk. I know it's a lie, and it's extreme, but if you're intent on doing this, we have to protect ourselves."

Anya nodded, "Yeah, okay. I can agree to that."

The sisters returned to the shop where the woman stood waiting. "You'll help me? Please, tell me you'll help me."

Eilish looked her in the eye. "On one condition." She nodded eagerly, "Anything. I'll do anything." Eilish spoke firmly, holding her gaze. "You tell no one, you understand? My sister's healing spell can be withdrawn as easily as it is cast. Your daughter's health will revert to where it is now. There will be no second chance."

The woman broke into tears. "Yes, of course, yes. I promise you. I lost one child. I can't lose another."

Eilish went to the shop door and locked it, flipping the sign to read 'closed.' She turned off the lights and then guided the woman and the small child into the store room, where Anya had already started gathering the supplies she needed.

The woman pushed the small child forward as Anya laid out the altar cloth and lit three green candles. Anya looked up at the frail little girl and smiled. "My name is Anya. What's your name?" The little girl answered cautiously, "Ellie."

Anya took her small hands in hers and could feel her life force draining away. "We're going to make you better, Ellie, okay?" The little girl nodded as she spoke. "I don't want to be sick anymore. No more needles, please."

Anya shook her head. "No needles. Just stand in front of me, and hold your hands out to the side, palms up." The girl complied, wobbling a little as she regained her balance.

Anya kneeled on the floor, the altar between her and the little girl. As she began the ritual, she picked up the freshly cut stalk of an aloe vera plant, its sap oozing.

"Disorders to treat, ailments to cure. Healing magic, doth restore. Aloe vera, widely known." She placed the stalk of the aloe vera into one of Ellie's outstretched hands as she picked up an amazonite crystal and put it in the child's other hand. "Amazonite, a healing stone. Look deep within, sickness revealed."

Eilish stood with the mother as they watched the crystal glow in Anya's hand before placing it in the child's hand, and the air began to shimmer around the child.

Anya continued to chant. "Anoint with oil, healing sealed."

She dipped her thumb into a small basin filled with the oil of calendula and elderflower and marked a pentagram on the child's forehead. The oil glistened, and the pentagram cast a soft light in the room.

"Magic to mend as three candles burn. Illness now leave, for health to return." Anya observed the dark shadow above the girl's head, gathering in size before it drifted toward the ceiling.

"Gratefully, I accept the magic of the gods and goddesses for Ellie, for protection to assist in all that I do. Lend me the strength, build power in me. Assist my transcendence. So, mote it be."

Anya knelt in silence, her eyes closed, and felt the transference of energy from her to the child, and knew that she was healed. When she opened her eyes, the child's color had already started to improve, and the dark circles under her eyes were disappearing. She removed the items from the child's hands, then blew out the three candles.

She looked up at the mother, who stood with silent tears. "Take the crystal and the three candles. Take her home now and lay her in her bed. Place the crystal in her left hand, and let the candles burn for three hours."

The woman said, "That's it? That's all I need to do?" Anya nodded. "Her blood is cleansed. Let the candles burn as it drives out the last of the disease. Your daughter will be fine."

The woman broke into sobs, opened her purse, digging for her wallet. "How much do I owe you? I can go to the bank or write a check, whatever you want."

Anya shook her head. "Nothing. I want nothing. It is against our practice to take money for our gifts. Just remember your promise." The woman grabbed Anya in a hug, sobbing on her shoulder. "Thank you. How can I ever thank you?" Eilish answered, "You can thank us by keeping your promise. Exposing us could cost us our lives. It's one thing for people to speculate, quite another when they know the truth."

The woman nodded, wiping away her tears as she took the child's hand. "I feel better, mommy." The woman nodded as she led the child from the shop, and Eilish unlocked the door for them to leave. Anya shouted after her, "Remember, burn the candles for three hours, and have her hold the crystal..." The woman looked over her shoulder, "In her left hand. I won't forget."

After the woman left the store, the sisters stood in silence, as Eilish closed the door behind her. Eilish looked at her sister. "I couldn't let her die, Eilish." Eilish nodded. "I know, I understand, but this stays here. We tell no one, ever."

BOHANNON

Fina sat at the breakfast table, her hot tea steaming as she sipped. She looked across the table at her two sisters and watched Eilish pick at her food while Anya scarfed down her peanut butter on toast. "Eilish, I'll need you to go to Savannah today. Anya, you'll help me in the store." She watched as they both looked up at her. "We need honey from Bronwyn for the Litha ceremony; you can take the caddy. It's only about a 2-hour drive. You may encounter more traffic since it's Saturday, but you should have no problems. Bronwyn is expecting you. Can you handle that?"

Eilish knew Bronwyn well. She created unique wildflower honey that they used every year in the ceremony. Fina usually made the drive herself with Warrick, so she wasn't expecting this request. She immediately realized she'd have some free time away from her sisters and hoped that Ian could accompany her on such short notice. "Yeah, sure. I can do that." She cast a sideways glance at Anya, who appeared none too happy about being stuck in the shop with Fina all day.

Anya looked at her sister and felt jealous. She knew Eilish wouldn't waste this time, and she'd hook up with Ian somehow. Then she felt ashamed for feeling such things. Fina grinned. "Well,

I'm glad to hear it. I thought perhaps Zavian could go along, and keep you company."

Eilish looked up, pushing down the panic. "Please don't. It's been so hectic in the store; a long drive enjoying the silence will be relaxing and help me clear my head. You do realize I never have time to myself."

Fina stood up and set her teacup in the dishpan, contemplating Eilish's request. Against her better instincts, she gave in to her sibling's desire. "I suppose. But be careful. Now, make sure you get enough honey for us to make the ale for the ceremony. And don't rush, be polite and courteous to her. Now go before it becomes too late." She headed for the stairs. "Anya, be ready to leave in 15 minutes; it will be a madhouse today."

Anya grabbed Eilish's hand. "You lucky thing!"

Eilish gave her sister a quick kiss on the cheek. "I promise to finagle something for you and Carter to have some time alone. Now all I need is for Ian to be home!" Eilish picked up her breakfast dishes and quickly rinsed them off before placing them in the dishwasher. She usually just piled them in the sink, but she didn't want to do anything that might make Fina change her mind today. She returned to her room to grab a shawl to cover her arms in the air-conditioned car. She stood in her closet while she texted Ian. *Are you home today?*

Ian was still in bed, enjoying a day off, when he heard the ping on his cell phone and grabbed it from the bedside table, praying it wasn't their foreman deciding they could work today. He was pleasantly surprised to see it was Eilish. He looked at the time. She'd be getting ready to head into the shop. *Good morning my lovely enchantress.*

She smiled at his pet name for her. She was frequently referred to as a moon child because of her white hair and pale gray eyes. *Good morning. Please tell me you don't have plans for the day.*

Ian sat straight up in the bed as he responded to her text. *No plans. What do you have in mind?*

I have to drive to Savannah today to pick up some things for the Litha ceremony we'll hold on the summer solstice. Anya and Fina will be in the shop all day. Please tell me you can go with me.

Ian couldn't believe his luck. *Come to the house. You can park in the carriage house; then we can teleport to Savannah, saving us valuable time.*

Eilish was surprised. *You can do that? I mean, teleport to Savannah and carry me?*

Ian was moving around the room, grabbing some clean jeans and a nice shirt. *Yeah, sure, I have power too, you know. Just get here already. I miss you.*

Eilish grabbed her handbag and ran down the stairs, gathering some bottled water from the fridge. She shouted out to Fina, "Where are the keys?" She heard Seraphina answer, "In the flour jar." Eilish shook her head as she stuck her hand deep into the flour jar, fishing around until her fingers found the keys. She lifted the flour-coated keys from the jar and held them over the sink, turning on the tap and rinsing them off before drying them on a tea towel. She was muttering to herself, "Don't know why we can't hang them on a hook by the door like normal people." But then again, they weren't normal people.

She went out the back door, across the screened-in porch, and down the steps, walking across the courtyard to the garage. Like most of the old houses in Charleston, there were no attached garages. The old houses had a separate carriage house to keep their horses and a horse-drawn carriage. Eilish grabbed the handle on the carriage house door and pulled hard, hearing the rusted hinges creak as they resisted being opened. With a lot of effort, she got one door opened and then looked around to see if anyone was near. The rear of their property was enclosed and protected from the prying eyes of the tourists as well as their neighbors. She glanced at the upstairs windows of the houses on either side of them and didn't see anyone, so she used her magic to open the other door. With a flick of her wrist, the door opened easily. She climbed into the black caddy, drove the car out, and again willed the two doors to close. It was too hot out to be wrestling with uncooperative doors. She went the short distance to Beaufain Street and saw Ian standing on the porch, leaning against the tall porch post, his arms across his chest, his feet crossed at his ankles, waiting for her.

He walked up to the car, leaning down to greet her as she lowered the driver's side window. "Nice car. The carriage house is around the side. I'll follow you. The doors are already open; just drive in, but don't get out. I'll step inside, and maybe you could pull some magic and close the doors from the inside? We can teleport from inside the carriage house. No one will see you."

She nodded and followed his instructions, pulling the car into the carriage house. He leaned into the driver's side window and gave her a quick kiss before she looked over her shoulder and willed the doors to close behind them, leaving them in the dark. "Okay, the next move is yours."

He took her hand to help her out. "Nice piece of magic there, by the way." He winked and pulled her into his arms. "Close your eyes." He watched as her eyes closed and stood for a moment, staring at her and then kissing her. "Your kisses could shoot us to the moon. So, we're going to Savannah. Do you know the address? I'll need it, so we can find a safe place to touch down. I guess you'll be visiting someone, and I'll have to disappear for a while?"

She nodded as she opened her eyes. "Yes, I have to pick up some honey from a witch named Bronwyn. She lives in a house at the corner of Whitaker and Congress, near Johnson Square. Is that enough information? If you can land somewhere discreet, then I'll walk up to her house and tell her I had to park several streets away. Parking on the street is difficult anyway, so that will be believable. You can wait for me in Johnson Square. They have a lot of park benches. I'll make it as fast as possible, but she will want to talk. She'll ask about Anya and Fina and others in our coven. I'll rush it as much as I can."

He slid his hand along her cheek. "So, I'm assuming this Bronwyn knows you're driving down from Charleston, and that means you have two hours to get there. If you show up now, she might wonder how you got there so fast. Hmm, now what could a witch and a vampire get up to on a Saturday morning for two hours?"

Even in the darkened carriage house, she could see the mischievous twinkle in his eyes. "So, tell me, Ian Cross, do you have a double bed because your sofa was a little cramped."

Ian chuckled as he teleported her inside his house and led her to his bedroom. "For your information, it's a king-size bed and a very comfy one at that." He unbuttoned his shirt and threw it to the floor. Leaning his head down to her, he kissed her neck softly, taking in her scent. He could feel her heart beating rapidly as his tongue left a wet trail. "You are the temptress. Tell me, what's your pleasure this morning?" He continued to kiss and nibble at her ear.

Eilish closed her eyes and reveled in the sensation of his lips on her neck and ear. She felt the energy build in her crown chakra as she surrounded them in soft purple light. His lips found hers, and she returned his kiss, letting her tongue explore, tangling with his as her third eye chakra spun with energy, the light turning indigo. She broke the kiss to help him remove his jeans, watching as he kicked them aside, and she pulled the tank top off over her head. She had a slender build, and her breasts were small. She rarely bothered with a bra. He pulled her close against his chest as he bent his head to her, kissing her face and neck, bending her backward as he suckled each breast. The energy vortex from her throat chakra was activated, and the room was bathed in a soft blue glow. He was backing her up in the direction of his bed, his mouth still connected to her breast when she whispered. "My skirt."

He barely stopped what he was doing as he deftly helped her remove her skirt; just as her legs hit the edge of the bed, he backed her into a sitting position and climbed over her, easily pulling her across his bed. He kissed her again, and she let him lead as her heart chakra kicked in, and the light in the room turned green and sent out waves of energy, pulsing through the air. "I love you. Against every principle of nature, I love you, Ian."

Ian barely noticed the changing lights around them. Everything in his world spun out of control whenever he was with her. He heard her words, his fangs punched to their full length, and his eyes glared red against her white skin. His voice was almost a growl as his beast begged to play. "Show me, my enchantress." He slid inside her, and his beast howled with the energy that engulfed him. His body was inflamed with fire and sparks, and he felt her energy pull him closer. Her hands were entangled in his hair, and he plunged to her depths, slowly riding the building energy that was about to rip him apart. Grabbing her hands, he held them above her head and drove his cock harder. His beast went to her neck as he tried to push him down, but the beast now had control of the situation. He wanted all of her.

Eilish let him lead, pinning her hands down above her head. She could feel his strength, the muscles firm and hard. She gasped and threw her head back, feeling like there wasn't enough oxygen in the room. She felt her solar plexus chakra spin, lighting a fire inside her, as the room glowed a golden yellow. He rode her hard. There was a primal aspect to his lovemaking she'd never experienced. She was close to orgasm but wanted to push them both to the brink. Turning her head, her voice strangled, she whispered one simple word. "Feed."

Ian heard the words, and his beast let loose. His lips brushed the soft skin of her throat before he licked her neck. Inhaling her scent, he sank his fangs into her tender flesh as he continued to ride her. The blood rushed into his mouth, and he jerked from the powerful energy it contained. He swallowed and felt every drop as her energy rolled and wrapped itself through him. He felt her muscles tighten like a vice around his cock and drew yet another mouthful from her. His body felt like it wanted to rip apart. He threw back his head and screamed 'Eilish' as he came inside her. He felt her cum with him, and he held her close. His body was shaking, and he felt like he was ripping through time.

Eilish felt the sting of his fangs at her throat and the intense heat that sprang between her legs, sending her sacral chakra into overdrive as the room glowed a bright orange. She wrapped her legs around his hips as he pounded into her, and they both rode the wave of the orgasm. His beast was freed, and his eyes glowed red, but they were barely noticeable as the orange light turned red, her root chakra aligned, as her energy reached its full power. His feeding did not deplete her but empowered them both. She felt his body relax on top of her, his heart pounding, his skin damp with the sweat of the energy he exerted. She lay with her eyes closed, waiting for her breath to return to normal. She'd been prepared to show him a unique experience. She wasn't prepared for what he'd shown her.

Ian wasn't sure what just happened, but he knew one thing, someone should have told him a long time ago that being with witches was this fucking amazing. He could feel her breathing slow, and he rolled off her, pulling her on top of him. "I love you." He kissed each cheek softly, then her nose, forehead, and those beautiful soft lips. He felt a warmth and gentleness, a peacefulness he hadn't felt ever in his life. The world had stopped just for them. "My beast likes you very much, I might add."

Eilish smiled. "That was the beast? Look at how easily he was tamed. The beast will forever do my bidding now."

"With pleasure, I assure you."

BOHANNON

Eilish and Ian made use of every second of their extra 'drive time' before Eilish rolled out of bed and started getting dressed. "Come on, you. We need to get going. As much as I'd like to spend the day in bed with you, we must get to Savannah." She watched Ian slide across the bed, his dark tan looking even darker against the white of the sheets. He moved with the grace of a jungle cat, and Eilish wondered briefly how many women he'd brought back here. She tapped into her third eye chakra and realized the answer was none. He never risked exposing his lair. She smiled, glad to be his first at something at least. He dressed quickly as they prepared to teleport out.

"Hold on tight; it will be a bit longer than the carriage house trip." He laughed as she held him tight, and he lifted straight from inside the house. She'd given him the address, and he knew exactly where he would land. She felt so light in his arms, and he assumed it was the euphoria from their lovemaking still hanging in there. But before he even realized what was happening, they were in Savannah. Ian realized her blood had made changes within him; his strength and speed were almost double their normal. He landed them softly within a small alleyway between the houses about a block away. He shook his head about; damn, even that speed made his head spin a bit. "Are we safe here? I mean, we shouldn't run into anyone you know, right?"

Eilish felt a little light-headed as he set her down. She'd held on to him, unconsciously stroking the solid muscles in his biceps. "We probably won't run into anyone who knows me here. Bronwyn is from a different coven, but she's been a friend of the family for years. Fina worked a deal with her years ago for the honey. We make an ale for the summer solstice ceremony that includes the honey, and Bronwyn has the best honey in the Carolinas."

Eilish led him from the alley and onto Whitaker and pointed in the direction of the large grassy, tree-filled square filled with sidewalks and park benches. "If you don't mind, you can wait for me there. I'll try to be as quick as possible, but Bronwyn will expect a visit. Try not to attract too many girls while you're there."

Ian smiled. "There's only one witch I want. I have no use for humans except to feed, and I'm perfectly full right now. Go on. I'll wait for however long it takes." He began to walk toward the park, and a few feet along, he turned to see her still standing there staring at him. He grinned and then kept walking; yeah, she liked his ass.

Eilish blushed when he turned and looked back at her, and she knew she'd been caught red-handed. Ian could fill out a pair of jeans and looked good coming or going. He had a swagger that communicated absolute confidence and strength. It was a swagger that women would be drawn to, and men would cross the street to avoid. He was as different from Zavian as night was to day, and Eilish was enthralled with every aspect of him. She shook her head to clear it. "Get a grip, Eilish."

Heading down Whitaker to the intersection, she quickly found Bronwyn's house. Like the Bohannons, Bronwyn lived in the historic district and had to contend with tourists stopping to take photos of the unique architecture. She climbed the steps and used the old brass door knocker to announce her presence. It was only seconds before the door swung open, and Bronwyn had her in a tight hug. "I'm so happy to see you! Fina said she was sending you. Come in. I have some tea brewing. You can fill me in on the latest gossip from Charleston."

Eilish entered the cool, dark room; the heavy drapes closed to the hot sun. She spent an hour sipping tea and eating small tea cakes Bronwyn had made for the occasion. After chatting about all their mutual acquaintances, Eilish approached the reason for being here. "So, I hope you had a good yield of honey this season. You know Fina. She's a stickler for tradition. We must have the ale for Litha."

Bronwyn wiped delicately at her mouth with her napkin before standing. "Yes...a good year. Fina said she wanted ten jars. I threw in one extra for good measure. You must have quite the ceremony."

Eilish followed her into the kitchen. "I think Litha is Fina's favorite ceremony, and she likes the ale to be sweet to reflect the bounties of summer." Bronwyn carefully wrapped each jar in newspaper and gingerly placed the jars into a tote bag. "Do you need help carrying these to the car?"

Eilish shook her head as she pulled the money from her purse, laying the bills on the kitchen counter. "Oh, no need. Please, you've done enough." She slipped the heavy tote bag over her shoulder and gave Bronwyn a quick kiss on the cheek. "Thank you. I'll give your regards to Fina and Anya. And please, come see us soon. You know we have plenty of room."

Bronwyn smiled, sorry to see her company leave so soon. "Be careful on your drive home. I know that old Caddy of Fina's takes up half the highway." They both laughed as Eilish left, waving goodbye one last time from the front porch. As Bronwyn closed the door, Eilish walked down the steps and back in the direction of Johnson Square. She crossed the street and saw him sitting in the middle of a park bench, both arms extended across the back of the bench, his eyes closed and his face tipped back to the sun, his booted foot crossed over his knee. The women slowed down as they walked past, checking him out from head to toe. He gave no indication if he was aware of it, but Eilish knew Ian had never had to work too hard to attract his prey. She picked up her pace and slid beside him on the park bench as he lifted his head and looked back at her, giving her a smile that would melt butter.

Ian felt her presence as she approached. It was vibrant in him since taking her blood, and when he looked up, she took his breath away. Her hair was blowing slightly in the breeze, and she greeted him with a warm smile. He noted the large tote bag, weighted down with jars. "Wow, that's a lot of honey. I hope you had a good visit and Bronwyn wasn't suspicious. So, now we have the whole afternoon to do whatever you want. Anything come to mind?" The smile on his face had a touch of wickedness to it.

Eilish returned his devilish smile as she pulled one jar of honey from the bag and handed it to him. He easily twisted the top off the jar, and Eilish dipped her finger into the thick, golden concoction before inserting her finger into her mouth and withdrawing it slowly. "Lunch. But a witch needs an altar, something she can cover in honey. Any volunteers?"

Ian licked his lips and watched her finger slide slowly out of her mouth and a drop of honey clinging to her bottom lip. He took a chance and leaned in, licking her bottom lip. Whispering into her ear, "Vampires make a good altar, and you can torture us for a very long time." Ian knew this would be one of the best days of his life.

BOHANNON

44

Eilish maneuvered the large black car into the carriage house. She had spent the rest of the afternoon and evening at Ian's after they returned from Savannah, keeping an eye on the time. Ian had cleverly adjusted the odometer to reflect the round-trip mileage before she left, just in case Fina checked. She knew her sisters would be busy at the shop until it closed at eight. Still, she wanted to be home before they got there. She slid the tote bag filled with the jars of honey over her shoulder and carried them into the house through the back door. She carefully removed the jars from the bag and removed the newspaper wrapped around each jar. As she placed each jar on the counter, she noticed that the golden honey seemed to glow as if lit from the inside. She knew her body was surging with excess energy from the day spent making love with Ian. She shook her hands at her sides, knowing as she did so that she couldn't shake away the magic.

She thought maybe if she kept busy, she could burn off some of that energy. Fina, for sure, would notice it. She opened the fridge to find it well-stocked with fresh produce. If nothing else, Fina was an excellent cook. Eilish set about preparing a summer medley of zucchini, carrots, cauliflower, snap peas, and green, red, and gold bell peppers. She added butter and sprinkled in seasoning, wrapped it in foil, and set it to roast on the grill on the screened porch. She returned and set the table, adding an extra place just in case Warrick showed up. Checking the fridge, there were two pitchers filled with sweet tea. She heard her sisters as they came in the front door, Fina loudly criticizing Anya, and Eilish was glad she'd taken the time to fix dinner. She shouted out to them as she filled the glasses with ice, "Come on, I have dinner ready for you."

She went to the back porch to remove the vegetables, and as she re-entered the kitchen, she realized she was holding the steaming hot foil with her bare hands. She quickly placed the foiled vegetables on a platter as the steam escaped around the folded seams, just as her sisters entered the room. She looked at the palms of her hands which showed no evidence of being burned. They weren't even red. Anya called out, "Smells great!" Eilish picked up the oven mitts and carefully opened the foil before dumping the medley on the platter, realizing she'd narrowly missed being seen.

"I thought I'd fix dinner since Fina was in the shop all day."

Anya rolled her eyes and nodded to Eilish, letting her know Fina had been a pain in the ass all day. Fina grabbed a glass of sweet tea. "When did you arrive back? I thought you'd perhaps stop in the shop and give us a ride home. Tell me you got the honey from Bronwyn because if not, heads will roll." Fina sat down in her usual place at the table. "Well, this looks delicious, Eilish."

"Thank you, Fina. I doubt it's as good as your cooking." Eilish took her seat as her sisters scooped a heap of vegetables on their plates. "Bronwyn sends her love to both of you. I got the ten jars you asked for. She said the honey was exceptional this year. It should make a great ale for Litha; you may even be able to use some in the cakes." Eilish took the platter of vegetables as it was passed to her, and she filled her plate. She usually nibbled at her food, but her afternoon of lovemaking had generated an appetite, and she, too, filled her plate. "So, how was the shop?"

Anya stopped midway to her mouth with a fork of vegetables and cocked her head to the side. "Well, Zavian stopped in to help; always a treat." Her voice dripped with sarcasm, making sure her message meant the exact opposite. She watched as Eilish tried to stifle a giggle.

Fina spoke up. "You should be glad Zavian takes an interest in the shop and helps out. He will be bonded to your sister. It's important that he learns the business. We were busy, of course, with Litha; many of the coven were coming in for things. There's still a lot for us to do tonight. Stop chattering and eat. We'll be up most of the night preparing. Warrick and Zavian will be here later to help. I expect both of you to show them proper manners." She stared at Eilish to drive the point home.

Eilish sighed. "I'll be on my best behavior, which is more than I can say for Zavian." Eilish wondered if Rain had made good on her promise to move in on Zavian. She thought maybe Rain might need a little encouragement if she hadn't. Nothing like a little scandal to break up a bonding. Even Fina wouldn't be so forgiving of that. Eilish reached for the salt shaker, which flew across the table into her hand. She sat startled, not speaking, as Fina shouted. "You know I don't like you to use your magic un-necessarily! If you make it a habit, you will slip up in public!"

Eilish answered softly, "Sorry." The truth was, she'd made no attempt at magic. Her powers were operating with a will of their own. She made eye contact with Anya, who gave her a hard stare to reel it in. Eilish only wished she could. She quickly cleaned her plate and said, "I'll clear the table and clean up the kitchen. Why don't you get some rest, Fina? Maybe take a nice bath or something before Warrick comes."

Fina stared at Eilish. It wasn't like her to abuse her powers. Anya was a different story. But neither of them gave her much trouble about using their power without cause. Something strange was going on, and Fina had to keep a closer eye on Eilish. This day seemed to be steeped in odd things. As she stood up, she made a casual remark to see what response she'd get from Eilish. "You know,

Zavian made the strangest comment earlier today. He said he had taken Wynter and Rain out for an evening drive. Do you know anything about that?"

Eilish rinsed the plates at the sink, keeping her back turned. "I haven't talked to Zavian since the incident at the shop, and quite honestly, Fina, what he does in his spare time is of no interest to me. I think he should spend time with the other witches in our coven. If he likes Wynter or Rain, I think he should go for it. It would certainly get me off the hook, now wouldn't it?"

Fina walked up to her and spun her around. "Get you off the hook? Now you listen to me, Eilish, you *will* bond with Zavian, and there is no 'off the hook.' I don't wish to fight with you tonight; there's way too much to do, but hear me loud and clear; it *will* happen!" She spun on her heels and made an exit for the stairs. "When Warrick arrives, I want to know immediately. I think I'll take a bath after all."

Eilish wanted to throw a jar of honey at Fina's head, but she stood still, her hands fisted at her side. She knew her power was on overdrive and she dared not move right now. Anya looked at her with a frown. "Holy crap, Eilish! Turn down the volume! How Fina didn't pick up on your energy is beyond me. You must have electrified poor Ian. Is he still alive?"

Eilish took a deep breath, blowing it out slowly. "Ian's fine; he's better than fine. I let him feed from me."

Anya choked on her iced tea. "Are you kidding me? That didn't deplete you?" Eilish shook her head no. "Quite the opposite, for both of us. And I don't know how to turn it off. Let's just hope it doesn't last too long."

Anya stared at her with her mouth open. "You're pushing the limits here, Eilish. I mean, seriously. Did he go with you to Savannah?" She shook her head. "Never mind, I think I already know. Did he say anything about Carter?"

Eilish returned to rinsing the dishes in the sink before placing them in the dishwasher. "Uh... we didn't get around to talking about Carter. Sorry."

Anya sat at the table, her head in her hands. "What in hell are you going to do? You heard Fina. Nothing has changed as it relates to Zavian." Anya stood up and knew she needed to be by her sister's side no matter what. "I was just caught off-guard by how quickly things are moving. I only want you to be happy."

She looked at Anya. "I am happy. When I'm with him, I'm happy. I just can't figure out how to get away from Zavian."

Anya nodded and began to look at the list Fina had made for supplies. She was tired, but Eilish helped her, and before they knew it, they heard the front door open. Anya looked at Eilish. "Yippy, here comes Mr. Charm himself."

Warrick and Zavian walked into the kitchen. "Well, here are the Bohannon sisters preparing. Where is my lovely goddess?" Anya rolled her eyes. "Soaking her bones, the last time I heard from her." Warrick grinned and headed for the staircase. "No bother to warn her; I shall catch her off guard."

Zavian smiled and went to Eilish and hugged her. "I've missed you. I was hoping to see you at the shop once you got back from Bronwyn's. I hope you had a good trip. Miss me?"

Eilish shrugged free of his clutches. "Fina wanted me to visit with Bronwyn and not rush, so I did. Sounds like you've been pretty busy, though. You can't have missed me that much."

Zavian was beaming inside. Rain had been making some advances, and he'd fended her off, but he'd made sure Fina was aware, knowing that information would be shared with Eilish. Reaching out, he tipped her chin up with one finger and smiled. "If I weren't mistaken, I'd say you are jealous, Eilish Bohannon. Don't worry; I knew someone would eventually tell you I was with Rain and Wynter. It was nothing."

Eilish wiped her hands on the tea towel as she brushed past him. She looked over Anya's shoulder at the checklist of supplies and tasks to be completed before Litha. She spoke to Anya, "I'll gather the candles and make sure we have the fresh herbs. Fina likes to gather her supplies for baking the ceremonial cakes and making the ale, so leave that for her." She looked back at Zavian. "And you're mistaken. I'm not jealous. In fact, I'd encourage you to spend more time with the other witches in the coven. I think Rain has a crush. You should pursue it."

Zavian's temper flared. She was brushing him off as if he meant nothing to her. As Eilish stepped away to gather candles, he stepped in front of her and blocked her way. "Don't ignore me and brush me off as if I am nothing. You may be Bohannon, but I'm de Burke. We have an elevated station in the coven and standards to uphold. I don't appreciate Rain pursuing me, and neither should you!"

Anya spoke up. If Zavian only knew her sister could blow him off the Earth at this moment. "You know, Zavian, you aren't exactly on solid ground with Eilish. If you had even a pea size brain, I'd drop this and just step away." Zavian turned on Anya, his voice low and angry. "Stay out of this, Anya. This is between Eilish and me."

Eilish laughed. "You know we're a package deal, right? Do you think we'd be free of Anya if we were bonded? I'd never live without my sister. And Fina? Do you honestly think she'd give up control? Not to mention Warrick. There is no me and you, Zavian. There is an us...all of us. And it gets rather crowded if I do say so myself.

Anya sighed a breath of relief as Warrick and Fina walked back into the kitchen. Warrick looked at Eilish and Zavian. "Lovers tiff?"

Zavian ground his teeth and looked at his uncle. "Nothing of the sort, but it *is* rather crowded in here; I think I'll take a walk." He stormed out of the room, brushing shoulders with his uncle. Fina raised her head slightly. "Well, whatever *that* was, I hope it's nothing I should be concerned about." Warrick laughed and put his arm around Fina. "I do believe just some sexual tension, my dear. Young love always has its ups and downs." Anya couldn't help herself and burst out laughing.

Warrick looked at her with scorn. "I'm glad you're so amused,

Anya. But perhaps you should be putting in a little more effort to find your own beau. You're not getting any younger."

Anya grinned, "You got another nephew, Warrick? Don't worry; when my beau shows up, I'll know." She looked at Eilish and grinned. Fina shook her head. "Enough of this. Let's get these things prepared. I don't want to be working the entire night."

BOHANNON

What had started as a great day ended in a very tense evening. After going through the checklist of items needed for Litha, Anya and Eilish escaped to Eilish's bedroom, leaving Warrick and Seraphina in the kitchen. Eilish climbed on her bed as the cat jumped up beside her. Anya quietly closed the door behind her before crawling onto the foot of the bed. "Tell me everything."

Eilish gave her a condensed retelling of her day with Ian and watched as Anya's face reflected both happiness and longing. "The strangest thing, though. I invited him to feed, and I knew my blood would enhance his strength, just as Henwen said, but it also enhanced mine. Or maybe it was just the sex...I don't know. I know my energy is at a peak, and I have little control. I have to consciously hold back. And then I come home to Zavian, with his nose out of joint. I don't know how I can sustain this."

"I can't imagine what feeding must feel like, but you don't seem worse for wear." Anya stroked Luna and sighed. "Sustaining this is something we'll figure out as we go, sister, because you're in pretty deep now with Ian. I can tell by your face when you talk about him. You're in love, and it sounds like Ian is too." Anya stood up and paced the room as Luna wrapped around her ankles as she walked. "The hard part is figuring out how to hook up with them and remain undercover. It's great that Wynter and Rain are covering for us, but that can't be our cover all the time."

Eilish nodded. "I know. This is going to be a lot harder than I thought. We didn't go out very often unless it was to the shop, or for the coven. Coming up with believable excuses is going to be hard."

Anya flopped back down on the bed. "I envy you so much. I know it's wrong, and I should be happy that you're happy. But I'm envious of the time you spent with Ian, alone and without worries about who might see you, and all that crap. The way Ian looks at you is amazing. You're lucky; Ian can shadow and teleport and take you places where no one can see you. All Carter can do is fall off the roof, and then I have to save him!"

Eilish smiled at her sister's joke, but she knew Anya was aching for a way to spend time with Carter, too. "I have an idea. The guys get off work early. They usually start working around seven in the morning to beat the heat and knock off around three. Why not have him pick you up after he gets off from work? I can cover for you in the shop. Just make sure you're back before eight, so we can walk home together."

Anya grabbed her and hugged her, both of them almost rolling off the bed. "Oh, Eilish, thank you! I'm going to text him right now, so he's prepared. I promise to be back at the shop by eight! Besides, we should get some sleep; I'm sure you're tired." She giggled as she punched her sister softly on the arm.

Eilish smiled as her sister left the room. The truth was, she had enough energy to light up all of Charleston. She doubted she'd sleep much at all.

BOHANNON

Carter and Ian had been hard at it all morning, the girls had walked past in the morning heat on the way to the shop, and Carter smiled at Anya. He didn't attempt any contact. He'd told Ian the plan and joked about getting a booty call last night. Carter was off like a flash the moment quitting time arrived and headed home to shower and clean up. He'd packed a large cooler full of beer and picked up some cheese and fruit. He was trying like hell to put some effort into this afternoon date and be romantic. He grabbed a couple of blankets, took the pillows from his bed, and stashed everything in the truck bed before heading for Rhiannon's. Anya had been very specific about where he should park and not to get out of the truck when he arrived. That was too risky. He parked where she'd told him and texted her that he was there. He'd been waiting for what seemed like a lifetime to be alone with her again.

Anya had been watching the clock the entire day. It felt like the longest day of her life. The store was slow at first and then picked up with customers that had kept her preoccupied. She was finishing up with several ladies interested in some of the jewelry when her phone gave out its soft ping. She stepped back from the customers and read the text that Carter was waiting for her. "Excuse me one moment, ladies." She slipped behind the counter where Eilish was sitting on the stool. "Eilish, it's Carter; he's here. Do I look okay? Thank you again for doing this. I'll be back at eight and help close up."

Eilish quickly stepped in, moving to help the ladies with their jewelry selection. "Go. You look great. Have a good time!"

Anya wasted no time. Running out the door, she quickly looked up and down the street to make sure no one from the coven was around, then started walking toward the parking lot a block away. She had to contain her excitement and tried not to hurry, so it looked inconspicuous. She spotted the truck and casually walked toward it, and jumped in. "Hey, bad boy, looks like you found me without a problem. Are we going back to your place?"

He gave her a wicked grin and a wink. "Now, darlin', do I look like the kind of guy who can't think of a place to take his girl?" He leaned over and kissed her, feeling the electric jolt of her kiss. She got settled in her seat, and he started the engine, heading the truck away from the city and crossing the bridge over the Ashley River towards the intercoastal waterway. He cranked up the radio as "Fancy Like" by Walker Hayes blared loudly inside the cab of the truck, and Carter sang along. Anya laughed, holding her hands over her ears, "Country, I should have known!" Carter just laughed and sang louder. He drove a few miles before he turned off the two-lane highway onto an unmarked dirt road. "Hang on; it's a bumpy ride." Anya squealed as the truck bounced over the uneven road, and she held on to the dashboard. Carter found a grove of trees near the waterway and parked the truck, leaving the radio playing. "Here we are. It may not be paradise, but it will do until paradise comes along. Come on. I got some blankets in the flatbed and a cooler full of beer."

Anya was delighted, to say the least. Alone, at last, with her Carter. "Well, I'm impressed. Anywhere is paradise if you're here. And a cold beer sounds awesome!" Anya rolled out of the truck and looked up at the sky and trees. It was peaceful here, and they were definitely all alone. "So, how did you find this place? And how many times have you brought girls here with a cooler full of beer?"

Carter laughed. "Well, to be honest, I used to come here late at night with my buddies when I was still in high school. We'd come out here to drink before we were legal. I hadn't thought about this place in years, but I remembered it was secluded, and we'll have some shade. So, you're the first girl I've brought here. Don't tell on me, now. I'm breaking the bro-code." Carter climbed down from the truck and walked around back, dropping the tailgate. "Come on, let me lift you up. The grass is too tall for us to spread a blanket, and there are too many grasshoppers. I made a soft place for us in the truck bed." Carter grabbed her around the waist and easily lifted her into the back of the truck before climbing in behind her. He opened the cooler and lifted two cans of beer from the ice. He popped both tabs and handed one can to her, holding his can up for a toast. "To us, Anya Bohannon. It's official now. Drinkin' with a good ole boy in the back of his truck with country music on the radio. It don't get more romantic than that." He chuckled.

Anya laughed and clunked her beer can against his. "Well, I suppose I should feel honored, and now I'm in the good ole boy's club." She sipped her beer and kept casting glances in his direction as he chugged his beer. "I've missed you so much. I didn't know how we'd manage to see each other. Thanks to Eilish for covering for me today. This is a strange way to conduct a relationship, always having to sneak around." Anya took a long sip of the beer and laid back on the blankets, staring at the trees.

Carter stretched out beside her, taking her hand in his and looking up through the branches of the trees. There was a soft breeze coming off the water. "I'd take you to one of those fancy restaurants in town if I could. I know this has to be secret, but I can't help wanting everyone to know you're my girl."

Anya smiled. "I know you would. Maybe someday we can do that. But I want you to be safe. If anything happened to you, I couldn't bear it. But I love the idea of being your girl." Anya rolled on her side and snuggled up close, kissing him. "And you're my good ole boy."

He brushed her unruly hair from her face and removed her sunglasses before kissing her again. "You got that right, darlin."

Making love in the back of the pick-up truck while Little Big Town serenaded them with "Girl Crush" wasn't easy, but it sure was interesting.

BOHANNON

The Bohannon house was hectic as everyone was gathering the supplies for Litha. Seraphina was in her element, issuing orders like a drill sergeant. "Warrick, did the warlocks get the sacred oak for the bonfire? I don't want to have to interrupt the energy of the ceremony to deal with building a proper bonfire." Warrick took her constant queries in stride. "I promise you, my goddess, the oak logs were cut and aged months ago in preparation for this day. They have been carefully stacked with plenty of kindling. You won't be disappointed."

Typically, Litha is celebrated mid-day, at the actual time the sun enters Cancer, heralding the beginning of the summer solstice, but the coven had to shift their celebration to the late-night hours to avoid scrutiny from the humans.

For years, the coven had made the pilgrimage to Bulls Island, an uninhabited barrier island off the coast of South Carolina, to celebrate Litha and escape notice.

Seraphina had used Bronwyn's honey in the preparation of her ceremonial cakes and in the mead that would be served at the conclusion of their rituals. Both had been carefully packed and loaded into Warrick's van. She hurried from one sister to the next, double-checking their list, making sure everything was in order. "Eilish, you will conduct the ceremony this year."

Eilish looked up, surprised. "What?" Seraphina nodded. "You will lead the basic ceremony; I will enter near the end after the bonfire is set. I'll bring forth Beckett and Esca. Esca is ripe with child, and we must celebrate the fertility of the summer solstice and bestow the coven's blessings on this newest member of our coven. It's important that the entire coven sees the power of our fertility ritual from Ostara."

Eilish smiled, "You mean *your* power." Seraphina gave her a hard stare. "Don't get cheeky with me. Of course, it was my power. But it never hurts to remind the coven why I'm the High Priestess, now does it? Besides, you need to start taking a more active role. Involve Zavian more. Let the coven see how you work together and how your power can be enhanced through a bonding."

Eilish frowned. "I've never been with Zavian, and you know it." She had been with Ian, though, and she knew her energy was still being held at bay. She'd have to work hard to control that tonight if she was going to lead the ceremony.

"Just do as I ask for once, and don't argue. Anya? Have you packed everything?

Anya held up her list for the fifth time, the exasperation clear in her voice. "Yes. How many times do I have to tell you?"

Seraphina made one more sweep through the house before herding them all into the van. "Your gowns?" The sisters answered in unison, "Yes, Fina!" Eilish shook her head as Zavian climbed in the van next to her, and Fina issued instructions to Warrick. Eilish leaned over the front seat. "Drive, Warrick, before Fina makes us all crazy." Warrick was glad to get moving. Seraphina would calm down once things were set in motion. She usually used the drive time to meditate and center herself. He reached over and gave her thigh a squeeze. "It will go off without a hitch; it always does, my goddess. Settle yourself now; find your center."

Seraphina nodded as she looked over her shoulder at Eilish. "You too. Since you're going to lead the ritual, you need to focus your energy."

Eilish nodded in silence. She had been fighting to hold her energy at bay ever since having sex with Ian and allowing him to feed from her. She cast a sideways glance at Anya. She could feel her sister's power as well. Carter was human and wouldn't be able to increase Anya's power, but the very act of having sex would open the sacred feminine in her and allow her to use her energy with more focus. Anya looked back at her and smiled. Zavian wasn't unaware of the feminine energy in the van that emanated from all three women. He knew this would be a powerful Litha.

As they arrived at Bull Island at dusk, much of the coven was already gathered. Some were walking along the shoreline, getting their feet wet in the surf, while others were stretched out on beach towels, enjoying the wind off the water. As Warrick's van came into view, the coven members scrambled back to their cars so the women could change into their white, gossamer gowns and the men could don their black robes.

The men had worked with Warrick the day before to stack the wood for the bonfire. Oak was always used for Litha and dated back to the time of the Druids. Oak symbolized the doorway crossing the threshold into the second, waning part of the year. The wood had been stacked high and would burn brightly at the end of the ritual when each member of the coven would be asked to come forward and lend their torch to the fire. Warrick and Zavian stepped out of the van to undress and slip the black, hooded robes over their heads. They left the women in the van to disrobe in privacy. Seraphina tossed her clothing in the tote bag as she pulled the sheer gossamer gown over her head. Anya and Eilish were in the back, doing the same, when Seraphina called out, "The halo garlands! We forgot them!"

Anya sighed and shook her head as she handed her older sister the garland made of oak leaves and sunflowers. "You'd think this was the first time we'd done this. Chill out, Fina." Seraphina took the garland and placed it on her head. "You know I just want everything to be perfect." She stepped out of the van, standing next to Warrick as she inspected the wood stacked for the bonfire from afar. "That looks quite impressive."

Warrick smiled at her. "You expected less? Take a deep breath, my goddess. Everything will go off without a hitch. It always does."

Anya handed Eilish her garland, and the two sisters placed it on their heads, helping each other to center it correctly. Anya noticed her sister biting her lip. "Are you okay? You're not nervous about the ritual, are you? You know it backward and forwards."

Eilish shook her head. "It's not that. My energy..." Anya took both her hands in hers. "Just channel it. Let it work for you. You know the coven feeds off the power of the ritual. Besides, everyone knows your power is equal to Fina's already." Eilish nodded. She wasn't worried about her power being equal. They hadn't even started the ritual yet, calling on the energies that ruled the universe, and she already felt like she could raise an army of the dead. She answered nervously, "Yeah, okay."

The two sisters emerged from the van as the two men gathered the supplies for the ritual, and the women carried the baskets filled with ceremonial cakes and ale as they all walked together. The rest of the coven, having changed into gowns and robes, followed, forming a circle around the bonfire. They had each brought a torch they would later light to ignite the bonfire. They laid the torch at their feet.

Zavian pulled the cloth pouch from the box of ritual supplies and started making the rounds, his hood pulled over his head, shadowing his eyes. He held the pouch open as he approached each member, asking the coven to toss in herbs that represented their troubles, problems, pains, and sorrows. He then returned to the center of the circle, placing the pouch near the altar that Warrick had set up. Seraphina had placed a cauldron in front of the altar, with a red candle to the right and a green candle to the left. Warrick placed the container of fresh spring water near the cauldron. Seraphina sought out Beckett and Esca and went over to them to let them know they would be called upon near the end of the ritual, so the coven could bless the new life that grew inside Esca's rounded belly.

Anya placed the yellow cloth over the altar, and covered it with sunflowers and oak leaves, then looked to Seraphina for direction. "Do you want me to sweep, or will you do that?" Seraphina stepped forward. "I'll do it." She took the broom, and the others stepped back, joining the circle formed by the coven. She swept the area, starting in the North to cleanse the circle, sweeping away any negative energies.

"Sweep out evil, sweep out ill, where I do the lady's will. Besom, besom, lady's broom, sweep out darkness, sweep out doom. Witch's broom, swift in flight, cast out darkness, bring in light. Earth be hallow, air be pure, fire burn bright, as water cures. A sacred bridge this site shall be, as I will, so mote it be."

Warrick then placed the Quarter candles at points North, East, South, and West. Inviting in the energies of the natural world. The warlocks began their low drone, a deep baritone sound that vibrated with male energy. Seraphina gave Eilish a nod, letting her know she should take over now as she and Warrick joined the circle. Eilish stepped forward in her sheer, thin gown to begin the ritual. She laid her garland by the altar as she prepared for the ritual bath. There was a slight murmur from the coven, as this was something Seraphina usually did.

The circle parted as Eilish made her way toward the ocean, walking into the surf to cleanse her body. The ocean was calm tonight, but the surf picked up slightly as her foot touched the water. With each step, the ocean became more turbulent as she walked chest-deep into the ocean. The coven felt the soft breeze from the water turn into a more forceful wind as strong as a Nor'easter. They had to stand their ground against the force of the wind as it whipped at their hair and sent their gowns swirling. They watched with some concern as the waves grew in intensity until the ocean rose up and crashed over Eilish's head, and she momentarily disappeared from view. When the waves retreated, Eilish turned, facing the coven, and slowly walked back to shore, the thin gown clinging to her nude body. The ocean immediately calmed as she stepped back on the sand, and the winds died down. The drone of the warlocks had been temporarily interrupted as the coven was taken aback by the ocean's response to Eilish's power. Eilish felt her power build and knew there would be no controlling it. She returned to the altar, replaced the garland on her head, picked up her wand, and faced South. The drone of the warlocks resumed and grew louder.

Warrick glanced at Zavain, who stood next to him in the circle of warlocks. Had they bonded? He had never seen Seraphina have the power to control the force of the ocean. Zavian looked back at him with a frown and gave a silent shrug. Warrick re-focused his attention on Eilish. He and Fina knew that Eilish had never really tapped into her full potential, so perhaps that was what he was witnessing tonight. She'd never been asked to lead a ritual before. As she held her arms above her head, she spoke softly, but her words were carried on the wind. "I celebrate the Summer with this rite held in honor of the Blazing God of the Sun. All nature vibrates with the fertile energies of the Goddess and the God. As the Lord of the Sun blazes above, the fires of our celebration shall flame below."

Eilish simply looked at the green candle to the left of the cauldron as it flickered to life, the flame rising high before settling, and a soft murmur could be heard through the circle and another slight hesitation from the constant drone from the warlocks. Seraphina knew Eilish could light a candle without a match, but she usually touched her finger to the candle to do so, as Seraphina did. She kept her face neutral as some of the coven cast a glance in her direction.

Eilish continued with the ritual. "Oh, Green Forest Mother, Meadow Mother, great One of the Stars and Moon, Spinner of Fates, I give honor to you, and ask your Blessings here."

Eilish turned slightly, facing the red candle as the wick sparked and snapped before the flame rose up. She took a deep breath, trying to calm her energy. "Oh, Great Red Sun God, Forest Father, God of

Fertility and Plenty, be here with me now. I give honor to you, and ask your blessings here."

Eilish knelt before the altar and lifted the container of spring water, pouring it into the cauldron. The water swirled inside the cauldron and seemed to glow as if lit from within. She lifted the cloth pouch that Zavian had used to collect the herbs from the coven, representing all their collective woes, and held it above her head. "Oh, fiery Sun, burn away the un-useful, the hurtful, the troublesome, the painful, the sickness, and ill luck. PURIFY ME!"

Usually, the High Priestess would hold the cloth pouch over the altar candle to light it afire, but the pouch spontaneously burst into flames as Eilish opened her hands and let it drop into the cauldron of water. There was a collective gasp from the coven as they took in the power of the young priestess. Eilish called out as the pouch smoldered and burned in the churning water, which seemed to be coming to a boil.

"By the powers of the Great Goddess and the Great God, by the powers of the Great Spirit of All That Is, by the powers of Earth, Air, Fire, and Water, and by the powers of the Sun, Moon, and Stars...I BANISH THESE BANES FROM OUR LIVES!" The cauldron boiled over, the steam rising, even though there was no source of heat under the cauldron, and the coven looked nervously from one to the other.

Eilish stood and raised both arms to the sky with the wand in hand. Her eyes were closed, and she seemed oblivious to the reaction of those around her. She was centered now, her chakras aligned, and she had given herself over to the energies of nature, serving as a vessel to channel the powers of all the gods and goddesses she had called upon. "As the Phoenix rises from the ashes, so let this water be pure and new, for this is the sacred cauldron of the Mother Goddess. Bless this water, so that its touch may bless and renew, even as the midsummer sun nourishes and blesses all life."

The wind picked up again with a sudden fierceness as the waves started crashing on the beach, moving closer to the coven. The witches and warlocks stepped back cautiously, trying to maintain their circle. The warlocks grabbed at their hoods as the wind whipped them back from their head. Seraphina whispered under her breath, "Eilish," but knew her youngest sister couldn't hear her, even if she had shouted her name. She had entered a trancelike state and would be oblivious to those around her. Seraphina's heart was pounding in her chest. She had always known Eilish's powers were greater than her own, but this was something more. She knew Eilish had had sex with someone else who had power, and she was drawing on the power of the sacred feminine. She'd have known if the bond had been consummated with Zavian. That would be news Warrick would have rushed to tell her. Besides, Zavian's power was weak. There was no way Eilish was channeling her power through Zavian.

Eilish passed her hands over the boiling cauldron and the two candles as the water boiled over, spilling onto the sand, and the flames on the candles rose almost to the level of her hands. She called on luck, health, fertility, and prosperity for the coven. She knelt before the altar and removed a pinch of salt from the shallow bowl, placing it on her tongue. At that moment, she had a vision of Rhiannon, the Celtic Moon Goddess, draped in gold and riding a pale horse. Rhiannon spoke to her. "You are the blood of my blood, bone of my bone. You alone inherited my power. Show them. Show them all." Eilish saw her connection to Rhiannon in a flash, reaching back through time, from one generation to the next.

Henwen's words came back to her, and she realized this was about more than a book. Eilish knew in an instant she was the designated descendent of Rhiannon. She stood, her hands lifted skyward, feeling her full power, and spoke words the coven had not heard before. "I, Eilish Bohannon, daughter of Rhiannon, and the names of all my ancestors, rededicate myself to the Goddess and God who together form the Great Spirit, the All-That-Is, whose combined power is strong and vital. I give my word to follow the ancient paths that lead to true wisdom and knowledge. I will serve the Great

Goddess and give reverence to the Great God. I am a Wiccan, a stone of the ancient circle, standing firmly balanced upon the Earth, yet open to the winds of the heavens, and enduring through time."

The winds blew around them with a new fierceness, and storm clouds blacked out the full moon. The waves continued to pound the beach. Warrick grabbed Fina's wrist. "Stop her." Seraphina shook her head no. "It's too late."

Anya watched in awe as her sister's power was unleashed and whispered under her breath, "Fuck, yeah." Eilish turned to face the North, where the flames on the candles remained lit despite the winds but flickered wildly. "Behold, oh powers of Earth, Spirits of the North. I, the daughter of Rhiannon, rededicate this coven to the Lady of the Moon and the Lord of the Sun." She turned East, South, and West, repeating the same incantation with each turn.

Warrick leaned close to Seraphina again. "Why is she calling herself the daughter of Rhiannon?" Seraphina gave him a cold stare, not pleased to reveal the secret and even less pleased that Eilish had discovered it. "Because she is. We all are, but Eilish holds the seat of her power. My mother told me. I thought I would lead the coven, but she said no, it was Eilish. Eilish held the power and would be prepared to lead the coven." She stared hard at Warrick. "You know I couldn't let that happen." Warrick didn't know what stunned him more, to learn the source of the Bohannon's power after all this time or the raw display of energy coming from Eilish.

Seraphina pushed Warrick forward, "Go. Now. You and Zavian. You know what to do." The two warlocks locked eyes, not quite sure they wanted to enter the vortex of energy the young witch had created, but they had a role to play. Seraphina cast a cold glance in Anya's direction, but she was held spellbound by her sister's performance. They would both have some explaining to do when this ceremony was over.

Warrick and Zavian slowly approached Eilish and stood on either side of her. Eilish seemed only remotely aware of their presence. Warrick bent down and dipped his forefinger into the water of the sacred cauldron as Eilish tilted her head back, her hair and gossamer gown had been blown dry by the wind. He marked her forehead with a pentagram as Eilish spoke, "Let my mind be open to the truth."

Zavian dipped his forefinger into the water, then touched his finger to the lips he'd wanted to kiss. Eilish responded. "Let my lips speak the truth, except that they may be silent among the unbelievers where there may be harm." Warrick dipped his finger again and anointed her chest over her left breast with a crescent moon. Eilish spoke softly, "Let my heart seek the ways of the Goddess always." The winds settled back to a gentle breeze, the waters calmed, and the coven seemed to release a collective sigh of the tension they had been holding.

Eilish extended both arms to her side, and Zavian and Warrick bent over to wet their forefinger again and simultaneously marked her palms with a pentagram. Eilish responded, "Let my hands be gifted to work in magical ways." Zavian and Warrick exchanged glances, wondering just how much power was in those hands. They both knelt at her feet, dipping their forefingers one last time into the cauldron, as Eilish lifted one foot, then the other, as they drew a pentagram on the soles of her feet. She spoke as they finished. "Let my feet ever walk upon the sacred paths."

As that portion of the ceremony was completed, Seraphina nodded at Anya, and together they grabbed up the baskets of the ceremonial cakes and the small, sealed containers of ale. They each walked around the circle until every member of the coven had been served, then they each partook of a serving themselves. Warrick and Zavian returned from the sacred circle, ate the cake, and drank the ale before returning to the center to take the offering to Eilish. Eilish took a single bite from the ceremonial cake and drank the mead as the coven felt the earthquake slightly under their feet.

Eilish started walking in the direction of the stacked oak, and the members of the coven, picking up their torches, reluctantly began to follow. Seraphina joined Warrick at the altar, with Anya on her heels. He turned to her. "I usually start the bonfire. What is she doing?"

Seraphina answered him with annoyance. "I know as much as you do. Don't make a scene. The coven is already on edge. Follow behind her. I'm sure she'll give way to you."

Warrick picked up his torch and used one of the altar candles to light it. His torch had been dipped in kerosene, so it lit quickly with a loud whooshing sound. The coven had gathered in a circle around the stacked oak as one warlock lit his torch and then tipped his torch to his neighbor until every witch and warlock held a glowing torch in their hand. Eilish continued to walk in the direction of the oak logs, piled high, in the shape of a teepee taller than her, allowing the air to move up freely through the wood. She heard footsteps behind her and turned to see Warrick approaching with his torch. She held up her hand, and he was stopped in his tracks by an invisible force field, and the flame on his torch burned out, the smoke blowing in the wind. Seraphina grabbed Anya by the arm, "What's happening?" Anya smiled, amused by the events of the evening. "Don't look at me."

The coven grew nervous, looking at both Seraphina and Warrick for direction. Eilish returned her attention to the stacked oak and raised her arms to the sky. "I, daughter of Rhiannon, Goddess of the Moon, call on The Triple Goddess, the Maiden, the Mother, the Crone, and the Goddess of the Sun! Let my hands bring forth the fire of the midsummer sun!"

The coven watched in awe as the logs began to smolder, smoke arising from the top of the stacked wood, and the logs at the bottom started to burn, igniting those stacked on top. In seconds the bonfire was fully ablaze, lighting up the beach. The coven fed off the energy of the young witch's power and began to dance wildly around the bonfire, to sing and chant incantations, waving the torches in the air. Anya joined in, spinning in jubilation, feeling the heat from the massive bonfire. Seraphina stepped back, as did Warrick and Zavian, dumbfounded by Eilish's power. The fire burned brighter, reaching new heights as the coven danced wildly. Eilish stood still, silhouetted against the flames, her arms raised to the sky.

After what seemed like an hour, she slowly lowered her arms, and the flames dissipated as she did so. By the time her arms were at her side, the fires had died out, and only smoke and embers remained, carried on the wind. Eilish seemed to come out of her trance as she turned slowly to see the members of their coven staring at her in stunned disbelief.

Seraphina grabbed Warrick's arm, "Quick, close the circle. Now!" Warrick looked at her, "But Esca and Beckett?" Seraphina pushed him. "Now! Do it now!"

Warrick returned to the altar to release the Guardians of the Four Quarters, ending with "Depart in peace, and blessed be." The coven shouted out, "Blessed be!" Seraphina started to enter the sacred circle when Eilish appeared at her side, lifting her wand. "Circle round, now be unbound. I now dissolve this sacred space and send all powers back to place."

The coven felt the wind sweep through their circle and looked skyward. Eilish continued, "Circle round, now be unbound. Stay if you can. Go if you must, with love and perfect trust. My work is finished for the night, and now I end my magic rite." The flames on each candle flickered and went out, as did the flames on every witch's torch. The air was perfectly still and silent, the only sound the soft lapping of the waves against the surf. It felt like all the air had been let out of the balloon. The coven stood silent, wondering what they had just witnessed. They looked to Seraphina, who waved her hands and said, "Clear this away now. Pack up before we draw attention."

The coven looked back at Eilish, who stood by the dying embers of the bonfire, her hair glowing softly in the full moon that had emerged from behind the clouds and her eyes glowing with a soft gray light. No one from the coven felt brave enough to approach her. Wynter and Rain exchanged glances. Eilish and Anya had said they saw warlocks from another coven, and whoever Eilish had hooked up with was someone with power. They didn't want to draw attention to themselves by talking to her after the ritual, so they followed the rest of the coven as they all returned to their cars.

As the beach cleared, Seraphina issued orders to pack everything and return it to the van. They worked in silence as Eilish joined them and started returning the ritual supplies to the boxes and baskets. Seraphina looked at her youngest sister. "We'll talk about this when we get home."

Eilish stared back at her. "Really? You want to share all the secrets now?"

Seraphina was dumbstruck. "What?" Eilish brushed past her as she climbed into the van. "You heard me."

The ride home was made in silence, as Seraphina and Warrick wondered how much she knew, and Zavian felt like he was way in over his head. Only Anya gave her a nudge and whispered, "Fucking awesome."

BOHANNON

Ian had told Carter he was going to watch the Litha ritual and had asked if he wanted to come. "Won't they see us there?" Ian shook his head. "I can teleport you if you want. I stay hidden, usually in a tree. There aren't many trees on the island, but it has a lot of heavy brush. I can shadow myself, and I can block you with my shadow to an extent, but you'll have to be still...and quiet."

Carter scratched his head, a frown on his face. "So, what do they do exactly." Ian gave him a half-smile. "You scared, Carter?" He shook his head, "No, well...I mean, until a few weeks ago, I wasn't sure witches were real until Anya saved my ass. That was some weird shit, you gotta admit. So, I'm just wondering...you know, like what happens when they all get together."

Ian chuckled. "Well, that's the point, isn't it? To see what they do when they're all together? I checked them out shortly after I got here. They did a ritual on St. John's Island. I wanted to get a sense of how big the coven was and how powerful. The covens have leaders, a high priest, and a high priestess, although the woman is always in charge. Eilish and Anya's older sister is the high priestess who led the ritual. It's where I saw Eilish for the first time. I followed her home, shadowed her, and figured out her routine. That's when I took the construction job. I figured I could find a way to meet her since she walked past that house daily."

Carter nodded. "Yeah, but what do they do?" Ian rolled his eyes, "They're witches. They call on the powers of nature. Burn candles and incense, stand in a circle and chant, stuff like that." Carter shrugged. "Sounds kind of lame, but okay, not like I got plans or anything." Ian looked at him. "So that's a yes?" Carter nodded. "Yeah, let's do it. I might learn something."

Ian laughed. "Okay, well, I have to carry you." Carter backed up. "Come on, dude. You're not going to like, hold me and shit." Ian held out his hands. "You going, or not? I have to pick you up to teleport you." Carter had heard Ian talk about teleporting and knew he had carried Eilish around, but he wasn't so sure anymore. "Okay, but you don't tell nobody, or I'll punch you in the face."

Ian chuckled, knowing Carter could never move fast enough to punch him in the face or anywhere else. "Yeah, okay, brother. Like who would I tell? Come on; we need to get there and get settled before they all start rolling in." Carter reluctantly stepped towards Ian as Ian slid his arm around his waist and grabbed onto the waistband of his jeans. Carter was about to tell him not to hold him too close when he felt himself being lifted and transported through the air faster than his eyes could follow. He unconsciously grabbed onto Ian's arm, wondering how high up they were. In seconds, Ian set him down on a sand bar in the middle of a scrub-filled marshland. The beach was in the distance, and he could smell the salt air from the ocean as well as the brackish smell from the marsh.

Carter surveyed the horizon. "Is this safe?" Ian sat on the sand and yanked on the pants leg of Carter's jeans. "Sit. You stand out like a solitary tree in a desert. It's safe enough. Mostly a bird sanctuary, but they have a few alligators."

Carter looked around the ground. "Alligators? You shittin' me? Could have told me that before we got here." Ian clipped him behind his knees as Carter dropped to the ground. "I said sit, brother. You'll have to follow orders faster than that if we don't want to get caught."

Carter carefully checked the heavy brush surrounding them, looking for any alligators. "But what about when it gets dark?" Ian sighed, "Carter! I'm a vamp. I'll see them, I'll hear them, I'll smell them. Now sit your ass down and pay attention." Just as he got Carter settled, the first of the cars arrived over the causeway, and people Ian recognized from the last ceremony started to get out and walk around. It wasn't long before he saw the large van, and the warlock they called Warrick emerged. He was tall, slender, and with long dark hair. Ian thought he was a mirror image of Seraphina if she were a man. He saw Zavian exit the van, and the two men undressed and pulled the hooded black robes over their heads. He could see the women changing their clothes inside the van. Carter noticed the early arrivers were all making their way back to their cars to change. As the women emerged, they were all wearing the sheer gown that did nothing to hide their nudity. Carter muttered, "You left out this part."

Ian nudged him with his shoulder and shushed him. They had a clear view of the beach and watched as the ritual began. They could easily hear the voices carried on the wind across the barren landscape. Ian spoke up, "Eilish is leading. She only assisted last time." Carter nodded silently beside him, more interested in the bevy of practically nude female bodies that formed a circle around Eilish.

Ian heard Carter whisper "Fuck" when Eilish lit the first candle with a glance. Ian had seen her light the candles at Ostara with the tip of her finger, so he didn't know if this was unusual for Eilish or not. When she walked into the ocean for her ceremonial cleansing, he was shocked to see the calm waves shift in an instant to three-foot swells, and he and Carter both felt the force of the wind. Ian could see the reaction of the coven and knew this wasn't something they'd seen before.

Carter leaned over close to him. "Did she do that?" Ian nodded silently. The two of them stayed low behind the brush, silent observers of Eilish's new power, and watched when the bonfire sprung to life, the flames licking skyward. Carter muttered, "Fuck me!" Ian turned his head to look at Carter, his face illuminated by the flames. Ian squatted lower behind the brush, pulling Carter down so they wouldn't be seen. Ian could tell from Seraphina's response she wasn't happy with how things had gone as they rushed to clear the beach when the ritual ended. The two men remained silent until the last car left the island. When the island was cleared, they stood up, stretching their legs and back. Carter looked at him. "Was that like last time?" Ian was quiet a moment before he answered. "No, that was nothing like last time." He knew a power had been unleashed in Eilish, a power that wasn't going to go back in a bottle, and he had a feeling he was a part of it. Things were about to change.

BOHANNON

They drove home in silence, and the tension inside the van could be cut with a knife. Seraphina had never seen Eilish's unbridled power, and she knew it had, at least in part, been triggered by a sexual union, and she knew for damn sure it hadn't been with Zavian. She cast a sideways glance at Warrick as he drove the van, and his jaw was tight. As they approached the house, Seraphina turned to Warrick, "Help us unload the van; then I want you and Zavian to leave. I need to talk with Eilish."

Warrick gave her a hard stare. He'd like to be a part of that discussion but knew Seraphina wouldn't budge. "If you insist."

Eilish had held Anya's hand during the drive home. Zavian was quiet and placed as much distance between them as was possible on the bench seat. He had been pursuing Eilish for years, and it was now clear that she'd been with someone else. He felt betrayed, even though she had never committed to him or offered him anything more than friendship. The men helped carry the boxes and baskets back inside to the kitchen. Warrick gave Seraphina a quick kiss and said, "call me." The three sisters emptied the boxes, returning everything to the cabinets and cupboards. Seraphina was taking out her anger on the cabinet and pantry doors. She turned and looked at

Eilish when everything had been restored to order, speaking harshly. "So, who is it?"

Eilish knew she couldn't avoid this one, but she couldn't tell Fina the truth. "I met a warlock from another coven. I like him. I love him, actually."

Seraphina slammed her hand down on the table. "Who? Tell me who!"

Eilish shook her head. "No. I won't tell you because you and Warrick will go after him."

Seraphina huffed as she paced. "You can't do this, Eilish! What were you thinking? Do you think *his* coven wants to let him go? Or were you planning on leaving? A Bohannon, leaving her coven. Our parents would turn over in their graves." She shook her finger in Eilish's face. "End it. Now, before you do any more damage. Explaining your performance tonight to the rest of the coven is going to be difficult enough as it is."

Eilish shook her head no. "I love him, I won't end it, and I don't know where it will go. I haven't thought that far ahead." Seraphina screamed back at her. "Sounds to me like you didn't think about a lot of things! What about Zavian?"

Eilish shrugged. "What about him? I've told you a hundred times that I didn't love him and wouldn't bond with him. The only people in the world that wouldn't listen to that message were you, Warrick, and Zavian."

Anya had stood in silence but knew this was the time for her to speak up. "And you might as well know, I've been seeing someone from the same coven."

Seraphina glared at her. "You, I can handle." Anya looked back at her, "Excuse me?" Seraphina waved her off with her hand as if this revelation from Anya were of no significance. "Wait, what do you mean you can handle me?"

Seraphina sighed, "Anya, you were never going to lead this coven. I would prefer you bond with a warlock from our coven, but if you don't, and you leave, it's no big deal."

Anya felt like she'd been slapped in the face. Fina had basically just said she was expendable. Eilish spoke, "My whole life, I thought it would be the three of us. It has always been the three of us, but clearly, you don't see it that way. Anya and I are a package deal. Where I go, she goes. And when exactly was I supposed to lead this coven? I don't see you and Warrick giving up control any time soon."

Seraphina turned on her. "Don't try to make this about me. You're not ready to be a High Priestess. It could be years." Eilish shot back, "Or it could be never. Isn't that the point? Zavian brings nothing to the table. I won't draw power from Zavian, but being bonded to him keeps both of us under your and Warrick's control."

As Eilish took a breath, Anya stepped in and spoke her mind. "Wherever Eilish goes, I go. You need to know you won't push me around, Fina. I'm with Eilish on this."

Fina spun on her heels and went nose-to-nose with Anya. "You are no use to this coven in a capacity that gives you any right to speak your mind. Especially to me, so I would advise you to stay out of this mess. Your sister has apparently been a very bad influence on your judgment. You should feel fortunate that anyone from *any* coven finds you desirable, considering how you dress and conduct yourself."

Fina stepped back and returned her attention to Eilish, with her dark, intimidating stare that bored into her. "You are both going to be punished. You'll both stay within the confines of this house for the next few days. I'll run the shop with Warrick. We have much to discuss since you've decided you think you will replace me as the High Priestess." She laughed hysterically. "You'll never overtake me, sister. You are nowhere near ready to handle this coven, nor a warlock of any standing!"

Eilish shouted back. "We're grounded? What, you think we're twelve?" The dishes started to clatter inside the cabinets, and Anya stepped closer to her sister, placing her hand on her elbow. "Let it go, Eilish." Eilish took a deep breath, knowing it wouldn't take much for her to bring the whole house down around their heads. "Fine. We'll stay home, and you work for a change."

She turned on her heels and marched out of the room with Anya right behind her. Eilish stomped up the stairs and waited for Anya to enter her bedroom before slamming the door behind her. "I never cared about being High Priestess; it meant nothing to me, but it's clear now that was my destiny, and Fina and Warrick were going to hold me back as long as possible. It's what Henwen said. We need to find that book, Anya. We'll have a few days to look through the house and see where she hid it. It has to be here somewhere." She saw her sister sitting with her head down, wiping at her tears. "Anya? Are you okay? Don't listen to her. Her words mean nothing. She has used her words to hold us down all our lives."

Anya looked up with tears in her eyes, "I'm not crying about that; I'm crying because no matter what we do, they always find out. I'm worried about Carter. I love him. For once, I have someone to call my own, and I don't want to lose him." She stood up and walked around the room. "What exactly are we going to do? Ian and Carter can't help us, not like this. But at least we have time to look for the book. I hope we can find it, and you can figure this all out." She walked to her sister and held her in a hug. "I never thought I could hate Fina as much as I do at this moment. Promise me you'll take me with you wherever you go because I'll always need you."

Eilish squeezed her sister tight. As much as they had always complained about Fina, she never thought it would come to this. "I meant what I said; we're a package deal. I need you with me, Anya. Even if we find the book, I have no idea what the coven will do. Bohannon's have ruled this coven for centuries. The coven has never had to choose which Bohannon to follow. We could be exiled."

Anya smiled. "But if we're exiled, at least we have our guys with us. I know Carter loves me, and there's no doubt Ian loves you. So, let's get some rest, and we will begin our search tomorrow. I'm going to text Carter. Tell him why he won't see us walking to work in the next few days; you should do the same. Try to get some sleep." She hugged Eilish tightly and left her room, wondering how she'd ever be without Carter for days.

Eilish got undressed and slipped on her gown, climbing into her bed. She rummaged through her handbag until she found her phone and sent Ian a text. *Things got a little out of hand at Litha. Fina is pissed, and Anya and I won't be at the shop for the next few days. Please stay clear and make sure Carter does the same.*

Ian lay in his bed; his thoughts were spinning. He knew what he'd witnessed wasn't normal. Eilish's powers were raw and intimidating. His phone pinged, and he grabbed it quickly, hoping it was Eilish. He hadn't dared try to contact her, knowing that the Bohannon house was probably in an uproar. As he read the message, his heart beat harder. He texted back quickly, his fingers moving like lightning. *I saw everything, and so did Carter. We were hiding nearby, and I was shadowing. Tell me you're all right.*

Eilish was surprised by his response. *You saw it? And you still want to stick around? Listen, I'm fine, we're both fine, but things are really tense right now. I need some time to figure this out. I need to know if you have changed your mind. I'll understand if you have.*

Ian sighed; she didn't seem to understand that it didn't matter. He was in love with this beautiful and powerful witch. *I love you, Eilish, forever. Now get some sleep. I'll be waiting.*

She sent him a heart emoji and held the phone to her chest. She needed to sleep. She had used a lot of energy during Litha, and tomorrow, she and Anya would begin searching for the book.

BOHANNON

Fina arose earlier than usual, and Luna was under her feet for every step. She noticed the house was extremely quiet but could smell the aroma of the toast from the toaster. That meant Anya was having her usual peanut butter on toast. She dressed for work and made her way to the kitchen to find both sisters sitting quietly at the table, neither of them speaking. "I'll be walking to the store; Warrick is meeting me there. Neither of you will leave this house. I'll place a protection spell. I know you can break it, but I'll know immediately that you did. Don't even open an outside door. You're confined to the house until I decide when this punishment is over. By the way, that will include the nights as well. It will give you time to think of your gross error of thinking you're in love with anyone from another coven. I expect dinner prepared when I arrive back home." Fina looked on as she sipped her tea, both of them with their heads down, completely ignoring her. "I see there are no apologies. Do you have anything to say, Eilish?"

Eilish looked up, her face neutral. "Have a good day at the shop."

Fina chuckled to herself; so, it will be that way, I see. "I intend to, thank you very much." She grabbed her bag and made her way, walking alone to Rhiannon's. Her walk was brisk and no-nonsense. Seraphina wasn't one to 'stop and smell the roses.' She hadn't walked to the store in some time. She noticed the house on the corner under renovation as she slowed her pace. It had needed repair and looked rather nice; they were doing a good job. Perhaps she should check out this contractor and hire them; their house could use some repairs. She continued on her way to the shop, enjoying the morning and her walk.

Ian got to work a few minutes short of being late. He scrambled out of his truck and onto the worksite. Carter was already there, and he quickly made his way to him. Carter was adding rain gutters to the new roofing, and Ian jumped in, working alongside him. "Hey, did you hear from Anya last night?"

Carter wiped his brow on his shirt sleeve, already sweating in the morning heat. "Yeah, she texted me. Said we had to lay low for a few days. What's going on? Is it about that ceremony?"

Ian nodded, "Yeah, things went down at the house once they got home. I suspected as much. We just have to ride this out for a while until the girls give us the green light. I have a bad feeling about this. You have to stay out of sight, Carter, serious shit."

Carter nodded. "But I don't understand. I mean, I've never seen a ritual before, so I don't have anything to compare it to. So, what's the big deal?"

"Look, let me try to make this as simple as possible. The oldest sister is the High Priestess; she holds all the power and runs the coven. She calls the shots, like the foreman here. But I have to tell you, Eilish had much more power at this ceremony than the last one I witnessed. I know that sex increases the power of the females, and we had sex the night before. Females rule in the witch realm, and big sister isn't happy about what went down. Eilish displayed more power, and it happened in front of the whole coven." Ian shook his head, "We need to lay low, let them handle this, and just stay the fuck out of the way. If you don't, you are going to end up dead. I can't make it any simpler than that."

Carter had stopped working to pay attention to Ian. "You think they're in any danger... the girls?"

Ian shrugged, "At the moment, I don't think so, at least not that Eilish indicated. I told you this would be one bumpy ass ride, and it's just beginning. If you can't handle this, you need to say so; you need to tell Anya; it's only fair."

Carter shook his head. "No, I'm in. Hey, I've dated some crazy bitches; how bad could this be?"

Ian shook his head. "Yeah, well, it's not Eilish and Anya I'm worried about. It's the oldest sister we have to steer clear of." A female figure walking past the house caught Ian's eye, and he quickly saw it was Seraphina. "Shit, that's her. Seraphina. Don't stare, don't look, just keep working." Ian noticed she slowed her pace a bit as she walked past, staring up at the renovations....at least he hoped it was renovations and not them.

Carter cast a quick glance, recognizing the dark-haired witch from the night before. It was clear she was a bit older than either Eilish or Anya. She was beautiful, but she looked stern and carried herself in a way that clearly signaled, 'don't fuck with me.' He turned his head back to his work, then watched her as she walked away. "So that's the enemy then. Her, and that tall guy she was with." He chuckled as he nudged Ian. "Piece of cake."

BOHANNON

Fina arrived at the store and immediately turned down the air conditioner to a level Anya had labeled on the thermostat with a sticky note that read 'morgue.' It was going to be another hot day. She was already hot from her walk and it went further than skin deep with Eilish and Anya, and their reveal. She quickly set up the cash register and began to check stock and found herself slamming things around. Taking a deep breath, she hoped to calm down before Warrick showed up. He'd want details, of which, she intended to tell him as little as possible. Naturally, he'd hold her accountable for all of it. She heard the familiar jingle of the bell over the door and knew it was him, she could feel it. She put a false smile on her face and strolled out to find him standing in the middle of the store staring at her. She greeted him somewhat defiantly. "Well, good morning to you. I know that look. Say your piece and be done with it."

Warrick shouted back at her. "Be done with it? Don't brush this off, Fina! Eilish had sex with someone, and it sure the fuck wasn't Zavian. Something triggered her powers. Something big. I've seen you use your peak powers, and you can't control the wind... or the fucking ocean, for fuck's sake! I've been getting phone calls from the coven all night. They want to know what happened. They're nervous. They could see her powers came as much as a surprise to you as they did to them. You can't sweep this under the rug with your casual dismissal. The whole fucking coven witnessed what happened. They're wondering if there will be a changing of the guard if you're stepping aside to allow Eilish to step into her role. I made sure every male in the coven knew she was off-limits, that she was destined for Zavian. He's weak, and we could have controlled them. All you had to do was keep her away from other warlocks. What the hell happened?"

Fina stridently walked up to him and looked him in the eye. "Be very careful with your words, Warrick. Remember who holds the cards in this relationship. Zavian is weak, like a kitten, pliable and stupid. And since we're throwing daggers, he's your responsibility." She poked him in the chest hard. "Eilish says she's in love with a warlock from another coven, and Anya is saying the same. They both refuse to tell me who or from which coven. They're confined to the house until I decide what to do. Do you wish to be a part of the solution, or do you wish to stomp your foot and scream at me like a little child?" She turned and walked into the back room.

He grabbed her arm and spun her around. "Don't dismiss me! I'm not a child! I know who holds the cards, but you better remember who helped put those cards in your hand and kept your dirty little secrets all these years. She can topple both of us if she ever learns the truth. How do you plan on breaking up this love fest? A couple of days in time-out won't do it. They're grown women, for fuck's sake. Tell me you have a more thought-out plan than 'go to your room.'"

Fina shrugged off his arm. "Don't strong arm me, Warrick. I know them both better than you! She'll never find the book, and she'll never uncover our secret. She may have more power, but there's nothing she can do without the book. She can try to take over, but it will never happen. Besides, this is nothing more than a crush. Some handsome warlock is trying to convince her she's in love. It will pass, as does everything else. If Zavian had made more aggressive advances, we wouldn't be having this conversation. As for the coven, they'll follow me no matter what happens. They believe Eilish is second in line, and I'm training her. Let them talk. I'm the eldest Bohannon, the High Priestess of this coven, and *nothing* happens until I say so. If we both remain calm, they will follow." The bell jingled as a customer entered, and she lowered her voice. "Do as I say, Warrick, and keep yourself under control!"

She walked to the front of the shop, brushing past him. She found an elderly witch from their coven looking aimlessly about. "It's good to see you, Rowan. Is there anything I can assist you with?" Fina felt Warrick walk up behind her. She turned and looked at his stern face as she flashed a huge fake grin at him and returned her attention to Rowan.

Rowan made a show of picking through the baskets of herbs. "That was quite the show, Seraphina. The whole coven is talking. It seems to us Eilish should be the one leading us. Her powers clearly outpace yours. She's young and hasn't learned how to focus yet, which can be dangerous. Only thing is, no one can figure out who she's bonding with. Clearly not Zavian. He was as shocked as everyone else." She picked up some smudge sticks and carried them to the counter. "I suggest you get your house in order and do it quickly. I'd hate to see the coven turn against you... and Warrick." She cast a hard stare at Warrick.

Fina could feel the fire building inside her and knew she was being warned. She felt Warrick stir, sinking her long, sharp fingernails into his wrist to silence him. "Wasn't she marvelous, our Eilish? She has great power, Rowan, and she's coming along nicely. Of course, I have much more work to do with her. She has yet to learn to focus and control her powers. She's still very raw. We chose to let the coven see how well she's coming along. We're proud of her dedication and diligence toward her craft."

Fina scanned the smudge sticks on the counter and began to

check her out. "But of course, Eilish and Zavian may not be compatible. That's something we're still exploring, aren't we, Warrick? Still, there is a special place in Eilish's heart for Zavian, so the jury's still out on that one." She placed the smudge sticks in the bag and handed them to Rowan. "The Bohannon house is in smart order; we know our power is unique and forceful. Otherwise, you wouldn't be here. And I'm sure you'll spread the word faster than lightning to the others." Her eyes bored into Rowan, warning her that her comments and attitude weren't welcomed here, and if she had a brain in her head, she'd spread the word quickly. "Have a wonderful day, Rowan."

Rowan muttered under her breath and snatched the bag from Seraphina's hand. As she left the shop, Warrick turned to Fina. "What do you mean Zavian isn't compatible? Have you lost your mind? We can't give Eilish free rein to pick her own mate! We lose all control! I've worked too hard to be High Priest to turn it over to some upstart who, until yesterday, didn't even know she *had* power."

Fina laughed in his face. "Oh, my dear Warrick. You just need to remain calm; they follow like lambs to the slaughter. I'm in control, unlike you. Perhaps it's time you do *your* job and have Zavian show some backbone. Have you taught him nothing about seduction? She claims they are friends. Perhaps she'll confide in him, give him some hint of who the hell this other warlock is! Give me a few days... once Eilish can't be with her beloved, he'll grow tired of waiting and learn I have control. He'll move on to greener pastures. Men have no patience." She turned to him with her hand on her hip and smiled. "When will you learn to leave it to me, Warrick? You can pretend you rule this coven, but everyone knows it's me. And so far, Zavian has been useless to us. It's your turn to earn your stay in my bed!"

Warrick growled back at her. "I'll not be treated like a whipped dog, Fina. I'll send Zavian in person. It will be harder for her to turn him down. You just make sure you do your part." He turned on his heels and marched out of the shop, slamming the door behind him.

Fina watched him go and smiled. "Oh, she'll see him, and somehow I'll find out who this suspicious lover is and bring an end to it." Several customers entered the shop at once, tourists mostly, with no knowledge of the power that lay in the objects on display, but Seraphina trudged through; after all, it was money.

BOHANNON

The sisters waited until Seraphina was gone, then sprung into high gear, cleaning up the kitchen. Eilish rinsed dishes and put them in the dishwasher. "Let's hurry, so we can start looking. This is a big house. Where should we start? Fina is clever; it could be somewhere obscure or in plain sight... something we walk past every day and don't even pay any attention to anymore."

Anya sighed, "It will be like finding a needle in a haystack. I guess we should start from top to bottom; that would be the best plan." She scrunched up her nose and sighed. "That attic is a nightmare, but there is so much stuff in there; it could take a week!" She went to the fridge and grabbed two bottles of water, handing one to Eilish. "I said I'd be behind you, and I am, so get moving; we have a lot of work to accomplish."

The girls went to the second floor and down the hall to the door that led to the attic. Eilish couldn't remember the last time she'd even gone up there. She opened the door and could immediately feel the heat from this space that trapped the scorching hell of a Charleston summer. She climbed up the dimly lit stairs, looking for the pull chain at the top for the single bare light bulb. She pulled the chain, and the light turned on, casting shadows in every direction.

Anya stepped up behind her as they looked at stacked boxes, old furniture, and long discarded toys. Eilish wiped at the sweat already appearing on her brow as she opened the bottled water. "This will take forever."

Anya shook her head. "Does she ever throw anything away?" As Anya stared at the daunting search ahead, she turned to Eilish with hands on her hips. "Do you know how big of a book we're looking for? Anything?"

Eilish shook her head. "Henwen said it held ancient spells that had been lost to the covens, that it had been handed down from one generation of Bohannon's to another, it was the source of our power, so it will be old. Other than that, I have no idea. Look for any book or even papers that are tied or clipped together. You start at that end; I'll start over there; we'll meet in the middle. Save anything that could possibly hold the spells."

Eilish stripped down to her underwear in the heat and used her shirt to wipe the sweat from her face as she stepped over boxes and made her way through the clutter until she reached the far wall. Sighing loudly, she squatted down and started rummaging through the first box.

Anya began at her end and found that just getting to the space she was supposed to be looking through, made her drip with sweat. She had a hair tie around her wrist and quickly swept her hair up in a ponytail, and began rummaging. She sat on the floor, digging through one box after another, and found everything but a book of spells. Her ripped tee shirt was soaked and sticking to her skin. "I think my eyeballs are even sweating. Seriously Eilish, have you found anything yet?" She sat against a stack of boxes she'd already sorted through and took a long gulp of water. "I can't understand why she kept all this old stuff. I certainly never want any of this crap."

Eilish pushed aside boxes she'd already explored, trying to develop a system for what had been searched. "There's stuff here from when Mom and Dad were still alive. Maybe that's a sign. But I haven't found anything yet. Keep looking. The one box you skip will be the box we need."

"Right." Anya spent another hour moving old bed frames, cribs, and boxes of clothes and then found something that made her laugh. She picked up the old tattered witch hat and placed it on her head. "Remember when we were little, Fina made us dress up as witches at Halloween? Traumatizing!" She laughed and threw the hat at Eilish, who wasn't exactly laughing. "Right, the boxes."

Eilish tossed the witch hat aside. On a normal day, they would have dug out those old costumes and tried them on, laughing at the memories, but this wasn't a normal day.

Anya continued as the sweat ran off her face. She kept looking over at Eilish, making sure she hadn't passed out from the heat, and thought this was the most boring thing she'd ever done. She decided to talk about something to keep their energy up. "So, you missing Ian yet?"

"Ian, yes, I miss him. I hope we haven't pulled them into something they'll regret. Finding that book might help us keep them alive." Eilish opened a box and gasped as Anya stopped what she was doing and looked up. "Find anything?" Eilish lifted some books from a box, fanning through the pages, before rejecting them. "No. False alarm. Just a bunch of old novels. Jeez, this place is a fire trap, Anya."

"Well, I know I feel like I'm about to burst into flames. I wasn't this sweaty when Carter and I were making our own flames!" Eilish looked at her, and they both broke out into giggles. As the morning grew hotter and hotter, they finally had gone through everything and decided it was time to take a much-needed lunch break and grab some refreshing sweet tea. "Any ideas where we need to dig next?"

Eilish stood and stretched out her back, feeling the sweat trickle down her spine. "I need a quick shower; then we can grab a light lunch and start on the second floor. At least it will be cool." She grabbed her discarded clothes that she'd dropped at the top of the stairs and tugged at the pull-string to cut off the light. She and Anya descended the stairs, feeling the temperature drop with each step.

Eilish opened the door at the bottom of the stairs and felt the blast of cold air, which raised goose bumps on her skin. She heard the scratch of a record player needle against vinyl, followed by The Platters singing "Smoke Gets in Your Eyes" as she wiped the sweat from her own. "Emric's in your vinyl collection. At least someone is enjoying their day."

Anya smiled, "Yeah, he has his good and bad days. Oh well, take your shower. I'll fix us something quick to eat. " Anya heard her phone buzz and looked to see that it was Carter. "Oh no! Fina walked past them this morning! He said Ian told him not to look at her." She looked at Eilish. "You don't think she knows, do you?"

Eilish shook her head. "No. That's the quickest route to the shop. Besides, if she knew, they'd be dead by now. The fact that he can send you a text is a good sign. I'm going to rinse off quickly and tie my hair up in a bun. I'll meet you in the kitchen."

"Right." Anya quickly messaged Carter, telling him to ignore Fina and that she missed and loved him. It made her feel better knowing that all of this effort was to save his cute ass in the long run. Quickly slicing up some tomatoes, she rinsed some lettuce and cut some slices from the loaf of homemade bread they had made the night before. She fried a pan full of bacon, then made some sandwiches and poured two large sweet teas. She was finally feeling cooler as Eilish walked back in, refreshed and ready for round two. "Think of our next spot?"

Eilish sat down at the table and took a large gulp of the sweet tea before biting into her sandwich. "Well, I think we can rule out our rooms. So, let's focus on Fina's, the room that used to be our parents' bedroom, and the guest bedroom. Oh, and the bathrooms and closets, don't forget them." She snickered as she looked at her sister. "You have a mayonnaise mustache."

Anya grinned and licked her upper lip. "This house is just too big! Why don't we split up? That way, we can cover more ground and if we find anything, just yell." Anya took another bite of her sandwich and moaned. "At least this will give me some energy."

Eilish finished her lunch and cleared away the plates, rinsing them in the sink. "You want to take a quick shower? I'll clean up here; then I'll start in our parents' bedroom. That seems a logical place."

Anya stood up and stretched, "Yeah, a shower sounds delightful. Even I can't stand the smell of me." She ran upstairs to take her shower, quickly scrubbing clean and putting on some fresh clothes. She walked into their parents' bedroom to find Eilish hard at work. "Anything yet?"

Eilish backed out of the closet, shaking her head. "Nothing. All the dressers and wardrobes are empty. Fina keeps the Halloween decorations in here." Eilish closed the closet door, looking around the stark room, devoid of anything that held any memory of their parents. She'd only been three when they died. If not for photographs, she wouldn't even know what they looked like. "Let's go check Fina's room."

They both headed to the bedroom together. "Well, who knows what we might find in here. That trunk has been in here forever. Any chance it might be unlocked?"

Eilish removed the folded blankets from atop the steamer trunk that sat at the foot of Seraphina's bed. Both sisters knelt in front of it and tried to lift the top without success. "Locked. Maybe that's a good sign. She has a protection spell on it too. I can feel it. If we break it open, she'll know, but if we can find the key, I can open it without disturbing the spell. Any idea where she'd hide a key?" Eilish got off her knees and started exploring the contents of Fina's jewelry box.

Anya grumbled, and then she grinned. "I have an idea. Maybe. If she keeps the keys to the Caddy in the flour canister, I might have a clue." Anya took off for the kitchen and pulled out the canisters from the counter. She skipped the flour canister, knowing the car keys were already there. Next, she checked the sugar but found nothing. Then the tea tin, nothing again. "Damn you, Fina!" As she was putting the canisters back, she grinned. She went into the vast pantry and began rummaging through the shelves loaded with food. It was hidden in the back, behind the tall mason jars of canned tomatoes. There it was, the old tin that went with the canister set. It was used to hold cornmeal, and Anya had often wondered why Fina didn't keep this canister with the set on the counter. She pried the lid open and stuck her hand in, and grinned. Buried in the bottom under the corn meal was a key. She quickly replaced the tin and ran up the stairs yelling, "I got it! I know it!" She rushed into the room and handed the key to Eilish. "I think this is it. Try it. It looks like it would fit."

Eilish took the old key. "Where did you find this?"

Anya grinned, "She had it hidden in the cornmeal tin in the pantry. I always wondered why she never kept it with the set, just figured because we rarely used it anymore." Anya held her breath as Eilish inserted the key.

Eilish mouthed the words to appease the protection spell that boundaries weren't being broken and slipped the key into the lock, giving it a twist. They both heard the lock click open. Anya dropped to her knees next to her sister as they both lifted the lid of the trunk. Their mother's wedding dress, sealed in a clear plastic garment bag, lay folded on top. Eilish carefully removed it and laid it on the floor. "Pay attention to how things are positioned. Fina will notice if anything's out of place." They carefully sifted through some old photo albums of them together as a family. Eilish looked at a photo of herself sitting on her father's knee while Anya was in her mother's lap, and Fina stood tall next to them. "Do you remember this, Anya? I don't even remember them."

Anya looked at the picture and smiled. "I know you were only three, and I was five. Daddy loved you so much, Eilish." A tear rolled down her cheek. "Mommy looks so beautiful, doesn't she?"

Eilish touched her finger to her mother's face, wishing she had even the faintest memory of her. "She does." They laid the album aside and continued to look through the carefully arranged items in the trunk. There was a box with an elaborate design that Eilish lifted from the trunk and carefully opened. She first saw the yellowed newspaper clipping of their parent's obituary. She lifted the clipping, touching only the tip of a corner, and set it aside. There were sympathy cards, pressed flowers from their grave, and bits of ribbon, all mementos from a tragically sad day. Their parents had been killed, and they had never learned who the culprits were. Eilish remembered Henwen's words that they had died protecting the book. At the bottom of the box was a folded piece of paper that Eilish carefully unfolded. Anya leaned in close as both sisters recognized Fina's handwriting. It was the eulogy Fina had given at their parent's funeral. Neither of them had been old enough to remember the contents. "Look, it says they'll take their secrets to the grave. Maybe that means only they know who killed them, or maybe... Anya, do you think Fina would have buried the book with them? Placed it in one of their coffins? But how would she ever get to it again?"

Anya studied the paper, and her thoughts were varied. Memories of her parents mixed with the excitement of finding a possible clue. "I don't know. If she buried it, it would be with Mommy. Okay, let's think this through. Their secrets could mean the book or who killed them. Burying the book sounds like something Fina would do. No one would dare look there. But why put it there if she would need the book?" Anya looked up as she saw Emric leaning on the door frame. She nudged Eilish and nodded toward Emric.

Eilish looked up to see Emric standing in the doorway. She had been so absorbed in thought that she hadn't noticed he had stopped playing music. "Is something wrong, Emric?"

He nodded his head. "The book is not here, Miss Eilish. After your parents were killed, Miss Seraphina was desperate to hide it away. Keep it safe where no one could ever find it again."

Eilish looked at Anya, who shrugged. "Do you know where it is?" Emric looked dejected. "No, ma'am. Just know it's not in the house."

Eilish bit her lip as she pondered this new information. "Do you know who killed our parents?" He shook his head. "No, ma'am. Wish I did."

Eilish sighed. "Okay, let's put this stuff back. Carefully... exactly as we found it." The girls replaced the contents of the trunk, carefully stacked the items in the order and position they'd been found, then closed the lid and locked it. Eilish replaced the blankets on top of the trunk. "Better put that key back where you found it, and make sure the tin is in the same place. Fina notices everything." Anya stood and took the key. "Well, at least we know it's not here." Eilish nodded. "But where? I feel like I know less than when we started."

Anya took the key and shook her head. "I feel the same way." She looked at Emric. "Don't tell Fina we asked you anything; never tell her we were in this trunk." Emric shook his head. "No ma'am, I am no snitch."

They all left the room, and Emric wandered back to Anya's room. Anya replaced the key in the cornmeal tin and made sure everything was back in its proper place. She left the pantry, shut the door, and leaned against it. "We are so close; I can feel it."

BOHANNON

The girls had dinner waiting for Seraphina when she came home and decided to keep up the pretense of remaining angry. The less said, the better. Seraphina had asked what they had done with their time. Eilish responded, "Basically nothing, Fina. We did nothing. Luna was thrown off her schedule by having us home all day. Emric played music. We spent some time on the screened porch; then we fixed dinner. And how about you? How was your day? You and Warrick work things out?"

Fina looked from one to the other; it was as she assumed it would be, both of them still acting put out. She found it funny that Anya said little, and Eilish did all the talking. But, all of this was Eilish's fault. "Warrick and I are absolutely fine; I know how to handle him. But you did make quite a stir with the coven. His phone was ringing all night. Rowan made an appearance and had the nerve to warn me about the speculation and gossip." She brushed her hand in the air. "I take no notice of such things; everyone on the planet has been talking about the Bohannons for ages; it all passes. But I did set her straight, and all is fine. And, I suggest you clean this house tomorrow, instead of wasting your time. It would be a shame if I cut off your precious cell phones."

Eilish felt her temperature rising. She needed her phone to stay in contact with Ian, but she knew it would only antagonize Seraphina if she responded. Anya served fresh vegetables from the steamer, as Eilish brought in the corn on the cob from the grill on the back porch. She filled the glasses with sweet tea. "We made a peach cobbler for dessert. Eat before everything gets cold." The three sat down and ate in silence. When the meal was done, Fina told them to clean up; she was going to her room for a shower and was calling it a night.

Anya smirked, "Not used to working?" Seraphina shot her an ice-cold stare and left the room. The girls giggled softly as they cleaned the kitchen together after she was gone. When they were done, Eilish poured them another glass of sweet tea, and they retreated to the screened porch, with the ceiling fan on high and the sounds of tree frogs and crickets filling the night. Eilish looked at Anya, "That went well."

Anya laughed softly, "Yeah, quietest dinner we ever had. I would have loved to have been a fly on the wall in that store today. I bet Warrick was a real grouch." Anya sipped her tea and scooted her chair closer to Eilish. "So, have you been thinking about that clue in the eulogy?"

Eilish leaned her head back against the porch chair, closing her eyes and feeling the breeze from the fan. "Yeah, I've been thinking about a lot of things, but let's save the discussions for tomorrow when she's gone. I don't trust Fina not to be lurking behind some door eavesdropping." She sipped at her tea and pulled her phone from her pocket. "I'm giving Ian an update. You should touch base with Carter, too. If they're in the loop, they are less likely to worry and show up here unannounced. That is the *last* thing we need right now." She sent Ian a text, as Anya did the same. Eilish finished her tea, then stood and stretched. "I'm going to bed now too. As soon as Fina leaves in the morning, we'll figure out our next steps."

Anya nodded and stood as well. "I think I need a good sleep after this day. Plus, I want to be alone when Carter texts back." They both walked inside and locked the door. As they got to the top of the steps,

Anya gave Eilish the thumbs up. She knew they'd be on their phones for a few hours before sleeping. She couldn't think of a better way to end this miserable day.

<hr />

Eilish's alarm woke her early. She rolled over and silenced her phone, disturbing Luna, who had been sleeping at her feet. The cat gave a disgruntled chirp, then curled back in a ball to sleep. She pulled on a tank top and a pair of shorts, pulled her hair back into a loose ponytail, and walked barefoot down the stairs. She could already hear Anya rattling pans in the kitchen. "Seen Fina yet?"

"Oh, she's up, but she isn't down here yet. She already ordered breakfast." Anya rolled her eyes. "I'm making hoe cakes; you want some? I already made blackberry muffins; they're still warm, so eat up!" Anya stirred the buttermilk, cornmeal, baking soda, and eggs together to make a semi-thick batter. She had the iron skillet sizzling hot with grease and scooped a few of the southern pancakes into the grill. The house smelled amazing already. "Honey and butter are on the table. Did you get any sleep?"

"Jeez, did she want room service too?" Eilish poured a cup of hot tea and put butter on the still-warm blueberry muffin as she slid into a chair at the table. "I texted Ian for a while before I went to sleep. Tossed and turned a lot, much to Luna's dismay. She doesn't like it much when her sleep is disturbed. You?"

Anya flipped the hoe cakes in the skillet, and fried them to a perfect golden brown. "Oh, I slept great. All the exercise and a sweet message helped. Shh, here she comes!" Fina waltzed into the room and eyed the hoe cakes in the skillet. "Don't fry them so long, Anya; they will taste like cardboard. So, I'm assuming the both of you will put your energy to good use today and clean this downstairs. If I'm not happy with the results, you can stay home again tomorrow and clean the entire upstairs." As she sat down, Anya put the stack of hoe cakes in front of her. "Come to think of it, that attic could use a good cleaning; it has been ages since anyone has arranged that."

Eilish licked at the butter on her muffin, then took a bite. "I'm not going in that attic. Not in this heat. Don't get too carried away with your punishment, Fina. Right now, we're cooperating. You wouldn't want to see us turn against you, now would we?"

Fina took a bite of her hoe cake, dripping with butter and honey, and stared at Eilish and laughed. "Try if you might, Eilish; it will never work. This coven may have seen your power, but it wasn't perfect. And, of course, they know I am guiding you." She reached for another hot off-the-skillet hoe cake as Anya put them on the table. "And you wouldn't want the coven to know you'd found a warlock from some other coven. I think you'd find that they'd feel betrayed by you, no matter how much you wowed them at the ceremony. They do not take lightly to other covens poking their nose in our business."

Eilish rolled her eyes and looked at Anya, who shrugged. "Yeah, fine. Still not going in the attic." Eilish polished off the muffin and carried her mug to the sink, kissing the top of Anya's head on the way. "Good breakfast, sis. I'll get the vacuum and get started. Have a good day at the shop, Fina."

Eilish walked out of the kitchen, leaving her sisters at the table, as she dragged the old Hoover out of the closet and started vacuuming, the loud motor drowning out any chance of a conversation.

BOHANNON

Anya spent the rest of the morning scrubbing the kitchen floor, washing dishes and preparing a squash casserole for dinner, filled with fresh yellow and zucchini squash, red bell peppers, onions, and cheese with a bread crumb topping. She threw it in the fridge to cook for dinner later. She would make the biscuits later too. She then decided to dust and polish the furniture as Eilish vacuumed the entire joint. Finally, they had finished, and it was time for sweet tea and some lunch. "Come on, Eilish, let's grab some grub; if this doesn't satisfy her, she can go fly a kite. I'm so sick of cleaning!" They could hear the thunder and the rain beating down as they entered the kitchen. "Looks like a mid-day summer storm. Want to go eat lunch on the front veranda?"

"Great idea. I love thunderstorms." The girls took their tomato sandwiches and sweet tea to the front veranda. The steam rose off the streets when it met the cooling rain. The wind whipped the trees around, and the Spanish moss swinging eerily in the gray light of the storm. Thunder cracked loud, and the air tingled around them. Both girls settled into the oversized Adirondack chairs, silently eating their sandwiches. As Eilish finished, she wiped the tomato juice from her chin and looked at Anya. "We have a mystery to solve. Emric said the book wasn't in the house. I don't think Fina would hide it in the shop. It's not that large a space and we use every inch of it. We're all three in there. I can't think of a place she could hide it that we don't already access every day. Other than the carriage house, we don't own any other property. I was wondering if maybe she gave the book to Warrick, but that would give him too much power over her, don't you think?"

Anya listened as she finished her sandwich. "Yeah, I've been thinking about it a lot. Like, the whole damn time I've been cleaning. I thought about the shop too, but we know every space in there, and because we are in there so much, I'm pretty sure Fina wouldn't put it there. I can't imagine it is in the carriage house. Really nothing in there but old rusty lawn and garden tools, the Caddy, and maybe a gas can. It would have to be someplace she knew no one could get to but her, someplace close, so she could watch it or check on it often." Anya laughed and then snorted as she did so. "Let's get serious. Fina loves control more than anything in this world; she'd never give it to Warrick. She loves controlling him more than us, I think. Have you said anything to Ian about all this?"

"I haven't told him much. I hate to get them too involved. Fina and Warrick will be on high alert to try and figure out who we're both seeing. I've just let him know we're okay." The thunderclap was loud as they watched a lightning strike across the Battery. "I keep thinking about the eulogy. She said they would keep their secrets...meaning our parents. My brain keeps going back to that. Do you think there's any chance Fina buried the book with our parents? I mean, it would be safe. I don't know how Fina would be able to get to it, but maybe she doesn't need to. If she read it or memorized it... I mean, maybe she doesn't need to actually hold it in her hands to have the power. Or maybe she's more concerned with keeping it out of other people's hands than having it herself. After all, it's what got our parents killed."

Anya sat up and looked at Eilish. "You could be right, but let's think about this. If she put it in the crypt with our parents, she'd really take the risk of someone seeing her, wouldn't she?" Anya sat back and sighed, closing her eyes, smelling the rain, and feeling the breeze of the wind the storm was kicking up. "You don't think there's a trapdoor in the floor anywhere in this house, do you, or some secret panel that opens to caves or caverns below the house?"

Eilish pondered that idea. "It's possible. This is an old house—pre-Revolutionary War and here during the Civil War. People could have dug out places for others to hide. Let's check under the rugs today. All these old rugs have been here since we were kids. There could be a trap door underneath. I guess we should explore all possibilities. We can check the walls, especially behind the large wardrobes and china cabinets where a secret panel could be hidden. We can do that this afternoon."

Anya grumbled, "Sorry I mentioned it!" She finished off her tea and stood up. "Secrets buried with the dead. You don't really think she'd put the book in the crypt? It would have a hefty spell on it, that's for sure."

"For sure. But let's not go there quite yet. I have the power to raise spirits, but not sure I want to call our mother from her sleep to settle a family argument. Come on; we have a house to search."

Anya gave her a look and trudged inside the house. They spent the entire afternoon searching for trap doors or secret panels but came up empty. Anya finally gave up and looked at the time. "Eilish, this is hopeless, and besides, I need to get the biscuits made and the casserole in the oven. Fina will be here soon."

Eilish bit her lip as she nodded. "Yeah, we can't be seen looking for anything. I'll set the table. You realize we're running out of options, right?"

"Oh yeah, I'm well aware and pretty damn sure that book is nowhere in this house." She quickly rolled the dough for biscuits and cut them out, placing them in the greased iron skillet and throwing them into the oven alongside the casserole. She heard the front door and glanced at Eilish, who nodded. Fina walked into the kitchen, and right behind her was Zavian. "Set another place, will you, Eilish? Our dear Zavian is joining us this evening. Isn't that so sweet of him to come help at the store today, and I thought it only proper he join us for dinner." Anya looked at Zavian and gave him a fake grin.

Eilish glanced at Zavian, who was watching her expectantly. "Oh, of course, I'll set another plate. Have a seat, Zavian. I'm pretty sure Fina had you doing all the work." She filled his glass with ice cubes and poured the sweet tea over the ice, filling the glass to the rim. She tried to ignore the heavy air of awkwardness in the room. This was the first time since Litha that she'd seen or talked to Zavian.

Zavian was taken off guard; he'd expected rejection, or at the very least a bit of attitude from Eilish. After all, she'd led him down a merry path and kept him at arm's length for so long, only to find out she was sleeping with some other warlock. Warrick had ripped him a new ass after Litha, and now Zavian had been sent on some sort of spy mission. He'd been instructed to find out all he could from Eilish, especially who this warlock was. "Thank you, Eilish."

Fina smiled, "It smells delicious, Anya. Let's sit down and eat together. Isn't this just wonderful to have Zavian with us?" As Anya laid the casserole on the table, she smiled, "Oh, just peachy keen Fina, why didn't Warrick come along?"

Fina waved her hand, "Business to attend to; he's always running here and there." Anya threw the steaming hot biscuits in a basket, laid them on the table, and took her seat. "Dig in!" Fina passed the biscuits to Zavian. "The house looks marvelous; you two have been busy today. I hope it was no trouble for either of you."

Eilish scooped the casserole onto her plate. "Oh, no trouble. It was delightful. I can't remember when I've had so much fun." She flashed Fina an exaggerated smile. "In fact, I think we should be punished more often, don't you, Anya?"

Anya laughed, "Can't wait to do it again." Fina didn't respond to their sarcasm, and Zavian tried to fill the awkward void. "This is delicious, Anya. The biscuits are light and fluffy, just the way I like them." He looked up and smiled at her. As the meal progressed, the conversation was minimal and strained. When the girls got up to clean the table and do the dishes, Fina intervened, deciding it was time to put her plan into motion. "Anya, I'll help you clean up. Eilish, perhaps you and Zavian would like to take a walk or sit on the veranda. We have plenty of wine." The look she gave Eilish invited no comment.

Eilish gave Zavian a weak smile. She knew Fina was working him like a puppet master, and he was in way over his head. "Yeah, sure." She poured two glasses of wine and headed for the screened porch at the back of the house. "Let's sit out here. No mosquitos." She handed him his glass as she dropped into a wicker chair filled with pillows. "Hope Fina wasn't too hard on you today."

Zavian smiled, "No, she was fine; I don't mind helping, actually. I know this is uncomfortable for you, but I wanted to speak with you alone. Will you hear me out, please?"

Eilish didn't make eye contact. It was almost 9:30 p.m., and the sun had set. She was happy to be cloaked in the dark with only a little light spilling out from the kitchen window. "I'll listen to what you have to say."

Zavian reached over and squeezed her hand but didn't push the boundaries of trying to hold it. "Thank you. I know that you were against us having a relationship, and you just wanted to be friends. I understand that now, more than you can imagine. So, I hope we can at least remain friends. I'm willing to accept that, even though Fina and Warrick aren't. You were amazing at Litha. It's all anyone can talk about. I feel like the laughingstock of this coven for not seeing what was in front of me. After Litha, it's clear your power is far above Fina's, and you'd never get that boost in power from me. I may be a fool, but I'm not stupid. I know you're being punished because you've been with someone else, someone powerful, but I can help you. If you try to be friendly with me, maybe some of this will blow over and appease Fina. For the record, I do love you. I always have. I finally understand that love isn't going to be returned to me. I can see that now. You said we'd always be friends, and I hope that part is true. If you need to talk, understand that I'm here for you. I wish you'd let me share in your happiness about this warlock. He must have amazing power."

Eilish squirmed in her seat. She wasn't about to discuss Ian! "Thank you for being understanding. You know I've always considered you a friend. Things are a little up in the air for me now with Fina and the coven. I don't think I want to talk about it. I just need time to figure things out."

Zavian thought she'd want to talk to him, but he'd have to push. He stood up and stretched. "I understand that. I hope that whoever he is, he treats you well. This will stir up a really ugly mess, and I am scared for you. If you need me, I'm here. " He crouched down in front of her. "Eilish, look at me. Time is not going to solve this any time soon. Don't push me away. I can't stop you from loving him. Maybe I can talk to him, help somehow, please."

Eilish set her glass of wine aside. "Talk to him? No! Why would you want to talk to him? He knows what's going on. He understands the position I'm in. The less that is known about him, the better. No. Not happening, Zavian. Let it go."

Zavian stood up and sighed. "Fine, Eilish, if you don't want me on your side, then I have no choice. But do us both a favor, at least when I call, have dinner with me; it will help your situation at least. I promise to be a gentleman." He reached out to take her hand and lift her from the chair. "Come on, let's go back inside, and I will say my goodbyes. You know how to reach me if you want to."

She could tell he was angry and didn't want to worsen the situation. "I can't make any promises, Zavian. Let's take this a day at a time." As they entered the kitchen, Seraphina was still there, her eyes taking in the both of them.

"Well, that was short; I hope all is fine with you both." Zavian went to Fina and kissed her on the cheek. "Thank you for dinner, Fina; it was a pleasure. Eilish and I remain friends, always. " He walked to Eilish and kissed her on the cheek. "I'll call soon. Good night." He couldn't get to the door fast enough.

Fina stood there staring at his back, spun on her heels, and faced

Eilish. "Friends isn't good enough. You had better start toeing the line, sister. This is *not* over."

Eilish sighed as she placed the wine glasses in the sink. "Oh, it's over, Fina. It's way past over." She walked out of the kitchen, brushing Seraphina's shoulder as she passed, and headed up the stairs.

Fina watched her walk away. Zavian had failed again. Her voice was low and filled with anger that she barely held under control. "Maybe you think it's over, but when I find this warlock, he is dead."

BOHANNON

Fina seemed in no hurry to get to the shop as she sat reading the newspaper and leisurely sipped at her tea. Anya and Eilish had both finished their breakfast and had started cleaning up. Eilish kept glancing at the clock, wondering if she should say something. Fina had been quiet after last night's blow-up over Zavian, and she didn't want to start anything. Luna strutted into the kitchen and jumped into Fina's lap, nudging her head against the newspaper and demanding attention. Fina put the paper aside and petted the cat before putting her back on the floor. "I guess I should get to work."

Eilish picked up her empty tea cup and saucer and carried them to the sink. "So how much longer, Fina? How long do you expect Anya and me to stay in the house? Because I have to tell you my spirit of cooperation is running thin." Fina grabbed up her handbag as she headed for the door. "I'll let you know." As she left the house, the two sisters looked at each other. Eilish said, "Carriage house?" Anya nodded. "It's the only place we haven't looked."

The girls quickly ran out the back door and into the carriage house. The Caddy sat with dust covering her glorious old frame. Anya walked past and patted the car. "Good girl." Eilish giggled, then looked around and sighed. Anya scanned the walls of shelves. "This is almost as bad as the attic, but I seriously don't think it's in here. I'll look through this side; you do the other."

Eilish agreed, and both of them began the dusty job of digging through rusty lawn and garden equipment, boxes of old jars and bottles, and old tools. Anya growled, "I swear Fina never throws anything out! She is like a little ole miser." Before too long, they were soaked to the bone from sweating and leaned against the Caddy with no luck. "I would die if this book was in the car!" Anya stood up and popped the trunk as they both looked furiously for a book. All they came up with were a car jack and a moth-eaten blanket. Anya sighed, "Now what?"

Eilish wiped the sweat from her face, smudging it with dust. "I keep going back to the eulogy and the reference to our parents taking their secrets to their graves. It's the only clue that makes sense, but I hate the idea of it. We've never disturbed our parents. If I call on them, and there's nothing there, they know I don't have the book, and Fina and I are at odds with each other. Are we starting something between the living and the dead? I feel like I'm in over my head now."

Anya answered softly. "I know you think it's a lot, but after Litha, I believe in you. You are much more powerful than Fina, and she knows it. Henwen said you were more powerful. Fina is fighting as hard as she can right now to hold onto her position. Believe in yourself and your power, Eilish. The hard part is, how in hell are we going to get out of here without Fina knowing?"

They left the carriage house, closing the doors behind them. "We'll have to wait until tonight after she's asleep. Besides, we need the graveyard to be deserted anyway. I just wish there was another way." The girls made their way back inside the air-conditioned house as Eilish used a paper towel to wipe her face and neck with cool water, and Anya grabbed a glass and filled it with tea. "That gives us the rest of the day to kill."

Anya looked at Eilish, "Look, I know you never wanted to do something like this, but just hear me out. I could easily make a potion to put in Fina's sweet tea at dinner. It will make her sleepy and knock her out for a bit. I know we shouldn't do it, but it would be security." She waited to see how Eilish reacted.

"Actually, that's not a bad idea. She'd know if we placed a spell, but if you put something in her drink . . . and she's tired anyway. She's not used to being on her feet all day. It has to be subtle, Anya. She can't feel dizzy or light-headed. Just something that makes her sleepy, and when she goes down, she's out like a light. She can't be suspicious."

Anya grinned, "You don't know how long I've been waiting to do this. Just some valerian root and lavender." She shrugged her shoulders. "And maybe a few other ingredients; passionflower and chamomile. It will assure us she doesn't wake up, and if Warrick comes home with her, he also gets a dose. By the way, is the crypt covered by a spell?"

Eilish nodded. "Every witch's crypt is protected by a spell, more to keep the humans away than other witches, but I can remove it. I may have to read up on it. We have plenty of books on witchcraft. I'll do that this afternoon."

Anya nodded, "Good. I'll make the potion while you do that. I know we have passionflower in this house someplace. I need to look for that. Should we tell Ian and Carter we're going out tonight?"

Eilish chuckled at Anya's enthusiasm for mixing up a potion. "I thought I'd let Ian know. I've texted him every night to keep him in the loop."

Anya smiled, "Well, I won't tell Carter, but if my phone keeps going off, you will know why!"

Eilish left her sister to mix the potion and went to the study, browsing the books on witchcraft. She found the one she was looking for and re-read the process for removing a protection spell from a grave before going upstairs to shower. She was covered in a sheen of sweat and a layer of dust from the carriage house. After that, it was just a waiting game.

BOHANNON

Anya prepared a heavy dinner of pork chops with onions and gravy, macaroni and cheese, green beans with shallots, glazed carrots, and roasted tomatoes. She prepared a lavish strawberry shortcake for dessert and laced Seraphina's sweet tea with the potion. The girls took lighter portions for their plates while serving large portions to Seraphina. Anya was an excellent cook and made a point of commenting on how great the fresh produce was this year. They both knew Fina had a thing about leaving food on her plate, and she'd finish her meal.

Eilish suggested they sit on the screened porch with their dessert and sweet tea when the dinner plates were cleared. They gathered on the porch, under the soft whirring sound of the ceiling fan and the accompaniment of the crickets and tree frogs, the wind chimes gently ringing. Seraphina leaned back in the comfy wicker chair and placed her feet up as the night settled in, and she felt her eyes growing heavy. It had been a long time since she had worked the shop, and being on her feet all day for the last few days had taken its toll. She finished her dessert and set the bowl aside. "That was delicious, but way too much food." Eilish faked a yawn. "Yes, but there's nothing like fresh veggies in the summer. It would be a shame not to take advantage of it."

Anya put on Nina Simone singing "Feeling Good" as the three sat in the dark. Seraphina's head began to nod. "Goodness. I can barely keep my eyes open." Eilish curled up in her chair, tucking her legs under her. "I know, right? It's such a beautiful night. I think I could sleep right here." Seraphina stood and stretched. "Well, I hate to end this party, but if I don't get a shower and get in bed now, I will be asleep on the porch. Great dinner, Anya." Anya answered from her cozy chair, "You're welcome, sis. We'll be right behind you as soon as we finish cleaning up the kitchen."

The two sisters stayed on the porch for a few minutes as they heard Seraphina climb the stairs. In minutes they could hear the pipes creak as the shower came on. They waited until the sound of the shower ended before getting up to clean the kitchen.

They kept their voices low, and Anya turned off the playlist of ballads she'd prepared for the evening. They waited until they felt Fina was in a deep sleep, then Eilish gathered her few supplies as they headed out. The two sisters walked hand in hand to St. Phillip's Church on Church Street. Eilish could feel the moisture in her palms. "I've been nervous about this all day. I've conjured spirits before, but this is different."

Anya looked up at the moon, "Well, how different? And I didn't tell Carter what we had planned, but I'm guessing you told Ian?"

Eilish squeezed her hand. "Different in that it's our mother. Mom was High Priestess, so if either of them has the book, it would be Mom. When I call her forward, she'll know something is wrong. If she has the book, she will know Fina is keeping it from me. Plus, I really have no memory of her. Only photos." She shook her head. "I just hope we're doing the right thing. I did tell Ian. He offered to come along, but I said the last thing my mother would want to see was a vampire."

Anya shook her head. "You don't know that, Eilish. She may not have cared because he brings you happiness. And I'm pretty sure if you pull this off, Mom will be glad for it."

As they walked, a shadowed figure kept his eyes on them,

following but not too close. Ian had talked to Eilish earlier in the day, giving him the details of what would happen. But Ian heard the hesitation in her voice, her conflict over whether this was the right thing to do. He knew this was dangerous and could result badly for her. He intended to keep his distance but make sure things went as planned. He wasn't going to leave her out here on her own. He watched from the church steeple of St. Phillip's as the sisters entered the quiet and looming graveyard. She looked stunning in the moonlight, even from this distance. Ian made himself comfortable and remained shadowed so the girls wouldn't see him. Settling in, he waited to see what would happen.

The girls entered the graveyard beside the church, walking between the graves to the two crypts that sat side by side. Hamish and Evelyn Bohannon. They had been brought here on the anniversary of their death every year by Seraphina and left flowers and crystals. The three would always come together, then Fina would take them back home, and she'd disappear for a few hours afterward. She'd say she needed some time to be alone with her thoughts. The sisters stood next to their mother's crypt. Eilish ran her hand over the engraved name and dates. "Hello, Mommy. I hope you'll forgive me for what I'm about to do." She turned to Anya. "Are you ready? There's no turning back now."

Anya looked at the crypt and then at Eilish. "As ready as I'll ever be. Just have confidence; you can do this. It's our only way. Go for it."

Eilish hoped she was right. What if the book wasn't there? Then her mother would know there was a rift between the sisters, and that's something she'd never want to see. "Okay then." Eilish opened the soft cloth pouch she's prepared for the ritual. She removed the salt container and walked around the crypt, pouring the salt until she had created a closed circle, then stepped inside. She laid a celestite crystal on her mother's name and spoke her name out loud. "Evelyn Bohannon." She removed a small branch from a yew tree, used it to brush away any debris from the top of the crypt, and then laid the branch under her mother's name. She took camphor, clove, and mimosa incense and placed the cones on top of the crypt. With a touch of her finger, she lit a flame, and the fragrant smell of the incense was carried on the trail of smoke. As she spoke, she marked her chest with a pentagram, raising her arms skyward. "I have come that I may see you. I open the Netherworld that I may see my mother, Evelyn Bohannon, for I am beloved of her. I have opened every path which is in the sky and on earth, for I am the daughter of Rhiannon. To the gods of Earth, Water, Air, and Fire, clear a path for her." Eilish stood silent as she waited for her mother's spirit to appear. She could hear Anya breathing softly behind her. The wind stirred slightly, and they could hear an owl in a nearby tree, but no spirit appeared. Eilish lowered her arms and placed both hands on her mother's crypt. "Mommy?" She turned to Anya and spoke with alarm. "She's not here. There's no one here!"

Anya had been holding her breath as she waited, her palms sweaty, yet nothing happened. Her fear and concern grew by the second. As she heard her sister's words, she stared at her with disbelief and confusion. "What? What do you mean there's no one there? They're buried here, both of them. We need to open the crypt. I can't believe they're not in there." Anya tried to push the heavy concrete slab that topped the crypt aside as Eilish joined her, but with no luck.

Ian had watched the ritual and could hear Eilish's chant. He watched in anticipation for the apparition to appear. He had seen Eilish do this before and was shocked when nothing happened. He heard Eilish as her voice grew panicked. He felt his blood rushing in his veins. This couldn't be happening. He leaped from the steeple in a split second and landed behind them. "Need some help, babe?"

Eilish grabbed at her throat, startled by his sudden appearance. "You scared me to death! But yes, help us move the slab.

Ian smiled. "Stand back while I move the slab, both of you." As the sisters moved back behind him, Ian easily slid the slab at an angle so the crypt's interior was visible. The three of them leaned forward, looking into the empty crypt. There was nothing. No coffin. No body. No book.

Eilish couldn't hide her confusion. "Nothing. Close it up." She looked at her sister. "This makes no sense. Where are they? We had a funeral. I remember the funeral. The crypts were already sealed shut when the coven gathered for the ritual, but that's our custom. Where the hell are they?" She could hear Ian slide the heavy slab back into place as she turned to him. "Just to be sure, check my father's crypt." He easily pushed the slab aside as the sisters confirmed what they already knew. Both crypts were empty.

Anya closed her eyes and shook her head. "We've been coming here since we were little children; all this time, and they weren't even here. Why? Why would Fina do this to us? They have to be buried someplace, Eilish. Someplace close if Fina needs the book and Mommy has it."

Ian put his arms around Eilish. "There has to be a logical explanation. Just think it through. Visiting their gravesite is important to Fina if she brings you here every year. How does Fina react when she's here?"

Eilish shrugged. "We come every year on the anniversary of their death. We leave flowers, usually roses and lavender, and an amethyst crystal. Other members of the coven also come by, leaving tokens of sage. The coven revered our mother, and everyone was always so helpful to Seraphina because she had to raise us on her own. After every visit, when we were small, we'd be left with one of the women from our coven and, later, left on our own. Fina always needed some time to be alone. She'd disappear for a few hours. No one thought anything of it. She was the only one old enough to have any real memories of our parents, plus they had been murdered. She was the one who found them and had to endure that trauma."

Ian scratched his head. "Things aren't adding up here. If your coven members come here, someone is duping all of you. Where does Seraphina go to be alone?"

Eilish shook her head. "I have no idea. She just goes off for a couple of hours and then returns home. She seems at peace afterward. It's just something she's always done, and there was no reason to question her."

Ian ran his knuckles across her cheek. "Right now, babe, you must question everything she does or says. I know she's your sister, and raised you, but since I've known you, she's done nothing but lie and try to manipulate you. She has a reason for all of this secrecy. We need to find out where she goes."

He looked at Anya, "Any ideas?" Anya shook her head. "I've got nothing. She never seems to take anything with her that I can recall. What a mess."

Eilish looked around the graveyard, lit by the moon. "Okay, well, first we need to remove any trace of our being here. Fina will recognize this ritual." Eilish started to put the crystal and the yew branch back in the pouch and brushed away the remnants of the incense. "You guys scatter the salt."

Ian watched as Anya used her foot to brush at the salt, so it no longer made a circle. He followed her example. "By the way, when is the anniversary of your parent's death?"

Anya answered as he helped her scatter the salt into the grass and dirt. "Three weeks from today, why?"

Ian stopped pushing his boot over the salt. He looked at Eilish and smiled. "In three weeks, she's going to bring you both here. You need to act like nothing is wrong. But I can help. When she leaves to go wherever it is she goes, I can shadow myself and follow her. I can help you find out where she goes. Let me help you, please?"

Eilish looked at her sister. "Another gravesite? Do you think Fina had them entombed somewhere else? But why?"

Anya put her hands on her hips. "Look, sis, right now, she's not playing by the damn rules. Maybe she's always been like this, and we never paid attention. So, I think we cover all bases. If that's where she hid the book, having them entombed somewhere else would be perfect. Think about it; no one would ever see her getting the book. I can't believe I'm saying this, but I'm with the bloodsucker; let him see where she goes." Anya looked at Ian. "No offense."

Ian chuckled. "None taken."

Eilish felt so betrayed. All these years, she'd been coming here to honor her parents, and they weren't even here. What was Fina up to? "Yes, shadow her, please. It may be futile. She may not lead us to the real graves, but it's the only clue we've got."

Ian held Eilish in his arms. He kissed her softly at first and then with a yearning that bared his soul. "I have missed you. I love you. Go home; I'll follow you, then take off once you're close to the house."

As the girls began to walk back, he kept to the tree tops, and once they were within a block of the house, he headed for home. Following a fucking High Priestess around to find out what she was up to wasn't his cup of tea, but he'd do everything he could to help Eilish and Anya.

BOHANNON

Eilish and Anya had walked briskly past the old house under renovation, casting quick glances in the boys' direction. They had been ordered to return to work in the shop, but they both knew Seraphina had them under close supervision. They'd been back several days now, and Seraphina, or Warrick, had dropped in at random times every day. They had also seen more members of their coven popping in than usual and weren't sure if that was Fina's doing or if it was just the natural curiosity of the coven. Everyone had something to say about Eilish's performance during Litha, and she was trying hard not to make a big deal of it. Before they returned to the shop, Fina had laid down the law and made it clear that whatever they had going on with the warlocks from the other coven was over, or else. The 'or else' had been left hanging out there, a veiled threat of some punishment yet to be named. Other than boundary spells, which Eilish had quickly learned to dispel, Fina had never used witchcraft on her sisters before. But that didn't mean she wouldn't, and both girls knew it. They were also keenly aware of the danger they could place Ian and Carter in.

The store had seen a steady flow of witches and humans all morning, and the girls had been busy. Eilish was preoccupied bagging up a purchase when the bell over the door jingled, and she looked up to see Warrick. She smiled and thanked her customer before muttering to Anya. "Our jailer's here."

Anya looked up and smiled. "Good morning, Warrick; what can we assist you with today? Oh wait, let me guess, just doing your usual detective work." Warrick smirked and looked at Eilish, his voice reflecting his frustration. He hadn't liked being dragged into this mess that Fina had created, and now he was made to watch over them like he was the puppet and Fina the puppet master. At this point, he was willing to do whatever was necessary to hang onto Fina and the associative power he gained, but not without a grudge. "So, you have decided to listen to Seraphina and act like proper witches with responsibilities to this coven. Perhaps you are convincing her, but me, not so much."

Eilish had to bite her tongue. She knew the tighter she pulled against the reins held by Fina and Warrick, the longer this close observation would last. Still, she didn't have it in her to just lay down and roll over like a trained dog in their little dog and pony show. "Whatever do you mean, Warrick? When have Anya or I ever been anything but compliant to your will or the will of our beloved sister?"

Warrick walked closer to the counter and stared. "Well, lately, you haven't been very compliant. Zavian tells me you haven't been responding to him in the least. But never mind that. I see it's been busy since you both have been back in the shop. You've sparked more interest within this coven than I'm comfortable with. I think, perhaps, it's time you're seen out with Zavian." He chuckled, "Let's see how compliant you are, Eilish."

Eilish bristled and could feel the hairs on the back of her neck stand up. Her fingertips tingled, and she noticed the tiny blue sparks that emanated from her fingers as she straightened the bags behind the counter. She took a deep breath and shook her hands, hoping to cool down her temper. If they thought for one minute they could force a bonding with Zavian, they had another thing coming! "Yes, of course, Warrick. Whatever you say. You seem intent on wasting my time and Zavian's, but if it makes you happy."

Warrick grinned, "You have no idea what makes me happy, Eilish. But I'm sure the warlock you think you love is quite bored with waiting. I'll make sure Zavian knows to call on you soon. He won't wait forever."

Turning back to the door, he thought he'd won this small battle. As he opened the door, he looked back at Eilish. "Be very careful, Eilish; you play a dangerous game." He walked out and softly closed the door, laughing as he did so.

Eilish stared hard at his back as he left, and the wind chimes started to swing wildly. A couple of salt crystal lamps glowed so brightly that the crystal shattered and the pieces scattered across the floor. Through her gritted teeth, she spoke to Anya. "You need to seriously keep me from turning him into to toad."

"Well, as much as I would love to see that, sister, you need to calm yourself down. Warrick is just trying to stir you up, so you make a mistake, and if that happens, we're both done for. I'll clean this up; go make yourself a cup of tea or something and calm down." Anya watched as Eilish walked to the back room, and she sighed. This would be a very dangerous adventure with Eilish and her power.

Ian watched as the girls walked by every day. He'd decided against filling in Carter about the night he helped them at the crypt. He wasn't sure how much he should share with him, and Ian felt the less he knew, the safer he'd be. He'd secretly been watching the shop after he got off from work and had seen a lot of witches coming in and out. He also didn't miss that their older sister or her warlock came in at least once a day. Ian knew this was to ensure both sisters were toeing the line. He watched as the warlock named Warrick left, looking way too pleased with himself, and knew Eilish was probably his target. He waited a while before entering the shop to make sure the warlock was long gone, and business had seemed to slow. Now was the time to move in. He dropped from the rooftop into an alley and walked down the street and into the shop. He could feel the anxiety in the air and found Anya sweeping up the floor. "I just saw him leave. Is everything okay?"

Anya was startled when she heard Ian's voice and stopped sweeping. "What are you doing here? It's dangerous for you to be here! Look, she's in the backroom; go now, before someone else comes in." Ian walked to the back and found Eilish pacing the floor. "Whoa, a bit of energy vibe you got going on there, babe."

Eilish stopped her pacing and looked at him with tears in her eyes. "Ian." She almost tripped over a box trying to get to him, collapsing in his arms as he held her tight. "I don't know a way out of this. I'm so glad to see you, but you shouldn't be here. They can hurt you."

Ian held her tight, softly stroking her hair. "Calm down. I'm right here, and you're fine; that's the important thing. The only way out of this is to find the book, and we have a plan in place. Now we just have to get through a few more weeks. I'm here because I love you, and I'll fight through whatever they want to throw at me. You have to do the same. They're going to test you, Eilish. Try to cooperate. You can do this. What in the hell did Warrick want anyway?"

Eilish laid her head against his chest, listening to his heartbeat. Its rhythm soothed her as she wiped at her tears. "They want me to see Zavian. I don't think I can do it. I'm so tired of their games, of being manipulated. I never wanted this. I never wanted the power, and I could care less that Fina is the High Priestess. I would never have challenged her. She and Warrick can run the fucking coven. Why can't they just leave me out of it?"

Ian felt her struggle, she was losing hope, and he never wanted her to lose that. He pulled her back and kissed her hard and sweet. His arms tightened around her, and he looked into her gray eyes as he broke the kiss. "You have to fight for what you deserve. I've seen this power of yours, Eilish Bohannon, and you were born to be the

High Priestess and take this coven in a new direction. Build it, and make it your own. It's your destiny." He slid his roughened carpenter's hand along her cheek and kissed away her tears. "You can do this, whatever it is, because you're the most powerful witch in the world. As for Zavian, just do what you must. He's powerless. Even I can tell his energy is weak. He's easy to manipulate, which is why Warrick is so intent on you bonding with him. I doubt Zavian would strong-arm you; he's not the type, but if he did, I'm ready to take his ass out. You have me, Anya, and Carter, and we're behind you."

She nodded. "Okay, I can do this. Just don't give up on me. I don't think Zavian actually cares. I think he's as bullied in this situation as much as I am."

"Maybe you should point that out to the fool." Ian let go of Eilish and walked around the room. His brain was going way too fast, and he felt like Eilish wanted to give up. He was doing all this for her and her love. "Eilish, look, the anniversary of your parent's death is only two weeks away; I'm only going to ask you this once. Do you still want me to go through with following Seraphina after you visit your parent's crypt? Because I don't want to push you into this if it's not something you want to pursue, even though I think you should." He walked back to her and stood with his forehead against hers. "Just tell me. It's okay if you want to give all this up, babe."

She leaned into him. "I could care less about the book, but without the book, I can't have you. I remain under Fina's control if I don't claim my power. I have to take the thing I don't want to have the person I love most in this world. Follow her. It may come to nothing anyway, but it's the only clue we have right now."

Ian kissed her then and felt in his heart that she was ready to move ahead. She loved him, and they'd find this book no matter the outcome. Being in the shop was risky, and he knew he shouldn't linger much longer. "I should go, even though I don't want to. But it's dangerous for me to be here. Just outwit them, Eilish, you can do it, and I'm always right around the corner. I'll follow Seraphina as soon as she leaves the two of you back home, and we'll do whatever it takes to be together."

Kissing her once more, they walked back out into the store. Anya sat behind the counter, listening to her headphones. "You know, Anya, Carter is driving me crazy. All he does is talk about you all damn day. What have you done to him?" Anya giggled and winked. "Well, I'm not sharing my secrets with you!"

Eilish stood next to her sister as Ian left the shop. She hugged Anya. "Shit's about to get real, sister. I hope we know what we're doing."

BOHANNON

The weeks had slipped by as Eilish and Anya resumed their routine of working at the shop. Warrick, Zavian, or Seraphina continued to drop in unannounced to keep them on their toes. Eilish would exchange looks with Ian every morning on their way to work, and Ian would often be out on Tradd Street when they left in the evening, keeping a safe distance but making sure they saw each other. He mouthed the words "I love you," and she returned his sentiment, sending a spell that made his chest feel warm. Sometimes he felt a sensation like her lips brushing his. It was a slow form of torture for both of them. Carter had been able to slip into the shop a few times to see Anya. As a human, he drew no attention.

In the evenings, after dinner, the girls retreated to their rooms and spent time texting in silence while Anya or Emric played music from Anya's extensive vinyl collection.

Fina was starting to get lax, not having seen or heard anything more about the warlocks from the neighboring coven, and was paying less attention to them. She felt confident the young warlocks would grow tired of this waiting game and move on to more available females.

Tomorrow was the anniversary of their parent's death, and Fina had remarked at dinner that she had picked up flowers for the occasion and asked Eilish if she had remembered to bring the rose quartz crystals from the shop. "Of course, I remembered. Tomorrow is a special day. How could I ever forget?"

As the girls started to clean up after dinner, Fina stood and announced she was going out to meet Warrick and would be back soon. "That doesn't give either of you license to leave. I'm putting a protection spell on the house. I'll know if you leave." Anya sighed loud enough to make herself heard. "Whatever, Fina."

As Seraphina left, the girls exchanged glances, knowing what lay in store tomorrow. It would either change everything or change nothing. After all, they didn't know where Fina went after visiting their parent's grave. It was possible she really did just want time for herself. Anya placed the last dish in the dishwasher. "I'm going to shower, then talk with Carter awhile. I still haven't told him anything about the plans for tomorrow night. I'm afraid he'd feel the need to help somehow and get himself killed." Eilish nodded, "Best to keep him in the dark for now. Besides, there may not even be a book. This could be Henwen's joke on us both."

Eilish followed her sister up the stairs and went to her room, closing the door behind her. She grabbed her phone and sent Ian a text. She knew he'd be waiting.

Ian lay on the couch and waited anxiously. Tomorrow would be the day he'd follow Seraphina, and his beast was cranky, to say the least. He'd been scouring the heavily populated tourist venues for young females to feed on to keep himself alive. A few times, he'd met Ryker at the bar and hooked up with some willing, if not slightly intoxicated females, but nothing satisfied him like Eilish. Beyond that, it had been weeks since either of them could physically be together, and all he wanted was her. He rearranged himself again on the couch and wondered when she'd text. He knew Seraphina's presence dictated her schedule, so her contacts were random and sometimes really late after Seraphina went to bed. Finally, he grew restless, grabbed the phone, and started for the shower when it pinged in his hand. It was Eilish. *Hey.*

He smiled. *Just thinking about you, babe. You okay?*

Eilish responded to his text. *I'm fine. Nervous about tomorrow. Fina just left to visit Warrick, so Anya and I are here without our jailer for a change.* She re-arranged her pillows so she could lean against the headboard of her bed. With Fina gone, maybe she would even risk calling him so that she could hear his voice.

Ian smiled. Any contact with her usually soothed him, but tonight, nothing was taking this beast down a notch. *She's usually gone a while and gives you a break. No need to be nervous. I'm not worried about tomorrow. Everything will go smoothly.* Ian knew he was taking a huge chance, but he decided it was now or never. He teleported to her house, landing on the roof of the veranda right outside her window. *Babe, do you hear anything?* He tapped lightly on the window several times while the beast growled inside him.

Eilish heard a tap at her window, and Emric started to rush about the room, shouting, "Invader, invader!" Eilish told him to calm down as she got up and opened her door, telling Emric to visit Anya. She pulled back the curtain on her window to see Ian on the other side. She lifted the window but was careful not to lean out as it would break Fina's protection spell. "Stand still. I can't come out, or Fina will know. But I can reverse the spell so you can come in."

Eilish stood at the window and used her hand to cut a portal through the barrier, watching as the air shimmered around the window. "Okay. Climb through."

Ian grinned and followed her instructions. He went through the window and grabbed her hard. "Well, there are major advantages to loving a witch; I like it." He kissed her quick and she felt his hands fist in her hair. "This is killing me; I miss you, and so does my beast. I'm sorry, I know this is dangerous, but I couldn't resist. Where is Anya?"

Eilish left the window open but closed the drapes. "Anya's in her room, and you'll have to leave as soon as Fina returns. She'll break the protection spell when she enters the house, and then you'll be able to leave without her knowing. I have no idea how much time we have. I can't believe you did this."

Ian looked at her and knew she was worried about his hasty visit. "It's okay, Eilish; I understand what we're up against." He unbuttoned her shirt and placed soft, tender kisses across her breasts as they peeped above her bra. When he felt her touch his hair, he reached around and unhooked her bra as it fell to the floor. His mouth devoured a nipple, and he moaned as his hands gripped her small waist. He wanted to climb inside her. "I want you, babe."

Ian walked her back until her legs hit her bed. "Wait." She started to lift his black tee-shirt over his head, his dark hair falling in a tumble. He sat on the edge of her bed and pulled off his work boots before standing again and unzipping his jeans. She helped him slide the jeans over his hips as he kicked them aside.

Eilish could still hear Emric crashing about in Anya's room, bumping against her record player and making the needle skip across the vinyl as he continued to shout, "Invader, invader!" She heard her sister admonish him, telling him to settle down before she heard a light tap on her door and Anya's voice. "Everything okay, sis?"

Ian had crawled into her bed and was impatiently waiting for her as Eilish answered her sister. "I'm fine. Just an unexpected visitor." She heard Anya chuckle as she turned to leave. "Okay, well, call if you need me." Eilish climbed into the bed, a wicked smile on her face. "You're being a very bad vampire tonight."

Ian grabbed her and pulled her on top of him. "Aren't all vamps supposed to be bad? Besides, when did you decide to be the good witch? I think it's time you showed this badass vamp a little of the wicked witch in you." He watched as she shimmied out of her skirt. He knelt at her feet, kissing his way up her leg, nibbling behind her kneecap, before he continued to the inside of her thigh, nipping and kissing softly. He felt her overwhelming need for him, and he wasn't far behind. He knew they didn't have time to play around, and at any moment, the High Priestess of this coven would come back home. He moved up her body and kissed her mouth as he slid inside her. He felt her energy suddenly swirl around him and drove his cock deep inside her.

Eilish gasped, then wrapped her legs around his hips. Witches and warlocks had great power, but their physical strength was like any human's. She loved his physicality, the feel of the hard muscles beneath her hands, his weight on her, the power behind his thrusting hips. He moved her around the bed, changing their positions on a whim as if she weighed nothing. He kissed her hard, and she returned the kiss, riding the wave of passion that was crashing over them. She felt her energy level rise, and the lights flickered in the room. She felt his mouth at her throat, his tongue exploring before she felt the sharp, piercing pain of his teeth into her flesh. The pinprick of pain was followed by the powerful sensation of heat and the unquenchable desire that rolled out from her core. She turned her head slightly to allow him to feed as the lightbulb in the lamp shattered and plunged them into darkness. As he continued to ride her to orgasm, she generated her own light from her root chakra, and the room was lit with a red glow that matched the glow in his eyes.

Ian fed and filled himself with her blood, unique and quenching. Together, they were combustible. As he rolled off of her, they lay together in a light sheen of sweat; he moaned, but it was one of great pleasure. "I should go, but damn if I want to. I will be close by tomorrow, at St. Phillip's, and then back again here. She won't sense me; I'll keep my distance, high up, rooftop level. Once I see her leave, I'll follow, no matter where she goes. Just hope to hell she doesn't lead me to the warlock's den!"

Eilish laid beside him, her hand on his bare chest, gently stroking him. "All kidding aside, be careful. This may be nothing, Ian. A wild goose chase. It could turn out that Fina just does what she's always said—spending some time alone. She was the one who found our parents after they were murdered. She's had to live with that memory, so I can understand if she needed to be alone. On the other hand, if she had them entombed somewhere else and hid the book in their tomb, she would be alert to anyone following her. She may not be as powerful as me, but don't underestimate her. If she detects you, hears you, even senses you, she can still cast a spell strong enough to kill. You don't have to do this if you have doubts or second thoughts."

Ian turned on his side to face her. Kissing her softly, he smiled. "I love that you worry so much about me. But I've been around long enough to know how to keep myself invisible. Don't worry; if she gets wind of me, I'll bail, but unless that happens, I'll find out where she goes. I'm not giving up. I'm doing this for both of us."

He kissed her one last time, making it last. Finally, he got up and dressed, careful to step around the broken glass from the lightbulb. "Thank Anya for me, for keeping that ghost quiet. I love you, Eilish. I'll be around, so think about me and us because I'll be thinking of you."

They cuddled until they heard Warrick's car pull up in front of the house. Eilish sat up in the bed, her finger to her lips, indicating he needed to be quiet. They heard one car door close, and Eilish slipped from the bed, stepping over the glass from the shattered light bulb, and looked out the window, opening the curtains slightly. She saw Warrick walk around the car and open the door for Fina. He held her tight and kissed her. Ian stood close behind her, waiting for his cue to leave. Warrick watched as Fina walked alone to the house before he returned and got in the driver's side, closing the door behind him and starting the engine. Warrick waited until he saw Fina at the door before driving away. Eilish saw the soft shimmer in the air as the protection spell was lifted and heard Fina's key in the lock. "Now! Go now!" She pushed Ian towards the open window, holding the curtains back.

Giving her a quick kiss, he climbed out the window and teleported immediately before being detected. He followed the car the warlock drove until he returned home and knew that if Fina led him there tomorrow, he needed to be on high alert. He texted Eilish when he got back home. *I love you.*

Eilish lowered the window and, with a flick of her hand, blew the broken glass under her bed before she quickly climbed in. She heard Fina's footsteps on the stairs, and in a second, Fina opened her bedroom door without knocking. Eilish lifted her head from her pillow as the light from the hallway shone on her face. "What's wrong?"

Seraphina just stared at her. "Nothing. Just checking." Eilish answered her, her sarcasm on display. "Your prisoners are safe in their bunks, Fina. Go to bed." Fina closed the door, leaving her in the dark. As she laid her head back on her pillow, she heard the soft ping of her phone. She knew without looking that it was Ian and what his message said.

BOHANNON

The shop was always closed on the anniversary of their parent's death. The mood in the house had been quiet. Anya had started to play some music, but Seraphina put a stop to it. "This is not a day to celebrate, Anya. It's a day to reflect." The younger sisters had always tried to respect Fina's space on this day. Although they had few memories, they tried to honor Fina's feelings and the parents they barely knew.

Anya busied herself in the kitchen instead, and Eilish helped. After dinner, the three of them dressed in white. Fina gathered the white roses she'd picked from their garden earlier today, and Eilish collected the six rose quartz stones she picked up from the shop. As the sun set, the three witches left their house, walking the distance to St. Phillip's Church. Eilish stayed on alert. If Ian was about, she couldn't detect him.

They entered the church graveyard just as the sun fell below the horizon; the sky was still tinged a pale pink. The three made their way to the crypts Eilish and Anya knew were now empty. There were already some fresh flowers on the tombs, indicating that other coven members had visited today. Fina laid roses on each crypt, and they each placed a rose quartz crystal, a symbol of love, on top of the slab among the flowers. Fina tilted her head and cried softly. It was a scene that Anya and Eilish had watched her repeat year after year; only this year, they began to appreciate Fina's skill at play-acting. For a moment, Eilish wondered if Fina even knew the crypts were empty. Maybe some other coven had broken the protection spell years ago and stolen the bodies and the book...if there even was a book. Her mind was filled with questions and doubt. Fina bit her lip and ran her hand lovingly over the concrete slab covering their mother's tomb. "Pay your respects, and let's go. It brings me so much sorrow. I can't bear it."

Anya and Eilish kissed the crypts, telling their long-dead parents they loved them, then followed Fina out of the graveyard. They walked in silence back to the house.

Fina gave them instructions as they entered the old Victorian house holding generations of Bohannons. "Nothing has changed for you two. Don't leave the house. I'll know if you do. I'll be back later." She went to the kitchen and reached into the jar of flour, fishing out the keys to the car. Leaving through the back door and sealing the house with a protection spell, she made her way to the carriage house. Anya and Eilish heard the rumble of the Caddy engine as she backed the car out of the garage and drove away.

Anya turned to her sister. "What now?" Eilish wrung her hands together, hoping she hadn't sent Ian to his death. "We wait."

Ian kept his distance as he watched the sisters pay their respects to an empty crypt. He kept his eyes on his surroundings, alert for other coven members or the warlock, Warrick. But only the sisters appeared at sunset. As they left, he kept shadowing them on their path home and maintained his distance. He didn't intend to be found out before he even began. He sat high on the rooftop, three houses down, his senses honed into the Bohannon household and its inhabitants. He saw the black Caddy pull out onto the street and was slightly surprised. Wherever Fina was going, it was a distance, or she was picking up someone. He followed her car, keeping his wits about him. He followed the car for almost an hour as she drove into the Francis Marion National Forest. "What the hell are you up to, Seraphina?"

Once she parked, she got out of the car and headed down the Awendaw passage, a well-marked hiking trail. Ian kept tree top level to keep his eyes peeled for any moves she'd make. It was dark now, and he wondered what in the hell she was up to when she left the trail and headed into the woods. "That's it, Seraphina, lead me to something I can use."

Seraphina had changed into a pair of sneakers before exiting the car and starting her walk down the trail. She flipped on a flashlight she held and pointed it to the ground so that she could follow the well-worn hiking path. She had walked almost two miles down the passage when she saw the large moss-covered stone that was her landmark and veered from the trail. She pushed aside the undergrowth and found her way through the woods in the dark, tripping a few times on the vines growing along the forest floor. As she got closer, she raised her flashlight to illuminate the portal as it rose up in front of her. It was an upright circle, perfectly symmetrical and elaborately created from a maze of sticks and branches, standing at least six feet tall. She and Warrick had built the portal years ago after Warrick had helped her to kill her parents. She had argued with her mother after being informed that it was Eilish, and not her, who would lead the coven and inherit the book. Warrick had always been her eager lap dog, and it took very little to persuade him that if he bonded with her and helped her kill her parents, they would be elevated to High Priest and Priestess, and no one would be the wiser. For Seraphina, it had been a small price to pay.

The portal loomed eerily in the middle of the dense forest. If any hikers stumbled on it, it would be a curiosity. For her, it was a portal to the Netherworld. She looked about in the dark woods, then turned off her flashlight and stepped through the circle.

⁂

Ian watched as her flashlight came on, he didn't need it to see in the dark, but she did. He watched as she veered further into the thicket of the wooded forest. The night was humid, and the sounds of the night creatures made their music. Suddenly Seraphina shone the light on an oddly constructed circle of branches and sticks. It stood upright, creating an open doorway or portal, hidden deep in the forest's darkness, well off the trail. It was the strangest thing he'd ever seen. The flashlight went out, and what Ian saw next, he couldn't believe. He watched in disbelief as Seraphina carefully stepped through the portal and literally disappeared. He blinked several times, teleporting back and forth over the portal, but she was gone. He landed on the forest floor and wondered if he should try and follow her. What if he disappeared as well? What if he couldn't get back? What if Seraphina could see him once he went through? He felt like he was in over his head. He shook his head and knew this portal held some kind of magic, but he'd never seen anything like it. He gave it a wide berth and walked around the portal, even teleported above it, circling at least a mile past the mysterious construction, but she was gone. Taking a deep breath, he realized only two things. He had no idea where the portal led and had no protection against whatever witchcraft was used to protect that portal. "So, this is where you go."

He thought about waiting for her to return but knew that wouldn't give him any answers. He didn't understand what he'd seen, but he knew Eilish would, or at least, he hoped she would. He teleported out, returning to Charleston in minutes, making his way to Eilish and the Bohannon house. They had a mystery to solve.

⁂

Want more Eilish and Ian? Of course, you do!

Information on Book Two, Rhiannon's Revenge, is here:
https://emilybex.com/p/rhiannons-revenge
https://emilybex.com/

SAMPLING OF RHIANNON'S REVENGE - BOOK TWO

BOHANNON

Ian was teleporting back to the Battery in Charleston from the most extraordinary thing he'd ever seen. Granted, he was a vampire, but he'd just watched Seraphina, the High Priestess of the Bohannon coven, pass through a massive portal of intricately woven branches and sticks, standing at least six feet high in the middle of the forest, then disappear. He'd teleported in a wide berth, high above the portal, and even dropped to the ground, walking around, but not through, the portal. He had no idea what lay on the other side or if he could still shadow himself from Seraphina once he went through. He didn't even know if he'd be able to get back. He knew the portal was protected by witchcraft, and he was out of his league. But at least he'd found an answer to part of the mystery about where Seraphina went every year on the anniversary of her parent's death.

So many thoughts ran through his head as he sped back to the two younger Bohannon sisters at their home. He needed to talk to Eilish and Anya, tell them what he'd seen, and hope they had some clue as to where their eldest sister had disappeared to. Eilish needed that book of spells. It was the only thing that would help her finally take her rightful place as High Priestess. He loved her, and he'd die trying to help her.

He finally got to the old Victorian house and landed unnoticed on the back porch. He rapped hard on the door and heard the sisters running in his direction. Eilish whipped open the door, Anya right behind her. "You won't believe what I have to tell you. But I found where she goes."

Eilish held the door open and ushered him inside before he was seen. She was thankful he'd shown up at the back door. "Get in here, quick. How much time do we have? Is Fina right behind you?"

"Well, not right behind me. She's a good hour's drive from here. She drove to the Francis Marion Forest. Once she got out of the car, I shadowed and followed her. She took a clearly marked hikers trail into the forest a couple of miles, then veered off the trail. She went into the forest pretty deep." Ian began to pace back and forth. He kept shaking his head. "I was right behind her since I didn't know where she'd go, but she disappeared." Eilish and Anya both looked at him and, in unison, said, "Disappeared?"

Ian shook his head, his dark hair flying. "There was this... thing... like a huge piece of art; it was a perfectly symmetrical circle, made of sticks and branches. It was like, six feet tall, clearly carefully constructed by hand, and made to last. She walked through the portal, and she was gone." He threw up his hands. "At first, I couldn't believe what I'd seen, but she never came back out. I teleported high above and couldn't see her anywhere. She just disappeared into thin air. Then I dropped down and stood in front of it. All I saw was the forest, but she still wasn't there when I looked through it. I didn't know if I should try to go through; if it's bound by magic, I might not be able to get back out. Where the hell did she go, Eilish?"

Eilish held her hands over her mouth, trying to take in everything he was saying. "It's a portal to the Netherworld. She would have cast a spell to enter, and she'd cast another to exit. For anyone else, any human who should stumble upon it, it's just an oddity. They can walk freely through the circle. But if you'd followed directly behind her when the spell was still in play, you could have been trapped in the Netherworld. You made the right decision not to follow her." Eilish placed her hands on either side of her head as Anya bit at a nail. Eilish continued, "If she built a portal to the Netherworld, then that's where our parents are. Fina doesn't have the power to call forth spirits on her own, but the portal will grant her access. This explains a lot."

Anya nodded. "Yes, but it's still limited. She can't call their spirits up whenever she wants. She doesn't have that power, but you do. Fina can only use the portal and would have to call upon them on the anniversary at the exact day and time of their death. That explains why she always waits until sunset before we can visit their graves... or what we thought were their graves."

Ian was listening closely as he looked from one sister to the other. The fucking Netherworld? Good thing he didn't try to walk through. "So, what are you saying? There's another crypt beyond that portal with your parents? Can you and Anya get through? Will you be able to get me through because I'm not letting you go there alone?"

Eilish nodded. "Portals for the Netherworld are rare, but if we know where it is, we can pass freely through and back. And somewhere on the other side of that portal lies our parents. But why? Why this whole charade of empty crypts in St. Phillips, unless that's where she hid the book? And if that's where the book is, she can only get access today and no other day. What the hell is in that fucking grimoire?"

Anya stared at her sister. "What's in that grimoire is the history of the Bohannon's. Everything she needs to control the coven. But, if she isn't meant to be the High Priestess, some of it does her no good. Henwen said it's all you need. Why else would she have lied to us our entire lives, sis? The whole thing was a charade and a betrayal to us and the entire coven." She spun on her heels and walked right up to face Ian. "Can you take us there?" Ian looked down at the middle sister. "Well, you're shit out of luck running through the woods without me now, aren't you?"

Eilish responded, "We'll need you anyway. Getting through the portal is just the beginning. We have no idea where our parents are. I doubt she'd bury them because she'd have to dig up the grave every year. She comes home too quickly for that. I assume it's a crypt, but how would she remove the slab? If Warrick was with her, maybe the two of them could do it, but she always goes alone. Maybe she has a spell. Maybe the book gave her a spell to give her the strength, but I've never heard of such a thing." She shook her head. "This makes no sense."

Ian chimed in. "I can take you to the portal, no problem. And I'll go with you because I can move the slab over the crypt. Just make sure you can get my ass out of there. But right now, I need to get out of here. We have no idea how long she'll remain inside that portal, and the last thing I need is for Seraphina to find a vampire in her house. Do you have some spell to clear the air once I leave? I don't want her to pick up my scent."

Eilish nodded, "We'll burn sage; now go." She kissed him, and he returned the kiss with more passion than she was expecting. Anya threw up her hands, "Not now!" Ian broke the kiss and chuckled at Anya's panic. "I'm leaving! But I mean it; you two don't do this alone."

Eilish nodded, and he threw Anya a kiss as he stepped out on the back porch and teleported away, disappearing before their eyes. Eilish watched him go, then turned to Anya. "You've got to admit, that whole teleporting thing comes in handy."

"Yeah, yeah, I'll give the bloodsucker that much." Anya went to the fridge, grabbed the sweet tea pitcher, and poured them a glass. "You better get the sage before she comes home. Now we have another plan to come up with, and we'll have to act like we know nothing and everything is normal. We need to figure out how to sneak out of this place."

Eilish gathered the smudge stick and feather from the pantry, and with a nod, the smudge stick of sage, lavender, and roses started to burn, its sweet smoke filling the air. As she began cleansing the house, chanting as she went, she looked over her shoulder at her sister. "Sneaking out is the least of our worries. We'll need to find where our parents are buried, then I'll have to call up our mother's spirit, and I'm pretty sure we'll have some explaining to do."

Anya nodded as she watched Eilish cleanse the house. "We can always get Wynter and Rain to cover for us unless they're fed up with all this drama. We'll have to gather everything we need and keep it hidden, so everything is ready when the time comes. You can do this, Eilish, I know you can, and I don't think Mommy will be upset. But if she doesn't have that book, I have no idea what we'll do then. I wish Carter could come with us, but I don't want to put him in any more danger than he's already in. "

Eilish stopped the cleansing. "That's a hard no to Carter! We don't know what we're walking into. Ian at least has a fighting chance."

Anya shrugged, "Yes, my mere human bad boy is in enough danger as it is." Anya turned out the kitchen lights. "I don't want to face Fina when she gets back. It's almost midnight now; she should be arriving any minute. I say we go up and get in bed. Besides, I'm exhausted."

Eilish returned the smudge stick and feather to the pantry. "I'm right behind you. It's better if we're in bed anyway. I'm not sure how I'd react around her right now." The sisters climbed the stairs as Luna followed behind them, each retreating to their rooms. Luna followed Anya, jumping up on her bed.

Eilish pulled a clean gown from her dresser and noticed Emric pacing at the window. "You okay, Emric?" The apparition wrung his hands, "The soldiers! The soldiers! There are so many!" Eilish felt his despair. "It's okay. Everything will be okay." He nodded and stood guard at the window. "I'll keep an eye out, Miss Eilish. You sleep now." She smiled softly at him as she turned out the light. "Good night." She heard his voice in the dark. "Good night, Miss Eilish."

Seraphina arrived home and backed the Caddy into the carriage house. She placed a protection spell over the door and walked toward the house. A few lights had been left on for her, but most of the house was dark. "They had better be home and in their beds." As she walked to the back porch and went inside, she noticed the smell of sage, lavender, and rose. It calmed her instantly, and she turned out the lights as she went. Walking up the stairs, she was greeted with silence. Before heading to her bedroom, she checked on Eilish, opening her door. As usual, she saw Emric standing at the window, always looking for something only he could see. Eilish was sleeping under a mound of blankets. She softly closed the door and went to Anya's room. As she peered in, she found her in bed, with Luna at her feet. Anya sat up as Luna leaped for the floor and curled around Seraphina's feet. "Glad to see you both following instructions for once. I'm home now; all is well." As she closed the door, the smile on her face was one of total smugness that, once again, she had fooled them all for another year.

ABOUT THE AUTHOR

Emily Bex is the International Bestselling Author of the epic six-book Medici Warrior Series. As she says, "Why start small?" She worked for over twenty years in marketing, developing ad campaigns, catalogs, product launches and promotional literature. She figured if she could write creatively about products, then surely she could write something about these characters that were rattling around inside her brain. The Medici Warrior Series is paranormal romance, or as she calls it, pure escapism. She currently lives in Virginia, but has used her extensive love of travel, both foreign and domestic, to create the backdrop for her characters to play out their story.

Sign up for Emily Bex's newsletter here:
https://emilybex.com/

Be sure to stalk me!

MORE FROM FOUNDATIONS

www.FoundationsBooks.net

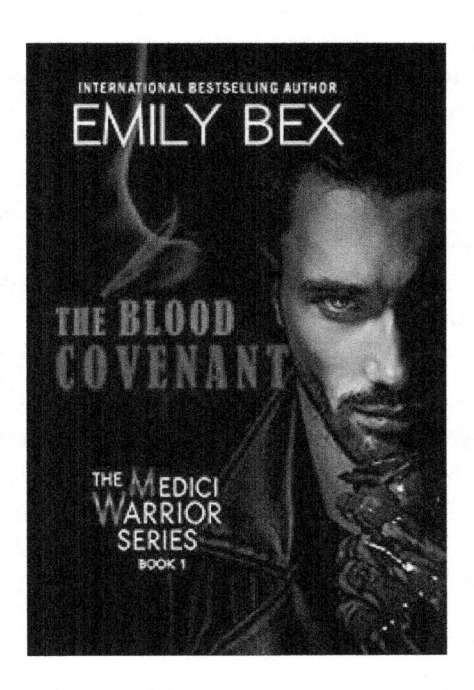

The Blood Covenant by Emily Bex

GET IT HERE

A top 100 Amazon Bestseller!

#1 Bestseller in Paranormal Fantasy and Urban Fantasy

Paranormal Romance and Urban Fantasy fans will become enchanted with this deliciously dark and scandalous series by International Bestselling Author Emily Bex. It's everything vampire romances should be made of!

*"Blood Covenant combines the hedonistic jet-setting pleasures of **BILLIONAIRE***

***ROMANCE** and the dirty little secret thrills of a **DEAD SEXY VAMPIRE!**"* - Katalina Leon, USA Today Bestselling Author

*"This series is going to **HIT THE CHARTS**... what an epic tale. Thank you Emily from a **NEW FAN!**"* - Cheryl, Amazon Reviewer

When he met her, he knew how it would end.

Shade Medici, a warrior king and sole male heir to the dynasty, is expected to mate and produce an heir to secure the continuation of the Medici coven. He's waited over five hundred years for the right mate, and when he meets Kate Reese, his attraction is more than primal - it's merciless.

She's also mortal.

Kate is fresh off a broken engagement and reluctant to open her heart, but her hesitations are no match for the unrelenting pursuits of the vampire king. Their passion for each other is searing...and not everyone is happy about it. Namely the ruling Council.

As they fight against deceit, treachery, and those who aim to see their love fail, Shade also struggles to control his impulses as Kate is immersed into his dark and dangerous world, but it's imperative he prepare her for the changes that will be demanded of her should she choose to bind herself to him through the blood covenant. All that scorches and glitters isn't gold, and she quickly learns that falling in love with a vampire comes at a hefty price:

It may just cost her everything.

"Scorching", "riveting", and hailed as "the NEXT BIG THING", The Medici Warrior Series follows the exploits of a vampire dynasty that spans four generations in a multi-genre novel with elements of paranormal, smoldering romance, and historical fiction. Get your copy today! Your vampire king is waiting...

Made in the USA
Middletown, DE
06 April 2023